Brisbane

Brisbane

A NOVEL

EUGENE VODOLAZKIN

Translated from the Russian by
Marian Schwartz

Plough

PLOUGH PUBLISHING HOUSE

Published by Plough Publishing House
Walden, New York
Robertsbridge, England
Elsmore, Australia
www.plough.com

Originally published in Russian as Брисбен. Copyright © 2018
by Eugene Vodolazkin. This translation published by arrangement with
the author and Banke, Goumen, Smirnova Literary Agency AG.

English translation copyright © 2022 by Marian Schwartz.

ИНСТИТУТ ПЕРЕВОДА

AD VERBUM

Published with the support of the Institute for Literary Translation, Russia.

ISBN: 978-1-63608-045-1

26 25 24 23 22   1 2 3 4 5

Library of Congress Cataloging-in-Publication Data

Names: Vodolazkin, E. G., author. | Schwartz, Marian, 1951- translator.
Title: Brisbane : a novel / Eugene Vodolazkin ; translated from Russian by
  Marian Schwartz.
Other titles: Brisben. English
Description: Walden, New York : Plough Publishing House, [2022] | Summary:
  "In this complex novel from the winner of two of Russia's biggest
  literary prizes, a celebrated guitarist robbed of his talent by
  Parkinson's disease seeks other paths to immortality: by authorizing a
  biographer and adopting an exceptionally gifted thirteen-year-old
  musician"-- Provided by publisher.
Identifiers: LCCN 2021043201 (print) | LCCN 2021043202 (ebook) | ISBN
  9781636080451 (hardcover) | ISBN 9781636080468 (ebook)
Subjects: LCGFT: Fiction.
Classification: LCC PG3493.76.D65 B7513 2022 (print) | LCC PG3493.76.D65
  (ebook) | DDC 891.73/5--dc23/eng/20211018
LC record available at https://lccn.loc.gov/2021043201
LC ebook record available at https://lccn.loc.gov/2021043202

Printed in the United States of America

*There is a reason to imagine that a continent,
or land of great extent, may be found to the southward
of the track of former navigators.*

— JAMES COOK, 1769

Performing at Paris's Olympe, I can't play a tremolo. Or rather, I can, but not accurately, not cleanly – I play it like a beginning guitarist, producing a muffled gurgling, not notes. No one notices, and the Olympe explodes in ovations. Even I forget my failure, but as I get in the limo to my admirers' shouts, I catch myself making the characteristic finger movement. My right hand now performs the no longer needed tremolo, as if atoning for its mistake. My fingers move with incredible speed. Touch imaginary strings. The way a hairdresser's scissors break away from the hair for an instant and continue cutting the air. As we pull up to CDG, I tap the poorly played melody on the window – nothing difficult. How could I have stumbled in concert?

I'm flying from Paris to Petersburg to shoot a video. My seatmate is buckling his seatbelt. He turns his head and freezes. He's recognized me.

"Are you Gleb Yanovsky?"

I nod.

"Sergei Nesterov." My neighbor extends his hand. "Writer. I publish under a pseudonym, Nestor."

I half-heartedly shake Nestor's hand. Half-listening. Nestor, it turns out, is returning from the Salon du Livre in Paris. Judging from the smell coming from his mouth, the book fair presented more than just books. Not that this writer has a very Chekhovian look: jug ears, a saddle-shaped nose with large nostrils, nondescript rimless glasses. Nestor bestows his card on me. I stick it in my wallet and shut my eyes.

Nestor to the supposedly sleeping me:

"I doubt you know my things. . . ."

"Just one." I don't open my eyes. "*Tale of the Interim Years.*"

He smiles.

"Oh my. That's my best."

I write, too, actually. A diary – not a diary – occasionally I jot down notes, during evenings at home or in airports. Then I lose them. Recently I even lost them in an airport. Pages covered in Cyrillic. Who would return them? Should they even?

The plane taxis onto the runway and stops, but then the engine revs hard. Snarling and shaking with impatience, the plane picks up speed instantly. Like a predator on the hunt – trembling, twitching its tail. I don't immediately remember which predator exactly. One of the cat family – maybe a cheetah. A fine image. A hunt over the distance between Paris and Petersburg. The airplane lifts off. Tilting a wing, it makes a farewell circle over Paris. I feel myself drifting off.

I wake up from a rattling accompanied by a turbulence announcement. A request for everyone to buckle their seatbelts. And I'd just unbuckled. I'd even loosened my own belt – too tight. The attendant approaches with a request to buckle up. I tell her I don't like seatbelts – not in cars, not in planes. No kind of contraption for a free person. The young woman doesn't believe me, chides me flirtatiously, and responds to all my arguments with a brief "wow." She is sincerely sorry that such a marvelous artist is flying unbuckled.

To end the conversation, I turn demonstratively toward Nestor. I ask whether it's hard to write books. Nestor (he'd been sleeping a drunkard's sleep) mumbles that it's no harder than playing the guitar. The attendant expresses not the slightest irritation, since it's clear the star is just being capricious. Oh well, stars can get away with it. She wags her finger at me and goes away.

Watching her, Nestor suddenly says, "I just had a thought. I could write a book about you. You intrigue me."

"Thank you."

"You could tell me about yourself, and I could write it."

I consider his proposal for a minute or two.

"I don't know what to say. There already are a few books about me. Decent ones, in my opinion, but they miss the point somehow. No understanding."

"Musical understanding?"

"Human, I'd say. I'd put it like this. There's no understanding that the musical stems from the human."

Nestor carefully considers what I've said. His conclusion is surprising.

"I think you'd like my book."

An alcoholic exhale proposes I believe him.

That's funny.

"Indeed? Why?"

"Because I'm a good writer. That's immodest, of course. . . ."

"It is a little. On the other hand, why be modest if you're good?" I tap out the tremolo on my armrest. "Go ahead. Write it."

The rhythmic tapping reminds me of how more than forty years ago, in Kyiv, Fyodor, my father, tapped out a rhythm to test his son's musical ear. Why shouldn't that be the start of the book? I turn to Nestor and briefly tell him about my very first test, and even reproduce the test question proposed then. At the time, I failed. Nestor, smiling, taps his armrest. He fails too.

1971

The night before the first day of school, Gleb sat in front of Fyodor watching his long fingers, and attempted to reproduce the rhythm. Outside, streetcars clattered as they made the turn. The china in the sideboard clinked briefly in response. Then Fyodor sang something and asked Gleb to repeat it. He couldn't repeat the melody, just the words: *paba-paba, paba-paba, paba-pa* . . . Pretty forgettable words – not exactly moving, and the only reason he remembered them was

3

because they sounded like "papa." Actually, Fyodor had asked him to use the Ukrainian, *tato*. Hardly anyone in Kyiv called their father that. It had been several years since Fyodor had lived with his wife Irina and Gleb: Irina had left him. Or rather, Fyodor had left after Irina asked him to move out of their place in the family dormitory. Once driven out, he'd rented a room in another part of town, and since he had a diploma from the music institute, he got a job at a music school teaching violin. For a while after the divorce he drank, preferring cheap stuff like 72nd Port or Bouquet of Moldavia. He didn't like hard liquor. If he did drink vodka, he'd fill a shot glass but wouldn't drink it right away; he'd bring it up to his eyes and his mouth a few times. Exhale a few times. Then pinch his nose and pour the firewater into his gaping mouth. His former wife considered this drinking purely for show, inasmuch as it took place primarily in front of people who could tell Irina about it. In one of her rare conversations with her former husband, Irina called this behavior childish. Without switching to Russian, Fyodor objected that the definition did not hold up to criticism, since children, as far as he understood, don't drink. Logic was on his side, but it didn't help bring Irina back. Three or four years later, once it was quite clear to Fyodor that his wife wasn't coming back, the drinking stopped. Irina allowed Gleb's father parental visits but derived no joy from them. Strictly speaking, neither did Gleb himself. When Fyodor took the boy for a walk, he was mostly silent or recited poetry, which for Gleb was worse than silence in a way. Sometimes, when Gleb got tired at the end of their walk, Fyodor would pick him up. Their eyes were on a level then, and the son would examine his father with a child's unblinking gaze. Under this gaze, tears would well up in Fyodor's brown eyes. One after another, they would roll down his cheeks and disappear forever in his fluffy mustache. Despite his obvious sobriety at the beginning of their walk, by the end, in some inscrutable way, Fyodor would be tipsy. Sitting in his father's arms, Gleb picked up the smell of cheap wine. In the boy's memory, his father's tears were firmly merged with this smell. Maybe they really did smell like that. Who has studied the smell of tears? When soon-to-be first grader Gleb announced his desire to learn to play the guitar, Irina herself brought him to Fyodor. She sat in the corner and silently watched Gleb fail to match the tones his father sang. "*Gleb*..." Fyodor poured himself half a glass of wine, drank it in three goes, and said, in Ukrainian, "*Gleb, my boy, you weren't made for music.*"[1] "Papa, don't drink," Gleb asked him in Russian. His father drank another half-glass. "*I drink because you weren't made for music – a first for the musical Yanovsky family.*" He noticed a heel of bread on the table and brought it to his nose: "*Prikro!*" "What's *preekro?*" Gleb asked. "*Preekro* means 'too bad,'" Irina said. "Yes, it's too bad," Fyodor confirmed. Without another word, the mother took her son by the hand and led him out of the room. The next day they went to enroll him in the nearest music school. There, Gleb was also asked to repeat a rhythmic phrase and a sung melody. Nervous, the boy performed even worse than the day before, but this didn't discourage anyone. Surprise caught Gleb in a different way: his hand turned out to be too small for the guitar's neck. So they suggested enrolling him in the school's four-string domra class – at least until his hand grew. Visibly distraught, Irina asked why they were talking about the four-string domra specifically. They told her that there was a three-string domra, of course, but typically the Ukrainian one (they replaced the guitar in Gleb's arms with a domra) was, after all, four-string. The boy's fingers gripped the domra neck without straining. Irina was also asked not to confuse the two domras with the Eastern dombra, and they were even about to explain the difference between them, but she didn't want to hear it. She wanted to ask why they didn't simply

---

1. Italics here and throughout the novel indicate a non-Russian language being spoken, in Fyodor's case, Ukrainian.—Trans.

choose a smaller guitar for Gleb, to ask whether they weren't trying to trick her son into going somewhere no one would go voluntarily – but she bit her tongue. She stood up and simply took Gleb by the hand. His other hand was still holding the domra. Irina indicated with a glance that he could put down the instrument, but Gleb didn't. "You want to play the four-string domra?" she asked. "Yes," the boy answered. That decided the matter because his mother was trying to spare him yet another no. They signed him up for the domra class. At the same time, Gleb started regular school. He always remembered the colors, smells, and sounds that came to him that September 1, 1971, because on that day his senses sharpened dramatically. The smell of his freshly ironed school uniform – brown, with knife creases in the trousers. Gleb thought it was the color and creases that made the smell. Exactly the same way the smell of his nylon jacket came from the material's waterproof qualities. At the first rain, the material turned out to be permeable, but this had no effect whatsoever on his memory of the smell. This was Gleb's first nylon jacket; up until then he'd only worn coats. The warm September day didn't call for a jacket, but the boy very much wanted to arrive wearing it, though his mother was opposed. Years later, examining his first school photograph, Gleb Yanovsky found the jacket quite shapeless. He never did understand what it was about this item he liked so much then. Maybe its smell intoxicated him, the way a carnivorous plant intoxicates insects. Whatever it was, on the first of September his mother met him halfway, as always. She helped him put on his jacket and satchel. She advised him at least not to button the jacket. The satchel smelled of leather, and also water and oil, and also his noxious plastic pencil case. When the boy moved calmly, the pens' and pencils' rattling was moderate, but when he broke into a run, the sound increased many times over. The precise rhythm he pounded out reminded him of a band's maraca. When he was a little older, the boy asked himself where people studied the maraca. Could there really be a maraca class at the music school, like a violin or piano class? And he found no answer because there was no such class. So there it was, his satchel, his school. At his father's wish, Gleb was sent to a Ukrainian-language school. His mother didn't object. She almost never objected. Knowing her ability to reconcile herself to circumstances, it was a wonder she'd had the character to separate from her husband. The real wonder, though, was that she and Fyodor had ever gotten together in the first place. Fyodor was from Kamianets-Podilskyi, Irina from Vologda. At one time both studied at the Kyiv Civil Aviation Institute, both landing there randomly, Irina after a failed attempt to get into the theater institute and Fyodor the conservatory. That's why they were allowed to stay in the city. They had not the slightest interest in civil aviation. This was one of the few things they had in common. As for the rest, they spoke different languages in the literal and figurative sense. People think dissimilarity breeds attraction, and that's true – but only at the start. Yes, the dark-haired southerner Fyodor was drawn to the northern beauty Irina, whose beauty was like the fog in a brief morning calm, like the dream of a tsarevna all too tempting to interrupt, like the quiet pond one wishes ripples would form in. Fyodor's invariable pensiveness made an impression on Irina; it implied experience and wisdom. She enjoyed listening to the Ukrainian words he uttered and demanded a minute-to-minute translation. Over the course of time, though, what had stoked their feelings in the first years turned into its opposite in Irina's eyes. Fyodor's pensiveness came to seem like sullenness, his wisdom did not manifest itself with the frequency she'd been counting on, and the incomprehensible words of the beautiful but foreign language began to get on her nerves. She stopped asking for their translation, waiting for Fyodor to guess and do it himself. Irina could have insisted he switch to Russian (as he did in important instances), but Fyodor's pronunciation mangled her native language.

And in bed, hearing his Russian words, she would laugh as if she were being tickled, push him away, and ask him to speak only Ukrainian. And then she left. After he was grown, Gleb heard many times about another reason for the divorce: Irina's "frivolous" behavior. He may have been able to believe in his mother's frivolousness (whatever that involved), but he didn't connect the divorce to that. The reason for the divorce, it seemed to him, was deeper and in a way more tragic. Gleb ascribed what happened between his parents to the particular pensiveness his father fell into from time to time. It was a pensiveness his mother, a vivacious person, came to dread. Those moments made Gleb uncomfortable too. It was as if his father had fallen into a deep well and was contemplating the stars from there, stars only he could see – even in the daytime, such being the optics of wells. When Irina left, the violin felt the fullness of Fyodor's emotions. Usually he played when he was alone. Gleb had once heard this playing when, with his mother's permission, he'd spent the night at his father's. Early in the morning, so as not to wake the boy, Fyodor shut himself in the bathroom and played. Turning on the water as well, to muffle the violin's sounds. These sounds, mixed with the water's noise, shook Gleb to the core. In 2003, he wrote several compositions that laid the guitar over the sound of water. This was his memory of his father playing. When he was writing them down, he'd had another thought, that in fact his father had turned the water on then in order to hang himself in peace. When Gleb finished writing his rain compositions, people told him they bore traces of despair. Gleb didn't respond. He remembered the particular expression in his father's eyes, an expression that could only be defined as despair. What really happened then? Was Irina frivolous? More likely, she took everything lightheartedly, showing a marked preference for the sunny side of life. And was disinclined to delve particularly into its shadowy aspects. She often repeated that she'd like to live in Australia; for some reason, that country seemed like the embodiment of the carefree life. Jokingly she would ask people to find her an Australian husband she could travel the world with. It was in one of those conversations that Gleb first heard the word "Brisbane." Talking about the city of her dreams, his mother named Brisbane. When asked why that city specifically, she said simply: it sounds beautiful. Her answer seemed silly – to everyone but Gleb. Brisbane. He easily linked the city with Zurbagan, Gel-Gyu, and Lissa, which the boy had read about in Aleksandr Grin. At the time Gleb had asked his mother whether she was going to take him with her to Brisbane. Of course she was. His mother kissed his forehead. How could she not? The time would come and they would live in Brisbane. Years later, when Gleb was graduating from high school, Irina wanted to buy a trip to Australia with the money she'd saved up. She was called into the Party commission, which had to give its consent – or rather, as it turned out, not give its consent – for the trip. She wasn't a member of the Communist Party, so it's an open question why the Party committee had any say at all. They proposed she name the members of the Politburo, asked what was discussed at the last congress of the Communist Party, and had her list the basic advantages of the socialist over the capitalist system. She answered the first, the second, and even the third. The third was the hardest for her, but she managed that one, too, because she'd prepared in the most painstaking fashion. And then Irina was asked one last question – as unstoppable as tank fire. They asked her whether she'd already seen everything in the Soviet Union. This question could not be answered in the affirmative; the country she'd been born in was too big. A negative answer implied that Gleb's mother should put off her trip to Australia until she'd fully gotten to know the Soviet Union – or so the commission members, at least, thought. She was denied permission. Actually, Irina took it lightly, as she did nearly everything. Maybe it was thanks to just this quality that soon after the divorce she got a room in a communal apartment, given to her by the design office where she'd been assigned after her studies, as a young civil aviation specialist. Had she taken this job opportunity seriously, they probably wouldn't have had to give her anything. A lot changed in Gleb's life with the move from the dormitory to the communal apartment. First and foremost, his grandmother Antonina Pavlovna showed up. She came from Vologda to help out his mother, who frequently went off in different directions. His mother called her absences business trips; moreover, each one ended in a present for Gleb. The presents – plastic toys usually – were quietly placed on the sleeping boy's pillow. He didn't give much thought to why his mother liked those toys particularly, he simply accepted them with thanks. Like a dog trained to search, he would wake up from the faint plastic smell touching his nostrils, because this was the smell of joy. He'd open his eyes and see his mother. She'd be sitting on the stool by his bed and smiling. Sometimes she'd cry. Her return was never an ordinary event. "Why do you take so many business trips?" Gleb once asked. His mother blushed and didn't answer. She glanced at his grandmother, who pretended not to notice anything. His grandmother wiped her hands on her apron – her saving gesture. When his mother left for work, Gleb repeated his question to his grandmother. Antonina Pavlovna fell silent and pressed a finger to her lips. "Tss," she told Gleb, "you see, she needs a reliable man by her side, only where are you going to find one?" "And my papa," Gleb asked, "is he unreliable?" "Your papa . . ." His grandmother sighed and shrugged. Meanwhile, his papa was very glad that Gleb was playing a Ukrainian folk instrument, and especially that his son had chosen it himself. Fyodor no longer saw Gleb's lack of absolute pitch as an insurmountable obstacle. He even said as much, that you didn't need absolute pitch to play the domra. To play the violin, which has no frets, yes, it's desirable, but for instruments whose neck is divided by frets, that requirement is superfluous. Not only that; in Fyodor's opinion, his ear could be developed (*to an extent,* he clarified). One day Fyodor took Gleb to the musical instruments store and offered to buy him a domra. The father demonstratively let his son choose; he considered assessing twelve-ruble instruments beneath his dignity. After running all over the store, Gleb settled on the darkest of all the domras and brought it to his father. Fyodor looked sternly at his son. "*It doesn't have any strings. Pay attention, son.*" After a slight hesitation, his father picked up one of the domras and ran his thumb over the strings. He frowned at the plywood sound, which reminded him of a toy balalaika's rattle. The other domra was the same, and so were all the rest. They chose the way Gleb had wanted to, by color – not as dark as the first, but with strings. When they got back, home smelled of a cooked dinner. "Will you stay for dinner?" Gleb asked his father. "*Ne. Ne zaproshue.*" "What does *ne zaproshue* mean?" the boy inquired. "No one's asked me," Irina explained, looking into Fyodor's eyes. His grandmother silently wiped her hands on her apron. It seemed to her that the man who not so long ago had been her daughter's husband should be asked.

July 18, 2012, Kyiv

Arriving in Kyiv on tour, I visit my father. He receives me good-naturedly but without any special fuss.

"*Hi there, Muscovite. What do you say?*"

He smiles. I smile back.

"I say, join the empire!"

My father sprinkles tobacco on a cigarette paper, rolls it, and running his tongue along it, seals it.

This is something new.

"*We can't do that.*"

"Why?"

He flicks his lighter and releases the first puff of smoke.

"Figure it out for yourself, son."

Galina, my father's second wife, walks in and nods at me apprehensively. Sets an ashtray down in front of her husband and goes out.

"I'm having some problems with my right hand." I bend and unbend my fingers. "I was performing in Paris and nearly screwed it up."

"You play with your heart, not your hand. Think of Paganini. He played no matter what the circumstances."

He looks at me with a half-smile.

"He still had one string. That's something. But without a hand, you know . . ."

"He would play without any strings at all, son. Even without a hand." My father thought and added, *"But in the meantime, go see a doctor."*

"Yes, I may well do that." Right before leaving for some reason I remember the Petersburg writer's proposal to write a book about me. I tell my father about it. He shrugs, and I already regret telling him. He rolls another cigarette, lights up.

"Music's music even in Petersburg. Let him write."

The released smoke does a somersault – as complicated as it is slow. My father seems to have slowed down with age. Softened. Or maybe he's become indifferent.

"It's not a matter of the music," I say. "It's the musician's life experience that needs describing, not the music. After that comes the music, or maybe the literature. I don't know whether the writer will understand that."

I walk back from my father's to the hotel. So as not to be recognized, I pull my cap down to my nose. This is better than sunglasses, which themselves attract attention. My route takes me through the Botanical Garden. Via a side path I reach the café where my grandmother and I used to have ice cream. The café's still there, the ice cream, too, evidently, but my grandmother isn't. Each time I visit, I go to the cemetery, where we're separated by two meters of dirt brown clay.

I sit on a bench and look at the café. There's a squirrel, a *belka*, right at my feet. On its hind legs, its front legs crossed prayerfully at its chest. I explain to it that I have no food with me, that I might have bought something, of course, and brought it, but that's so complicated. Words are powerless. I clap my pockets so the squirrel can see I have no treats for it. To make my point, I get out my wallet and even open it. There's an excessive theatricality to this, unquestionably. In the sense of food, the wallet has nothing whatsoever to offer. The limit of my dreams is a cheese slice.

I notice Nestor's business card. Why did I start telling him about my childhood? Why would he write all this? It occurs to me to toss the card to the squirrel – let the squirrel call him. He can write about the squirrel's life. Isn't that interesting? A half a dozen books have already been published about me, but not a one about the squirrel, I bet. Except for *Tales of Belkin*. I take the piece of cardboard in two fingers, all set to let it fly. And hesitate. In essence, not a single one about my *life*, though. They've written about all sorts of things, just not about my life. Hmm, that's something to consider. I put the card back.

1972

Gleb spent the entire fall with Antonina Pavlovna. After school they would go to the Botanical Garden, which was right across from their building. No one called this fabulous spot the Botanical Garden; they said "the Botanic." There Gleb and his grandmother collected bouquets of maple leaves, bright yellow and bright red, which they put in milk bottles all around their room. They collected rosehips, which his grandmother used to brew tea. In and of themselves, rosehips aren't all that attractive, so she would mix it with something to enrich the tea's flavor. But the tea's main interest, of course, lay in the fact that he had collected the rosehips with his own hands. This was an open section of the Botanic, where you were allowed to gather anything you liked. The garden sloped down from the hill in terraces, and squirrels lived on one of the terraces. Or rather, they lived all over the Botanic, but on this terrace they could be fed. They took food right from your hands. Antonina Pavlovna brought hazelnuts for them in the pocket of her demi-season coat. She'd bought the coat in Kyiv, and for a while she pronounced the word "demi-season" very nasally (evidently having heard it from someone), but then she stopped. For all the rest she had a strong Vologda accent, with a heavy stress on all her o's: *khO-rO-shO* (good), *mO-lO-kO* (milk), *mO-rO-zhen-O-ye* (ice cream). Yes, *morozhenoye*. That was the Botanic's main pleasure, and its day was Sunday. At about two, grandmother and grandson would come to the open air café above the University metro exit. Everything here was round: the metro exit, the café, to say nothing of the ice cream scoops. What else could they have been? They were served in little plastic cups and eaten with little plastic spoons. These marvelous items were the café's inalienable property, inasmuch as the era of disposables had yet to come. Meanwhile, Gleb liked the little spoons very much. One time, he licked one after his latest portion of ice cream and stuck it in his pants pocket. He told his grandmother about his acquisition at home. His grandmother said nothing right away, but her response was imprinted on her face. Everything in it literally fell: the wrinkles over her eyebrows, the bags under her eyes, the corners of her mouth. It turned out that he had stolen the little spoon – and tomorrow, after school, they would go return the little spoon together (after all, we stole it together, his grandmother made it clear). Gleb conceived of the return as a solemn and terrifying act, involving the entire café staff and maybe even the police. That night he barely slept, though then it turned out that he did after all, but his dream was worse than his vigil. Here they are, he and his grandmother, entering the café, they sit at a little table. Before they can order anything, policemen pretending to be ordinary ice cream lovers come running toward them from neighboring tables. In civilian dress, but they look too casual: Panama hats, neckerchiefs, shorts. From this alone you could tell it was an ambush. The policemen rush at Gleb (his grandmother's horror-stricken eyes), and this is the most terrifying episode of the arrest. When they bend his arms behind his back, he's not scared, and when they click the handcuffs and lead him to their Volga GAZ-21, he's not scared. But when they leapt up and rushed at him – he was. Bastards! Freaking cops! Gleb shouts, transitioning to a wail. This is how their neighbor Uncle Kolya shouts when they take him in – he shouts and rolls around on the floor, and the whole apartment looks at him censoriously. Looks down at him. Gleb rolls around, too, catching his grandmother's look: so it's come to this, has it? What, you couldn't have sat tight at home? His grandmother is crying because now she understands everything. Sitting in the car with his hands cuffed behind his back is uncomfortable, but the fact that they're driving him in a Volga takes some of the edge off the situation. Gleb had long dreamed of riding in a Volga (the deer hood ornament alone!), only somehow it wasn't working out quite right. Yes, some of the night he didn't sleep – and then he dozed off in class. After school, he and his grandmother really did go to the café. The boy's expectations notwithstanding, everything went fairly simply and even without unpleasantness – probably because the worst had happened that night. His grandmother ordered two portions of ice cream and while they were bringing them put the ill-fated spoon on the next table. Many years later, Gleb recalled that little spoon on planes while stirring tea served by a flight attendant. At that time he was flying almost weekly (his grandmother was no longer by his side – she lay, dead, in Kyiv's Berkovtsi cemetery) and had, accordingly, expanded his opportunities for taking whatever spoons he cared to. But he didn't take even a single one. Life is a good teacher. Now about his studies. As was said, Gleb attended a Ukrainian-language school. This choice was welcomed not only by his father (which is understandable) but also by his mother, who felt you should know the language of the land in which you live. True, a practical circumstance did influence the choice. While all the Russian schools had more applicants than they could accommodate (five classes per grade, with forty-five pupils in each), calm and intimacy reigned in the Ukrainian ones. Gleb's class had twenty-four pupils, and there was only one class per grade. The children of Ukrainian writers studied in this school and – since it was next to the train station – so did children from the villages closest to Kyiv. Gleb wasn't either, and his Ukrainian was limited to individual words heard from his father. Actually, in important instances it became clear that the writers' children didn't know everything either. When in the first lesson the teacher, Lesya Kirillovna, asked what the Ukrainian was for *pebble*, only the village children knew it. *Ochyeryet,* said a pupil whose last name was Bdzhilka. *Ocheret,* Gleb whispered, enchanted. He thought bitterly that there was no place for him among people who knew such marvelous words. He was doomed to drag along at the back and admire those who were ahead. Gleb was mistaken, though. In all the years that followed, Bdzhilka did not give a single additional correct answer. *Ochyeryet* was his shining hour. Subsequently, Gleb tried to remember why Lesya Kirillovna had started talking about pebbles in their first lesson. Evidently, it was an explanation for something. Although not necessarily. Inexplicable things did happen in general education institutions too. Enigmatic things, even. Thus, in a moment of anger, Lesya Kirillovna, moving her lips, would say something soundlessly. That is, in these instances she did say certain things out loud, but what was audible had, on the whole, a happy character – at least compared to the expression on her face. What had no sound remained a puzzle, and her facial expression evidently corresponded to that. Once, when Gleb's ear happened to be right up to Lesya Kirillovna's lips (she was leaning over him), some of the puzzling words became clear. There are times when a solution does not bring consolation. Or joy. Generally speaking, joy in life is a rare visitor. Of all the joyless things during those years there was nothing more joyless than Russian lessons. Lesya Kirillovna began each such class with a warm-up that, following the methodology's recommendation, included a tongue-twister. In essence, it was always the same very sad tongue-twister: *zhutko zhuku zhit na suku*. Dreadful for a bug living on a branch. First, each pronounced it in turn; then they all did in unison. After listening to everyone with a gloomy look on her face (what other look can you have listening to a text like that?), Lesya Kirillovna would lick her lips and prepare to demonstrate the standard pronunciation. On the first *u* she slid smoothly into a moaning *oo*, and the rest were not much prettier. In this performance the tongue-twister lost in speed but palpably gained in dread. Only after listening to Lesya Kirillovna could one fully appreciate how the bug felt. Some cried seeing their teacher standing by her desk and letting one *u* after another fly uncontrollably (and dreadfully) through the classroom. Generally speaking, things weren't all that simple when it came to Lesya Kirillovna. Once, in the middle of the school year, a pupil, Plachinda, looked through the cracked door and saw Lesya Kirillovna sit down in the seats of different pupils in turn and, imitating them, give answers to the teacher's questions in delicate, childish voices. Each time, the pedagogue returned to her desk to ask the question and in an intentionally crude voice addressed her next victim. In and of itself, her voice was sufficiently crude that, strictly speaking, no amplification was required. What struck the pupil most were two things. First, in answering in the role of Plachinda, Lesya Kirillovna would make faces, gesticulate heatedly, and from her squeaking make it clear that the lesson had not been learned. Second, after returning to her desk, Lesya Kirillovna would unleash on the respondent a stream of choice curses. Yes, the pupil was unhappy that someone viewed her this way, and yes, she was upset that she hadn't learned the lesson, but why the obscenity, she asked herself, and obscenity like that to boot! When she recounted all this at home, her parents, to her surprise, showed restraint. Chewing his lips, Plachinda père murmured that ultimately it was a general education school, that schoolchildren's studies were conducted along the most varied lines. . . . Meanwhile, in addition to regular school, Gleb continued to attend music school. For the first two weeks he studied only with Vera Mikhailovna, a plump young woman. A few times the boy heard that she was his teacher "in his specialty." He liked that he now had a specialty and had a teacher working with him individually and "training his hand." In Vera Mikhailovna's hands his own little hand was like putty: his teacher sculpted from it the hand of a genuine domrist. She would give his fingers the correct position and sometimes shake them, as if shaking off all their mistakes and imprecisions, and kneaded, kneaded, kneaded. It was this part of his lessons that Gleb liked most of all. Vera Mikhailovna's touches sent a low-voltage current down his arm and spine. Maybe that's why he learned quite quickly the right way to hold the pick, the small plastic petal that touches the domra's strings. Unlike guitar strings, which are long and pliant, the domra's strings are short and stiff, so you had to use a pick. You have to hold it with the right thumb and index finger, while the hand itself has to have the shape of a little house. You have to play – and this is a very important point – by moving the hand, not the whole arm. It was the hand movement that wouldn't come together for Gleb. For some reason his entire arm would start moving. But by early October, come together it did. In October, Irina wasn't living with Gleb and Antonina Pavlovna. She stopped by nearly every evening for tea, but went off to spend the night somewhere else. Unlike her business trips, this was a long-lived story, and most of all – much more serious. Where are you always going? Gleb would ask her, but his mother wouldn't answer. She would smile. Happiness shone in her eyes. In November, she came home, oddly, and, moreover, in the middle of the night. She looked downcast. Gleb and his grandmother didn't ask any questions, and she didn't explain. From that day on, Irina spent all her nights at home, which made Gleb unspeakably happy. Not that he minded being with his grandmother, not at all, he just liked it when they were all together. Moreover, Antonina Pavlovna, no matter how you slice it, was a grandmother in every sense – age and status – while Irina was a young woman who he found much more interesting. That fall, though, a woman appeared in Gleb's life who turned out to be even more interesting to spend time with: his music school teacher Klavdia Vasilievna (privately, Gleb called her Klavochka), who became his first love. Klavochka was essentially just a girl herself still, but even in these circumstances she was three times her admirer's age. And approximately twice as tall. Actually, that wasn't what bothered Gleb most. Klavochka taught what a beloved woman should in no instance teach: solfeggio. Heading off once a week for his lesson with her, Gleb experienced two conflicting emotions: love for Klavochka and revulsion for her subject. Before solfeggio, music seemed to have flown down from the heavens, possessing no explanation for its beauty. But explanations existed, and they looked more like mathematics than music. The airship in which Gleb had set sail had a fairly dreary engine compartment, it turned out, where flywheels slapped and there was an acrid smell of grease. Most surprising of all was the fact that Klavochka was in charge in this hellish world. The properties of this world did not make themselves clear to Gleb right away. While Klavochka was explaining the duration of notes and the characteristics of the staff, he had no inkling of anything bad. His first worries began creeping in when she moved on to triads. She informed him that a triad was a chord made of three sounds spaced in thirds. His sole delight was in watching Klavochka's slender fingers when she demonstrated triads on the piano: do-mi-sol. Then she would also sing: do-mi-sol. A gentle voice, velvety – he honestly wished she would sing something else. . . . What else was bad about solfeggio was that Klavochka didn't teach Gleb alone: there were seven others in class as well. And everyone, by the way, except for Anna Lebed (specialty, cello), disliked solfeggio. For instance, Maksim Kleshchuk (accordion), who shared a desk with Gleb, was constantly twisting his feet, and at the word "triad" would become covered in sweat. Once, Klavochka devoted an entire lesson to the inversion of triads, which consists of moving the bottom note up an octave. The first inversion is a sixth chord, the second inversion a six-four chord. "Kleshchuk," she said at the end of the lesson, "construct a tonic sixth chord in C major for me." Kleshchuk, who had already been sitting with a tense face, positively turned to stone. Big tears rolled silently down his face. A quiet gurgling was heard under his seat. Everyone looked under Kleshchuk's seat because, however big his tears were, they certainly couldn't gurgle. The accordionist's right hand lay on the desk and held a pen while the left squeezed something under the desk. From his seat, which had a bend in it, a thin stream was running into a puddle forming on the floor. Klavochka never asked Kleshchuk about triads again, limiting herself to questions about note duration. This meant the other pupils had to talk about triads more often. Gleb had little to tell his beloved girlfriend about triads, and this upset him greatly. At home he would sit for hours over his textbook with just one goal: not to disgrace himself in front of Klavochka. From time to time he would pluck the chords he was studying on his domra. Occasionally he would look up and watch the snow skidding along outside, since winter had arrived unbeknownst to him. It was hard for Gleb to concentrate on triads – and not only because of the snow. There was a lot at home to distract him. At home. Homeward. Home. Maybe the only one in his life. Later he had lots of homes – so many that they lost their homelike quality and became residences. But an umbilical cord connected him to this one: home. A small, two-story building on Shevchenko, formerly Bibikovsky, Boulevard. On the second floor – a balcony hidden behind the branches of an old chestnut.

JULY 19, 2012, KYIV

I go to where my building once stood. Rising in its place is something glassed – a five-star hotel, to judge from the sign. A window-washer cradle is sliding down the glass wall. There are two window washers standing at opposite ends of the cradle making energetic arm movements. The window reflects them, and also the sunset's orange rays, which pour down the glass with the cleaning fluid.

My grandmother washed windows very differently. First she wiped them with a rag, and then she made the final swipes with a crumpled newspaper. A fresh layer was added to the soaked newspaper time after time, forming this sort of onion, which squeaked and squealed when it touched the window. String instruments make a similar sound when the nails of the thumb and index finger run down a string together.

I turn my back to the hotel and examine the poplars on the boulevard. Unlike my building, they've lasted. If I don't turn around, I might think my building is still behind me. That they're just about to call me to supper, for instance. Or bring out a warm sweater, because it's evening. No, they won't. No one calls out to me. Something's gone wrong. My mobile rings, lights up: *Mama*. From my long ago, as from oblivion. The voice is muffled, broken up by static.

"Gleb, how are you?"

"Thank God you called. Thank God. . . ."

I walk into the hotel lobby. People recognize me, and a crowd gathers. I tell the hotel management that's run up that I once lived here. The management nods politely, although (he finds this strange) he remembers nothing of the kind. It's even stranger because they usually make precise note of this type of visit.

"You've misunderstood me," I say. "I lived in the two-story building that stood at this location."

"Now isn't that something," management marvels. "Remarkable. Rather unprecedented even."

"The building's gone," I continue, "but the address stuck in my memory: 28 Shevchenko Boulevard, apartment 2. Like the leash of a dog that died long ago."

Everyone smiles with restraint. The staff of an expensive hotel aren't supposed to laugh out loud.

"A remarkable comment. Showing a love of nature, as they say."

"As a child, I very much wanted a dog. Very much, but the neighbors wouldn't allow it. And now – I don't."

1972

"*The boys are all right, but the girls are stupid,*" Lesya Kirillovna reported at the parent meeting. By way of illustrating her idea, she imitated Lyusya Mironenko, who thought about anything and everything except the lesson: chin on her palm, eyes unfocused and basically gathered somewhere on her forehead. And she wrote her own last name with an *e: Meronenko.* Lyusya's mother smiled, embarrassed.

Noticing the smile on another mother's face, Lesya Kirillovna switched over to her: *and Sidorova writes 'hopework.' Hopework – simply brilliant!* Everyone knew Sidorova was beaten at home, so the slip of the pen might be called Freudian, but in the seventies no one knew that author – not Sidorova, not her parents, not even Lesya Kirillovna. When it came to Sidorova, her life experience had led her to two simple conclusions: she liked being at school and she didn't like being at home. And this made perfect sense. As for Gleb, he liked music school most. Now that he'd mastered the basic techniques of domra playing, he and Vera Mikhailovna had started thinking about the aesthetics of the matter. Play with nuance, Vera Mikhailovna never tired of repeating to her pupil, and the very word "nuance" captivated Gleb. It was so expressive, so refined that it required no refinement. Playing with nuance became the young domrist's favorite activity. Sometimes, carried away, he would put his fingers in the wrong place or pluck the wrong strings, and then Vera Mikhailovna would shout: *cringe!* But in her cry one sensed an understanding that the technical flaw was a necessary sacrifice in the name of beauty. The performer knew he would be forgiven his cringe, whereas an absence of nuance – never. Maybe this was why Gleb loved music school. Actually, that was not the only thing he loved. Unlike Sidorova, Gleb, who knew no beatings, liked his home in the communal apartment. Everything there was simpler than at music school, and more modest when it came to nuances, but this was his beloved home, which no school could replace. Three other families lived in the apartment, besides Gleb, his mama, and his grandmother. Their names were listed under the doorbell with a note saying how many times to ring for each. These names greeted the boy every day, and even after his neighbors were gone, let alone the building itself, Gleb firmly remembered that the Pshebyshevskys had to be rung once, the Yanovskys twice, the Kolbushkovs three times, and the Vinnichenkos four. No one rang for the Kolbushkovs or Vinnichenkos because they never had guests. You could have put a zero after their rings and made it thirty and forty without disturbing anyone. But the single and double rings were firmly imprinted on Gleb's ears. The boy could easily tell from their volume and duration who was ringing. It turned out that even a single ring (and this was where the real nuances came in) could be made with limitless variety. For instance, a momentary touch of the button – and the bell was like a puppy's yap. You could ring without pressing the button too much – and timidity would creep into the ring. When, on the contrary, they rang until their finger turned white – there would be a scandalous sound full of crackle. Two short rings sent the listener to an ethereal staccato, two longs engendered thoughts of a bomb shelter. This was excellent training for note duration, Kleshchuk's favorite topic. Beginning in second grade, Kleshchuk would sometimes come over to Gleb's after school. His brief brushes against the doorbell yielded two exemplary eighth notes. Generally speaking, the old fifties button possessed the expressiveness of a violin, and because of this the full spectrum of its possibilities was utilized only by Fyodor – when he was a bit tight. From the characteristics of his ring you could immediately determine how drunk he was. But it wasn't only the bell that made a sound, there was also the door, which had its own range: from the latch's quiet click (the morning departure for work) to the hurricane slam that shook the double doors in the evening hour. Slams like that usually accompanied a stormy departure or a stormy return. The latter was a rarity because, after spending a while outside, the person would cool down. This person was Uncle Kolya Kolbushkov. Actually, he rarely went out either: he preferred driving his wife Katerina out of their room. In those instances, she would bed down and curl up on the big rug-covered chest in the vestibule. In the middle of the night she would go up to the door to their room and ask in a dispirited voice: "Mikola, let me in!" Abbreviated but harsh curses would follow from the other side of the door. Sometimes – if Mikola came out to the vestibule – a muffled blow; Katerina's abundant body absorbed all the sound. One time, in front of the neighbors, he lunged at Katerina with a handsaw, which pierced Gleb's door and for a while oscillated with a brief, mournful melody. It even seemed to Gleb that a minor sixth dominated there, like in Francis Lai's "Love Story" (dó-mi-mi-dó-dó and so on). Evdokia Vinnichenko called the police, but nothing came of it. Uncle Kolya managed to stash the surprisingly musical instrument in time, and Katerina did not press charges. Uncle Kolya's wife expected nothing else. Ultimately, he'd played her "Love Story." Katerina herself was no namby-pamby and – give her credit – she never missed an opportunity to wrangle with her husband, most often when Uncle Kolya, a war veteran, tossed a few back after his factory shift, went out into the yard in a T-shirt, sat down at the table under the crooked olive tree, and started chatting with the public. A light hung on a wire over the table, so that the socializing could continue in the dark too. In his right hand, Uncle Kolya held a pack of Belomors, and in his left, matches, which he pressed to his palm with his pinky and ring finger. Those two fingers of his were always bent: they held the matches, which were extracted as needed. After he started one of his cheap cigarettes, Uncle Kolya would tell stories about how he, yesterday's Voronezh peasant, had been in the front ranks that liberated Kyiv. *Anyone who walked in the front ranks is long gone,* was the invariable debunking from Katerina, who didn't seem to have been there a minute before. Retribution was not long in coming. If the woman was within arm's reach, Uncle Kolya would give her a good smack; if not, he'd stick to elaborate obscenities. After an instant's flare-up, Uncle Kolya would calm down just as instantly. A minute later the smoke from his cigarette would cozily envelop the burning lamp and vanish in the olive tree's dark branches. His war stories would continue. Nothing could stop him, even Katerina's interventions, which remained a puzzle to everyone. This woman's longing for truth was combined with a taste for suffering, inasmuch as the two were clearly intertwined in her life. It may have been she didn't get enough feeling from the now old Uncle Kolya and she was trying to elicit it, like an artillery spotter who despairs and brings down the final volley on himself. What was important here was not the feeling's nature but its strength. Many years later, when the district authorities started resettling the communal apartment, people in the know advised the spouses to divorce temporarily. Then they would get two one-room apartments instead of one, and after that one of them could sell or, say, exchange their apartments for a two-room. And remarry. Opposed to this clever plan was Katerina, who refused to divorce, even fictitiously. She was afraid Mikola wouldn't marry her a second time. By the way, Gleb never saw any weddings in the apartment, although he did once see a funeral, when their neighbor Evdokia Vinnichenko died. Despite her mellifluous name, Evdokia was not remarkable in any way. Her sole distinguishing quality, perhaps, was that she never left the apartment. All chores outside the house, including the shopping, rested with her husband, Silvestr. No one had ever seen Evdokia in street clothes; she was always wearing a floral flannel robe and fur slippers. She walked quietly and spoke quietly – and mostly not at all. She and Silvestr barely talked either. They communicated in gestures and looks but didn't waste words. Most likely they had no children because how can you conceive them in a silence like that? Silvestr's silence was so profound that his voice seemed to have disappeared. Ultimately, Silvestr himself disappeared. Evdokia provided no explanations for what had happened. Maybe she didn't have any. To questions of Silvestr's whereabouts she would answer briefly: d'speared. After this event, her life didn't change in any way. Amazingly, she never did start going outside – at least, so it seemed to Gleb. In his imagination she was one of those people definitively tied to a specific place. Evdokia's place was by the kitchen table. She spent more time there than in her own room; washing something, cleaning something, moving things from place to place – from the left side of the table to the right and back again. She would do this in an odd way, picking up one foot off the floor and balancing on the other. Evdokia herself would sway as she did this, reminding him of a roly-poly toy, or a ballet dancer. A dancer, more likely. Observing Evdokia once from under his own table, unseen by her, Gleb noticed that her standing leg bent beautifully, balletically even. A sad and beautiful melody would pour barely audibly from her lips. He had no more doubts: Evdokia was dancing. Gleb badly wanted to ask what exactly Evdokia was singing, but even as a child he understood that if a lady of pension age is dancing and singing, it's better to pretend you haven't noticed anything, and under no circumstances ask questions. The boy recognized this melody on the day of Evdokia's funeral, when a brass band played it. The music breathed, each breath accompanied by a stroke of the cymbals and drum, making it heartrending, tragic; it had lost that shining sadness he'd heard in her quiet singing. Gleb asked his father, who had come to accompany Evdokia on her final journey, what the melody was. *"That's Chopin's Piano Sonata no. 2,"* his father replied, *"part three, the Funeral March."* "Evdokia used to sing it when she was alive," Gleb said, astonished. *"That's evidence she dreamed of dying,"* Fyodor said. "Does that really happen?" the boy asked. Fyodor looked at his son closely: *"People usually sing about what they dream of."*

AUGUST 28–31, 2012, PETERSBURG

On tour in Petersburg. En route from the airport, I stop the car at a bookstore and send the driver in to buy all the books they have by Nestor. He comes back with two. There had been five others, but they were sold out. I think two will suffice.

27

In the hotel I take a shower and unpack. Knocking timidly, the maid wheels in a cart with Veuve Clicquot and fruit, a gift from the establishment. The young woman blushes and asks for an autograph. As I get out a tip, I come across Nestor's card. I put it by the phone. I dial the first digits and hold down the hook.

I get out the package of books purchased and quickly look them over. *Aeronaut*, as the title says, is about the history of aeronautics in Russia. Flawed flying machines and selfless aviators. Fur jackets, leather helmets, safety goggles. A full catalog, it seems, of monoplanes and biplanes. "The list of ships I . . ." For the enthusiast.

Some things are more important than a shot. In the crude language of summary, the reader is informed that this is the story of a nurse who became a chief physician. Her rises and falls. Relations between patients and staff at a medical institution, difficult hospital days, where love and death live side by side. I open the book at random – short, choppy sentences, precise descriptions. I like the rhythm, but most of all, the gaze. Her rises and falls. . . . Judging from the theme, the first book is about falls too. This reminds me of something. There are things more important than music. . . .

The card is by the phone. Why should I call? I ask myself. I have three concerts in Petersburg, three evenings in a row. Nestor is certain to show up at one of them.

He doesn't. The last evening, after the concert, I call Nestor after all. To the long beeps in the receiver I doodle squares on his business card. Just as I'm about to hang up, he picks up at the other end. Nestor is very happy I called; he knew nothing about my tour. I draw a fat exclamation point on the card.

Nestor suggests we meet the next day, but my plane is in the morning. Right now then. Nestor thinks we need to meet right now. He and his wife Nika invite me over. I'm still acting undecided, but inwardly, I may well be ready. The thought of entering someone's nighttime coziness fills me with joy.

Nestor dictates the address. He plans to pop out for vodka too. And also, Nika asks the guest to grab his guitar. I report that this will be done and put a second exclamation point on the card. I call a car and grab my guitar. Approaching the door, I notice the cart the maid brought – they refresh it every day. The Veuve Clicquot and fruit go straight into the bag of books.

Nestor lives on Bolshoi Prospect on the Petrograd side. It takes exactly ten minutes to drive there from the hotel. As I'm getting out of the car, Nestor is just returning from the store. We go up to the apartment together, where we are met by Nika, a lady with a low, husky voice. Nestor, Nika, and I, by all accounts, were born the same year or very nearly so. You usually feel at ease with people like that.

The table is set in the kitchen. Cheese, sausage, sardines, vodka. Before sitting down, Nika shows me the writer's quarters. All as it should be: bookshelves packed to the limit (her husband is given many books, we haven't bought them in a long time), vertical and horizontal placement side by side. In addition to the books, room has in some inexplicable way been found for many knick-knacks. Books on tables, on beds, on the floor, on the microwave and washing machine (the writer likes reading in the bathroom). Nika refers to Nestor as a writer and is very proud of him.

The Veuve Clicquot goes into the freezer, but no one here seems to have any particular interest in it. Nestor pours vodka for everyone, including his wife, arousing no protest in Nika. We drink to our meeting. Nestor recounts to Nika in detail how it began. He acts out our airplane conversation. He shows her how arrogantly I answered him and put his card away without a glance. I applaud Nestor.

"Is that really me?"

Narrowing his eyes, Nestor shakes his head.

"That's the view from the outside," Nika reassures me. "I wouldn't trust it."

"And I don't." I drain the shot I've been poured. "But I do want to say that your writer is pretty darn good. A decent writer."

Nika's phone rings. Covering the mouthpiece with her palm, she says it's their son. She lights a cigarette and goes out into the hall to talk.

"Your son doesn't live with you?" I ask.

"He lives nearby." Nestor also lights up. "And I've already started writing, you see. . . . Are you truly agreeing to the book? That's an outside view too."

Three decisive noes come from the hall.

"I've looked at myself so long from the inside."

With the fourth no, Nika appears.

"Get lost," she whispers and hangs up. She sits down at the table. "I'm sorry, an educational moment." To me: "Do you have children?"

"No."

A phone rings – Nestor's this time. After a brief, dry greeting there is yet another no. They have a taste for that word here. Nestor leaves the call unexplained. The topic of children is not revived because Nika makes a toast:

"To collaboration!"

Everyone drinks.

"We have just clarified . . ." Nestor sounds depressed, like someone who hasn't joined in yet. "We've clarified just how seriously Gleb regards this undertaking."

"How seriously is that?" Nika asks. "You know, even I'm amazed. You always speak so well about life through your music, why do you need his words?" She nods to her husband.

I take a cigarette out of Nestor's pack. Nestor offers me a light.

"It's hard to explain. I think music . . . and painting, too, probably . . . Ultimately they exist only because the word exists."

Nika nods at the guitar lying in its case.

"Will you play?"

I suggest we all switch to informal address, the familiar "you." I get out the guitar and tune it for a few minutes. Nika points out the empty glasses to her husband.

"Whereas at the edge of the word I experience fear." Nestor is about to pick up the bottle but puts it back down. "You know, where the word ends, that's where the music begins. Or, well, yes, painting. Or silence in general."

I start playing a Ukrainian song, "The Sun Is Setting" – first the theme, then variations. I hum along quietly. The words aren't entirely clear to my audience, but it's obviously a sad song. It's night. A young girl's beloved comes to her. As she let him in, she *squeezed his hand*. And as she let him go, *she asked him the truth*. Voice and strings resonate. *"Do you love me?"* she asks. "Might you be seeing another," she asks, "and won't admit it?" "No," he answers, "I love you, *only you, but I'll not marry you*." Guitar solo. Pizzicato on the high notes – all the way up the neck. *"Oh, my God, my God . . ."* Clearly he's telling her everything. The height of sound shifts to the height of suffering and dwindles until it is completely inaudible because grief has no expression. His fingers are now still, but the music keeps pouring out.

I leave at dawn. At the open door, Nestor embraces me firmly and Nika's arms rest on top. The three of us stand there like that at the open door, the night's lingering chill on our backs. His eyes dropped delicately, a neighbor walks by with a fishing rod. There's a car waiting for me by the front entrance.

1972

Soon after Evdokia's funeral, Gleb heard the cymbals and drum once again. This was at the opera theater, where his grandmother took him to hear *Evgeny Onegin*. What struck him first was the way the orchestra started up. The enormous hall filled with melody fragments. A grandiose torrent of sounds freed from the music forever, it seemed, creating a new fellowship. That was only how it seemed, though. In the darkened and stilled hall the fragments were gathered up by the very first sweep of the conductor's baton. And Gleb burst into tears – at this harmony, at this fullness and power of sound such as he'd never heard before, because, plunged into darkness, the hall slowly soared, and he was part of that flight. An incredible journey began for the select – those who had had the courage to sit in the dark hall. The boy sobbed, covering his mouth with his hand, although no one could hear him over the loud music, and in the darkness no one saw his shoulders shaking. Gleb and his grandmother were sitting in a first-tier box, while two tiers above Sergei Petrovich Brovarnik, who taught compulsory piano at Gleb's music school, lay on the floor. Sergei Petrovich believed that music should be listened to by tuning out not only the surrounding world but even one's own body. He would bring a sheet to the theater and spread it on the floor, where the rows ended, lie down on the sheet, and close his eyes. He didn't miss a single opera performance. Keen on opera, Gleb very often saw Sergei Petrovich in the theater. Once, when Antonina Pavlovna and her grandson were sitting in the third tier (they were performing *Ivan Susanin*), Sergei Petrovich was lying directly behind them. From time to time muffled sighs could be heard from where he lay, and the audience, alarmed, not versed in the various ways of perceiving music, would look around into the darkness behind the seats. In Gleb's memory, Sergei Petrovich was an example of true devotion to music.

As for *Ivan Susanin,* the boy liked the opera, but it wasn't a patch on *Evgeny Onegin.* Singing over the cacophony, Lensky with maximum precision: "I have simply asked Mr. Onegin to explain his actions. He does not wish to do so, so I ask him to accept my challenge!" Oh, how harsh this was; *Ivan Susanin,* for all its tragedy, had nothing like it. Especially that "simply." And the cry of the mistress of the house, "Oh, my God!" musically repeating the exclamation "my challenge!" Plus, of course, the word "Mr.," which Gleb liked tremendously – so elegant compared to unkempt, unwashed "comrades." An extraordinary item was the top hat, filled with aristocratism, instead of the worn, here-we-go-again cap. Nonetheless, in Gleb's eyes, what hit hardest was the duel scene. He acted out this scene endlessly with Kleshchuk, whose parents, it turned out, had also taken him to *Evgeny Onegin.* Kleshchuk-Lensky would sink slowly to the floor after Gleb-Onegin's shot. Tubby Kleshchuk sank awkwardly and unnaturally, and each time Gleb had to show him how people usually fall after being shot. Gleb took some satisfaction in this – as an artist and a teacher. Despite all his efforts, progress was imperceptible. Kleshchuk, overcautious, would manage to look at his feet a few times, although what did he actually expect to see on the highly polished parquet? While instructing Kleshchuk, though, Gleb tried not to go overboard. He knew what comes from excessive pressure on people, and he didn't want to spoil his impression of *Evgeny Onegin,* which became the chief delight of his first academic year. The fullness of this delight was reached when, as of that winter, the boy was able to listen to the opera on record. For New Year's, his mama and grandmother, after long consultations in the evenings, gave Gleb a record player. Even Fyodor was drawn into this expensive purchase, and, impoverished though he was, he came up with the last twenty rubles. Along with the record player there was a cardboard box in which lay three records: *Evgeny Onegin.* And although subsequently other records were bought as well, Gleb listened to *Onegin* almost exclusively. In a couple of months he knew all the arias by heart. At family parties, the boy, at the guests' request, would sing them all in order or at random – with feeling, although, according to his father, who was once invited, not entirely in tune. His mother, indignant, objected that *how* the child sang the arias wasn't the point, the point was that he was *singing* them, and that instead of supporting him, his father was spouting all kinds of nonsense. Being out of tune isn't *nonsense,* Fyodor muttered, but he didn't get into an argument. Gleb pretended not to eavesdrop, but deep down he was hurt. He very much wanted to impress his father. And didn't. On the other hand, he did impress the others – his classmates, for example. Although not all. His aria performances did not impress Bdzhilka, who had known the magical word *ochyeryet.* He asked Gleb to sing folk songs and even sang one himself – "Oh, in the grove by the Danube" – one especially beloved in his village. The song was beautiful (Ukrainian songs are fabulously beautiful), but this did not induce Gleb to change his repertoire. He continued to sing his arias under Bdzhilka's mocking gaze. Meanwhile, Bdzhilka would ask questions to which Gleb could not always find an answer. Listening to Gleb's performance of Lensky's aria, Bdzhilka asked what an "aurora" was ("aurora's ray will shine come morning"), why the "biss" was slow ("the young poet's memory swallowed by the slow Abyss") and the urn early ("shed a tear over the early urn"). Outside, sometimes, he would stop over an urn and start collecting imaginary tears in his hand. Actually, when it came to laughter, Bdzhilka couldn't come close to Gleb – Gleb and another classmate, Vitya Kislitsyn. Gleb and Kislitsyn were called the laughers because they were constantly guffawing. If they looked at the passing bursar (squint-eyed, fat-lipped), they'd laugh. If they looked at a dog (one ear up, the other drooping), they'd laugh too. Whoever they looked at, they'd laugh, because there's something funny about everyone, it just takes an eye. An eye and company, since you're not going to laugh alone. The English teacher, as long as a stork, arms and legs like the blades of a pen-knife, was walking down the hall. Walking stiffly: in lockstep, her head thrown back. Irina Grigorievna. Gleb and Kislitsyn started laughing. Irina Grigorievna complained to Lesya Kirillovna. At her very next lesson, Lesya Kirillovna, an unsmiling person, called Kislitsyn to the board. Without warning, she picked up the pupil by the nape (his legs quietly swinging) and prompted him: *"Laugh!"* Kislitsyn didn't laugh – evidently that's hard to do dangling. It had the exact opposite effect: tears started rolling down his cheeks. Gleb realized that he was probably next, which was scary. Scary and funny, as can happen. He looked at his dangling comrade but got no look back. Kislitsyn had no thought of exchanging looks, he was looking at the ceiling. Gleb was the first to notice that Kislitsyn had an incredibly big head over his small swinging body. His friend looked like an eighth note on the top line of the staff – the one with stem and tail pointed down. D, apparently. Or F. Gleb smiled at this thought, and now it was hard to imagine what punishment awaited him. But once she'd set Kislitsyn down, Lesya Kirillovna unexpectedly smiled too – for the first time in a year, maybe. Something had touched her, either Kislitsyn's tears or Gleb's smile. Lesya Kirillovna turned out to have quite a few gold teeth in her mouth. Gleb thought her smile was blinding and was amazed that the possessor of such wealth had never smiled before. Actually, she didn't smile much afterward either, except for one strange instance Gleb was told about by Plachinda, who continued observing Lesya Kirillovna. This time, sitting at Kislitsyn's desk, the teacher smiled shyly, evidently depicting the pupil's smile. Then, after she was back at her desk, she burst into laughter with a brutality compared to which all her former swearing dimmed. Lesya Kirillovna pulled an imagined Kislitsyn off the floor and demanded, *"Laugh!"* But the real Kislitsyn wasn't laughing anymore. He never did recover from that dangling at the board, you might say. From time to time he would still smile, but his smile would sometimes turn to tears. Maybe this was why Plachinda told Gleb, not him, what she'd seen. As for Gleb, he also got what was coming to him, only in a slightly different way. Seeing Gleb laughing, Lesya Kirillovna once advised him to hide his *buck teeth*. From the standpoint of pedagogy, this advice might raise questions, but the comparison certainly did hit its mark. By the middle of second grade, Gleb's upper teeth had shifted noticeably forward and become exactly what the teacher described. The sole advantage of teeth growing in wrong was their acoustic properties. By clicking his thumbnails on his teeth, Gleb learned to do a virtuoso rendition of Gershon Kingsley's "Popcorn." He could play other things, too, but nothing could compare to that staccato, xylophonic melody. After what the teacher said, Gleb's amazing gift was forgotten overnight. Everyone in class repeated what Lesya Kirillovna had said. Kislitsyn, who didn't want to be known as the only one to dangle, had an especially good time with it. Listening to the new teasing repeated in different ways, Gleb wondered at what cruel creatures children were after all. Why, Gleb thought, were they (we) considered angelic? The only person who expressed sympathy for Gleb was Bdzhilka. Sensibly, he didn't comment on Lesya Kirillovna's statement, but he did give practical advice. "*If you lick your teeth, they'll straighten out,*" he told Gleb, and he even showed him how it was done. Bdzhilka's tongue – surprisingly long and agile – moved freely across his teeth. At one point his tongue even seemed to latch on tight to his front teeth and drag them back by force. And although upon closer examination it was discovered that Bdzhilka's teeth remained in their former position, his power of persuasion was so great that for several days Gleb did in fact lick his teeth. Without results. No, that's not entirely true. The result was his grandmother became aware of the problem. She took Gleb to the dentist. Before she could put the boy in the chair, the dentist said he needed a retainer. Gleb had the discouraging thought that his bad bite could be seen from the threshold. So as not to lose time, they decided to take measurements for the retainer right away. The nurse took a metal form and filled it with wet plaster. The doctor shoved it deep into Gleb's mouth, telling him to bite down as hard as possible. With his lower teeth the boy felt the metal, but his upper ones sank into the mildly malodorous mass. It felt as if this mass was growing, that soon it would block his throat and he might suffocate. He started to feel sick. He tried to hold on, told himself it would all be over in a moment, but nothing was over. The fear that if he started to vomit the vomit would have nowhere to go rolled over him in uneasy waves. He threw up a second after they removed the form with the set plaster from his mouth. A couple of weeks later, when the retainer was ready and Gleb put it on for the first time, he threw up again. The plastic palate looked disgusting, touched his real palate disgustingly, and unstuck with a disgusting sound. The one more or less acceptable part of the gear was the double wire that grasped the teeth that deviated from the right position. When touched with a finger, the wire made a quiet but melodious sound. That alone reconciled the boy to the teeth-straightening process. An outside observer saw only the wire, not suspecting the construction, physiologically repulsive, that held this fragile detail. Sometimes Gleb's patience ran out. He would look around, take the retainer out of his mouth, and put it in his desk. And honestly (though perhaps not very) would forget it there. Be that as it may, the next morning he would invariably receive the retainer from Lesya Kirillovna and put it in his mouth under her stern gaze. Gleb wore the retainer for nearly a year and – who would have thought! – his teeth were fixed. Now they were big and even, qualities that undoubtedly constitute beauty for men's teeth. This did not happen without loss, though. Now that his teeth were even, for some reason they lost their musical properties. They no longer played "Popcorn." On the other hand, how his domra played! Little by little it was becoming clear to everyone that the boy possessed great talent because he alone was capable of playing with such impressive nuance. At times his technique betrayed him – he didn't always keep to the tempo – but when it came to nuance, he had no equals. This was what made Gleb the pride of the music school. Yes, his ear was still far from perfect, but he wasn't playing the violin, after all! Strictly speaking, Gleb's current domra was nearly a violin by now. Seeing her pupil's success, Vera Mikhailovna presented him with his own instrument for his studies, a custom domra made from Caucasian fir. To carry it, Gleb was given the brown case originally ordered with the domra. The boy was enchanted by its velvety sound, and he admired the amber relief of the old wood. Everything pleased him – except for the case, because the case reminded him of a coffin. Each time Gleb opened it, the domra looked like a broad-hipped beauty brought not from music school but from the Berkovtsi cemetery – then still deserted but already enormous. Putting the domra back in its case, he pictured it as his lost beloved taken away to the cemetery forever. The case poisoned his life.

SEPTEMBER 15, 2012, MUNICH

Our building on Am Blütenring. Katarina and I are reflected in the evening window. Katya. I'm sitting at my desk while Katya stands behind me, her hand on my shoulder. My desk lamp is turned on, and in its yellow light the reflection in the window is fabulously beautiful. Painted by the lamp, we remind ourselves of an old photograph and look to ourselves vaguely posthumous. Actually, there's a painting hanging in a hotel with the same composition (including the reflection), but we prefer resurrecting it every evening. We appreciate the details – the turn of the head, the bend in the arm, the placement of the fingers on the shoulder.

"It's long since time for you to have your hand checked out," Katya says.

"It is."

I find a lighter in the malachite desk set and flick it. One more point of light appears in the window.

"Barbara will help. She'll set it up at her clinic."

"Let's try to get along without Barbara."

Katya's lips graze the top of my head and she sighs mournfully. I feel the warmth run through my hair. I'm irritated that her sister Barbara comes up no matter the subject. A tall, red-haired German with a loud voice. Everything about her is excessive: her voice, her laugh, her movements. She also likes to drink.

An hour later, as if on cue, Barbara arrives, already a few sheets to the wind. I need to answer several letters urgently, so I go into the other room. When I return, I see Katya and Barbara over a bottle of vodka. I call their interest in alcohol unhealthy. Katya, vindicating herself, starts talking about some reason they needed a drink today, but Barbara interrupts her.

"There is only one reason, my friend: no children. And all we have left is to show an interest in alcohol. And cry." She wipes her eyes with a hankie. "Wet tears."

Katya and I speak Russian. This doesn't work with Barbara. Switching to German, I summon resolve. I pour the vodka into the sink, pick drunk Barbara up off the floor and, despite her size, carry her to the sofa. She calls me a Russian brute, but she's fine with this brutishness, basically. On the sofa, Barbara offers some resistance. Subduing the woman, I sit on top of her and inform her that she's a lush. They're both lushes.

"Possibly," Barbara replies. "But on the other hand, take a look at *what* we drink: a purely Russian beverage. Because even while displaying unhealthy interests, we want to make a good impression on you."

"Without much success, though."

Barbara to her sister:

"Looks like we're not winning him over this way. Too bad."

Katya sighs.

"Alas. But maybe" – she points up – "maybe we'll win over the Russian writer coming to see us."

Barbara's look is full of surprise.

"A Russian writer?"

"His name is Nestor." Katya smooths her imaginary beard. "He's going to write a book about Gleb."

"He's already writing it," I say angrily.

"Already writing it!" Barbara throws up her hands. "How timely!"

"We agreed that every few months Gleb would send him tickets and Nestor would come see us. They'll be working on the book." Katya draws a book in the air with her index fingers.

"A Russian writer might come see us!" Barbara slides to the floor and leans back against the sofa. She flaps like a crane a few times. "That's marvelous! That's simply wonderful, that a Russian writer can come visit!"

1973

That summer, Gleb and Antonina Pavlovna went to Kerch and stayed with his grandmother's friends on Cooperative Lane. Gleb's eye linked the two cooperative *o*'s with the b*oo*m of the front entrance. And the c*oo*l when you came in from the scorching street. To his ear, those two *o*'s cascaded deliciously from the long to the short *o* – in everyone but

40

his grandmother. Antonina Pavlovna pronounced them the Vologda way, with two long *o's*. Cooperative Lane ran into Lenin Street, which went off to the right – interlaced overhead by old acacias. On the left was a large square (also Lenin Square, apparently: there was a low-slung statue of him there) with the municipal theater and the Seagull department store. Running behind the square was a shady little side-street that led to the sea. This was the first sea Gleb had ever seen – full of fishing boats, not a tourist sea, and even, as it turned out, not a swimming sea. A couple of years later they shut down the beach due to cholera. But at that remarkable time the beach was still in the center of town, and you could only get there straight from the embankment. The beach and embankment were separated by a stone balustrade that stretched the full length of the beach. Towering over the balustrade was a gazebo, also made of stone. A kingdom of stone. The water splashed against the concrete shore. Bathers took the concrete steps down to the water. They held on to the metal railings because the steps were slippery, covered in green seaweed that echoed the rhythm of the waves. Gleb knew how varied this rhythm could be and how abruptly it could change. After frequent stirrings from the breeze, the slow power of the big incoming waves would suddenly surge, and the sea would drone like a gigantic swinging bell. On stormy days, when there was no swimming, Gleb and his grandmother would stand on the sand-sprinkled slabs of beach and watch crystal garlands by the thousands rocket skyward following the strike of a wave. But this happened rarely. Usually the sea was calm. They (his grandmother first) would descend the steps cautiously. The bottom sloped, and the first few days Gleb, who couldn't swim, tried to walk on it. He didn't get far. The entire bottom was scattered with rocks big and small. And since it's difficult to move around in water even without rocks, Gleb eventually preferred just standing. Throwing out his arms and balancing, swaying with the water, sometimes slapping at it. Sometimes he got cold from not moving. When she saw Gleb's blue lips, Antonina Pavlovna would bring her grandson to shore and rub him down with a terry cloth towel. But even rubbing didn't warm him completely. The gooseflesh went away only after several minutes of lying on the mat – actually a fringed tablecloth his grandmother's friends had lent them to take to the beach. Burying his nose in it, Gleb smelled mothballs, so unlike all the beach's smells. In that odd apartment where they stayed, mothballs were a notable, if not the only smell, generally speaking, and was mixed with the smell of the sea, which came from the many curios: dried fish, starfish, seashells. The apartment also smelled of propane – even, for some reason, when the burner was off. This made his grandmother wonder about an explosion, but calmly, in her Northern, rather fatalistic way. The tap water had its own taste too. Or rather, it tasted amazingly terrible, unthinkable to use for tea, you'd think, although the locals did. They probably didn't think water could be any different. But Antonina Pavlovna and Gleb had come from other lands and knew a thing or two about good water. Instead of tea, they drank lemonade or mineral water. They would chill their beverages in the refrigerator and take them along on their outing. They would walk to Mithridates Hill, where it was hot even late at night, when the stones gave off the warmth they'd absorbed over the course of the day. In the tall, nearly burnt grass, they would discover traces of archeological digs here and there. Grandmother and grandson looked at the fragments of stairs and walls, trying to imagine how Mithridates lived here. From the grass came the chirring of grasshoppers, and in the rare acacias the chirring was overpowered many times over by cicadas. To Gleb it was like listening to a huge orchestra playing in unison. An apotheosis of sawing, a triumph of bows. The ultimate devotion to music: the musician's body as his instrument. The thought of this devotion was a support for Gleb when he returned to music school in the fall. He managed his études with aplomb – not that he liked them. The boy felt more in tune with melodic pieces and folk songs, especially those with tremolo, using the pick. Actually, everything on the domra used the pick. Gleb began to feel it physically as the extension of his hand, kind of like an artificial nail growing out of his thumb and index finger simultaneously. In his favorite pieces, the pick merged with his fingers without the slightest effort and didn't slip out of his sweaty hand. His hand movement was free and powerful simultaneously – and the tremolo came out luscious and dense, never for a moment falling into separate strikes of the strings. If before, when listening to Gleb perform classics, Fyodor had just smiled, now more and more often he gave specific advice. His father was listening in domestic surroundings, understandably, without the piano accompaniment. The boy wanted to stand before his father in all his musical beauty, and definitely with accompaniment. He got such a chance one day when the music school's best pupils were invited to perform at Pushkin Park. Gleb was supposed to play Mozart's "Turkish March" – just the piece to be performed before this sure-fire audience. Gleb, who usually wasn't shy in front of listeners, already had a foretaste of how, accompanied by their rhythmic clapping, he would play the famous Mozart grace notes. The rhythm's solemnity was the very essence of the "Turkish March" and manifested itself in everything, up to and including the way the weeping willow's branches swayed in the wind to the music's beat. That wind, as became clear, held a danger too. Gleb's fingers froze. How differently musicians are made. Some play calmly in the freezing cold; others lose all mobility in their fingers from a slight breeze. Gleb lost his. He lagged behind the accompanist, and although a couple of times he tried to catch up, they finished separately. This picture solidified in Gleb's memory forever: the loosely filled seats on benches, like on a chessboard, his father's sad eyes in the last row, and the absolute impossibility of playing. He never performed on outdoor stages again.

43

And still doesn't. After that day and for a long time, Gleb lost his taste for playing *beautiful* pieces, as if the Mozart hit was the reason for his failure. He came to like those which at first glance did not seem beautiful – études, for example. This love was a special kind of feeling, an attraction to beauty through complexity because complexity has its own beauty. He also became aware that he truly did love the domra. If previously this little instrument had seemed to him merely a step on his way toward the guitar, it had now taken on independent significance. The domra reminded Gleb of a snail with its neck extended; abandoning it would be a betrayal. It was decided to continue domra classes. Then his father told him, "*Now, my son, you will work for Leah for seven years and then for Rachel for seven years.*" Gleb studied the folk instrument for five years, but he understood his father's biblical parallel.

October 1, 2012, Munich

Nestor is flying in to work on the book. I have four days free of touring. That's not a lot, of course, but it's enough for a first time. Our housekeeper, Geraldina Kästner, a skinny forty-year-old woman, greets him at the airport with a sign that says "Nestor."

Conversation en route probably does not go well. Nestor doesn't know German, and Geraldina's English "*is very limited.*" She informs him of this without taking her eyes off the road. And smiles with restraint, I think. Further communications to Nestor are less intelligible; it's merely clear that the Yanovskys aren't home right now. They're at their *dacha* in the mountains, Geraldina explains, but will be back for dinner. They may already be back.

Very near the house a car sits on their tail and warbles a honk at them. It's Katya and I. Looking in her rearview mirror, Geraldina responds with a short stern beep. She is aware that her position does not give her the right to a warble. She clicks open the gate. Both cars drive into the courtyard.

I embrace Nestor and introduce Katya to him. She gives Nestor her hand:

"Katya. Mr. Yanovsky's driver, and also his wife." She laughs. "He still doesn't know how to drive a car."

"Nor do I," Nestor says.

Everyone washes up after their journeys and then sits at the table on the front lawn. Geraldina brings lap robes, but we don't need them. On a sunny day, a Munich October is still practically summer. Dinner is brought from the nearest restaurant. The waiter pours the wine into glasses and lights two candles. The first goes out over the salad, the second lasts until the soup. The waiter lights them again, but this time the candles go out immediately. You can tell the boy's no arsonist. Smiling, he makes another attempt – and the wind blows out the candles again. The wind rustles Katya's loose hair.

After dinner, Nestor and I sit on the veranda and get to work. Nestor takes out his dictaphone.

Turns it on silently.

"One, two, three. And we're off. . . ."

He hits rewind. The dictaphone responds in the same Gagarin cry. "How did your musical career begin?"

My career. I answer as if from a written text.

"The night before the first day of school, I sat in front of my father watching his long fingers and attempted to reproduce his rhythm. Outside, streetcars rang their bell. The china in the sideboard clinked in response. Then Fyodor sang something and asked me to repeat it. I couldn't repeat the melody, just the words: *paba-paba, paba-paba, paba-pa.* They sounded like 'papa.' But Fyodor had asked me to use the Ukrainian, *tato.* Hardly anyone in Kyiv called their father that."

45

"I think you said all this on the airplane."

"Practically word for word. That's how I always answer this question. I've been asked it a good two hundred times."

"All right. Let's take this from another direction. Was Ukrainian forbidden?"

"No. Quite the opposite. All the signs were in Ukrainian, the radio, all that sort of thing."

"You mean there was no nationality issue?"

"I don't know. Russian was the more prestigious language, shall we say. Everyone realized you couldn't get anywhere without it. I'd put it this way: The question of prestige stands above national identity. When that identity becomes a matter of prestige, then that's another matter."

Geraldina brings in a coffee tray. Pours us each a cup of coffee. In a whisper ("Pretend I'm not here") asks for permission to add cream. Tiptoes out.

"As you realize, I'm not writing a history of Ukraine. What's important to me is your story. It's just that you combine two nations, and I want to understand exactly how."

"I wish I understood that myself."

I top off our coffees. A brown spot spreads over the tablecloth.

"Well, what do you consider yourself?" Nestor blots the spot with his napkin.

"I could say Russian, of course."

"What's stopping you?"

"Nothing, probably. I just don't distinguish between those nations very well."

Nestor lights up. Clouds of smoke take on the image of Geraldina and an ashtray. Placing it in front of Nestor, she looks reproachfully at the coffee stain.

46

"Tell me about your father."

"My father . . ." I pensively squeeze Nestor's pack of cigarettes. "I'm going to bum cigarettes from you, okay? It's important I don't buy them for myself. I'm afraid I'll start smoking again."

"Had you already started?" Nestor offers me a light.

"Yes, at about fourteen. I'd save my lunch money and buy cigarettes. I had no money. . . . You were asking about my father. There was someone who had no money. Ever." I take a sip of coffee and inhale deeply. "A lover of grand gestures without the slightest wherewithal for them. Well, isn't that a drama?"

Nestor shrugs. He probably doesn't think so.

"From time to time he'd buy my mother fancy bouquets." I run the tip of my cigarette across the ashtray's bottom. "From time to time – because he'd save up for them. He'd come home with a bouquet and present them casually, as if to say, Look what lovely flowers I found on my way home. And she knew approximately when she'd get the next bouquet since she knew his rate of saving."

"But a bouquet bought on scrimped money is more precious than a bouquet you don't have to save for. Isn't that obvious?"

"Yes, yes, it's obvious, but my father, I repeat, he loved grand gestures. Gestures, understand? And a grand gesture doesn't necessarily mean saving. It means ease, but since that's something he didn't have . . . One day – this was after their divorce – he took my mother and me to an expensive restaurant. He ordered everything himself because he was keeping a running total. Moving his lips. But in the end they brought him a much larger check. He immediately made the waiter recalculate everything. He did, quite deliberately, and my father sat there red-faced. My mother proceeded calmly to tell me some story, as if she didn't notice what was going on. That's who had the ease."

"How did it all end?"

"It turned out, of course, that the waiter had added extras. And still the check was bigger than my father had expected. There was something he hadn't counted, some sauce. My father settled the bill, turned out all his pockets, but there was nothing left for a tip. And the waiter stood there, the scoundrel, the towel over his arm, and smiled: 'So, are we tipping?' I felt like strangling him, basically, and I remember that scene to this day. My father sat there so defenseless. And you know, at the time I suddenly felt how much I loved him."

My mobile plays "March of the Aviators." I answer in German, sternly and briefly. I explain to Nestor that it's a newspaper. Another question from an idle mind.

"For example?"

"What do you think about multiculturalism?"

"What do you?"

"Nothing."

1974

In the middle of summer, Fyodor's relative Galina and her son Egor paid him a visit. This greatly surprised Irina because they were from Kursk Province. It wasn't that Fyodor seemed like someone who couldn't have relatives in Kursk Province, it's just she'd never heard about anything of the kind. Galina moved in with Fyodor. What surprised Irina even more was that her former husband asked her to put Egor up. Fyodor wanted Egor (he and Gleb were the exact same age) to have company while he was in Kyiv. Given that Galina looked Romani, her son's hair was inexplicably blond – inexplicably for Gleb. Not thinking about a possibly blond father, Gleb privately decided Egor was a foundling. This was why people treated him badly, Gleb thought; it was no accident that upon his arrival in Kyiv he was

48

handed off to the Yanovskys. But Egor wasn't a foundling. As he himself stated when Gleb, delicately, he thought, asked him about this. If he wasn't he wasn't. Gleb's question wasn't idle. It's just that if Egor were in fact a foundling, Gleb would have asked his mama and grandmother to adopt him: Gleb wanted a brother. In his father's absence – as Gleb already knew – he couldn't even dream of a real brother's appearance. Actually, dreams of a brother visited the boy only on the first day of their Kursk visitor's stay. That whole day Egor was quiet and pensive. But by the next day his behavior had changed, and Gleb's dreams of a brother flew out the window. Egor started ordering everyone around, from Gleb to Irina. He decided what to make for dinner and how, what to read for the night, and the right way to pronounce the letter *g*. He disqualified the occlusive *g* on the grounds that people in Kursk Province didn't say it that way. Also, according to him, people there didn't call it a *tele*phone – only a tele-*phone*. When Irina expressed doubts about this, he demanded an immediate trip to Kursk and was prepared to accompany Irina. No one had the nerve to be firm with Egor because he was a guest. Within a day he was bossing kids around in the courtyard. For the Ukrainian children, Egor had somewhere got a hold of a Ukrainian counting rhyme. He lined them up and told them to memorize it: *Tsutsyk went into the bog / Told Froggy, "Get to work!" / Froggy said back, "Keep your job!" / and Tsutsyk, "Lose that smirk!"* The rhyme determined who would be "it" in a game of hike-and-seek. Egor's new friends liked the story about Tsutsyk the troublemaker and foul-mouthed Froggy. It did not lack drama and a certain protest even against the existing state of affairs. But Egor taught the Kyiv children to hide as well as count. Or rather, he taught them to appreciate and utilize the dark because they played in the dark too. Before, the children had hidden far away from whoever was "it." They would climb onto low branches of trees, scramble over fences, and clamber onto shed roofs. *One, two, three,* *four, five* ... Whoever was "it" would open his eyes so he looked like Vii, the Spirit of Evil. *Ready or not ... here I come. ...* He always knew where to seek and where to find. When everyone jumped out of their hiding places, he easily cut them off. And was first to slap the pole. With Egor's arrival, it was made clear that you could hide differently in the dark. For instance, if there was a lamp at the corner of a building, then the darkness around the corner became pitch dark. Without hiding anywhere – just leaning up against the wall – you became completely invisible. There turned out to be quite a few places on the cusp between light and dark, but only at night did they acquire their magical properties. One of those evenings something awful happened. The boy standing at the cusp between light and dark nearly died. Artur Akopyan, a boy from the next courtyard. He came out of his hiding place before the count ended and, swaying, walked toward the boy who was "it." He was about to ask why Artur had come out ahead of time, but the question stopped at his lips. Artur was walking with a frozen gaze and half-open mouth. His neck and chest were bloody. A second later he threw up and slowly dropped to his knees, smearing vomit over the asphalt. He was on all fours, and he kept vomiting, but that wasn't the scariest part. When Artur lowered his head, in the light of the streetlamp you could see the bleeding wound on the back of his head. Egor dragged him to the spigot in the yard and started washing his head. Artur's mother ran out from somewhere, someone said he'd called an ambulance, and Gleb looked at Egor and admired his decisiveness – especially the fact that he hadn't been afraid to get close to the bloody person. Then Egor felt around in the shadowy place where Artur had been standing and found a poker there. Examining it, Egor found blood and Artur's tar-black hair at the bend in it. He was a real Sherlock Holmes, this Egor, and he liked it that people called him that then, since the night before he'd been reading Conan Doyle. Without a doubt, the boy had been struck with precisely this object. In the courtyard, where they had long since switched from a furnace to steam heat, by way of an instrument of crime they had used a poker, and this amazed Egor endlessly. Where did the poker come from? The fact that Artur had been struck, and from behind moreover, amazed him less. Artur took more than a month to recover. One day (it was early fall already), Gleb's mother met Artur's mother at the trolleybus stop. They talked about this and that. My son told me, Artur's mother said suddenly without any transition, that your Egor had been walking around with a poker a few days before all this. Mowing down burdock with it. What of it? Gleb's mother asked. Nothing, and Artur's mother looked down. By this time, Egor was already in Kursk Province. Actually, he didn't stay there long. Six months later he and his mother moved to Kyiv. Galina, who had been passing herself off as Fyodor's relative, was in fact no such thing. More precisely, she wasn't that summer, because a few months later she was: Fyodor married Galina. Galina turned out to be an amazing soul, good-hearted and selfless, which even Gleb had to admit, having been set against her at first. In the beginning, Fyodor more than likely had had no intention of marrying her, otherwise he wouldn't have called her his relative. When he got to know Galina better, everything changed. After his failed marriage, Fyodor decided to make one more attempt. Everyone who knew of Fyodor's complicated attitude toward Russia was amazed that both times his marriage was to Russian women. Here again the word "complication" arose – this time applied to Fyodor's spiritual world in general. In his hometown, in Kamianets-Podilskyi, people talked about him "overcoming," although without specifying whom or what. More than likely, himself, because there was no need whatsoever to overcome Galina. Striving to cement their union even more firmly, she learned Ukrainian with incredible speed, a speed explained, one can't help but think, by her healthy foundation in the form of her fricative *g*.

Galina spoke Ukrainian not only with her husband but with everyone else, who spoke Russian, understandably. Egor, too, learned Ukrainian, demonstrating great flexibility: he conversed in Ukrainian only within the family. In her new position, Galina existed between two far from simple men, Fyodor and Egor, and tried to please both, each in his own way. Irina knew this from Gleb's stories of visiting his father's, and she would tease Galina. Despite her indifference to Fyodor, the appearance in his life of a new woman irritated her a little. The tiniest bit. Not so much as to prevent her, for example, from eating the pies that Galina sent her with Gleb each time. Looking at Galina, Gleb thought how lucky his father had been with her after all and dreamed of a similarly quiet and sensible wife. Actually, even at his early age he realized that men marry women like Galina, of course, but fall in love with imprudent women. Such was Gleb's new love interest, Elena Markovna – like Klavdia Vasilievna, a teacher at the music school. She was a year younger than Klavochka (and he was a couple of years older now), so the age difference that had so grieved Gleb before was, in this instance, slightly less. Elena Markovna taught not the depressing solfeggio but the intriguing musical literature, which is why his feeling toward her was not suffering-love but pleasure-love. The main thing that drove Gleb crazy was Lena's very imprudence. Lena. Straight to the point. No diminutives or patronymics here. Despite school rules, she demanded they call her by name, Lena, and this was the first point of her imprudence. The fact that she taught in a Soviet music school wearing jeans was the second. The third – she did without a purse and tied her books and lectures together with a raggedy gray string. Class began with its untying and ended with its tying. Lena also did without things in a way that probably added another hundred points right off to her imprudence – and in this respect her rating shot up when she told them she'd spent her two-month teaching break in the Caucasus with hippies. So. Musical literature. It all started with Grieg, whom

Gleb didn't want to hear about because he was playing battleship with Maksim Kleshchuk. Lena said, "*Peer Gynt* is about true love." Although otherwise occupied, Gleb and Kleshchuk laughed out loud: the name "Peer Gynt" reminded them of something. And at that Lena approached. She grabbed Gleb painfully by the ear and whispered into that same ear: "You little pisser, what do you understand about love?" She let him go and stepped away. But he still felt the touch of her lips. It was painful, hurtful, and . . . intimate. Pisser. What did that word actually mean? A little pissing person? That part of his body, too, accordingly small? Probably the body part connected to love (as Gleb already knew) in the most immediate way. All this passed through his mind later, but at the time, in class, there wasn't a thought in his head. Not a one. There was a burning and hard-to-define feeling for Lena that in one moment flooded him, splashed out, and made him blush. Hatred, pain, shame, love? All of those at once? Gleb watched Lena nonstop, but on her face he read nothing but her attraction to *Peer Gynt*. After talking about the piece, she put on a record. While they listened to "Death of Aase," her eyes filled with tears. During "Anitra's Dance" she conducted, barely perceptibly, with the tips of her fingers. Kind of like "Lena's Dance." Not a dance, just its denotation, and because of this maximally sensuous. Lena. Olive-skinned, raven's wing hair. Daughter of a Bedouin chief. She pointed upward: "Listen! The cellos and double basses are playing pizzicato. What rapture!" She made a few plucking movements. Rapture. But what Gleb liked most was "Solveig's Song." Lena would wait for him always, at least until he grew up. After class was over she asked him to stay back. She sat him at a desk and herself sat on it. She straightened his twisted collar. Lena's finger brushed his cheek, and myriad goose-bumps began a descent down his spine. You weren't hurt? After she asked, she patted his chin. No, Gleb answered and started to cry. Tears of love, not hurt. She kissed him on the same ear she'd pulled in class.

It doesn't hurt anymore? No, it didn't anymore, but Gleb kept silent. Let her be punished. After that, musical literature was his favorite subject. Listening to Lena's stories about composers, he lived their lives, composed their music, and was amazed that all this had existed before him. When in the next quarter Lena talked about Haydn, Gleb watched her with pride because he was Haydn. Actually, "Gleb" sounded like "Gaidn" – Russian for "Haydn" – and Lena couldn't not understand that. Surely she was grateful to her pupil for all his 104 symphonies, of which her favorites and Gleb's were two: Symphony no. 103 (with timpani drumroll), and especially the "Farewell" Symphony no. 45 in F sharp minor. Two oboes, clarinet, two French horns, first and second violins, violas, cellos, and double basses. They stop playing in the following order: winds, double basses, cellos, violas, and second violins. Each places his instrument on his chair, each snuffs out his candle and leaves. All that remain are the two first violins, which conclude the symphony. They snuff out their candles and leave as well. Once, when Lena had taken her group to hear Haydn at the Philharmonic, the oboe's candle wouldn't go out. He blew on it and moved toward the exit, but before he had gone a few meters, the candle started burning again. The hall let him know. Whistles, claps, and shouts rang out. The oboe waddled back, kind of crookedly even (his smile was just as crooked), and blew out the candle. When he was already backstage, the candle summoned its strength and ignited again. The hall hooted. The oboe looked at the conductor, who was standing with his back to the hall, hiding his face, evidently, because the second time the oboe returned without a smile. He blew on the candle long and gloomily. To general laughter, he waited for it to renew its burning. It seemed strange to Gleb that the person whose main life's purpose was to blow was having so much trouble with a candle. But maybe – who knew? – this was about the candle, about its indomitability. Eventually, naturally, it went out.

What did not go out was Gleb's feeling for Lena. He thought he felt
the feeling returned. Sometimes, pacing around the classroom, she
would stop next to him. She would put her foot on the crossbar of his
chair and rock it. She would go on talking as if nothing was going on.
The boy's throat would dry up from the proximity of her slender leg
and that rocking. He couldn't take his eyes off her leg, it was so beautiful – and not only that, he was simply afraid to look up. Once he did,
though, and caught Lena's gaze, imperious and moist. She seemed
embarrassed; at least she took her foot off his chair. When he went to
bed that night, Gleb pictured Lena lying next to him, very close, and
feeling her soft skin. Lying together like that the whole night – just
lying, with no thought of anything else. Lena would look at him with
the same imperious and moist gaze, and this gaze would be stronger
than anything that could ever happen. In the morning, Gleb got up
with an unusual feeling, as if something very shameful and very sweet
had happened in the night. Morning's a hard time. It's always been
that way.

OCTOBER 2, 2012, MUNICH

Nestor turns on his dictaphone.

"In your interviews, Brisbane often comes up, and Australia in
general. Why?"

"Because when we have winter they have summer."

"And when we have summer?"

"Then they have summer too. By our standards, it's summer.
That's the whole joke, get it? In our family, that place was considered
paradise."

"There's a much too specific population there for paradise.
Convicts' descendants."

"So what?"

"For paradise you need a good biography."

"Have you been there?"

"Where? Australia?"

"No, paradise. How do you know what kind of biography one needs?"

Nestor shrugs.

"I wanted to ask you about Irina. Did she go to Brisbane after all?"

"At some point she started corresponding with someone from Brisbane. I don't know where she got his address, but she just wrote to him for many years."

"And did he propose to her?"

"Yes. It was a touching correspondence. From time to time my mother would relate his letters to me. Very fine ones. Mostly about General Thomas Brisbane, in whose honor the town was named. Unfortunately, she took them with her."

"What's her friend's name?"

"James – like Cook. She would call him Cook. 'Cook wrote me that besides the city, there's a crater on the moon named after Brisbane. The general was an astronomer by education.' Or: 'Cook writes that in his free time General Brisbane discovered more than seven thousand stars. Just imagine: in his free time!'"

"You've lived abroad for a long time. What do you think, those who left – are they finding a solution to their problems?"

"Hard to say. The decision is relatively . . . well, superficial, I think. If you look at it more broadly, I think even paradise is largely an internal state."

"In other words, what's the point of someone entering paradise with all his pain?"

"I'm afraid that on a backdrop of universal happiness he's going to be doubly unhappy. And eventually will probably run away."

"Have you and Irina stayed in contact?"

"Yes. We have. That's exactly what we've done."

1975

One morning on the way to school, Egor intercepted Gleb. He was standing there, leaning against a chestnut tree, and smiling. His arm holding his schoolbag was swinging like a pendulum, which made Egor look feeble. That was only how he looked, though. Egor was all will and determination. He'd come to suggest Gleb play hooky. This was an offer Gleb couldn't refuse – and not because it was so attractive. There wasn't anything particularly attractive about it; this was all about Egor's pressure. He laid out his plan as if it were a great gift to Gleb that he, Egor, was offering up in all selflessness. Understandably, Gleb had no choice but to accept the gift. First thing, Egor led his friend down Shevchenko Boulevard, where he knew a first-class gap between two apartment buildings. They hid their schoolbags there. In the time he'd lived in Kyiv, Egor had learned the city thoroughly; he was his own man in it. When he talked to Gleb he sensibly switched to the occlusive *g*. Given Egor's character, this was exactly the *g* that suited him. After hiding their schoolbags, Gleb's new relative marched off to the nearest dump and found two chair legs among the broken furniture. Gleb couldn't imagine what they might be needed for, but he didn't ask questions. Both boys knew that a question was a show of weakness and an answer was somehow the opposite. The legs turned out to be simple: they were needed in order to knock down chestnuts. To collect them, the foresighted Egor had brought along a canvas bag. Chestnuts grew on Shevchenko Boulevard alongside the apartment buildings, and pyramidal poplars rose in two parallel rows down the middle of the boulevard. Kyiv chestnuts were inedible. They weren't roasted on street corners, and they weren't in any way Parisian, but Egor and Gleb liked them. These chestnuts hung on branches like little green, sometimes yellow, hedgehogs. When knocked down by a well-aimed stick, the hedgehogs fell apart in flight, breaking in half and freeing the polished chestnut beauties. They struck the asphalt with a melodious sound, took a few hops, and stopped somewhere near the curb. Smooth and shiny, always with an unpolished crown. The chestnut's muffled pizzicato was followed every time by the stick's ringing grace note. Although the stick landed last after everything that flew from the tree, it still didn't get by with just one note. And one time it came like the strike of a drum: it hit a branch, flew off toward the road, and fell on a parked Zhiguli. When Gleb picked the stick up off the car's hood, he saw a dent. A small one, but a dent. He studied it for a minute or two until he felt Egor's hand on his arm dragging him toward the nearest archway. He would have liked to grab the bag of chestnuts under the tree, but Egor's hand pulled him forcefully toward the archway. From another archway, having heard the sound of the strike on his hood, the Zhiguli's owner was already running toward them. Egor and Gleb ran into the courtyard, rushed through the first open door, and flew up the stairs to the top floor. This was the building's back stairs and was appropriately pitch-dark: there were no windows or electric lights on its first three floors. A light glimmered only on the top, fourth floor, where there was a window that opened on the gap between the buildings. In the murky window light they could make out the back door to an apartment – a narrow door with peeled paint. The back way was, evidently, used. People went out to smoke at the half-open window, witness the massive granite ashtray full of butts on the windowsill. Muffled voices could be heard through the door. Holding their breath, Gleb and Egor waited to see where the car's owner headed. He'd seen them go through the archway but didn't know where they'd fled after that. The boys heard his cautious steps. At a certain moment they even thought someone was coming up the stairs, but that was just for a few seconds. Their pursuer probably thought better of searching for them in the dark. Judging from the grating sound of broken brick, he'd decided to check the gap between the buildings. Gleb was about to feel relief but discovered no joy on Egor's face. Our schoolbags, Egor said with just his lips. He's noticed our schoolbags. Through the open window they saw the car owner's bald spot slowly move toward their schoolbags. This guy had guessed who'd left their things there. Gleb saw Egor's hands reach for the ashtray and dump the butts on the floor. Slowly he lifted it past the windowsill. Gleb watched the strange, rocking motions of Egor's arms, horrified. He shifted his gaze to Egor's face – and Egor was smiling. Gleb realized this was a joke, and his fear passed. When the bald spot was exactly under the window, Egor let go. But it's not that easy to hit a bald spot with an ashtray. The ashtray fell for an inexpressibly long time, with Gleb still hoping it would miss. It didn't. It struck muffledly the bone covered in hairless skin. The man standing below didn't fall. He took a few more steps and slowly sank to the ground. Then fell over on his side. He started rummaging around on the ground as if looking for something. He touched one of the schoolbags but didn't try to open it. He clearly wasn't looking for anything. He let out a sound like a bellow. Egor nodded to Gleb and they went downstairs. They cautiously entered the space between the buildings. To collect their schoolbags, they had to step over the bald man – and that was scary. Even in the half-dark they could see his face was bloody. Egor stepped over the man lying there, picked up both schoolbags, stepped back over him, and walked toward the exit. Gleb thought about it and also moved toward the exit. The swath of light broadened and they came out into the sun. But the bald man remained in the gloom. "Come on, let's drag him out," Gleb said. Egor grinned crookedly and followed Gleb. With the same smile he observed how Gleb was afraid to touch the man's jerking arms. He walked up and grabbed his right arm. Told Gleb to grab the left: "We'll drag him!" The bald man's legs trailed limply on the ground. Egor and Gleb laid him on the grass, but he didn't quiet down. In slow motion, he turned over on his stomach and crawled to the nearest tree. He looked like a big, clumsy bug. A bald bug – bugs are often drawn bald. Only there was a deep wound on his bloody bald spot. Gleb thought those only happened in the movies. It was scary to look at. As they left by way of the courtyards, the boys exchanged looks. Turning around one last time, they saw a woman with a stroller unhurriedly approach their former pursuer. Evidently she thought he was drunk – and would soon sort out what was what. And call him an ambulance. Gleb and Egor never did find out whether she did. Dreadful for a bug...

NOVEMBER 9, 2012, MUNICH

I'm lying in the Jacuzzi, my entire body reveling in the warm jets. The bathroom is spacious and light. Knowing my habit of taking long baths, when we bought our house Katya set one condition: enlarge the bathroom. The light is bright but diffuse; it spills from recessed ceiling lights. The major decisions in this house rest with Katya. The minor ones with Geraldina. In the bathroom, Katya has created a kind of office for me. A reception room.

Sitting on beach chairs, Katya and Barbara observe my bathing, glasses of liqueur in hand. I feel so comfy and calm that I don't reproach the sisters for their alcohol use, although at some other time I might. Actually, I'm holding a glass of liqueur too. The glass is shaking barely noticeably.

Barbara: "Your tremor worries me."

Katya (uncertainly): "It's from the gushing water."

Barbara stands up and turns off the water. My glass keeps shaking.

Me: "My right arm doesn't move at the shoulder." I finish the liqueur and put the glass on the Jacuzzi's edge. "I think it's all about my spine."

Katya looks at Barbara. There is doubt in Barbara's eyes. She asks me to close my eyes and touch my nose with one hand and then the other. The task is completed with slight imprecision.

"The liqueur's effect," I say.

A bus goes by outside. In the murky glass we can see only its contours and lights.

"Why don't you say something, Barbara?" Katya asks.

"In Gleb's place, I'd consult a neurologist."

Barbara has an absent look.

"Do you hear what the doctor's telling you?" Katya addresses me.

"This doctor is a gastroenterologist." I am emphatically calm.

"But first and foremost, she's a doctor!"

Katya makes an abrupt gesture and the liqueur splashes out. I smile. The smile lets them know unambiguously that both instances with the glasses have the same cause – the liqueur. Continuing to look into the distance, Barbara speaks.

"I'm afraid this might be Parkinson's."

Creating a tsunami, I jerk to a sitting position and wrap my arms around my knees. A wave splashes on the floor. Katya calls for Geraldina, who comes with a bucket and rag and concentrates on collecting the water. The rag has traces of cleaner in it, and Geraldine's hands get covered in foam. She doesn't look at me naked, although she's not particularly shy. Finished wiping the floor, Geraldina stands up and tugs at her jeans, which have slipped down. Katya comes close and runs a finger over my wet shoulder.

"Gleb, darling, you really should get checked out."

I abruptly step over the side of the Jacuzzi. Throw on my robe without drying off. Another big puddle forms on the floor.

1975

Declension of the noun *put'*: "way." There was a section like that in my Russian textbook published for Ukrainian schools. The Russian forms – *put', puti, puti, put', putem, puti* – were contrasted to the Ukrainian ones: *put', puti, puti, put', puttiu, puti*. The main difference: in Ukrainian *put'* is feminine. Grammatically feminine. Once Gleb asked his father how it came to be that *put'* was a she. *"Because our way,"* Fyodor replied, *"she's like a woman, soft and gentle, while the Russian way is harsh and unpredictable when it comes to life. That's why we can't have a common path."* Suddenly Fyodor sang a song about an armored train shunted off to the side. The song was very much to the point because that morning in school they'd dictated a list of outside reading in Russian literature, and it included Vsevolod Ivanov's novella *Armored Train 14-69*. Bdzhilka, who wrote slowly, didn't manage to note the train's number and so after class went up to the teacher to get it. There was a danger the pupil might read a novella about an armored train with a different number. Gleb worried about grammar, not numbers. After a week of thinking, he brought Fyodor a list of Ukrainian words of masculine gender, contrasted to the feminine gender in Russian: pain, rattle, dust, dishes, manuscript, Siberia, and dog. He asked his father to comment on those instances too. Did the grammatical gender mean that Russian pain is femininely gentler and Russian rattling finer? Finally, what did it mean that in Ukrainian a dog was a he? After thinking over the list for a while, Fyodor was forced to admit that grammatical interpretations had their limits. With respect to the difference between the Russian and the Ukrainian "way" (and no grammar entered into this), Fyodor, with his characteristic inflexibility, held to his opinion. Actually, there was one topic where his opinion did change. Gleb's ear. Fyodor noted with satisfaction as his son's ear developed more and more with every passing year.

Not once was anything said about this as a result, but the process was obvious to Fyodor and delighted him. He came to Gleb's graduation exam, where Gleb played Vivaldi's Concerto in G Major. The boy performed it without a single hitch, and in doing so did not simply follow the great Italian's indications but added something inexpressible that moved Fyodor. The beginning notes (G, F#, G), which many performers tend to swallow, Gleb accentuated, on a defiant fortissimo, which sounded almost tragic. This beginning worried Fyodor, who thought that, by playing the first notes at such a high point, the performer would devalue all the concerto's subsequent emotions. Because an entire piece can't be played at this strength of emotion (which can be achieved only once), and concluding on a level lower than the initial level is a failure. A failure in the literal sense, a movement down. But something inexplicable happened. As he played the concerto, Gleb claimed a height even higher – but it was a different height now. He (and this was what seemed inexplicable to Fyodor) didn't attempt to storm the same peak twice. At a certain point another, previously unseen peak appeared or – this was becoming increasingly obvious – yet another dimension formed on the original peak, and now his son was striving toward it. Here Fyodor mentally corrected himself: the dimension didn't just form, Gleb formed it. And now he looked at Gleb with new eyes. If his previous attitude toward his son's musical studies had been condescending, and a compassion had been born toward his son's attempt to lift the unliftable (as Fyodor explained it in his conversations with Irina), now he saw the unliftable being lifted. Gleb's childish fingers were creating something that hovered over Vivaldi's music. This something was still quite small, but it was palpable because it allowed the music to be born anew each time, because only on that condition could it continue to live. Fyodor couldn't express this properly himself, he simply knew that sometimes even a virtuoso performance doesn't give birth to music. It merely repeats what is written on the staff with the dispassion of a harpsichord. And absolute pitch gives way to another – internal – pitch that allows him to penetrate to the thing's very essence. Gleb's inspiration was conveyed to the accompanist as well – an elderly woman with eyes faded from longstanding indifference. Everything about her was unmusical: her short fat fingers, her ever-present knit top, and her hennaed gray hair – but she, too, was transported. After playing the last note, she stood up from the piano and embraced Gleb. Fyodor wanted to embrace his son, too, but at the last minute he was embarrassed, perhaps because he was embarrassed to copy the accompanist. The hand extended toward Gleb dropped to the domra's fingerboard. He squeezed it for a while, as if it were an inalienable part of Gleb, and then let it go. *"That was fine, son."* It wasn't much, but it was enough for Gleb. There were many congratulating him, but he really had been waiting for what Fyodor would say. That day the music school graduate received another gift as well: a Raketa watch. The watch had a silver-plated body, and the dial, executed out of some semi-precious stone, was unexpectedly crimson. One might think that a gift like this would warn the graduate of the difficult, perhaps even somehow crimson time to come, if his mama, grandmother, Fyodor, and Vera Mikhailovna hadn't clubbed together to buy it. The givers' names were engraved on the watch without any warnings, naturally. True, Vera Mikhailovna had wanted to engrave something about graduating in domra, but there was only room for either the names or the note about his graduation. They preferred the names, especially since Gleb hadn't graduated at all but rather was beginning: he was moving on to the guitar. And he was going to study once again with Vera Mikhailovna. Gleb started first year of music school anew. And experienced perfect happiness. This feeling wouldn't allow him to wait for the beginning of the school year, and now, in June, as five years before, he and his father went to the instrument store and bought a guitar manufactured in Leningrad. By Soviet measures, it was a decent guitar, but in the greater scheme of things – Gleb understood this much later, collecting instruments – it was a blunt instrument. Vera warned him that this time she didn't have a custom guitar, but this didn't upset Gleb in the least. He admired its looks and stroked the strings of the guitar they were able to buy. He felt pride that such an elegant instrument was now in his home. And that before – it was hard to imagine – his home had somehow gotten along without it. All summer, Gleb pictured performing famous pieces, tossing his hair to the side, and running his fingers over the strings. This was perhaps the best music of his life because it did not bear the curse of embodiment. Pure idea. A dream not weighed down by reality. Actually, Gleb had a teach-yourself book, and certain things he could have learned on his own (especially since he wanted it so much!), but he didn't. The young musician treasured purity of style so much that he preferred to take even his first steps under experienced guidance. Thus a virgin guards herself for her future husband because the first caresses should be blessed by marriage. The household was somewhat surprised at this musical chastity. Gleb's mother said it was as if her son, while waiting for his swimming trainer, was practicing in a pool without water. Inasmuch as playing without sound looked unusual (Gleb looked at his fingers, exactly that – looked!), he started producing sounds himself. These sounds imitated the melody but more often simply the rhythm. Regardless of whether the original had words or not, any melody was performed in the form of a furious di-di-di-di, accompanied by tiny drops of spit. Added to this gradually were da-da-da-da and du-du-du-du, so that Gleb approached the summer's end with a rich arrangement. Subsequently, of course, he learned to play the guitar as well, but the habit of vocal accompaniment remained. Became Gleb's trademark. And that summer entered his memory in the audio design he had conceived. It was also memorable because Fyodor's son, Oles, was born. Although, *also* hardly fits: this was the main news of the summer! And the main surprise because up until the last moment Galina's abundant body had concealed the conception of a new body in it. To say that Oles's birth was a joy for everyone would be an exaggeration. Irina, at least, experienced no such joy. She didn't regret parting with Fyodor for a minute, nonetheless, she wasn't thrilled about Galina showing up in his life and, as a consequence, Oles. Gleb and Antonina Pavlovna took the news calmly. The person who became truly upset, by all accounts, was Egor. One day, when Fyodor and Galina were out, he took the infant to the kitchen, put him in the oven, and turned on the gas. Over the hissing gas he didn't hear his parents return. They rushed straight to Oles, who, fortunately, was lying on the stove's clogged burner. Thus they gained the seconds that allowed him to survive until the adults' arrival. Fyodor and Galina were so shaken that they didn't lay a finger on Egor. When he realized they weren't going to beat him, Egor walked behind his parents and in a whining voice talked utter, terrible drivel. He said flies had covered Oles all over and he, Egor, out of stupidity, had decided to put the baby on the gas for a few seconds. Seeing no response, Egor started genuinely crying and saying it all happened because they didn't love him anymore, that all their attention had switched to Oles. This was the sole point where Egor came close to the truth, and Fyodor rewarded him with a slap in the face. Smearing the blood coming from his nose, Egor hoped they'd beat him some more (he realized this was the least evil) and maybe forgive him. But they didn't beat him anymore. Egor's parents put him in the kitchen, shut themselves up in their room, and started discussing what they should do with him now. Clearly, they couldn't leave the children alone together for a minute. For Fyodor, this meant that the adults had to triple their attention, but Galina viewed the matter differently. Looking at her husband dry-eyed, she said, *"He can't live with us."* Fyodor was silent for a long time. Eventually he asked, *"Why?"* *"He has a killer inside him,"* Galina answered. Seeing that Fyodor was about to object, she put her hand on his shoulder: *"I know it."* A week later, Fyodor took Egor to a boarding school. This wasn't a place for juvenile delinquents (they told no one about what happened); it was an ordinary institution for orphans and children from broken families. Soon after, Gleb visited Egor there – he went with Fyodor. Apparently, Fyodor took Gleb along only because he didn't really understand what he was supposed to talk to Egor about. When he'd left the boys alone, Egor told Gleb, "I'm better off here. I'm sick of that pair." And he told him what had in fact happened. In parting, Egor whispered to Gleb, "Too bad I didn't wipe out their infestation." Gleb looked up at him, and his eyelids looked leaden. Egor laughed. "I'm joking!" That was August 31. The next day Gleb was sitting at his desk and thinking that in a few hours he would have his first guitar lesson. Which he'd been looking forward to for five years, by the way. He had his lesson. And it was given by the same Vera Mikhailovna – in her old skirt and her old jacket, which was getting shiny at the elbows. Gleb realized he was expecting an upgrade, if not in Vera Mikhailovna as a whole (that was hard to imagine) then at least in her wardrobe. Unfortunately, she had not fully appreciated this and had not come upgraded. Despite Gleb's subconscious expectations, life did not find a new beginning with the beginning of his guitar studies. This realization saddened the boy. Shining with joy just that morning, at music school he had a look that Vera Mikhailovna immediately defined as *limp*. She even asked Gleb whether he was ill. No, he wasn't. In love maybe? Gleb looked closely at his teacher: maybe. That was a nice idea. A feeling, to be exact. It had visited Gleb before, but his chosen one was older and, most important, taller. This morning the situation started evening out. A new girl was standing next to him in the opening day line. They'd known her last name long before classes began: Adamenko. The class monitor had said that Valya Adamenko would be joining them the next school year. To the question of whether this was a boy Valya or a girl Valya, neither the last nor the first name provided an answer. Attempts to clarify the matter with the monitor proved unsuccessful. "I said. Valya Adamenko," the monitor replied sternly. Nor did she know any details about Adamenko, though she wouldn't admit that outright. Valya Adamenko turned out to be a girl. A beautiful girl. Despite her Ukrainian last name, her features spoke of the East: a special cast to the eyes, a slight swarthiness. They didn't even say this, they hinted. Her father was military, and Valya had ended up in Kyiv with his latest service transfer. Valya's classmates had seen him a couple of times – he had a typical Slavic look. Responsible for the Eastern touches in Valya's appearance, most likely, was her mother, whom no one had seen. In the lineup, Gleb picked out barely distinguishable little hairs on the tender skin of Valya's face. Not hairs even, but the lightest fuzz, like on a peach. At the thought of a peach, he unexpectedly thought about something absolutely forbidden, and a warm and wet wave swept over him. He'd experienced this for the first time the way Adam had when he ate – no, not a peach, an apple. *It* was unfamiliarly tenacious, and the more obscene it became, the sweeter. It rose like well-proofed dough coming from the depths of his belly, born out of everything – the semblance of shapes and sounds . . . especially sounds. For instance, nails sliding down the E string reminded him of passionate cries. And the wood inlay on the body surface was like a woman's naked body – maybe even Valya Adamenko's body – and Gleb fixed his eyes on it. Often he imagined Valya without clothes, especially at bedtime, and after that he would toss and turn for a long time. Who could sleep . . .? Even Valya's last name was linked in his consciousness with Adam. He'd heard the story of Adam more than once from Antonina Pavlovna, and each time, he'd asked why he and

Eve had been so severely punished for that apple. He and Valya. If they'd eaten an apple . . . Gleb felt perspiration cover his body.

DECEMBER 20, 2012, MUNICH

I'm on my way to see a neuropathologist, Frau Fuchs. Last night I searched the Internet and found a doctor not far from home. I want to make this visit part of my walk. It's not as if I was going to see a doctor on purpose – no, I was just out walking, saw it, and dropped in. Going to see Barbara in her clinic is somehow too formal and, clearly, fraught. They might find who knows what there, they might come up with a diagnosis that could well dispatch me to the crematorium. I press the intercom button. There's a Christmas wreath on the door and under it a bronze plaque with the office hours of "Frau Fuchs, MD" She meets me on the threshold to the buzzing of the door. Surprisingly young for a medical doctor. The nurse peers around her. Frau Fuchs smiles.

"Have you really come to see us, Mr. Yanovsky?"

Her voice is low and quiet.

"Yes, in a way."

I pretend to be self-conscious. In fact, I haven't been self-conscious about anything for a long time. I tell them I've started having problems with the fingers of my right hand. The arm doesn't move well, and I can't raise it above a certain height. During my attempt to raise my arm, Frau Fuchs's face expresses mild distress. She asks me to undress to the waist. On Frau Fuch's command, I shut my eyes and touch the tip of my nose with my index finger – first with my left, then my right. The doctor and nurse whisper an excited *hurrah!* and raise their hands as if to applaud. Clearly they are linked by years of work.

Then they have me lie down and Frau Fuchs starts bending my arms and legs. Checking for sensitivity, she presses various points

69

on my arms. Next act: I stand with arms held out. I abruptly throw my fingers forward and gather them back into a fist. Frau Fuchs grabs my fists and tries to bend my arms, but she can't. After that she pulls on my arms again (the way people, when moving away from a closed door, give the handle another tug) and releases air through her slightly parted lips: exhausted. Vanquished. A strong, healthy patient. A brilliant musician and frankly an attractive man.

Frau Fuchs suggests discussing the results of her examination over coffee. We sit in the full light (tall windows) of the waiting room. Outside, a raven is hopping across the greenish-brown, frost-flecked grass. Occasionally it switches to a walk – and rocks comically from foot to foot. As if it has its hands in its pockets. It doesn't have pockets, though. It doesn't even have hands (I put brown sugar in my cup), but now, you see, it's as if... Yes, the doctor understands her patient's fears. The patient has been told he may have Parkinson's. No, that's highly unlikely. In Parkinson's the so-called resting tremor is characteristic, when the hands tremble in the absence of muscle effort, moreover, the amplitude of that trembling is fairly large. A slight trembling of the right hand is indeed observed in the patient, but its amplitude can't be compared to Parkinson's. It's nerves, which given Mr. Yanovsky's demanding performance schedule and intense social life comes as no surprise. What will help here is a therapeutic course of modern medicines. As for his shoulder problems, this is in all likelihood his spine. He needs a good osteopath.

It goes without saying that he already has a good neurologist. Frau Fuchs takes the prescriptions for the medicines I need out of the printer and signs them with an elegant fountain pen. I, in turn, take out of my bag two CDs with my performances and sign them as well – for the doctor and her assistant. I cast a parting glance out the window: the raven is gone. Emptiness.

1976

Sometimes, when Gleb picked up the guitar, he imagined it was Valya. The guitar had essentially feminine shapes. Only touching the strings had a cooling effect on him: the strings so delicate they canceled out the corporal. And produced sounds of unearthly beauty. As he practiced articulation, Gleb grasped techniques he'd never known before. The bar, for example, which isn't used in domra playing. The difficulty of the bar is by no means in pressing the index finger firmly against the neck. It's all about being able to feel each of the pressed strings. Those who use force rather than skill focus the pressure on the middle of the finger. As a result, most of the strings don't get held down and are muffled. Or take the tremolo. On the domra, the tremolo is played with the pick, and the entire hand moves. On the guitar, the hand is fixed – and the fingers move. Gleb spent more time working on the tremolo than anything else. On Vera Mikhailovna's advice, he turned on the metronome and started playing simple melodies in tremolo. In his daily practices, he devoted about an hour to this alone because he accented each of the fingers in turn. When he had achieved absolute mastery in producing sounds with all his fingers, his tremolo became magical. And this was not merely a method of playing taken in isolation. Gleb learned to inscribe it into the overall canvas of a piece. It is well known that the tremolo, like all colorful phenomena, stands out from the overall musical texture and that unifying it with the rest of the piece's text is no simple task. So you see, the boy managed that as well. For instance, he would slow the tremolo exaggeratedly, thereby draping the seam to the next musical fragment. This astonished even his teacher. Gleb may have been in the music school for more than five years, but he was just a first-year guitar student! Her astonishment notwithstanding, Vera Mikhailovna brought many of her older pupils to his lessons to show them what a true tremolo was. To Gleb himself

71

it reminded him of time: it was just as steady, and it swallowed the notes the way time does events. Gleb discovered time for himself at thirteen or fourteen. Not that long ago it hadn't moved, it was an eternity, you might say, and now everything had changed. At first the years came up and each was special in the sense that it had nothing in common with other years. As if it had flown in from outer space, rootless and unpredictable. But this last year had suddenly found its place. It was dependent on the previous years and determined the character of those to follow. Nor was it boundless, as previous years had been. It was foreseeable. For Gleb, years started not on January 1 but on September 1, as in ancient Rus. Of course, he didn't know when ancient Rus's year began. His year was the school year, which was now moving into its calm summer phase. That summer, Gleb and his grandmother took their vacation in the small town of Klavdievo outside Kyiv. They stayed with the Polyakovskys, mother and son – Pani Maria and Pan Tadeusz. The Polyakovskys, in full accord with their last name, were Poles, descended from the Poles who had come to build the South-West Railway and ended up staying in the home they had originally considered temporary. The summer in this house, which had leaned over and gradually grown into the earth, almost a half-basement by now, was a fairytale for Gleb. Here an amazing old-timey life still ticked along such as he'd only seen in the movies. But this life hadn't been created for film. It had just gone on, continued to exist in just this one Klavdievo home, as if it had arisen out of a music box, because the Polyakovskys' house looked like a music box. Pan Tadeusz used the formal "you" with Pani Maria and called her *mamo*. This sounded so noble that Gleb decided to use the formal "you" with Antonina Pavlovna. She was somewhat taken aback but did not object. Her grandson kept this up for just two days because it's no easy task – using the formal "you" with your grandmother. And although he went back to his former address, his informal "you" was different now because it included the two-day formal "you" experiment in Pani Maria's home. There was also a very old piano in the house that took up almost the entire big room and was completely covered with cypress-framed photographs. Pani Maria's numerous kin. The full complement trembled the tiniest bit when anyone started playing the piano. As the volume increased, the portraits went into motion. At fortissimo, they moved freely across the piano's lid, trading places, and from time to time even falling to the floor. When Pani Maria played, the music was accompanied by a special sound that came from touching the keys with her rings. A precise silvery sound – distinct from the diffused, corporal sound from her fingertips. The pedals' squeak. The floorboards' creak. There were lots of extra sounds, but they didn't get in the way. They may even have helped. Thus, sitting in the first row of the parterre, you gratefully hear the ballerinas' footfall, and you think how good it is that art has a place for the body. That it's not specters dancing but muscular, sweaty women. Otherwise art would drift off like a helium balloon. Pani Maria's music was beautiful primarily because of her face's exalted expression. It trembled with all its wrinkles. Her eyes stopped moving, they looked up somewhere, and there was something unseeing in this. Her lips lived a separate life, first firmly shut, then rolled into a tube, mobile like on anyone with very few teeth. Her head tilted slightly to one side, and she nodded rhythmically to each strike of the keys, or maybe she was simply shaking because the sweep of Pani Maria's hands was filled with power. All this enchanted the village girls who took piano lessons from her. They copied Pani Maria's manner of playing and even her movements, including her head shaking. They didn't understand that there are movements born of experience, of life itself, if you like, and you can't repeat them in a vacuum. To conduct yourself this way takes living your whole life in a dusty village as a grande dame, which is hard, very hard. No easier, we would note, than having a father capable of going to Petersburg to speak with the Minister of Railways. The story went like this. During the construction of the South-West Railway, in honor of Minister Nemeshaev, stations were given the names Nemeshaevo-1 and Nemeshaevo-2. The engineers often confused them, so Pan Anton (*bardzo* elegant!) goes to see Klavdy Semyonovich Nemeshaev personally and suggests changing Nemeshaevo-2 to Klavdievo. An excellent idea: Klavdievo. Klavdy Semyonovich's soul approved it even after his death. Tadeusz would recount how he'd seen many times the souls of Klavdy Semyonovich and Pan Anton strolling through the garden arm in arm. Being a fine draftsman, Tadeusz drew them like that – in the garden, arm in arm. The portrait of the two railway men hung over Gleb's bed. Lying there, Gleb would examine the two men. Nemeshaev's round face framed by several chins. When the artist was asked whether a soul could have so many chins, he admitted that he hadn't really gotten a good look at Nemeshaev's face. He had no access to a portrait of Klavdy Semyonovich here so he had to draw him on the basis of Pan Tadeusz's general notion of ministers. The other face, Pan Anton's face, was long, with deep-set eyes and thin lips. Sharp temples. Tadeusz obviously had these features too, especially when he sang to his mother's accompaniment. Like the frog-prince, with the first notes he cast aside his windburn and calluses and resurrected his ancestral elegance. Pani Maria spent nearly her entire life in the village, but she didn't become a peasant. Tadeusz did, though. He was the first peasant in the family. Singing may have been the only thing that lifted him above ordinary village life. Naturally, not only the Polyakovskys sang in the village; singing could be heard on weekdays and holidays, and it was definitely no worse than in the city. But in the village they sang folk songs or something from the Soviet stage, whereas Tadeusz sang sentimental songs. There's a difference. And he didn't sing – he performed. He stood, elbow propped on the piano, and looked at his mother, who was also the conductor in this duet. Naturally, he could have performed himself, but he always did this at her nod, caught it – which evidently was how they had set it up from the start. Tadeusz had a low, pleasant baritone. Glinka's "Doubt," and Schubert's "Serenade," and Abaza's "Foggy Morning," and much else that made his heart beat faster entered Gleb's soul encased in precisely this voice. *Be soothed, unrest of passion. . . .* After evenings like that it would take him a long time to fall asleep. Antonina Pavlovna, hearing Gleb tossing and turning, even briefly considered putting a stop to the evening concerts, but she drove out that thought. She understood and took pride in the fact that her grandson had a delicate nature. True, after falling asleep late, Gleb would get up fairly late, but his grand-mother didn't waken him. On days like that, he would get up when the garden was already filled with stuffiness and the scent of sun-warmed apples. But Klavdievo had other mornings, too, so early that the sound of the washstand on the post pounded into the earth was like a tocsin. At that early hour the apple trees were wrapped in fog, and only the sun's rays gave the scene any sharpness. Sitting in the leaning summerhouse at the samovar, they drank tea with jackets thrown over their shoulders. Steam rose from the samovar. From the tin mugs of tea too. And from the mouth of each participant in the tea-drinking. Beyond the trees, right by the fence, Pan Anton and Klavdy Semyonovich Nemeshaev stood arm in arm. They watched the dacha dwellers finish their tea and head off into the forest. At first, Gleb and his grandmother started out down the dirt road and went around the puddles left in the ruts after the night's rain. In open spaces, where the forest stepped back from the road, the wind roamed and rippled the puddles' surface. Where there were trees, the shadow retreated, and the sun's rays were already truly hot. Gleb felt their weight on his shoulders – as if they were bending him toward the ground – and he would walk along, hunched over. The wind had lost its freshness and held the slightest hint of a sultriness borne from parts unknown. Gleb and his grandmother would leave the road for the forest. Their feet sank into the deep moss. The pines were improbably tall and mighty, in some way the opposite of Pani Maria's house, which held a whole world in a music box. Whereas here the world seemed to smooth itself out and show how enormous it could be. But there was more to it: in the night, when the light went out on the summer veranda, the world revealed its true dimensions even in the Polyakovskys' garden. Stars came out on the black of the sky, and under them, in the flickering of signaling lights, planes, small and defenseless, flew by without a sound. Calling on the pilots to be careful, Pan Tadeusz quietly talked to them from the ground about how simple in those instances it was to slip into the black abyss. The earth is cozy, after all, and so is a good conversation on the porch, and night fishing. . . . It would be a shame to be deprived of all that, you know. To say nothing of the blows from apples falling to the ground. Muffled though they might be, taken separately at night they make an impression, I'm here to report, especially when a big Antonovka goes flying. A meteorite! And the gate's creak on rusty hinges – it's gone at 11,000 meters' altitude, it only exists here. Tadeusz walked toward the gate and started opening and closing it. Well? What? Where else are you going to find such a first-class creak? I could oil it a hundred times, but I couldn't care less, I'm not oiling it, I want to preserve the sound's purity. Meanwhile, it's under UNESCO protection. That's the kind of creak it is. Squinting, Pan Tadeusz looked at the carefree airplanes, and deep down he was bitter that he'd never flown. Occasionally he'd make circles with his cigarette – his order to the airplanes to descend. With rare exceptions, they listened to him and descended. Where could they go? From time to time he would pensively approach the gate, and a muffled gurgle would come from the gloom. Returning, wiping his lips, Pan Tadeusz in his conversation with those flying by would shift to a whisper. Yes, gentlemen, you might say that my life has been spent on these thousand square meters. It didn't work out the way I'd planned, shall we say. Though maybe it simply worked out. Flopped out. Flattened out like this matchbox (the sound of a matchbox being taken out). It got too cramped, if I can put it that way. Raising his open palm, Pan Tadeusz showed the flying train the crushed matchbox, and even the flat . . . But God forbid you should climb to heights from which there is no return. That is what I say to you, gentlemen, and I understand better than others what the absence of limits means.

FEBRUARY 3, 2013, LONDON

At my concert at the Royal Albert Hall I can't play a single grace note cleanly. This is followed by the evening of my insanity. Celebrating my performance in a Russian restaurant on Wellington Road, I drink a lot, joke loudly, guffaw, and even meow. Such is the form my despair takes. Katya, who guesses the reason for my jollity, puts her hand on my knee under the table. When her hand squeezes in warning, I meow and stab her with a toothpick. Katya shrieks and jumps up, and this is accompanied by a new outburst of laughter. Someone says quietly that this is the first time he's seen Katya quite so jolly. For some reason, everyone hears what he's said. Laughter. A toast to Katya follows. Her glass is empty. Katya's neighbor on the left notices.

"What can I pour you?"

"I don't know. Champagne, maybe."

"But what happened to your hand? Is that blood?"

Katya looks at her hand.

"I got stabbed somewhere."

The waiter brings disinfectant, sprays it over her hand, and covers the wound with a bandage.

"To wounded Katya!"

Smiling through her tears, Katya raises her glass and clinks with everyone in turn. After a pause, she turns to me. I crash my glass into hers, spilling the wine.

"You're going to be ashamed of this," Katya says with her lips.

I already am. I'm already in pain.

"You're wounded. Hell. . . . Get out of here!"

I'm dying for the world to come crashing down. In its most important and precious parts. Unto death.

Katya sets her glass on the wine-stained tablecloth, wipes her wet fingers on her napkin, and gets up from the table. The waiter calls her a taxi and she leaves.

"Well there, you're wifeless," Mayer, my producer, says sadly. "What's so good about that?"

He's a German, but in today's company he's speaking English. Everyone today is speaking English.

"But I'm not wifeless!" I cast my gaze over those present and stop at a woman about eighteen years old. As if I'd only just noticed. In fact, I'm playing games. I noticed her long ago. "Will you be my wife?"

"For today," Mayer clarifies. "Because he already has one wife. And forgive me, who do you represent at this table?"

The young woman, briefly: "Femen."

Mayer frowns theatrically, as if trying to recall something. He covers his face with his hands and says through slightly separated fingers, "I don't think we invited that movement."

I start hearing Ukrainian:

"Nobody invites us. We just come."

They translate for Mayer. Everyone laughs.

"Mayer, lay off her!"

I head for the young woman, take her hand, and lead her to my end of the table. I seat her in Katya's chair. On the way it's clarified that the young woman's name is Hanna, and everyone drinks to Hanna.

"Being in Femen is a major responsibility, Hanna," Mayer says, lighting up, "but not everyone realizes that. Membership in the movement assumes more than ideological agreement, right?"

"What are you talking about?" Hanna lights up too.

I try to translate her question, but my tongue won't obey me. Someone does it for me.

Mayer nods.

"I mean that not just any breast can be bared. When a woman with sagging tits jumps up on stage, any idea fades. Do you understand me?"

Hanna puts out her butt in the ashtray and starts unbuttoning her blouse, in no hurry. The young woman isn't wearing a bra – and her breasts are ideally shaped, firm. Dark brown nipples, a tattoo with the movement's name. What she's demonstrated provokes applause. Hanna's right to belong to the movement is unanimously recognized. I kiss the young woman on the lips and feel her respond. Or maybe I don't. Sensations are becoming increasingly deceptive.

At around midnight, when everyone goes home, Hanna and I end up in the same taxi.

"To a hotel!" I order the Arab driver.

Waiting for my kiss with Hanna to end, the driver asks, "Which one, sir?"

"Any!"

The car takes its time getting going. Those seeing us off pull away in the rear window at the same speed. When they've disappeared nearly entirely, they start waving their arms energetically, as if they'd forgotten something. A telephone call catches up to me. They had all the many bouquets I was given. I tell them to hand them out to beggars. Hanna and I drink champagne from the bottle.

Half an hour later another call comes. They describe to me how Mayer, tottering, is going around to all the beggars on Wellington Road. He's finding them on benches and ventilation grates, sleeping under piles of blankets and in cardboard box shelters. Walking behind him are three more people carrying armfuls of flowers. Each time, Mayer pokes the tip of his shoe into the rags, trying to uncover the owner's face. Looking into their goggling eyes, he bows respectfully and confers on them flowers from Gleb Yanovsky. The roused men silently take the bouquets, but there is no joy on their faces. Nor gratitude for Gleb Yanovsky.

At the hotel, Hanna asks me whether I cheat on my wife often. I say never, and it's the truth. Hanna sits thoughtfully on the bed. She doesn't seem to be saying anything, but I hear her voice from far away. If something happens between us, I'm going to regret it. She puts me on notice. She does. That's the last thing I remember. I'm not sure anything happened between us.

1977

It was a gorgeous Kyiv June – warm evenings, boat rides down the Dnieper, and the first swims. As it happened, friends going away on leave asked Antonina Pavlovna to stay in their apartment in Rusanovka, a new district on the left bank of the Dnieper. The reason for their request was their cat, fish, and plants, which needed tending. The reason for Antonina Pavlovna's agreement was her desire to take Gleb to the river. The building was on an embankment on an arm of the Dnieper. The embankment, contrary to the usual, ran not right next to the water but at a slight distance, about a five-minute walk. For those five minutes we had to walk through osier thickets, small jungles with a head-spinning mixture of smells. The bouquet included leaves (fresh and last year's), sand, water, and empty river snail shells, which gave the bouquet a certain acerbity. This was the optimism-full aroma of death giving birth to new life. Each morning, Gleb and his grandmother would walk to the beach, and the smell was the first thing with which the river greeted them. Halfway to the beach, as the sand was starting, they would remove their footwear and walk barefoot. The sand was dirty, now and then something in it would scratch or jab, but this didn't diminish the pleasure of sinking his feet in the warm, crumbly element. At some point the river would begin to sparkle through the osier branches. Seeing the sun dancing on the water was Gleb's main morning delight. More even than the swimming, because touching something is often less significant than dreaming of it. But the swimming was indeed wonderful, generally speaking. The river water may not have held him up like seawater, and it wasn't clear, but on the other hand it didn't form great waves (there were small ones from motorboats). This was domesticated water, and you didn't have to travel hundreds of kilometers to get to it, it ran through the city. Even the beach was different from the South. No tents or chaises set out on it with geometric precision; just the osiers' spreading shadow. Trunks and roots you could hang your clothes on, wound around each other, trying to tear away from the earth. The beachgoers lay on towels and blankets, moving them from shadow to sun and vice versa. This river life continued even at home, because their apartment windows looked out on the Dnieper. Gleb would drift to sleep to the sound of motorboats. In the evening, they were rare and therefore precious. The boy would catch an engine's noise on the distant approaches and mentally follow it until its echo had disappeared. If the boat was going upstream, he could imagine its final goal – the Russia he loved but had never seen. His mama and grandmother loved that land with the beautiful feminine name, so how could Gleb not? If the boat was going downstream, Gleb understood it had the Black Sea ahead, in which he had never swum and which he loved no less than he did Russia. He liked the Dnieper then, too, but this feeling lasted only so long – until a certain morning that was etched into Gleb's memory forever. He and his grandmother were walking through the osiers to the beach. Morning-cool air, sharp shadows on the sand. In front of them on one of the paths, a young woman emerged. A very, oh, what a very unsuitable word, but on those paths, which wound through the bushes, someone would in fact emerge from time to time. A young woman. Seen from behind: light brown hair flowing over her shoulders, a red and black swimsuit, and a long sheer scarf tied at her waist. On her right arm, a bracelet woven from sky-blue wire. Gleb and Antonina Pavlovna were walking barefoot, carrying their sandals. The young woman was also barefoot. She was carrying a straw beach bag on her shoulder – maybe her sandals were in that. She took broad steps, somehow even ballet-ish, and Gleb copied her walk, trying to step in her footprints. When he did, it excited him. At the nearest fork, she turned onto the right path, while Gleb and his grandmother took the left. Reaching the water, they spread out their blanket – an old curtain – part of it in shade (Antonina Pavlovna preferred shade) and part in sun. Gleb dozed off basking. And awoke to shouts. Someone was being carried out of the water. Who – he couldn't see because so many people were involved. Gleb only saw a freely swinging arm, a woman's probably, but even that was impossible to say for sure since the arm kept being hidden by all the people. Suddenly he noticed the blue woven band on her wrist. It was the girl he'd seen on the path to the beach! They carefully placed her on the sand, and one of the men started rhythmically pressing on her chest. He performed artificial respiration, mouth to mouth. For a few instants, Gleb envied him. But then he saw her eyes – and they were open. There was no life in them. The young woman's body was still shaking under her rescuer's hands, but for some reason it was clear that life had quit her. Never to return. After a while, doctors appeared from the bushes. With abrupt motions they started opening and closing the young woman's arms across her chest, but not for long. They felt for a pulse. Stepped aside and conferred softly. Watched as the same man tried once again to resuscitate her. No one noticed when they disappeared. Gradually the crowd around the drowning victim began to thin out. Antonina Pavlovna wanted to take her grandson away, but he resisted. He couldn't take his eyes off the young woman, who seemed no longer to be of any interest to anyone. Those who remained talked more about their own things. Striking matches in the morning wind, they lit up, tapped off the ashes with exaggerated caution, and stubbed out the butts in the sand. It's morning, Gleb thought, the morning's still not over, but the person I saw this morning is gone. No – how can that be? She'd felt the same wind and seen the same clouds at the sky's edge. They hadn't been swept away yet, after all. Never again would she feel the wind, the rain, the snow. The snow would be different, falling slowly from the skies, stinging, hitting you in the face. She wouldn't feel any kind of snow. Wouldn't see that the river would be different – ice-covered, leaf-covered in the fall, or the way it was now. Wouldn't look for her slippers by her bed. Wouldn't sit down to breakfast. Wouldn't come in out of the cold. How awful. When Antonina Pavlovna . . . When Antonina Pavlovna said it was time to go, Gleb suddenly shouted at her, loud enough for the whole beach to hear. Then, without saying a word, she collected their things and left, rolling from side to side like a bear. "Old fool," Gleb hissed. For a moment he hated his grandmother. Because (it seemed to him) she was incapable of grasping the depth of the drama played out. The beauty and death hadn't touched her. And he couldn't understand how someone could just have been alive and an hour later be dead. How? His grandmother came back to collect him after all, and he shouted, "Go away!" His shout turned into a shriek. She left and didn't come back again. Someone brought the young woman's things and covered her face with her scarf. Gleb had seen that scarf tied around her hips. The beach emptied out – not entirely, but the part where you could see the drowned woman. Only Gleb remained by her side. He thought something more should have been done to save her. That there wasn't enough love in what was done. Some effort of the heart needed to have been made by the people around her, but there weren't any. They chose to leave the young woman alone with her misfortune. With her death. The light scarf was blown off her face by a gust of wind. Gleb examined that face and found it beautiful. A straight nose. Delicate, slightly parted lips. Only in the changed color of her lips was there death, and in her stilled gaze. Not in anything else. But her eyes said absolutely for sure that her life had ended. Why hadn't anyone closed them? Gleb had never seen this young woman's face alive because he'd been walking behind her. All he'd had to do was run ahead and look. She would have expressed surprise. She would have laughed and waved him off. She might even have snorted – you never know what a person is capable of when someone notices her. Now it was pointless to surprise her. She was completely devoid of expression. It all had to have been done while she was alive. Returning home, Gleb expected a hard conversation with his grandmother. But that didn't happen. His grandmother hugged him without saying a word, and Gleb realized she understood him better than anyone. The transition from life to death was, for her, a question of the near future. His angry shouts on the beach still rang in Gleb's ears. His anger melted into a wrenching feeling for his grandmother and fear of her impending death. Lying in bed, Gleb began to weep. Tears flowed from his eyes until he fell asleep. Just before dawn, he woke from the parquet creaking: standing at his bed was the person he'd been weeping over. She said her name was Arina. He realized that in instances like this he had to be dreaming, but Arina's wet hair and the fact that she held herself so uncertainly convinced him he was dealing with reality. Arina was thinking about how fragile life is and how easily it can be cut short. He could tell that from her face, which had regained expression. And Gleb thought about how little love a person receives in his lifetime. Arina nodded: Maybe nothing would have happened to me if I'd been truly loved. Maybe the water pulls down those not held by anyone's feeling. That's probably how it happens, Gleb agreed. I should have embraced you lying on the sand and the beats of my heart would have started your stopped one. One heart responding to the rhythm of another's. It was growing light outside, and to Gleb it seemed like the light of a dream come true. Arina pressed her forehead to his. He felt the water from her hair run down his face, neck, and chest. Gleb's soul, filled with happiness, became light. It flew over the beach, announcing to the sunbathers Gleb and Arina's coming marriage, or some kind of union even stronger than marriage. Exactly what Gleb's soul announced didn't seem all that significant. Arina's return to life was a thousand times more important than those details. The beachgoers waved osier branches in response, but a little uncertainly. Voices reached Gleb that considered the information premature. That made him laugh. He woke up with a smile and a heart full of light. When he realized his joy was a dream, his mood darkened. The few days left until the apartment owners' return grandmother and grandson spent in a depressed mood. They would go down to the courtyard occasionally but not to the beach anymore. When, as they were leaving Rusanovka, the metro car crossed the Dnieper, Gleb turned away from the window. He stared at the ceiling and sat perfectly still until he stopped seeing the play of sun reflected from the water. He dropped his head on his arms and his hands covered his face so he couldn't feel any of the river's traces. Once home, Gleb seemed to forget about the death on the river. At least so it seemed to Antonina Pavlovna. But when a month later she suggested they go to Crimea together, he refused. The problem wasn't his refusal but its categoricalness. Antonina Pavlovna realized that for now, visiting beaches was contraindicated for him. Gleb spent the rest of the summer in town. He read a little but spent most of his time outdoors. Started smoking. In the evenings on the deserted playgrounds it was impossible not to smoke: everyone there did. They sat on the backs of the low benches and spat foaming spit through their teeth onto the ground. They burned their names into the seats with their cigarettes. Or, twisting the swing chains tight, spun on their axis. What with all the burning and spinning, Gleb didn't hear a single complete sentence; in the scheme of things, their speech was mumbling. They went around with mouths dangling and eyes rolling senselessly. Did Gleb act that way? Evidently, yes. Those were the terms for going to the playground. Why he acted that way, Gleb didn't exactly know himself. More than likely, he had a subconscious desire to be among others like himself, lost and unhappy. Because teenagers are usually unhappy.

FEBRUARY 15, 2013, MUNICH

Nestor is visiting us once again, this time for two weeks.

It's morning. He and I are working on the book in the winter garden, the large conservatory attached to the house. Actually, it's part of the house because the wall between the residence and the conservatory is glass. Huge darkened beams break off artistically at the wall. In addition to his dictaphone, Nestor has a notepad with questions in front of him. He reads off the first of them in a mechanical voice. Like a reporter for a district newspaper.

"In your memoirs, you often mention rivers. Do rivers occupy a special place in your life?"

"Rivers are movement, they bring something, they take something away. Most often, they take away."

Nestor looks up from his notepad.

"The Lethe? The Styx?"

"Perhaps. Well, maybe the Dnieper and the Neva too."

"Very different rivers, it seems to me."

"Very. The Neva isn't swimmable, it's cold in every sense. Whereas the Dnieper is warm, joyful, if you like."

Nestor raises his head.

"Even after Arina's death?"

"Well, yes. You see, certain events in life balance out others. The same melody can be played in the beginning in a minor key and later in a major. Or the other way around."

Directing, I hum both versions. Nestor nods to the beat. Not without surprise.

"Then tell me about the major."

"Fine, the major. Picture that apartment on the embankment I told you about; my mama's brother Kolya and I renovated it. This was a year or two before Arina's death. Kolya came from Vologda to do this." I see Nestor's polite smile and I'm overcome by laughter. "Pfah, it sounds so silly. Ask me something!"

"I don't even know what I can ask here. Well, all right. Why were you renovating this apartment, or rather, why was it you renovating it?"

"I don't remember. Things happen in this world without beginning or end. All I remember is that neither I nor, I suspect, Kolya, had ever renovated anything before in our lives. So we won't be hot, we open the windows and energetically paste the wallpaper."

"But you don't paste wallpaper with open windows."

I look respectfully at Nestor.

"Lacking your experience, Nestor, we make up the paste. It's full of lumps. We apply it to the wallpaper strips with a brush that's losing its bristles. Sounding like an old hand, Kolya tells me to push out the air bubbles under the pasted wallpaper. We do this with the help of rags."

"You can use brushes. Powerful motions from the central axis of the wallpaper to its edges." Nestor demonstrates the motions for me. "Slightly downward. It's like drawing a Christmas tree. What then?"

"Then Kolya points out that the main thing about wallpapering is carefully papering the corners of the walls."

"Exactly. If there's anywhere you should press down the wallpaper properly, then it's in the corners. That's where the wallpaper pasting can get in trouble."

"We selflessly press the wallpaper down in the corners. The paper tears. . . . Listen, how do you know all this about wallpaper?"

"In my university years I made money on the side as a paper-hanger. But you stopped at the most interesting part."

"By evening we're finishing up papering the living room and we go out to buy some draft kvass. The store's closed. Kolya says he has an idea. We go to the grocery store and buy a few packs of kvass concentrate. Back home, we turn on the soccer game. At the first strike of the ball we hear a crack in the room."

"Logically."

"Kolya surmises that that must be what's supposed to happen when wallpaper dries. A little while later, the first strip of wallpaper separates from the wall . . ."

Geraldina walks in with mineral water and pours it into tall wineglasses.

". . . separates and curls up on the floor. A massive deluge of wall-paper – Kolya turned out to be right about this – it does start from the corners. We aren't discouraged and decide to drink some kvass. Unfortunately. The kvass concentrate doesn't dissolve in water."

Nestor laughs out loud.

"It never did! Or rather, it did, but not completely. You got a cloudy, tasteless liquid with crystals settled on the bottom."

Geraldina asks whether we need anything else, but her question goes unanswered.

"At that moment Kolya gets a remarkable idea: eat the concentrate dry. Amazingly, the taste lost when the pellets are dissolved was there in full in its dry form."

Nestor nods to Geraldina and raises his wineglass.

"You could eat it and wash it down with water!"

"We stayed on the Rusanovka embankment for about a week and nearly every evening ate that concentrate, pellet after pellet. Every evening there was a soccer game on television and the pyramidal poplars swayed through the windows. And also, there was the sound of motorboats off the Dnieper."

I signal to Geraldina that we don't need anything else. Geraldina goes out slowly and sadly. It's clear to everyone that there's nothing harder than inattention. Nestor interrupts the pause.

"Did it get dark late in Kyiv?"

"Yes, but even when it did get dark, for a while the steep right bank still glowed. The sun was setting beyond it."

I want to add that a feeling of boundless happiness was flying through the windows with the moths, but I'm afraid I can't put any of that into words. I fall silent. I think I hear music capable of expressing it. In A minor, two-quarter time: happiness rising from the smell of the river, from the awareness that ahead lay my entire life, and, as I now understand, from the absence of any notion of death.

1978

At the very end of August there were a few rehearsals for the concert in honor of September 1st, the traditional first day of school. At the second rehearsal, Gleb was sitting next to the cellist Anna Lebed – *lebed* meaning "swan" in Ukrainian and Russian both – who was preparing to play – what else? – "Le Cygne" by Saint-Saëns. We braced ourselves for the school director's playful song about two swans, one of which turned out to be Anna. The melody and words were a frank reference to the Ukrainian song "Two Colors." The song had popped up a year and a half before, when Anna started on Saint-Saëns, and each time (as happens when directors joke), everyone laughed as if they'd never heard it before. They laughed this time too. Anna usually wore her school uniform, but at the rehearsal she wore a short skirt. And a short T-shirt. Sitting to her side, Gleb watched her stomach tremble from the forced laughter. The T-shirt rode up, revealing a strip of skin, and the observer's head started to spin. To fill with blood, and spin, and become someone else's. "I've heard this masterpiece somewhere," Gleb's lips pronounced unexpectedly and loudly, "approximately a hundred and twenty times." No one was laughing anymore. In total silence, the director walked up to Gleb, and Gleb thought quite calmly that he was going to hit him. But the director didn't. After a brief silence, he said, "You're taking on a lot, Yanovsky." Gleb looked him calmly in the eye. He thought about Anna and her trembling stomach. The director quickly left, accompanied by Gleb's gaze. Anna gripped the cello with her legs and started playing "Le Cygne." Gleb shifted his gaze to Anna, who'd changed over the summer. It wasn't just a matter of body changes (there was no doubt about those); she had a new gaze, adult and womanly. Most of all, she played differently. People play like that, Gleb told Kleshchuk quietly, only after losing their innocence. "You mean the movement of her hands?" Kleshchuk asked, perplexed. "Her legs," Gleb hissed. Turning around, he watched Anna's bare legs first release her instrument, then squeeze it with new strength, and "Le Cygne" resonated with the observer in a strange way he'd never experienced before. Gleb already knew he wouldn't leave without waiting for Anna. The dim and moist feeling that had made him insult the director now robbed Gleb of his will and drew him after her. And Anna knew it. She collected her music with exaggerated deliberation and put her cello in its case. Without even looking at Gleb, she felt the full strength of the thread connecting them. Anna wasn't surprised that Gleb had left without saying goodbye, just as she wasn't surprised at running into him when she turned the corner from the music school. Silently – holding his guitar – he looked at Anna. With his free hand he took her cello (an electric shock when their fingers touched). "A one-man orchestra," Anna joked, but Gleb didn't laugh. He followed her, hanging back half a step, and the cello case's handle creaked in time to their progress. Anna lived in an ugly new apartment building on Vladimirskaya, directly across from the opera theater. Her parents were musicians. "They're performing in Moscow today," Anna explained, closing the front door from the inside. So they were in Moscow. The whirlwind that drew Gleb after Anna would have blown any parents out of the apartment. When they went into Anna's room, she got out the cello and arranged it between her legs. With an offhand gesture she flipped up her skirt and started playing "Le Cygne." She smiled: only for you. She played sloppily, not always playing the notes precisely. All her efforts may have been spent on her performance at the music school, but maybe she was simply nervous. After all, she was playing only for Gleb. And her legs squeezed the cello again, and under her bravely flipped back skirt the edge of her panties flashed. "You embrace the cello like a man," his mechanical voice said. Anna set aside the cello, stood up, and turning toward Gleb, sat in his lap: "I can embrace you. . . ." Her breasts were right at Gleb's face. The stretched fabric fully reflected her virtues, but Anna peeled off the T-shirt too. Gleb touched her breasts with his lips. Inhaled the smell of her skin. In the Land of the Soviets, deodorant was not common property at the time, but that didn't bother anyone.

Quite the opposite. Whenever he remembered his first experience of love, Gleb invariably smelled the aroma of her youthful womanly body. People say the memory for smells is the most durable. Women he was involved with later were remembered by their deodorant brand, no comparison with the fragrance of Anna Lebed's flesh. For a few infinite minutes, that flesh belonged to him. Anna squeezed and released his hips, and lying on her bed, he felt like a cello. Then they smoked. The ashtray, placed on Gleb's stomach, rose and fell to the beat of his breath. Resting on Gleb's shoulder, Anna blew a thin stream of smoke. Gleb looked at the ceiling. "What are you thinking about?" Anna asked. "Death." "That's odd." She rubbed the back of her head on Gleb's arm. "That's odd you're thinking about death now particularly. It's like thinking about death at the beach." Gleb ran his finger down Anna's nose. "I did see death at the beach." "Phoo!" Anna brushed away his hand. "If we're going to love each other forever," Gleb said, "then death isn't scary. It isn't, do you understand?" "Yes." Anna stood up and took the ashtray from his stomach. "I'll go wash up?" Stretched out on Anna's bed, he studied the opera theater. The theater took up the whole window, which made it seem to be continuously increasing in size. Gleb thought about how he was lying there looking at this theater for the first time. He didn't know this time was also his last. But the saddest part was something else. Anna went out of his life along with his view of the theater. After that passionate tryst, he saw her only once – at the general concert. Gleb went up to ask when they were going to see each other, but Anna put her finger on his lips. She answered with just her eyes, and her eyes expressed a plea for patience. At least that was how he understood it. Patience, in Gleb's imagination, was measured in hours, oh, a couple of days, but a week passed and Anna didn't show up at the music school. When he didn't see her at their shared classes, Gleb checked on the cello classes, but she wasn't at those either. Finally, Gleb summoned up his nerve and went to the apartment where he'd studied the opera theater (and not only) in such detail – and no one answered the door. Then, embarrassed, he went to the cello teacher and asked what had happened to Anna. "You mean you don't know?" the teacher was surprised. "Anna's parents were accepted into a newly created group. It's called the Violins of Moscow." "They're violinists?" Gleb asked for some reason. "Yes, violinists." She smiled. "Good ones, if that interests you." It didn't. The teacher moved toward the teacher's lounge. "They just learned about it recently," Gleb clarified, catching up to her. "About the move?" She frowned. "They knew it back in the spring." In that first moment he felt like rushing to the train station and going to Moscow. He would find Anna through her parents. There couldn't be that many groups called the Violins of Moscow, he reasoned. But a minute later the urge passed. He was disgusted. Knowing she was leaving, she allowed herself to let down her guard, Gleb thought. Allowed herself a little adventure. Now he was irritated at himself for thinking about Anna all this time, learning her schedule, running around to her building, running to her teacher. Most painful of all was that to himself he'd been calling Anna his wife. He'd made his life's choice. What had started as a call of the flesh had become the basis for a long ladder leading to heaven, a ladder he'd created in his imagination. At first he thought it had come crashing down. Then it became clear that it hadn't – he'd only heard the crash: there had not in fact been any ladder. Gleb remembered Arina who perished and realized she'd been his one and only love. How had he dared not stop her on her way to the beach? Why hadn't he grabbed her hands and dragged her out of the water? Yes, that would have been rude and probably surprising, but what significance did that have compared to a saved life? Without explaining anything, he would have covered her face in kisses, and she of course would have forgiven him. They would have merged into one, the way he had with Anna, but there wouldn't have been an Anna, at least not the Anna that had come into his life. On other days, Gleb would forget about Arina and think of no one but Anna. He burned with desire. At times he would wake up in the night and imagine Anna's body distinctly, to the point of trembling. He would feel her rhythmic movements and be covered in sweat. Sometimes he was on the verge of running off to Moscow, where no one was waiting for him, actually. He didn't plan to ask Anna for a permanent relationship (how could that even happen at their age?), but he was prepared to beg her for a repetition of what there'd been: for *one* more time. Dreaming of this, he despised himself because his dreams were born exclusively of lust. There was nothing of what he'd thought about after Arina's death.

FEBRUARY 28, 2013, MUNICH

The smoke from Nestor's cigarette is streaming through the glossy tropical leaves. Occasionally even I light up. Although she changes out the ashtrays from time to time, Geraldina does not approve of smoking in the garden. Her entire sorrowful look makes it clear that nothing here is up to her. In her free time, she tells the Bavarian gardener about the interminable Russian conversations and overflowing ashtrays.

The gardener comes three times a week. He listens politely to Geraldina, but smoking in the garden doesn't bother him. He is a calm, mustached man who looks like a walrus. His equanimity is conveyed to the plants, which do everything at the right time: bloom, bear fruit, or simply entwine around the planted poles. Sometimes, Geraldina wishes she could entwine herself around him, and everyone in the house knows it, including our visitors.

Nestor asks me about the relationship between Geraldina and the gardener. In a whisper I say that the only thing that interests him is flora, not fauna. Stormy tropical love in this garden seems unlikely. On the other hand, the garden is magnificent. The degree of its grooming can be compared only to the grooming of the Bavarian's mustache: the same hand is felt in both.

"By this example do you mean to say," Nestor searches for the words, "that genuine art requires asceticism?"

"I think Balzac once said something to the effect that a night spent with a woman is worth a page of good prose. But it might not have been Balzac."

Nestor looks at me dubiously. A night spent with a woman . . . That probably never impoverished his prose. But then he isn't Balzac.

After dinner, Nestor, Katya, and I go for a bicycle ride, since in Munich this can be done even in February. Nestor is given my light jacket; he would be hot in his own. At the entrance to the Englischer Garten I determine the order: Nestor and Katya in front, me in back. At first we ride down the paved central allée, where oncoming bicyclists wave to me in greeting. We turn and find ourselves on the bank of the Isar, a minor but swift river that rises in the Alps.

"There are fewer bicyclists here," Katya explains to Nestor, "and it's more serene."

"In my opinion, all Munich is serenity itself."

Katya nods.

"Perhaps. But maybe that's characteristic of cities where there's lots of greenery. Greenery is calming."

"Katya, darling," I say, "you're overfond of generalizations. If that's true, then the serenest of all should be jungle inhabitants."

Speeding, we descend toward the Isar. At this spot the river goes over a small, artificial threshold and then flows in flocks of foam.

"But Katya's right." Nestor stops on one of the rocks by the bank. "When was the October Revolution? When the leaves had fallen!"

I'm about to inquire what we're to do about July 14 and its greenery but think better of it. Superfluous questions only spoil handsome theories. We laugh, and I see us in black and white, like in an old photograph. I often see pictures like that. Nestor squats on his rock and scoops up water from the river, splashing his face. The water runs off his chin. Nestor is left with a shining wet face. Me leaning against a maple trunk. And Katya – the main thing is Katya, the reason why it's all stuck in memory. Her face is shining, too, from tears. A red nose. I think these are tears of happiness, that at that moment we're all happy. But Katya suddenly cries out: "How awful life is!"

Reaching for me, her legs half-bent, she cries out.

1979

One day – this was in February – Anna Lebed's teacher went up to Gleb, held out a piece of paper, and said, "Anna sent me a New Year's greeting, here's her address. You can write to her." The teacher had no idea the storm she was stirring up in Gleb's soul. Had she guessed, she would have handed over the letter without delay, not waited a month and a half. She suggested he write. Ha . . . Of course, he went. At home he said he was going to visit Bdzhilka in his village. Antonina Pavlovna knew of Bdzhilka's existence but had never seen him. She saw her grandson off at the station, where Bdzhilka himself met them, as he was supposed to. He asked Gleb, "*Where are you going?*" to which Gleb, pretending he was joking, replied, "*That's a secret*" – and hurriedly said goodbye to his classmate. His grandmother, unaware that they had just said goodbye to the real Bdzhilka, naturally could not have guessed that her grandson was going to see a fictitious Bdzhilka. And if she'd dug deeper, then not even an invented one but Anna Lebed, the cellist who had her grandson so worked up.

His grandmother watched thoughtfully as Gleb boarded and the train started moving. She waved to him until the train was out of sight. When her grandson reached the next station, he got off and transferred to another local heading for the town of Konotop. There he could take a train to Moscow. The journey with multiple transfers was inconvenient but cheap. Gleb rode the entire way in a gloomy mood and felt his uncleanness almost physically. Below, under his wooden seat, an electric furnace roasted him mercilessly. Gleb quickly started sweating, and the stickiness of his clothing felt like the stickiness of sin. Special pain was inflicted by the memory of his grandmother waving: that picture stayed with him the whole way. For the first time he had deceived her in a major way. Getting out at Konotop, Gleb went into the cold station, and his damp clothing became almost intolerable. The train to Moscow was leaving in two hours. The gloom thickened outside. He tried to nap, but each time sleep crept up, the door would slam on its rusty spring. The door was off-kilter and didn't close all the way, which was why the station was so cold. Finally Gleb managed to fall asleep, and he dreamed of crossfire, the shots being made by the slamming door. He nearly missed his train – woke up at the last moment. As soon as he hopped on, the train doors slammed shut. Once he was settled in by a window (he couldn't see anything through it except for flying snow), he instantly fell asleep. He woke up from a stream of cold air and saw the doors to the landing were open and on the landing – he remembered this only now – a broken window. There was no hope anyone would close the door. Looking around, Gleb realized he was alone in the car. The situation was hopeless – he would have to deal with the doors himself. Gleb slowly stood up and swaying in rhythm with the knocking wheels moved toward the jammed doors. As he should have anticipated, they wouldn't yield to any effort; evidently they'd frozen tightly to their channels. Gleb perched on the bench by the door and now rocked sitting up, rocked and rocked . . . now not by the doors . . . now in his previous seat . . . because he hadn't gotten up . . . he hadn't gone anywhere . . . but rocking, of course, he was rocking. This was a special rhythm that had nothing to do with Glinka's "Traveling Song" because Glinka's music was written with the thought of a locomotive (then called a steam engine) and definitely not train cars with their pensive rhythm. Definitely not about those. No matter how you slice it, train cars don't have that steam engine whistling in the dark. Gleb woke up for real only at Moscow's Kievsky Station. Entering the station building, he found a spot on one of the benches in the waiting room. Morning was far off, as was the start of public transport. Not only that, Gleb thought, drifting off, he wasn't going to go to Anna's on the first metro. He wasn't about to awaken the entire family with his early arrival. And he didn't need the entire family – he just needed Anna. And why was he so sure, actually, that her parents would leave and Anna remain? More likely, the opposite: Anna had to leave early for school, whereas musicians are late risers. Sleepiness fled Gleb for a minute. But after checking his watch, he realized there was still a lot of time left, even for an early meeting. Once again he started drifting off, and through his sleep he felt himself getting sick and reassured himself by saying he was dreaming it. He woke up at around six o'clock utterly done in. He made an attempt to stand, but his legs wouldn't bend and his temples were throbbing. He sat back down. He wondered whether it was worth visiting Anna in this condition. Maybe not. But maybe . . . He pictured Anna putting him in her bed, giving him pills, bringing him warm milk with honey. He realized he'd fallen asleep again, stood up in a single burst, and looked at the clock. Six-thirty. If he didn't leave now, he might not catch Anna. How to get to Anna's building Gleb had clarified back in Kyiv. He went into the metro and took the ring line to the Belorusskaya station. From there he could go a couple of stops on a trolleybus, but he preferred not to wait and set out on foot. A blizzard had started up, but to Gleb's delight, the wind was at his back. Actually, there was no special delight because he had no strength left for it: this walking person was filled with quiet gratitude that he didn't have to overcome the elements as well. Rather the opposite, the elements themselves were pushing him along from behind. Gleb walked down Leningradsky Prospect to Pravda Street, where the cellist he valued so highly lived. When he'd been given her address, it had felt a little strange that Anna's life was now passing on a street with such an unexpected name, but he'd grown used to it back before he left for Moscow. He thought not about the newspaper *Pravda* but about truth as such, of which each person has his own: Anna, her parents, he himself. . . . His *pravda,* his truth, now was that he no longer wanted anything from Anna but sympathy and warmth – emotional, mainly. Well, and milk with honey. Passing under the arch of Anna's building, he pictured taking the hot mug from her hands. Her entry was in the courtyard, and the door to it was locked. Life had already begun in a courtyard. A man was walking his leashed dog over the snow-covered lawn, and nearby a young guy wearing a sports jacket with the letter D for the Dinamo soccer team on it was sitting on his sports bag. Gleb decided not to ring the bell. He waited for the dog to finish its business and go home. He kept the door from slamming and slipped through behind the dog and its master. Went up to the seventh floor. Got close to the apartment door – no sound. He was about to get into the elevator and wait for Anna in the courtyard when the lock clicked. Gleb barely had time to jump back. With an indifferent look, he moved up the stairs, as if continuing his way on foot. A way that between the seventh and eighth floors, of course, was anything but natural. Gleb continued without turning around. He relied on his hearing. The person who came out rang for the elevator a few times but the elevator was in use. Then wearily put something on the floor. A cello case? Gleb turned around: yes, exactly, a cello case. Anna (it was she) slowly looked up and froze: "You?" She didn't rush into his arms, and there was no joy in her question. "Me," Gleb confirmed. She went up a few steps but stopped two or three short of him. "You know, I'm late for class." She took one more step and stared into his face. "What's with your eyes? They're red, tearing." In these words Gleb imagined he heard concern. Maybe even tenderness. "I got sick on the way," he said, almost whining. "I have a fever." Gleb really wanted her pity, if not her bed and a cup of milk then at least a warm word. But he got nothing. Anna went down the stairs to her cello and called the elevator. "You have to go back to Kyiv right now" – the intonation of a loving but stern mother – "and take care of yourself there." She invited him into the elevator and held the closing door with her foot, not without a certain generosity. When they stepped outside, Dinamo man left his bag and headed toward them. When he got close, he kissed Anna on the lips. Took the cello from her hands. Demonstratively ignored Gleb. "Cheers, buddy," Gleb said defiantly. The young man looked at Anna, who shrugged. The two headed for the arch, in no hurry. "Get better," she called to Gleb over her shoulder. "I will," he replied soundlessly. Following their stately movement with his eyes, he noticed with glee that Dinamo man had forgotten his bag. Wearing track pants, his wool socks neatly folded down over his boots – he'd forgotten it. It might be more interesting to wrap your legs around someone so athletic, as she would a cello, than him, Gleb, but . . . He didn't even know what to put after that "but." There didn't seem to be anything. Dinamo man appeared from the archway and jogged toward his bag. Anna was probably waiting for him there. He was just about to run back when he saw Gleb's smile and braked. Gleb was standing, leaning against a streetlamp, and the shadow on his half-face turned his smile into a sneer. "What, did you freeze in place?" Dinamo man inquired. Gleb tried to be ironical, but his voice wouldn't obey: "No . . . hah . . . your tramp girlfriend –" Gleb was going to add something else when a quick jab in the face laid him out on the ground. Now he was looking up at Anna's new friend, who seemed huge. Dinamo man swung his leg at him but didn't connect. He said, "If you run your mouth about her one more time, I'll gouge your eyes out." He put his foot on Gleb's face, and left his footprint on the lying man's lips. And vanished with his bag. Gleb slowly stood up, walked over to a snowdrift, and scooped up some freshly fallen snow. Rubbed his lips and nose with it – bloody, of course. At the train station he took a quick look at himself in the mirror. In addition to the bloody streaks on his chin, he sported a leaden bruise under his right eye. Gleb took two local trains back too. Twelve hours later he was home, and when she saw him, his grandmother gasped. After hastily rinsing off her grandson's face and hands, she put him to bed, where he lay for a little over two weeks, felled by a serious flu.

MARCH 12, 2013, MUNICH

I'm at an appointment with Professor Wentz. The professor is a leading specialist in neurology. He asks me to stretch both arms out in front of me and looks at them closely. He asks me to clench and unclench my fists. He bends my arms at the elbow, especially the right. Standing behind me, he grabs my shoulders and pulls me toward him. He asks me to sit on the examination table, remove my shoes, and move my feet. He takes a chair and sits across from me. He smiles. He says, as if continuing a long-running conversation:

"Yes, Mr. Yanovsky, you have Parkinson's disease. Don't be upset. People live with it."

Professor Wentz's office and Wentz himself flip to the negative and back. No more guitars in my ears whatsoever. A drum solo.

"It's hard for me not to be upset." I switch suddenly to a whisper. "I'm a musician."

The smile on the professor's face is replaced by a momentary sadness.

"Yes, yes, I know. A famous musician. But I'll tell you this. There are illnesses even worse when, forgive me, music is the least of your troubles. Not only that, you have to have happiness even in unhappiness. You have classic . . . mmm . . . symmetrical Parkinson's, and we know what to expect of that." I make a movement with my left hand, and Wentz nods. "Yes, your left is substantially better than your right for now. Over the next three years, it may catch up, if I can put it that way. Generally speaking, you have to realize that this is not a disease of the arms or, you know, the feet, it's a disease of the brain."

The smile returns to the professor's face. In an odd way, it doesn't offend but rather instills hope.

"You say it's a disease of the brain. . . ." I don't know how to express my thought without offending the doctor. "But there is such a thing as magnetic resonance imaging. For you it . . . I mean to say, can you establish a diagnosis without it?"

Wentz nods good-naturedly. He's used to people doubting his diagnosis in the beginning. They suggest to him, to Wentz, how to conduct his examination. It's a normal reaction.

"I understand what you're getting at. An MRI – yes, it's what we will certainly do. But imaging . . . mmm . . . can only clarify certain details. It will scarcely affect the diagnosis."

Katya is waiting for me at the office door. I gesture to her: let's go. And we head for the exit at the end of the hall. Running down the stairs, I turn for a second:

"Parkinson's."

Katya groans muffledly, slows down, and stops. Hanging over the railings, she looks at me stopped a flight below. I'm reflected in her eyes. My face is a bright blurry oval in the staircase's quasi-gloom.

There's nothing left in it of the face on hundreds of posters. Just pain and distress.

"Gleb, how can he establish everything so simply, without tests or imaging?"

"Katya, let's go, for the love of God."

She starts descending slowly.

"I understand all that, he's a specialist, but there's also common sense, which suggests to me –"

I turn around once more, this time with a finger to my lips. Katya's German accent has increased five-fold. Outside, she throws herself on my chest. People look at us.

"What, am I dying? Dying? What's this scene?"

Her hands link around my neck. If it's going to be absolutely terrible, she's not going to let me depart for the next world so easily. Not that that seems to be what this is about. Wentz did say there are diseases much worse.

"You know," I whisper in her ear, "let's go somewhere for a drink."

Katya nods. She asks whether we should pick up Barbara on the way; Barbara, too, is awaiting the results from my doctor's visit. "No" – I turn my head – "not today. We can just call Barbara. I want to be alone with you."

We take a taxi to the Karlsplatz-Stachus neighborhood. Rush hour is beginning, and the car goes slowly. I roll down the window. Warm air penetrates to the inside of the car. I point out an SUV with a Petersburg license plate to Katya: affixed to the back door is a Saint George ribbon and the inscription "To Berlin!" Katya smiles.

We find an appealing little restaurant next to the Marienplatz and sit on the terrace. The waiter brings lap robes, though they're not really needed. We order ice cream. Wine for Katya, brandy for me. The waiter lights the candle on the table, but Katya asks him to take it away. I find that funny. Looking at me, the waiter smiles with restraint. The sun pokes through the still sticky chestnut leaves, and there are flecks of light on the tablecloth.

A woman gets up from a neighboring table, apologizes, and asks for my autograph. Two staff carry a harp onto the terrace. The harpist comes out, takes her time – black dress, bare shoulders, boa. Full-figured. This only embellishes her as a harpist. On her way to the harp, she makes a detour, approaches our table, and bows. I respond with a bow, and those around us applaud. The harpist takes her seat and begins to play.

"We'll get through all of it together." Katya puts her hand on top of mine. "All of it."

I cautiously free my hand from hers.

"Remember the Russian restaurant in London? My madness. I didn't spend the night at home then. I want you to know . . ."

"Don't say any more. I want to forget that." I do too. Silently, I kiss Katya's fingers.

1979

Gleb was slow to recover. Sometimes Antonina Pavlovna began to think he didn't want to. In fact, that wasn't so. Not at all. Gleb had no desire to get up. He lay covered by a blanket from the head down, leaving only a small hole for his nose. After breakfast, which he was served in bed, he would burrow back under the covers and by an effort of will drive himself to sleep. Yes, Gleb had no desire to get up, but above all he had no desire to wake up. Never before had he slept so much and so pointlessly. Gleb started confusing the time of day, and mostly – his dreams. Dreams he hadn't finished before now appeared as a component part of new dreams. One dream plowed into another, they intertwined bizarrely, like the dragons on his window curtains.

This connection between his dreams and dragons became so strong that with one glance at his curtains, Gleb's dreams would swoop down from above. When the reptiles started to move, one of his dreams would pick up the sick boy's hands and lull him to the rhythm of the curtains flapping. One could only speak for sure of Gleb being awake when he was eating. Chewing Antonina Pavlovna's steamed croquettes, he thought with anguish about the day he would have to appear at both schools. For the first time in all his years of study, Gleb didn't feel like going to either. When sleeping became impossible, he turned to reading. It turned out that books correctly chosen fenced him off from reality just as well as sleep did. He started with *Robinson Crusoe,* and as soon as he'd finished he reread it twice. True, he reread it from the spot where the hero ends up on the island. From this book it was a natural transition to *The Mysterious Island,* and from there to *Twenty Thousand Leagues Under the Sea,* which were also reread. Willing himself to sleep at night (now he found this very hard), he pictured himself on an uninhabited island. Or sailing in a submarine. In all instances, a thickness of water separated Gleb from the surrounding world, and he felt relatively calm. But even when he was in his safe place, the sick boy thought anxiously about how on weekday mornings he would once again hear the radio that hung on the wall. Hating it with all his heart, Gleb at the same time felt sorry for it: it was making an effort, after all, continuously making noise. Whether it rasped like an old Bolshevik or squeaked like a young Pioneer, it did what it could to help the child wake up, get up, and start getting ready for school. Children's choruses and their soloists' voices, which rang like aluminum plates, had a particular effect. Listening to one or two choral songs made it impossible to go back to sleep. Gleb, who still hadn't properly woken up, recognized weekends by the absence of radio, and these were days of quiet happiness. His illness became a kind of weekend for Gleb. Which eventually came to an end. And once again the radio started up, and the Bolsheviks, Pioneers, and choristers were back at it, plus, of course, calisthenics to the piano, the tiresome folk songs in all the languages of the peoples of the USSR, plus something else, but the main thing was those songs performed once again by choruses that made Gleb sick to his stomach, naturally. Years later, after a triumphal performance of folk songs, Gleb was asked to share the secrets of his artistry. He was asked what was required to have such a subtle understanding of that music and, most of all, to perform it. It's essential, Gleb replied after a moment's thought, to hear it year after year early in the morning, before school. Preferably over the radio and performed by a chorus. The secret of his artistry, according to Gleb, was that the strength of his hatred for the radio performance had given birth to an unprecedented desire to finally play it differently. All that said, this doesn't mean that the future virtuoso had disliked choral singing since childhood. Listening once to a chorus in a concert, the boy was amazed because the chorus sounded quite decent. The vocal collective pushed through the radio at 7:15 cast him into the deepest depression. Actually, given a similar statement of the question, the depression that in fact had Gleb in its grip could be written off to the choral singing in the mornings, but that would be unfair. The reason for Gleb's unstrung condition lay much deeper. The memory of the tragedy at the beach would not leave him, so that one might think that the reason lay in the drowned Arina. Or maybe in the undrowned Anna. This was closer to the truth, but it still wasn't the truth itself. What happened that summer had revealed death to Gleb. No, that's wrong. . . . Death as something that happens to someone else had been revealed to him long before, at Evdokia's funeral. Death as the dead man's personal failure. But after Arina's death, he suspected that death had something to do with him too. The more he thought about this, the more he was convinced. Even worse, Gleb became aware that death did not simply cut short a wonderful life, it turned what had already been lived through and achieved into senselessness. Sense-less-ness – six whole *s*'s, plus four *e*'s, plus two *n*'s, and one *l* – even such a rich word ultimately passed into oblivion. The word vanished in the absence of someone to say it, revealed to Gleb a bottomless abyss, and took away any joy in life. For a long time this discovery kept him from recovering. And did he really recover? To Antonina Pavlovna, who knew her grandson so very well, this present vigil of his seemed like a form of sleep. For fear of irritating him, his grandmother asked him no questions, although she saw he had lost interest in his studies and even in music. He would struggle to get up in the mornings, complain of weakness, and say he couldn't go to class. Soft-hearted Antonina Pavlovna would leave her grandson at home, and he would immediately drift off. Waking up after noon, he would read or go outside. When the snow was mostly gone, he started riding his bicycle. The next day he presented his teacher with a note from his grandmother explaining the reasons for his absence. The teacher nodded her head, but for a long time she wouldn't accept the note. When their frequency exceeded reasonable limits, she summoned Antonina Pavlovna. Walking past the glass doors of the teacher's lounge, Gleb saw his teacher talking to his grandmother. Listing Gleb's delinquencies, evidently, the teacher bent her fingers, and his grandmother stood in front of her, her head bowed – the worst of the worst students. Gleb felt a fury rise to his chest and a red color spill across his face. On the one hand, the helpless and pitiful figure of his grandmother; on the other, those picturesque fingers being bent. Gleb burst into the teacher's lounge, grabbed the hand with the bent fingers, and started forcing them open. But this wasn't to be: the pedagogical worker's fist was like iron. The woman herself couldn't have explained why she squeezed so firmly. Possibly she thought that each unbent finger would no longer be counted as an argument, or it might have been pure reflex. Whichever it was, not one of the whitened fingers was unbent. A few moments later, Antonina Pavlovna, who had come to her senses, was hitting her grandson on the back. Without saying a word, Gleb ran out of the teacher's lounge, rode the handrail down to the first floor, and shot out of the school like a bullet. At the end of the block he stopped: he had nowhere to go. He thought a minute and headed home. His grandmother wasn't there yet. To avoid running into her, Gleb took his bicycle outside through the service entrance. And he rode, standing on the pedals, dismounted, climbed some shaky stairs (carrying the bicycle), and wound up in the next courtyard. Handsomely, leg over, he mounted his bicycle and emerged on Pirogov Street. Remembering that Pirogov lay somewhere embalmed – in Vinnitsa, he thought – he envied him. His back fender clunked and his bicycle left the sidewalk for the street. The rhythm of the motion made him feel better. Movement always makes you feel better. In the midst of the despair that beset him on all sides, the bike ride was a small and totally unexpected happiness. There wasn't anything special in the ride, seemingly, but it stuck in Gleb's memory. Maybe because it kept him from drowning in the abyss that was already sucking him in. His hands froze on the handlebars, so he put on his gloves. Nonetheless, the wind was already springlike – in smell if not temperature. Behind him a trolleybus sounded its horn, angrily and at length. Gleb hugged the curb, but the trolleybus passed very close to him. Trying to scare him, obviously. Where did that hatred come from? Gleb thought that dying right now under the trolleybus's wheels would in some sense be a solution. For him. But for his grandmother? What would happen to her life? What would happen to his mother's life and their trip to Brisbane? She wouldn't be able to go if it meant leaving behind her son's grave. Or (even sadder): his mother would bring his zinc coffin to Brisbane to commit to the earth at the municipal cemetery there. Visiting his grave every day, she would be unbearably pained that her son got to the city of universal happiness only posthumously. But native Brisbaners would come to this grave as well. Gradually a memorial would take shape there dedicated to those who never did find happiness. Gleb felt a tear roll out of the corner of his eye and stop on his eyelid. A warm tear. It trembled, like a diver – at the very edge of the diving board. Pausing, it fearlessly took the plunge and smashed on the asphalt. That day he covered the city from east to west, crossed to the left bank of the Dnieper, and sat for a while where Arina died. The spring beach was totally deserted. The place looked even more hopeless than the summer before last. Gleb got home late that night, and his grandmother didn't say a word. She hugged him. She heated his dinner – the boy's favorite roast potatoes. She was happy because she'd been afraid she'd never see her grandson again, and he knew it. From that day on he went to school without any absences, but these were strange attendances. He showed no great interest in any one subject except maybe biology. Actually, even that interest was fairly unusual. Gleb was interested in the time it took different types of organisms to decompose: people, birds, lizards, snails. The teacher, who did not have all the facts, tried unsuccessfully to elicit from her pupil why he wanted this information. Placing her hand on his neck, she leaned toward Gleb like a priest taking confession, while at that time he was thinking that her pudgy cheeks would probably be first to fall victim to decomposition. They wouldn't last a week. During the days when Gleb's attendance gradually became more regular, a notice arrived from the music school. Taking advantage of the fact that Gleb had missed classes, the director had expelled him. Vera Mikhailovna, remembering how insolent Gleb had been to the director, considered his expulsion retribution. In the evening, she went to Gleb's apartment and announced that tomorrow morning she wanted his grandmother to go with her to see the director and ask for Gleb's reinstatement. Vera Mikhailovna felt that the director was, in essence, a forgiving person and the school had a shortage of pupils, so that if he were to apologize . . . "No need," Gleb stopped her. "What do you mean? No need to apologize?" the teacher asked. All words failed Gleb at once. "To reinstate me. I don't need it." Vera Mikhailovna looked at Gleb in amazement and slowly, almost syllable by syllable, said, "Why don't you need to be reinstated?" The boy pulled his head into his shoulders. "Because I'm going to die." Silence. The radio kept murmuring – and it was odd that it didn't fall silent too. Vera Mikhailovna was at a loss how to react. "But we're going to die too. Me, your grandmother" – Antonina Pavlovna nodded – "and, by the way, even the school's director. And that's all right; we're not canceling what we're doing." Gleb looked hard at a dark spot on the wallpaper. He said, "Why do we need to do anything if everyone's going to die?" Behind his back, his grandmother made a calming gesture to the teacher, whose eyes showed she understood. She stroked Gleb's shoulder and with exaggerated caution, on tiptoe, left the room. She was sure Gleb and his grandmother would come see the director the next day. But they didn't. Not the next day and not later. Gleb quit music school.

March 20, 2013, Munich

Morning, the doorbell. Geraldina goes to open up. Obviously she's encountered someone unexpected or even undesired because quiet negotiations go on for a couple of minutes. Eventually, the visitor loses patience. Comes in and to Geraldina's cries of protest goes up to the dining room.

In the doorway is my London acquaintance Hanna. She's dressed like a hiker: a big backpack over her shoulders, jeans rolled up almost to her knees, sneakers. A Ukrainian embroidered shirt. Which might go with jeans and sneakers, but on Hanna it doesn't.

"I'm *vagitna*," Hanna says.

"What does *vagitna* mean?" Katya asks, although it seems she already knows.

Standing in the doorway, Geraldina watches the draft stir Hanna's loose hair. It spreads throughout the room – and the sun illuminates it from beneath. Illuminates the embroidered shirt too.

"It means she's pregnant."

I say it without expression so as not to shout.

"*Sie ist schwanger.*" Katya for some reason translates for Geraldina.

"*By him.*" Hanna nods toward me.

Katya freezes. There is emphatic bewilderment on Geraldina's face. Hanna's nod is eloquent, but it's hard for her to imagine Herr Yanovsky . . . Something not quite proper flashes in Geraldina's eyes. No, Herr Yanovsky had never so much as looked at other women, she can't believe this. Geraldina glances at Hanna. That is, she can, of course, but with difficulty.

Katya goes up to Hanna and lifts the backpack by its side straps, allowing their guest to free her arms. She hugs Hanna awkwardly and seats her in an armchair. Hanna, who had been expecting a scene, continues to hold herself stiff, since anything might happen still.

"Hanna" – Katya's eyes are shining – "dear Hanna."

"Khanna," Hanna corrects her vigorously.

"Something between a g and an h," I explain to Katya.

"Khanna," Katya repeats readily. "What happiness that you've come to us with your little one."

Looking at the ceiling, Hanna shrugs one shoulder. Where else was she supposed to go?

"What I mean" – Katya draws geometric figures in the air – "is that you haven't done anything irreparable."

Hanna's pursed lips make it clear that the question of that hadn't even come up. Geraldina serves lunch.

Hanna barely touches any of it.

After lunch Katya suggests we go to the Englischer Garten. She thinks it will be a little easier there than at home. We find ourselves on the main allée in the middle of Munich bicycle life. Our usual walk is exactly the same as it's been hundreds and hundreds of times – except for Hanna's presence. Bicycles come toward us and overtake us from behind, come out from behind trees and, unlike Hanna, disappear behind them. They brake, honk, rattle their leather toolkits, and keep us from talking. Which suits everyone, basically. Some bicyclists dismount and ask permission to take a selfie with me.

When we turn onto a side path, quiet falls, and we can talk. We *need* to talk. The path is narrow, the strollers can't walk in a single row, so I let the ladies go ahead. I feel like a bigamist. The word sticks to my tongue and melts it. Yes, Katya is nobility such as can be counted on the fingers of one hand. She suggests Hanna stay with us – it's just not clear as what. Junior wife?

For Katya this is all about the baby. If it was conceived with Hanna, that means Hanna is my wife. And the one I didn't conceive with – that means . . . disaster. I slow my pace and lag behind the women. Katya turns around and looks at me helplessly, but I'm closely watching a squirrel on a pine trunk. The squirrel is watching me just as closely. It knows that life's troubles arise primarily due to men.

Imperceptibly, I increase the distance, and neither woman has the nerve to call out to me. Snatches of their conversation, which is going on in Russian, reach me. Katya doesn't know Ukrainian. Neither does Hanna, apparently. In London, that didn't strike me somehow, but now her ignorance of her *native tongue* is increasingly obvious.

Her Russian is far from irreproachable, either, to put it mildly, especially that fricative g she's already managed to teach Katya. It's Russian that's taken a lot from Ukrainian phonetics. Losing that accent is extremely hard, and reading a paragraph of a textbook isn't enough; this isn't just about declining *put*. Hearing Hanna's speech, I feel like getting even farther away from her. She's some kind of Eliza Doolittle. Only I'm no Professor Higgins.

Katya does most of the talking. The words "our duty" and "on the third floor" reach me. Katya is planning to put Hanna on the third floor. They're already walking arm in arm. Katya is wearing something ethereal and black; Hanna her embroidered blouse. Returning home, they get ready for dinner. Katya brings Hanna a silk robe.

"I want it all to be homey, because you're home now."

Hanna changes clothes. Looks at me inquiringly.

I say, "That robe looks good on you."

"For sure?"

Of course. She's taking everything seriously. Dark blond hair and a nearly ideal oval face, except that her cheekbones are more prominent than on Ukrainian women. However. This is exactly what makes her enchanting. If you can't understand what she's saying, you can genuinely fall in love with her – marry her, for instance. But if you can, then you might do the exact opposite – go your separate ways, let's say.

Katya, at supper:

"It would be right if Gleb spent the night with Hanna today."

She says this with a cheerful face, as if this went without saying. With all her nobility, Katya does not want to stand in the way of my and Hanna's love. Which (love) never was, in essence. Katya smells of alcohol. Hanna doesn't quite understand what's going on and says nothing. I do, but I say nothing as well.

When the time comes to go to bed, Katya takes me by the hand (my half-hearted resistance has been broken) and leads me to Hanna's room. And tiptoes out for some reason. I pull Hanna close, kiss her on the forehead, and wish her a good night. I go down to the front hall. Lie down on the sofa and pull a lap robe over my head. I think about the baby Hanna's expecting. Is it mine? I'm gasping for air – I pull the lap robe off my face. But even if it isn't . . . Since Hanna says it is, that means there's no one else to care for the baby. Which means it's mine in either case.

In the middle of the night I wake up from the creak of footsteps. Katya is coming down the stairs. She waves to me to come into our bedroom.

1979

Fyodor found out that Gleb had quit music school. With some delay, a few months later, but he did. And got upset. It was a surprise for everyone who remembered how reserved he'd been about his son's decision to study music. For the first time in years Fyodor asked Irina if they could meet. Hearing that Gleb had abandoned music in view of the death that awaits each of us, Fyodor became agitated and said that this was the act of a genuine musician. That the distinguishing trait of a musician was not the dexterity of his fingers but the constant thought of death, which should instill us with optimism, not horror. Meant to mobilize, not paralyze. "*In other words, true creativity must balance between life and death,*" Fyodor summed up. "*It has to see a little beyond the horizon.*" But this was only the beginning of the conversation. The actual conversation took place later – and not with Fyodor but with his father Mefody, who had come from Kamianets-Podilskyi to visit his son. Mefody was tall, broad-shouldered, and gray, kind of like Turgenev. The resemblance was heightened because, unlike Fyodor, his grandfather switched to Russian once in a while. And although his language might not have been Turgenevian, his readiness to speak it was much more important. To his grandmother's question of what he thought of Mefody from their first meeting, Gleb said without thinking: well-meaning. The definition was exceptionally precise. Mefody meant well with every word he spoke. With every wrinkle, one might say, of which his face had many. Tiny ones spread around his eyes like a cast net, but there were also large ones as deep as trenches traced from his bridge to the corners of his mouth. Yes, Fyodor wanted the boy to meet his grandfather, but he himself hadn't anticipated that this would be the start of a longstanding friendship. Gleb wouldn't let Mefody go for a minute. It's hard to say what this was: a longing for male company, which Gleb had been deprived of, or the qualities of his grandfather himself. Most likely, this was about his grandfather, since life without a father hadn't nudged Gleb toward his own father. Yes, sometimes Gleb wished he could make an impression on his father, but he had no desire for constant communication. With his grandfather, though, he did. His grandfather turned out to be gentle and easygoing. Unexpectedly, Gleb played the part of grandfather in the interactions between these two people. He led Mefody through his favorite streets and told him about them. His grandfather was a grateful listener. Listening to Gleb, he would nod, but at the end of the story sometimes would ask a question or two that made it clear he knew a lot more about the subject than Gleb. "So you know everything," Gleb said with slow amazement. "*Come now.*" His grandfather gave him a funny blank look as he switched to Ukrainian. "*I don't know anything.*" "Yes, you do!" Gleb would say playfully. One time his grandfather didn't try to vindicate himself and said, "If there's something I definitely do not know, it's why you quit music school." Caught flat-footed, Gleb fell silent. Then he repeated what he'd already said once: "Because I'm going to die." Uttered the first time, those words had been hot, like breath, but now suddenly they seemed like cardboard. Not to Mefody, though. To Gleb's great surprise, his grandfather considered this line of thinking natural and even praised the boy for his philosophical approach to life. But he didn't forget Gleb's words. They surfaced a few days later, when grandfather and grandson were sitting by the fountain in Zolotovoritska Park. "*If you're going to die,*" Mefody said thoughtfully, "*then why should you go to that music school?*" Gleb heard new notes in the question and so nodded cautiously. His grandfather stood up from the bench, moved closer to the fountain, and put his large hands under the stream. When they were full, he washed his face. He turned back to Gleb. "*But what if you're not going to die?*" "How's that?" Gleb asked. Mefody's face took on a puzzling expression: "There's this idea . . ." Gleb looked at his grandfather and smiled. An idea. That's what a progressive grandfather he had, then. Progressive and even in a way sophisticated. Mefody waved and a taxi stopped in front of them. Like a fairytale! In the blink of an eye! Handsomely. A Volga GAZ-24, which Gleb had never ridden in before. He'd only ridden in a Volga GAZ-21, which Fyodor talked about often, saying it wasn't quite a tank but it wasn't quite a car either. The taxi Gleb's magician-grandfather seated him in had a quiet engine and a smooth ride. His grandfather did in fact remind him of a fairytale character because the waves of his hands produced things he'd never seen before. A small church popped up by the Holosiiv Forest as from the sleeve of Vasilisa the Wise, and in that small church, Father Pyotr – fair hair gathered into a bun, neat beard, eyeglasses. The church was straight out of a fairytale, but Father Pyotr more than likely wasn't. He smelled of eau de toilette, and it was obvious that, unlike folklore characters, Father Pyotr took care of himself. After he and Mefody embraced, Mefody smelled of eau de toilette too. Observing these dissimilar men, Gleb realized they were linked if not by personal friendship then by firm, longstanding acquaintance. Mefody told Father Pyotr that his grandson had discovered death for himself, and this, understandably, had made him give up music school. Father Pyotr also found this act natural, inasmuch as what in fact did anyone need music school for if everything was ending in we-know-what. Once he'd received Father Pyotr's approval, Mefody noted that, on the other hand, it was too bad the boy had given up school. Yes, perhaps it was too bad, Father Pyotr agreed, since music links the school to eternity, after all. "Is music eternity?" Gleb asked. Father Pyotr shook his head. "Music is not eternity. But it reminds us of eternity – profound music does." "What is eternity?" Gleb asked. "It is the absence of time," Mefody conjectured, "which means the absence of death." "Ultimately it is God," Father Pyotr said. "The One you are seeking." The priest gave Gleb a New Testament, a catechism, and a prerevolutionary textbook on "Divine Law." In parting, he asked him to learn the Symbol of Faith, which was marked in the textbook with a piece of velvet. When he got home, Gleb put the three books in front of him and read them in turn. One of them (Divine Law) he took to school the next day. Sitting in his social studies class, he read it under the desk. His teacher, walking along the rows, silently stole up from behind and plucked the book from Gleb's lap. To general laughter, she read the title, and her first reaction was surprise. That was not what she expected to find in a lap under a desk. She opened the book to the bookmark and tried to read it out loud and stumbled. Obviously, knowledge of social studies was inadequate for that kind of reading. She closed the book. "So, maybe we go to church?" she asked Gleb. The first person plural, it occurred to Gleb, how self-centered. Not only would he not have gone with her to church, he wouldn't even have gone with her to . . . She came right up to him and inquired, "Do we pray and beat our brows?" Gleb tried to snatch the book from his teacher's hands, but she deftly turned away. "Do we beat our brows?" she asked again.

"That's none of your business," Gleb snarled. "That is where you are mistaken, Yanovsky. It is my business and the business of the Young Communist organization, if, of course, you are a Young Communist." Gleb actually did belong to the Young Communists. At first he hadn't planned to join, but Fyodor called that step a bad omen. From his observations, those who didn't join the Young Communists later did not get into university or conservatory. During the break, the social studies specialist took the Young Communist member to see the principal, an elderly, good-natured lady. Placing Divine Law on her desk, the teacher said, "Here is what our school's Young Communists are reading. Young Communist Pilgrims." Leafing through the book, the principal thanked the teacher for her vigilance, and this gratitude, it seemed to Gleb, was not without irony, as the "You may go" tossed casually to the social studies specialist attested. The elderly lady did not believe in God but did not like tattle-tales. She decided not to complicate Gleb's future and so limited herself to an informational conversation. The principal directed Gleb's attention to the fact that Gagarin flew into outer space but did not see God. From this, it seemed to her, followed the inescapable conclusion that there is no God. She asked that someone from the Yanovsky family come to pick up his Divine Law – which was a mild summons to the school. The boy gave this a couple of days' thought and then reasoned that the best thing to do in this case was go to his grandfather. After all, the confiscated book, ultimately, had come through him. When Gleb told Mefody what had happened, he showed no concern whatsoever. He only asked whether Gleb had managed to memorize the Symbol of Faith. No. That's fine, too (his grandfather smiled), maybe now the principal will. He asked his grandson for a piece of paper and in a calligraphic hand wrote the Symbol of Faith on it. He explained the unfamiliar words and chanted it from beginning to end. He held it out to Gleb: *"When you've learned it, tell me."* An hour later, Gleb had it by heart. He explained to his amazed grandfather: the music. The music of words. He memorized the Symbol of Faith as musical phrases. When his grandson recited it without a single hitch, Mefody waved his hand again and they found themselves at Father Pyotr's. At the doors of the church he greeted them with an exclamation: *"Behold, one born for eternity is coming!"* He blessed his visitors and slowly set about the christening. It was a sunny day, and the splashes spilling from the fount sparkled in the sun's rays like jewels. And hung in the air for rather a long time. After christening God's servant Gleb, Father Pyotr intoned, "In the name of Our Lord Jesus Christ I release you from mortal fear and counsel you to return to your current affairs – for example, to your studies at the music school. Work, my friend, to the glory of God! While remembering that eternity lies ahead, do not neglect time, for only in time can something be achieved. Your parents asked that you not be registered in the church book to avoid problems with our militantly atheistic state – and so I am not registering you. Know that you are registered with the Lord, and that is what is most important. In difficult moments, rely on me and on your grandfather Mefody." At these words, the newly christened young man remembered that Mefody had before him his meeting with the principal, and his heart sank. He worried in vain, however. The eldest in the Yanovsky clan took full responsibility for his assignment and headed for school the very next day. Mefody's gray hair made the most favorable impression on the principal, who began her conversation with him with what seemed to her an irrefutable argument. Returning the confiscated book to Gleb's grandfather, she took him by the elbow rather theatrically and led him to the window. Pointing to the sky, she said, *"Yuri Gagarin flew in space but did not see God. You agree?"* Mefody politely bowed his head: *"True, Yuri Gagarin did not see God."* Not tearing himself away from the sky in the window, the old man smiled broadly. *"But God saw him. And blessed him."*

It's good when troubles start in the morning: you have all day to deal with them.

The bell. Geraldina opens up. In the doorway is a plump woman in a track suit, a suitcase in each hand and a pack on her back. Pointing to herself, she says: "Liudmila."

Before she can cross the threshold, Liudmila is explaining to Geraldina the meaning of her name. She (she points to herself) is *mila* – dear – to *liudi* – people. She gestures with her entire arm to signify people. Encountering bewilderment, Liudmila signals to the foreigner: "It's too complicated. We have our own history, our own names." A big smile, a collection of gold teeth. Geraldina takes a step back in astonishment.

Liudmila notices me.

"And I'm Anya's mama from Melitopol." She gives me a kiss on the cheek. "Hello."

"Hello. Hanna will be right down."

Liudmila laughs.

"Why Hanna? No one's ever called her that!"

Hanna appears, wrapping her robe around her as she goes.

"Anya, daughter dear! What scared you into being a Hanna? That's a good joke! A circus on a wire, not a daughter."

There is no joy on Hanna's face.

"Mama, what on earth have you come for, I have to wonder? Is this what I gave you the address for? And with those trunks – you could fit all Melitopol in them."

Liudmila darkens too.

"You know where you can stick that tongue of yours? You were a vulgar girl before, and you still are."

"And you're a professor."

Liudmila mutters something in offense, but her lightning bolts have already petered out. Indeed, she's not a professor, and that's hard to reconcile herself to. Her anger has evaporated. Liudmila is forgiving. Looking closely at each other, mother and daughter start to smile. A minute later they're hugging. Hanna agrees to be Anya.

Geraldina serves dinner on the lawn in front of the house. She lists the dishes to Katya: Greek salad, broccoli bisque, trout with potato puree. A 2009 Mosel. Ice cream. Coffee. Liudmila surveys the coniferous exotica growing along the lawn's perimeter.

"But where are the apple trees, the pear trees, the plum trees?"

"*There aren't any,*" I answer.

Everyone laughs. Liudmila slaps her forehead and rushes into the house. She reappears with a two-liter bottle and something wrapped in foil. Moonshine and fatback, it turns out.

"Mama, what have you done, damn, why . . ." Anya blushes. "Who's going to eat that?"

"Hel-lo-o-o! If no one else is going to, then I will!"

"I will, too," I say.

"Excellent, son-in-law!"

Anya looks at Katya, but she keeps her cool. Liudmila unwraps the foil and cuts thin slices of fatback. Geraldina watches the proceedings with interest. Liudmila notices and picks up a slice of fatback with two fingers and brings it up to Geraldina's mouth. Geraldina rolls her eyes and giggles. Liudmila (an animal trainer of major proportions) shakes the fatback by her mouth. Geraldina the little dog cautiously takes the slice with her lips. And groans lightly as if from pleasure.

Seeing this success, Liudmila pours her half a glass of moonshine. Geraldina watches the cloudy protuberance in the bottle with trepidation. She picks up the glass with an elegant movement, raises it to her nose like a sommelier, and draws in the air. An expression of horror appears on her face. *Nein, danke.* Without saying a word, Liudmila takes the glass from Geraldina and downs it in one go. Noisily sniffs a piece of fatback, practically sucking it in with her nostrils. And then eats it. Pours me some moonshine. I repeat what Liudmila has done.

"A drink?" Liudmila asks Katya.

Katya nods. She sips the moonshine, savoring it. The homebrew makes her frown, but she drinks. Liudmila wants to tell her exactly how she should drink the moonshine, but she holds her tongue. She still doesn't fully understand the nature of her relationship to Katya. After dinner, Katya, I, and Anya (in precisely this order) sit on the swing and slowly swing. Liudmila, shown the way by Geraldina, goes to take a nap; she's swinging noticeably too. She stops on the threshold and sends everyone an air kiss, her gold teeth flashing.

"Mama is silly, of course, but well-meaning," Anya says.

Geraldina returns. She pours white wine and serves us. Taking a glass from Anya's hands, Katya returns it to the tray. Silently kissing Anya on her temple, she hands her a glass of orange juice. Anya shrugs, also silently. All you can hear is the swing's rhythmic creak. There's something operatic in this solemn swinging. Katya's helpless look is like a stab of despair. I stand up and look away. It's a dream-operetta, I just have to wake up. I can already see Katya touchingly worrying about Anya's baby. A baby belonging to the three of us. Wake up or die.

"*Guten Morgen,* son-in-law! And *hände hoch!*"

Liudmila appears in a second-story window in her flowery nightgown – above the sill, as if it were a puppet theater. Waves gaily. Her breasts sway majestically under the nightgown.

"Go away!" Anya orders.

Liudmila throws her arm out in a salute:

"Hitler kaput!"

And disappears. She sleeps until supper.

In the evening, as everyone is getting ready for bed, I go into my study and turn on the computer out of habit. I have to make a decision. I look at the screen, as if I could expect an answer there. But I haven't even formulated the question. I search for "Parkinson's." "Parkinson's disease is a slowly progressing neurological illness." So . . . "The neurons that process dopamine die in the brain." Parkinson's is a pain, and Anya is a pain. Combining two pains does not make things easier.

I lean back in my chair. Up until now I hadn't let myself read a line about Parkinson's. And hadn't asked the doctor anything. And the doctor hadn't tried to tell me anything. "Dopamine. It conveys the brain's commands to the muscles. When it stops being produced, the muscles . . ."

Liudmila's quiet song reaches me from the hall. I rest my head on the keyboard and the screen runs through the development of Parkinson's disease in a mad rhythm – symptoms, complications, prognosis for longevity. I compute this information with the back of my head.

My mobile plays "March of the Aviators." I lift my head: "Mama" comes up on the screen. No, not now. She senses me and guesses everything right away. She'll understand everything at "Hello." Why upset her? The phone vibrates, revealing a total absence of dopamine. The hallway announces heavy steps, and the commander speaks in Liudmila's voice:

"A call for someone!"

This could be recorded as a ringtone. The voice is just so-so, of course, but it can be heard everywhere. I press "answer" and say hello to my mother. The floor creaks outside the door. Without interrupting my conversation, I abruptly open the door. Instead of crashing into Liudmila's forehead, the door runs into something soft: the woman, lost in thought, is sitting on the floor. I wave goodbye to her.

"Don't read all that muck," my mother advises. "Disease is a person's condition, and people, my son, are different. You have a lot of durability in reserve."

She tells me about Michael Fox and Mohammed Ali, who've been fighting the disease for decades. Perfectly correct. She always calls at the right time.

1980

Beginning in the ninth grade, Gleb attended church on Sundays. Most often with Mefody, now a frequent visitor in Kyiv. Each time he appeared, Mefody explained he had business to attend to, but Gleb became increasingly convinced that the old man was coming for his sake. Father Pyotr was transferred away from Kyiv, and then Gleb and Mefody moved to St. Makariy's on Lukyanovka, where another priest Mefody knew served, Father Georgy. Gradually Gleb got in the habit of attending church even without his grandfather. Father Georgy was like a grandfather to everyone – equally close and loving. Gleb had never seen this kind of collective kinship before. Nor had he ever seen birds perch on a person's head and arms, and not just pigeons (they'll perch anywhere), but also sparrows and tits. They perched on Father Georgy. Coming out from the church, he would fling his arms wide and stand motionless. Birds would come flying to his bald, fringed head and then to his arms, which trembled from the tension. Slowly they would lower along with the birds. Father Georgy would gather his strength and straighten out his arms again, and it would be like flight – very slow and, at his advanced age, clearly the only possible kind. So then, Mefody. He truly did come for the boy's sake because he sensed the boy needed support. They would go to museums and take walks in parks. Also, Gleb could smoke in front of his grandfather, and to him this seemed to make him an adult and equal to his grandfather. True, once Mefody said, "*You'd do better not to smoke, son.*" He was giving advice, actually, not forbidding him. "I can't quit," Gleb, who by this time was smoking a pack a day, replied. "Don't quit" – Mefody switched to Russian – "just don't smoke. Those are different states." He explained to Gleb that someone who's quit smoking is constantly thinking about the fact that he quit, and that's intolerable. "And a nonsmoker?" Gleb asked. "A nonsmoker" – Mefody spread his arms – "doesn't smoke." When Gleb realized he was a nonsmoker, he really did stop smoking. Without any particular effort. But at the time – at the time Gleb's smoking brought them closer and injected a note of trust. All their serious conversations began after a cigarette appeared in Gleb's mouth. He would take his time lighting it with a lighter (a gift from his grandfather!), and his first words would come out with clouds of smoke. His nonsmoking grandfather would watch with regret the practiced way his grandson handled the lighter. At each flick, Mefody experienced doubts as to the correctness of this gift. And each time he told himself that the gift was correct if it helped pull his grandson out of the hole he'd fallen into. And Gleb had in fact started to climb out. He felt that although death was inevitable, it wasn't final. Etched in his memory were Mefody's words about death being a door to eternity. Should he be afraid of a door? Standing at the Sunday service, Gleb experienced full liberation from death. His legs ached for want of habit, but it was a pleasant ache, physical evidence of his movement into eternity. Sometimes his attention wandered, and Gleb would start to get bored. In the winter, when the church doors and windows were closed and there wasn't enough air, he would get sleepy. The boy would pinch his hand so it hurt, but that didn't help for long. Then he would exit the church, sit on a bench cleared of snow, and feel its frozen wood. After the hotly heated space, the cold felt good. Upon his return to the warmth, he would get even sleepier. For a little while sleep would drive out his thought of overcoming death, but a few minutes later it would draw him in because death is sleep. Nearly drifting off, Gleb would suddenly wake up, since it's hard to fall sound asleep while standing. None of these difficulties stopped Gleb. On the contrary, overcoming them seemed to him a small but essential sacrifice. And anyway, this wasn't the hardest part about attending church. Perhaps the hardest was confession, which touched on his intimate acts and thoughts. Gleb tried to imagine just how repulsive he seemed to Father Georgy after all his stories. What was most frustrating was that in the priest's eyes he appeared much worse than he in fact was, since he only told him the bad parts. One day he surprised himself at confession by saying to Father Georgy, "I could tell you something good too." "Well, the way confession works," Father Georgy replied, "people talk about what's bad, but the fact that you're good, son, I already know that." Son. Usually it was "child," he called everyone "child." Child, go back to music school (he said), it's not good that you left it. Gleb thought that then he would have to ask forgiveness from the director with his stupid jokes. Father Georgy, reading his thoughts at that short distance, said, "Well, so ask forgiveness. What's wrong with that? Maybe his jokes are better now. A person doesn't stand in place, after all. Asking forgiveness never hurts, and moreover, you do want to go back, don't you?" Yes, Gleb did want to, he wanted to very much. He called Vera Mikhailovna, they went to see the director together, and Gleb apologized. It turned out not to be difficult at all. The director even seemed to have become a little embarrassed by his jokes; at least during their conversation he didn't joke once. Returning home, the reinstated music school pupil decocooned his guitar, which was completely out of tune. He neatly turned each peg and delighted in the floating sound of a string being tightened. It was like turning a radio dial. But if the radio's light signaled a precise landing on a radio program, the sole testimony to a string landing in the overall harmony was his, Gleb's, ear. Or more simply: he, Gleb, did have an ear. Or: Gleb had an ear. The boy repeated this mentally to various tunes – he even sang to himself, it seemed to him. In fact, he was singing out loud. He saw his grandmother's lit-up face and realized that. Gleb's return to music school filled her with happiness. Looking at his grandmother, Gleb thought about how she might soon face death and that thought might have poisoned her existence, but here this minor detail was delighting her. But what if his grandmother had already said goodbye to her life and transferred it to Gleb's life and now was experiencing happiness at his return? To say nothing of how happy Gleb himself was. All evening he went over the repertoire he had played before. Despite the extended hiatus, his fingers remembered the music of Carcassi, Giuliani, Carulli, and Sor. They remembered Roche's "Habañera." Once Gleb had changed the rhythm and played Roche as a tango, and his teacher had liked it. He'd played it like that for a joke, but she suggested he perform it at the academic concert. Gleb did. He was nervous. The audience applauded for a long time then – everyone, including the school director. On the whole, he's a decent guy, this director, Gleb thought as he plucked the strings, and he shouldn't have been like that with him. . . . The next day, he performed brilliantly all the things he played for Vera Mikhailovna. Yes, exactly so, because none other than Vera Mikhailovna said, "Brilliant! As if there hadn't been a long hiatus. Simply brilliant." To the next lesson she brought a list of pieces comprising Gleb's new, fairly difficult program. It included a fugue from Bach's Sonata in G minor transcribed for the guitar by Francisco Tárrega, and Introduction and Variations on a Theme of Mozart, Op. 9, by Fernando Sor. Also proposed were Tárrega's Capricho Arabe, Isaac Albéniz's Asturias, and Heitor Villa-Lobos's Etude no. 1. The teacher asked whether Gleb agreed to this repertoire. Yes, he agreed. His joy at returning to music school was so complete that he agreed to everything, even to attending classes in solfeggio and musical literature, which he'd been excused from, having already taken the full course. Actually, upon reflection, he did reject solfeggio (in his eyes, there was still Kleshchuk constructing triads), but he did attend musical literature. The subject, alas, was now taught not by Lena, who, as was clarified, had gone on maternity leave. After what there had been between them (in Gleb's dreams), her pregnancy was tantamount to betrayal. But the classes, and most of all the new teacher, proved so interesting that Gleb quickly forgave Lena. The teacher's name was Pavel Petrovich Sergeyev, who outwardly was as unremarkable as his name. An older man of fifty who wore unfashionable and crooked glasses. His voice was thin and raspy, such as would tell you a spring had broken, but when in this very voice Pavel Petrovich began to talk about music, he was transformed. He became taller, younger, and tidier, and his glasses sat noticeably more evenly on his nose. When Gleb got to his class, he was talking about polyphony. Pavel Petrovich put the stress in the word on the second "o" and considered that the sole possible option. Lena had somehow left out polyphony, maybe because she was of a determinate nature and alien to dichotomy. The topic of polyphony completely captivated Gleb, who had the vague sense that life consists of repetitions and parallel statements. Although he covered various types of polyphony, Pavel Petrovich dwelt in detail on two. The first had to do with *subsidiary voices,* which accompany the main melody, altering it slightly. Subsidiary voices are characteristic above all of the folk song. Pavel Petrovich lowered the needle on a record, and they heard a Georgian song with a faint crackle. Breaking it off with obvious regret, he moved on to the second type of polyphony, which is distinguished by the fact that the main melody is first heard in one voice and then appears in other voices. In the process, the melody may change – not unlike what happens in the fugues that came so successfully to the incomparable Bach. A quick change of record: the Toccata and Fugue in D minor. The same crackling now sounded like a salient quality of polyphony. The needle broke off like an airliner taking off and smoothly shot upward. When the melody was repeated unchanged, it became a form (search for the next record) rather grandly called a "canon." The next record was a total surprise for Gleb. It was the duel scene from *Evgeny Onegin.* In the orchestra, the somber booms of the basses. First Lensky, followed by Onegin: enemies, the thirst for blood had led them away from each other long ago. What Gleb knew by heart was, it turned out, a canon. Which you can't sing alone. And you can't turn to Kleshchuk for vocal support; he didn't know how to fall back properly. All that remained was to listen, which is what Gleb did, with a new ear. And he loved this music even more ardently than before; the hiatus worked to his benefit. In the intervening time, a certain experience had taken shape in Gleb's soul that allowed him to look on life and music in a new way. To see in music not a reflection of life but its continuation, its higher self, perhaps. Thus, Mozart's Requiem was for him not a description of departure but the departure itself, not a depiction of suffering but actual suffering. He listened to the Requiem innumerable times. Previously he'd imagined a dark figure coming to Mozart with an order. He might as well have been ordering someone to dig their own grave. Now he imagined nothing because the music entered him without images or conception, the way October's raw sharpness enters us when we view fallen leaves – reddish brown, disintegrated into harmless leaf skeletons. Tears come to your eyes – because of the wind, the cold, the smell of rot – especially in old people. Old people are weepy. Any falling of leaves seems like a requiem to them, connected in their minds to we know what, so we don't even need Pushkin's man in black. Old people are also garrulous. They don't talk to report something important or to be liked, the way young people do. They wish to assure themselves one more time of their connection to this world and ultimately to enjoy this world. Any conversation of theirs could be their last because it costs those leaves nothing to separate from a branch. This image led Gleb to thoughts of his grandmother. But Antonina Pavlovna had no plans to separate from her branch. Nothing so prolongs life as being needed. She went to the stores, cooked, did the laundry. And she did something more: in the absence of copy machines, she would copy out music for Gleb. This was a double feat since she was not musically literate. To be more precise, Antonina Pavlovna didn't rewrite the notes, she redrew them. Very rarely – mostly before academic concerts – she would write homework assignments in literature for her grandson, who would copy them without understanding them particularly well. He was praised for them, and a couple of times they were read out to the class, and he listened to them as if for the first time. Yes, his grandmother wrote quite decently, but this was done not for Gleb's glory but so her grandson didn't steal precious minutes from his musical studies. He now devoted all his time to music and spent hours studying études and various pieces. Previously, Gleb had tried to figure out and memorize a piece as quickly as possible. He got bored after half an hour because the work of his fingers didn't engage his mind. His mind found work for itself, but work unrelated to the composition being studied. Now everything was different. It wasn't Gleb's fingers playing, it was his whole being, and his mind was no longer a part distinct from it, untethered. The performer dissolved in the music without residue, erasing any distinction between emotion and thought: both became the music. Gleb was the music no less than the composer because the composer is nothing more than curlicues scattered over the musical staff, whereas the music, ultimately, is what sounds. No longer did his time in class drag; it simply flew. Or put it this way.

When he picked up his instrument, Gleb was transported to where there is no time. That was when something arose in his playing that one music scholar later defined as "Yanovsky's supermelody." Critics compared it to the supertext of Joyce or Proust, by which they meant the additional meaning that took shape upon reading their texts. Not merely a sum of the words or descriptions. The supertext spoke about something beyond the scope of the basic text. Gleb's supermelody arose during his school years and was expressed in a quiet vocal accompaniment – odd but undoubtedly pleasant. One monograph devoted to Gleb even spoke about how the supermelody arose in him before the melody. Grounds for saying this was that memorable summer when Gleb performed his supermelody without touching the guitar strings. Without having the least notion of playing the guitar. This continued during his studies as well. His teacher would involuntarily start nodding to him to the beat and only minutes later seemed to shake herself off and tell him to quit his *humming*. Ultimately, humming became the generally accepted signature of Gleb's unique style. Gleb really did hum inasmuch as it was hard to call the sound he made singing. The point wasn't even that no words were envisaged here (there is such a thing as singing without words, after all). What came from Gleb's lips was more like the sound of a musical instrument than a human voice, as became perfectly obvious when the boy's voice changed. Another change took place as well. The previous supermelody had not gone beyond the bounds of the tonality of the composition being performed, but the new one did. This humming was like a prototype of the music, its heavenly *eidos*. It did not precede the music and was not born of it but rather both preceded and was born of it, inasmuch as it was totally independent of time. Gleb was addressing that heavenly matrix from which the music he was playing was cast. This kind of casting could not be ideal because only the matrix is ideal. Gleb's humming restored the places the composer hadn't written out and made the composition deeper and more three-dimensional. It was polyphony, essentially, but an unusual kind, not based on the complicated rules for creating polyphonic music, which Gleb didn't know anyway. Years later, critics conjectured that the strange magic of these sounds was born not so much through musical harmony as through the combination of timbres, the guitar's and the voice's. This shifted Gleb's performance to the sphere of the unrepeatable, in the narrow sense that repeating it required the exact same voice that had sounded. But those who preferred to explain the Yanovsky phenomenon as a different two-voice texture were right after all. This was about a mystical polyphony that combined in music what had been manifested by the composer with what remained closed to him in the heavenly archetype.

MARCH 30, 2013, MUNICH

Nestor has come for another visit. The house on Am Blütenring has never been so full. Never have we awaited Nestor so impatiently. Katya even insisted he bring his wife, but Nestor refused. It seems important to him to preserve the professional nature of his visits, but he promises to bring his wife later. Nestor knows nothing about Anya and her mother.

In order to catch Nestor up on the latest news, Katya and I meet him at the airport. Nestor (seated in front) reacts to the news with restraint, as befits someone impartially setting down events. He tries to clarify the age and occupation of the new arrivals but does not get an intelligible answer. Somehow not even Anya's age has yet been made clear.

"It's just been awkward to ask," Katya explains.

Nestor's arrival feels like a support for us. A kind of hope, even, for a resolution of what so far has seemed unresolvable. We're stuck in traffic, and Katya is looking straight ahead, tensely, as usual. She speaks in an even voice.

"I very much wanted children. Always. When it finally became clear I couldn't have them, I remembered the story of Rachel, incidentally, as it were." She looks at me. "Gleb immediately realizes where I'm going with this."

"Katya, darling" – I put my hand on her shoulder – "you're putting our friend in an awkward position."

"He told me I'm not Rachel and so from the standpoint of morality there are questions."

Nestor loosens his seatbelt and turns toward Katya.

"If this isn't directly related to our work, I do in fact feel awkward."

"It is. Directly. So, Gleb didn't want to but I insisted. That was how my sister Barbara came to be in our house." Katya starts the stalled engine and goes about fifty meters. "Nothing came of that crazy plan. To put it biblically, Barbara's womb was also shut. And now the story has been repeated. Only not the way I'd wanted."

Nestor's finger slides down his seatbelt.

"This girl is refusing doctor's visits." Katya's lips are trembling. "She says they don't do that. That if she does feel bad, she'll consult a doctor herself."

Nestor smiles barely visibly.

"Apparently she feels fine. . . . She and her mama."

"When I tried to insist, she said it was her baby, not mine, and I shouldn't interfere."

Katya buries her face in Nestor's shoulder. Nestor strokes her head. The cars ahead move, the cars behind honk. Katya starts up abruptly and nearly rams a black Audi. When she slams on the brakes, their seatbelts save her and Nestor from smashing into the windshield.

Upon arrival, a dinner-introduction. A bottle of moonshine appears on the table. Geraldina brings it in in outstretched hands at Liudmila's request. Katya looks questioningly at Nestor, but he is distracted listening to Liudmila. She's telling him about how you predict the weather from anthills.

"I'm sorry, but are you from Leningrad?" Liudmila suddenly breaks off.

"I am."

"But there aren't any anthills there!"

Liudmila's surprise presumes that this is not her first drink today.

"Just imagine, not a one," Nestor confirms.

Pursing her lips, Liudmila sets the glasses out in two rows and in a single movement, without raising the bottle's neck, fills them with the cloudy liquid.

"So why the hell am I telling you all that then?"

"I don't know, Mama, oy, I don't know." Anya turns to Nestor. "Are you really a writer?"

Nestor smiles politely. Anya gives her mother an angry look.

"So you're going to write about my mama, eh? She's a real find for a writer. And don't forget about the anthills."

Katya stands up, intending to take away the shots of moonshine, but Liudmila nimbly covers them with her hand.

"Do you know the seminary regulation?"

Katya freezes. Anya stands up.

"Mama!"

"Anya, quit mama-ing me! The seminary regulation: drink it up, put it down."

With her free hand, Liudmila raises her glass, drinks it up, and puts it down with a bang. Demonstrating the right way to put it down, she bangs it on the table a few times. The glass makes a powerful, muffled sound that fully corresponds to the word "put."

Liudmila takes a piece of Roquefort from the plate and not without delicacy (pinky out) places it on her tongue. She swoons from the inexpressibility of the taste.

Anya is holding a glass. Everyone falls silent.

"You can have just one." Liudmila radiates calm. "Moonshine is pure tears."

"*Nein*," Katya exhales in fright.

Liudmila is starting to lose patience.

"Hey, son-in-law, who's the boss in this house? Is she going to be busting our chops for long?" She points to Anya. "She's your wife, she's expecting your child, and just who is this?" She turns to Katya. "What are you doing here anyway? Am I going to have to fucking stick you somewhere?"

Katya covers her face with her hands. I take Anya's glass and drink it down. Slowly I walk up to Liudmila. She looks at me with disquiet. A stranger to democratic values, she's expecting a blow.

Anya stands up so abruptly that her chair falls behind her.

"I'm leaving!"

"Anya, what's wrong? Too much to drink?"

"Me? Too much to drink? I'm sick to death of all of you!"

"Even your mama?"

"You especially."

Anya pours herself some moonshine and polishes it off.

"Think of your baby!" Katya cries out heartrendingly.

"What baby? There is no baby!" Anya shouts at me. "There isn't! I made it all up."

She kicks the fallen chair, and it skips across the floor a few times. Geraldina, who has walked in, picks up the chair. She doesn't understand what's going on, but she's guessing this isn't the time to ask questions.

Only Nestor is calm.

"May I ask why you made it up?"

"Maybe I wanted to get hitched! Or at least shake the money tree."

Anya pours herself more, but now no one stops her. "You thought I loved him?"

Everyone looks at me.

"Oh, Anya. . . ." I pour myself some moonshine.

"He didn't 'oh, Anya' me when he picked me up in the restaurant!" Liudmila slaps her hips.

"Picked you up! Now all these people are going to think . . ." She turns to all these people. "I'll tell you what. I'm sh-shocked."

"You can just shut up now. You've disgraced the entire town of Melitopol!" Suddenly, to Nestor: "I don't fucking need him or his money! You can write that down, writer."

Anya walks slowly toward the door. At the threshold she turns around, and her eyes lose their anger.

"The person I feel sorry for, Katya, is you. I wish you all well. . . ."

Liudmila thoughtfully chews some sausage. She watches Anya go.

"She should feel sorry for herself, the dummy. She doesn't have enough to buy a bra." She sighs and turns over her glass.

Nestor shrugs.

"I don't think that's required for Femen."

"What Femen are you talking about? That's all bullshit."

Liudmila stands up and, swaying, walks up to me.

"Virtuoso, are you going to render material assistance? It's not like she'll ever ask."

She gives me a loud kiss on the cheek.

"Yes."

An hour later, Geraldina is revving the engine, offering both women a ride to the station. I go with them. At the train car, I hand Liudmila a check. Before I can turn away, Liudmila gives me another kiss on the cheek. She unfolds the check in the train car and blows me a dozen more kisses – air kisses, fortunately. Anya is sitting at the window perfectly still. Liudmila tries to get her to blow me at least one kiss. She touches two fingers to her daughter's lips and blows it herself. The train starts.

I get out my mobile and wait for a connection.

"Mama, they're gone. My God. . . ."

1980

This year was the last in Gleb's musical education. Everything he achieved subsequently was due to his own efforts because he did not graduate from music school or conservatory. Moreover, quite unexpectedly for Vera Mikhailovna, he didn't express the slightest desire to go to conservatory. After Gleb's return to music school she was certain his principal studies lay ahead. Yes, Gleb played the program Vera Mikhailovna proposed brilliantly, but it all ended at that. There is the opinion that music receded into the shadows in his life in general. This, in particular, is what the authors of most of the works devoted to the musician think. According to one music critic, Gleb left the highway for a moment and lost his way for years. Gleb didn't agree with that handsome statement. He believed he'd just left the highway behind and started straight for his goal. There was no reaching it by the highway. It all began with a trip to Leningrad, where he went with his grandmother after ninth grade. Gleb knew from films and photographs that the city was beautiful, and he loved it before he got there. Even its current name didn't seem to spoil it. It had separated from its historical face and begun a new, perfectly unstained life. Actually, most of the city's inhabitants Gleb saw preferred "Piter," short and sweet, to "Leningrad." Unlike the films and photographs, the real Piter was full of smells. The smell of a great un-southern water – the Neva or the sea. Rain, the deck of a pleasure boat, the paintings in museums, the old furniture in the palaces. The smell of museum guards (the iron, camphor, Red Moscow perfume), their hair pinned at the nape. Paints. A separate delight (where the clouds thicken over spires and cupolas) – the gold and lead. Among Piter's sounds you could pick out the noon firing of the cannon, but that wasn't what knocked Gleb out. He was shaken by the Russian language such as he'd never heard it, with its own exquisite melody and, of course, words. Here, no one needed to be told how to decline the noun *put.* He and his grandmother stayed with Liza, his grandmother's cousin's daughter. Liza had been born here, and the marvelous Russian language was her birthday gift. This one fact could have instilled respect for Liza in Gleb, but the story didn't end here. Liza taught the Russian language that so enthralled him at the university. She never said "Piter": stinting on neither time nor effort, she painstakingly pronounced "Petersburg." In an official setting, she would use the expression "the city on the Neva," which her colleagues took in with some surprise. Actually, everything connected to Liza was surprising. She had seventeen cats living in her small, two-room apartment. Veterans of catfights, pensioned-off fighters, each was missing something: a paw, a tail, an eye, an ear. Liza collected them on the street, healed them, and then kept them. For the time of her visitors' stay, they were all locked in the big room (where Liza lived with them), and her visitors were given the smaller room. The cats loudly expressed their displeasure, and from time to time their howling – and even worse, their smell – would seep through the locked doors. Unlike her cats, Liza locked in with them abided in serenity. In the morning, when Gleb and Antonina Pavlovna were just waking up, they could already hear her cheerful singing in the kitchen, accompanied by the whistle of the kettle, which chimed in last, trying to match Liza's key, a hopeless attempt because within the bounds of one song the key changed frequently. Only Liza's mood didn't change – it was always upbeat – and her divine language. Crystalline Russian, the best Gleb had ever heard. He fell in love with its individual sounds, its overall intonations, its rhythm – everything that comprises the music of the Russian language. Compared with the music he played, its nature was completely different. And this music was performed by Liza. Gleb might have said he'd fallen in love with Liza, too, had he dared admit it. The fact that she was much older than Gleb didn't bother him; nearly all the women he'd loved had been that. But Liza was his relative, albeit a distant one, very distant even. This fact left the boy in his flight of fantasy. What stopped him was something else. Liza, slim, ethereal Liza, whose language he loved so much, had a weakness for sharp perfume and used it liberally. Recalling what Chekhov said, Gleb noted with chagrin that not everything about Liza was wonderful. One of those days, he and Antonina Pavlovna, while waiting for Liza, attended her class with external students. Her lecture was devoted to the development of the meaning of words. A word, Liza lectured the students, is like a person. It has its own history and has not always been as we now know it. For example, in olden times the word *uspekh*, now understood as "success," had three basic meanings. The first and most important meaning was "benefit" (Liza wrote the word on the board), especially spiritual benefit. Good deeds were committed "for people's *uspekh*." The second meaning was "forward movement," "advancement" – in service, for example. Finally, the third meaning of the word *uspekh* is conveyed by the modern word (very similar to *uspekh*) of *pospeshnost'* – haste. Thus, the expression "rising with *uspekh*" meant not a successful rising but a hasty one. Dictionaries of the contemporary language usually single out two meanings for the word *uspekh*. The first is defined as "a positive result, a successful conclusion"; the second, as "public recognition." Neither meaning has anything to do with benefit. A positive result can be achieved in a far from positive matter and from the standpoint of benefit may turn out to be the most negative possible. And we know who (Liza winked at her students) gets public recognition in today's world. The other two ancient Russian meanings come closer to the word's modern meanings, especially when it comes to haste, which is often connected with achieving success in our present-day understanding. To use a word with the same root, *uspet*, meaning to manage to accomplish something. "Why wasn't the word's main medieval meaning preserved?" one of the students asked at the end of the lecture. "I think," Liza said, "the answer should be sought outside the sphere of language. Most likely, issues of morality ceased to be central in society. Mankind's development in the New Era was connected to a deepening of the principle of the personal. Any development, though, has two phases, the constructive and the destructive. The construction of the personal in man made the individual subtler and opened new horizons. The gaining of these horizons and moving beyond them began to destroy the individual. Personal rights, set above morality, transformed modern man into a pleasure machine. He was presented with the deceptive right to sail past the buoys, and humanism turned into its opposite." The students filed out of the auditorium in silence. Perhaps they, like Gleb, were afraid of their new, abundant knowledge spilling out. All that remained on the board was the first meaning of the word *uspekh*. Liza hadn't written down the others. Walking down the University Embankment, they came across the students again. They waved, and Gleb felt pride in his kinship to Liza. In a certain sense, he himself was an external student come from far away who had received this city as a gift, if only for a couple of weeks. It was then for the first time that it occurred to him to go to university here. That evening he shared his idea with Liza. For some reason, Gleb had expected his plan to thrill Liza and her to start doing everything in her power to support it. Moreover, viewing the presence of cats as a manifestation of loneliness, he made it clear he might even move in with his relative.

Subsequently even Gleb himself had no idea why he'd said all that. He probably believed, as is typical of people in love, that his own attraction for Liza was mutual. For some reason he was certain she dreamed passionately of having a man in her home, regardless on what grounds he appeared – friendship, family, or something else (exactly what wasn't specified) – just so there was this man. Imagine Gleb's disappointment when Liza reacted coolly to his plans. Yes, she thought studying in Leningrad was a possibility, but studying in Kyiv seemed to her even more of a possibility and even more convenient. As for housing, it was suggested that Gleb initially count on a dorm, inasmuch as she, Liza, valued her solitude highly (an apologetic and touching smile) – if you could call a life with seventeen cats solitude. Gleb's feelings were hurt, although, to give him his due, he tried not to show it. He even asked whether he could attend her next lecture and got her consent. Obviously, Gleb's feelings were manifest enough because Liza felt she had to respond to them and did so in a supremely elegant fashion: the lecture Gleb attended was devoted to the word *obida* – offense. Historically, this word meant damage of the most various kinds, but primarily moral. But ultimately *obida* goes back to the root for seeing, its point doubtless being in the gaze. A special gaze: as when we say someone looked the wrong way. Said something wrong – and so it began. In essence, *obida* is a feeling based on the unexpected. Only someone you expect to say the right thing can say the wrong thing. Only in childhood do you assume that everyone loves you and has to say the right thing; only later do you realize that the world works the exact opposite way. And in this sense, *obida* is a very childish emotion. At this, Liza shot Gleb an eloquent look, and he realized this had been uttered for him alone. But he no longer felt any *obida*, his feelings were more complicated and fell more into the category of "mixed." When he and Liza were going upstairs to the auditorium, Gleb smelled an acrid, feline smell from her dress, the sharp smell of acetone, which meant that the contact between Liza's charges and the dress was fresh. The smell even permeated the perfume curtain that enveloped Liza. That was when Gleb realized why his relative perfumed herself so immoderately. Her cat proximity restored to the perfume its original purpose of knocking out other smells. Unfortunately, it didn't do the trick. And Liza, brilliant Liza, who knew the history of Russian words like the back of her hand, was instantly transformed into a sufferer worthy of his pity. Poor Liza, if you like. From that day on, that was how he always thought of her: poor Liza. Poor. And never felt any *obida* toward her again. After they returned to Kyiv, he and his grandmother tried to call Liza to thank her for her hospitality but couldn't get through. They didn't have a phone, so they went to the call center, where they ordered a call. The operator dialed Liza's number, but no one picked up. The young woman made three unsuccessful attempts at reaching Leningrad, and when Antonina Pavlovna asked her to try a fourth time, the operator refused. She said it was useless. That she never dialed more than three times. There was no point insisting. Then Antonina Pavlovna wrote Liza a letter in which, in addition to her gratitude, she mentioned her attempt to call. Soon after a reply came from Liza, who wrote that Gleb should come to her if he needed any kind of help in applying to university. The impossibility of reaching her was due to the fact that the cats (she wrote "kitties" in the letter) had gnawed through the telephone wire. Now the line was fixed and we could call again.

April 5, 2013, Munich

Nestor and I are sitting on the front lawn. It's hot in the April sun. The neighbor's car door slams over the garden wall. Steps ring out far back in the house. I tense. It's Geraldina bringing us juice. For a moment I thought Liudmila was coming out of the house.

Nestor slowly exhales the cigarette smoke.

"I hadn't expected them to shove off so simply."

"Me, neither," I agree. "Although, you know, there's something to that Anya. Do you remember what she said to you at the end? Writer, write that I don't need him or his money."

"What of it?"

"How can you not understand? She wanted to go down in literature looking dignified. Not a train station whore but a Turgenevian young woman."

"Lovely. Only I doubt she's read Turgenev."

"But it doesn't matter whether she has or not. She's in this cultural field . . ." I depict reading with my palm in front of my nose. "Have you ever seen a metro where so many people read?"

Nestor shrugs and finishes his juice.

"Not long ago I'm riding the metro at seven in the morning. The car's packed. The crowd rides half-asleep, rocking back and forth, and there's the reek of alcohol."

"And in the corner a girl is sitting reading *First Love*. Haven't you seen that? And she's wrapped up in the book, not the train car . . ."

". . . and her name is Anya. I wonder when the last time was you were on our metro? Who are you trying to convince? Yourself?" Nestor looks at me carefully. "Maybe you want to return to Russia?"

"I don't know. I don't know much of anything anymore."

My hand jerks abruptly and my glass flies off the table. It doesn't break, just lies there in the grass. Nestor leans over and carefully places the glass on the table.

I clap him on the shoulder.

"For some reason I'm very tired."

That evening I sit at the computer and go through my mail. I get twenty or thirty letters a day. Confessions of love, agent reports, invitations to perform, but mostly, of course, requests – for an interview, to help a charity, and simply for assistance. Usually Katya and I go through the letters. She replies to the German and English ones, and I dictate the replies to the Russian ones to her.

Today I'm answering the letters alone – and limiting myself to brief sentences. Or not answering. This goes on for about fifteen minutes. Exiting the mail program, I slip onto the forum I'd actually turned the computer on for. Just yesterday I came across a discussion by doctors on the problems of Parkinson's. I read slowly, disconnecting from the fact that this is about me. *Involuntary salivation.* I lean back in my chair. All this lies ahead.

I hear steps behind the door. Not very firm ones. Katya's. I recognize them unmistakably. I can't get the cursor on the x. Katya comes in and hugs me from behind.

"Gleb, darling, you promised."

"You also promised something."

But I didn't promise. Professor Wentz simply told Katya and me that it was better not to read anything about the disease, and we agreed. He said it would only scare us and there was zero to be gained from that knowledge. He, Wentz, would tell me everything I needed to know.

"What do you think of my involuntary salivation?"

I feel Katya's tears on my neck. It occurs to me that involuntary tears are romantic, but saliva isn't, although what's the difference between them actually? We live in a world of conventions.

1981

This was Gleb's last Kyiv year. In view of Petersburg's existence in the world (he only called it by that name), staying in Kyiv was impossible. Gleb studied for his graduation exams and prepared essays on likely test topics, but mentally he was already in Petersburg. Generally speaking, it was the essays that transported him then to the banks of the Neva, where he felt with full force the beauty of the Russian language or – in concepts more familiar to Gleb – its far from simple music. *"You've made your choice, and I respect it,"* Fyodor said when he learned of his son's decision to attend Petersburg University. Gleb might have thought he was talking about his choice between music and literature, but Fyodor immediately clarified that he meant the choice of language and culture as a whole: *"It's the same choice our namesake Mikola once made."* Gleb didn't respond because he had made his choice long ago – so long ago that he didn't even remember making it. As for Mikola, he apparently hadn't chosen anything. He'd simply combined the two elements in his consciousness and lived in them. What did he feel when he left his native land? The same thing Gleb did – a thirst for the new, fear, the pain of parting? At graduation, all these feelings converged in the boy's throat into a single lump, and he lost his voice. Not for long, about twenty minutes, but he did lose it. So no one would notice, he left the auditorium and went out into the hall. Standing facing an open window, he waited for his voice's return. He pretended to be looking at something that required concentration (his future?); in fact he saw only the poplar fluff collected in the windowsill corners. When he heard steps behind him, he waved out the window at someone who wasn't there. He did this so convincingly that eventually he saw him. It was him, Gleb Yanovsky, only decades later. This wiser Gleb already knew that this standing by the window would be remembered – with the fluff, the poplars, the piano's muffled sounds coming from the auditorium – everything (the end of childhood), which slid by like film titles. The end of childhood, both Glebs whispered – and then parted for several decades. Both thought about those who had experienced these same evenings decades before, with the sounds of the piano and the poplars. Where were they now, one wondered? On mosaics of the Moscow metro, wearing wide pants, taking giant steps. And not only there: in the elegant, old expansive graves, in their rolled-up white shirt sleeves, in their jackets draped over their shoulders, in what was left of their hair combed back, in their unnaturally long, to the wrist, finger-bones – drafting cases, astrolabes and compasses, and, on the women's skulls, daisy crowns, gaping eye sockets looking selflessly into the future. The thought of these graduates occurred to him on his graduation day. But this wasn't the only reason that day entered his memory. There was his enchanting ride down the Dnieper too. An ordinary ride, as envisioned (the *Raketa* hydrofoil, the dressed-up graduates, a pair of plump teachers); its enchantment consisted in the fact that for some reason the bar on board was open. Marlen the bartender, who had been regretting his lost day, proposed that the teachers drink at the establishment's expense, and to his surprise, he did not get a refusal. Marlen asked their names (Ruslana Rudolfovna and Neonila Nikolaevna) and proposed a toast to friendship. Then the teachers drank at their own expense. After their third, Marlen asked, by the by, whether there were any reliable people among the graduates. He wanted to offer them, without damaging the educational process, the same drink that the teachers liked so much. Indicating his interest, he poured them another. He was a sly fox, that Marlen. The mysterious drink, if one is to call things by their real names, was wheat vodka, but by leaving it unnamed, it dulled the trusting teachers' vigilance. They quickly drew up a list of reliable people, and Marlen started inviting them to the bar in alphabetical order. No one turned down his invitation. A small line even formed that – as is natural for a fast ship – moved fairly quickly. Until the very end of the list, Gleb didn't know whether he was one of the reliables. To his enormous relief, he was. Ruslana Rudolfovna proposed a toast to Marx and Lenin, but all the graduates understood that she was obliquely toasting Marlen. Squeezing her hand in his, the bartender asked in a whisper, "Ruslana, where is your

146

Lyudmil?" A squeeze of the hand in reply followed immediately. Ruslana Rudolfovna was easily moved to tears. The reliable graduates were followed to the bar by the unreliable ones, moreover these latter ordered much more and much more eagerly. Hearing the lively intonations in the saloon, the crew members started going down one by one. With each such visit, the *Raketa's* speed increased. Half an hour later, the hydrofoil was poised for liftoff. Lent wings by the holiday atmosphere, Ruslana Rudolfovna and Neonila Nikolaevna left the saloon for the open area astern. Feeling an irresistible urge upward, Ruslana Rudolfovna moved toward a staircase not meant for passengers. She unhooked the chain blocking the stairs and prepared for her difficult ascent. On the very first step, the woman was nearly knocked off her feet by a gust of wind – the *Raketa* was racing at the limit of its capabilities. Ruslana Rudolfovna was saved by the fullness of her new emotion – or maybe just by her fullness. Observing the spectacle from the pilothouse, the *Raketa's* captain announced that the first step, which was shaking very hard, was separating. But his statement was premature. Both the step and the teacher standing on it (she was clutching the metal railing) held. Flapping deafeningly, her long skirt struck her legs, and her bun lost its pins and her hair streamed loose in the hurricane wind. This is how Gleb saw her when he emerged from the saloon, and it shook him. Despite the elements' resistance, the woman was not only ascending but also declaiming something in hexameters. He couldn't make out the words; the verse had turned into pure rhythm. On the last step, her skirt flew up and covered Ruslana Rudolfovna's face. Now she, or rather her upper half, resembled a self-propelled smokestack, while her lower . . . Gleb was the only person who saw this. Saw it and chastely turned away. Only for his glance to fall on Neonila Nikolaevna, who was hanging on the deck railing, swaying over the Dnieper's foam. Nor was she silent either, rather she was reciting something a little simpler: *catch yourself a great big fish, catch yourself a little one . . .* Neonila was simpler all around. Now dragging her away from the railing, Gleb saw two sailors leading Ruslana Rudolfovna down the stairs. They'd tried, laughing, to lower her skirt, but unsuccessfully. Maybe they didn't want to. When both teachers were given a brandy antidote in the saloon, Ruslana Rudolfovna told everyone that up top she'd been reciting Sophocles' *Antigone.* At Marlen's request, she recited those lines once again: *Many are the world's strange things, / And the strangest of all is man, / The wind may lash and cut his face, / Yet boldly he goes his way.* Everyone applauded, especially Marlen, who had no idea of the any-thing-but-simple conditions in which this had been heard for the first time. He proposed a toast to Sophocles, who he'd never heard in Ukrainian before. He drank and clarified that, if his memory hadn't failed him, he hadn't heard him in any other language either. Nor had he read *Antigone.* Observing her colleague's success, Neonila would have liked to recite something, but immediately changed her mind. Just before their return, at the request of those present, Gleb played the guitar. A day later he flew to Leningrad, where university entrance exams awaited him. In August the news came that Ruslana Rudolfovna had married Marlen. As he admitted at the wedding, this woman's erudition had knocked his socks off. Ruslana Rudolfovna vaguely remembered that there, on the *Raketa,* something similar had nearly happened to her. Gleb sent the newlyweds a congratulatory telegram and thought about how crucial it can be to recite Sophocles at the right time.

JUNE 15, 2013, NEW YORK

I'm performing at Carnegie Hall. A month before the concert, after the posters had been made, I informed Mayer about a change in the program. Instead of my usual repertoire (popular classics plus modern pieces), it announced the performance of folk songs. Mayer resisted with a stubbornness unusual for him. He was upset not so much by the need to reprint expensive posters (this kind of thing had happened before) as by the fact that I had made the decision unilaterally, without consulting him. And without any explanation whatsoever.

Only what could I explain? That for three months I hadn't been able to play a single difficult piece? That I'd doubled the number of rehearsals but my fingers only seemed to move worse because of them? Maybe not because of them, but that it was worse was definite. Mayer tried to reach me, but my telephone was silent. Living in the same city with his client, Mayer could have gone to see him, but something told him he shouldn't. The sophisticated intuition of someone who has been working with people for a long time.

Mayer heeded it.

All he had left was e-mail, to which I rarely responded. As long as we were corresponding, my producer would not back down. When on one of those days he did reach me by phone after all, he realized that it was pointless to insist. I spoke calmly, but behind that calm Mayer sensed despair. He didn't understand the reason for it, but the depth of the despair knew no bounds. We composed the program as I'd wanted.

Katya and I fly into New York the night before the concert. At the airport a limousine drives right up to the ramp, so my many admirers in the arrival hall are left empty-handed. Those greeting me are told the maestro has left. The bouquets and posters soaring over people's heads here and there gradually merge into a single procession. My mind's eye sees the parade head for the airport exit with sighs of (star-struck) disappointment. That is no way to treat fans. Some of the bouquets land in the garbage can; for their owners, Yanovsky the virtuoso no longer exists.

The virtuoso himself spends the evening in his hotel. We even ask them to serve dinner in the room. The next evening we go downstairs and get into a Cadillac. Mayer is already waiting for us in the front seat. He examines me closely, as if expecting a catch. He's obviously worried he'll see me somehow different. Concealing the loss of an eye or a leg, for example. Or, what would be perfectly awful, a hand, without which you couldn't play even a folk song. No, all is in place. Mayer calms down a little and nods to the driver. The car begins to move – it's not far.

Ten minutes later we're pulling up to Carnegie Hall. We moor majestically, something only expensive cars can do. Carnegie Hall staff open the Cadillac's doors. Katya emerges from the left side, and a second later, from the right – I do, with my guitar in its case. A buzz of greetings rings out from many voices, and we wave to those who have come. The director of Carnegie Hall kisses Katya's hand and embraces me. Cameras click away. As I head for the door, I give autographs and stop several times to let people take selfies. Concert hall employees follow behind with the bouquets I've been given.

I know Carnegie Hall like the back of my hand, but (tradition is tradition) the director takes the lead, showing the way. In the makeup room, I'm brought strong tea in a glass with a silver glass-holder (once upon a time, the director was told that this is how it's done in Russia). On the train. They left out the part about the train. Actually, in the narrow makeup room it's almost appropriate: it's like a large train compartment. I hear the brisk metronome of the wheels. Exactly what's wanted for études.

I rub my hands and sit down to play. Between études I take a few sips from the glass. I lie down on the sofa and shut my eyes. 19:07. A precise knock at the door: "Mr. Yanovsky. . . ."

"Don't worry," Katya whispers to me as I go, "it's all going to be fine."

"I'm not worried. I truly am not worried."

Before walking out from the wings, I kiss her on the forehead. Katya won't sit in the audience, she'll stand here the entire concert. That's how it always goes. I attach the microphone antenna to the guitar and give the sound director a sign. When I get a sign in response, I start toward the lit area of the stage. The hall explodes. I walk, head down, as if concentrating. In fact, I'm adjusting to the stage's blinding light; I never have learned how to deal with it. I stop next to the tall chair on the proscenium and raise my head. I smile. My smile is relayed to the big screen. My half-lowered eyelids make it look like a blind man's smile.

The chaos shifts into a rhythm. The incredible sound is replaced by harmonious waves of applause. They're on their feet greeting me. My guitar gleams in my hands. I sit on the edge of the chair (my feet on the bottom cross-bar) and strum two chords. In a strange way, the tall chair and my pose create a bar scene. It wouldn't seem unnatural, in fact, if I were to order something right now. Some good Russian drink, say.

A teddy bear flies onto the stage as an expression of sympathy for Russia. I stand and bow. I pick up the bear and put him on one of the stands and go back to my place. The noise gradually dies down. Without waiting for total silence, I start playing a Belarusian song, "Kupalinka." Only the guitar. No voice. The light on stage goes out leaving just a sharp, bright circle, at the center of which is the musician. He's alone, and his song is sad. Its words in English translation pan across the huge screen.

The concert organizers doubted the need to provide the lyrics, but I insisted. Without that, I said, no one would understand anything. *Kupalinka-kupalinka, dark night . . . Oh, dark night, where is your daughter?* Even with the words (they objected) no one will understand anything. After all, you need to explain that on the eve of Ivan Kupal Day, young women wove wreaths and put them on the water to learn their fate. And then, whose daughter is this, and why is she weeping? What's there to explain? I wonder. It couldn't be clearer. *In her garden, my daughter's rose she weeds. Her rose she weeds, though her white hands bleed. The flowers picked, a wreath she weaves. Twists the flowers and weeping, grieves.* What difference does it make whose daughter she is? What's important is she's weeping. In art it's better to say too little than too much. The audience will weep over their own sorrow.

On the last note I raise my eyes and look at the hall to see wet cheeks glistening in the light reflected off the stage. Handkerchiefs flash in the applauding hands. I can only see the first few rows, but I know that there, in the dark depths of the hall, my music has been felt just as keenly. Maybe even more so. Such things often happen to those who can't afford good seats.

I stand up and (my guitar on its strap) walk downstage. When I perform "The Old Linden" with voice accompaniment, the audience stands up too. My strange humming comes through. I never begin with it. Let them first hear how it is without it – with just the strings. My voice resonates with the guitar, and I feel their harmony. I lose my body and turn into sound, a fine, almost imperceptible energy. Before my hand tires, I decide on a difficult variation of the song and play it nearly without a mistake. I glance behind the wings and see Katya's thumbs-up.

Neither Katya's thumb nor her shining face can fool me. I know how worried she is. Today's performance has been structured in a particular way. I began with pieces that are usually the concert's culmination. They're played when the degree of tension has seemingly reached its limit. The audience is raging. And suddenly – a new peak that seemed impossible just a moment before. Is that possible now?

This time the songs follow by degree of difficulty. First come the technically difficult pieces, and in the final part, when my hand is thoroughly exhausted, I'll perform the simple ones, moreover with an orchestra. From the producer's standpoint, this is a permissible progression because difficulty does not necessarily lead to the greatest effect. The danger lies elsewhere. The trance into which the audience usually dives gradually has already set in. From the very first song. And there's no assurance that this state of mind can be maintained.

As I play "A Moonlit Night," my heart aches to see the Carnegie Hall audience walk barefoot through the cold dew in an unknown direction. I pick them up and carry them. The sparks flashing in the stalls build to full-fledged ball lightning. I watch continuously as a glowing cluster of electricity slowly sails over the hall. The variation changes key, and this is like a turn on a rollercoaster – and the audience gasps. I know for certain that I can think about anything I like but not my actual playing. Caresser, think not of your caresses. If you compare the hall to a woman . . . That's not right: because of her ability to respond. . . . I nearly falter switching to the tremolo. In short, a lot depends on the hall.

After intermission, the orchestra appears. In the first part, elegance and technique; in the second, emotion and power. I play song after song. The question is whether the hall is capable of such indefatigable love. Such (three grace notes in a row) insatiable love. Yes, it is. It turns out to be capable of insatiable love too. Such continuous love, because I play without stopping.

Two people run down the center aisle carrying a stretcher atilt. They lift someone off the floor, lay him on the stretcher, and secure him. The movement toward the exit (I'm playing "The Ducks Are Flying") is unhurried and matches the song's mood. Those who remain see what fully dissolving in the music threatens. The danger of pleasure makes it even more beguiling. At "On the River, on the Fontanka" the hall can't sit still any longer. Its vast body sways, entering perfectly into the rhythm. This is now one shared body, one shared ecstasy. And now no one knows how all this might end for us. No one can even guess. No one.

1981

August 30, a train platform flooded with Kyiv sun. Gleb's send-off to Leningrad. He started in the Philology Department in July, moved into the dormitory, and now was on his way to study. Gleb had stepped into the train car. Standing by an open window, he was amazed at the morning air's transparency. Fyodor once taught him that morning is the best time for picture taking. The train platform, photo from above. The figures' proportions are distorted. In the first row: his mama and grandmother, worry in their eyes. The second row: Fyodor. A white ironed shirt with rolled-up sleeves. He's worried, too, though he's trying not to show it. So they stuck in Gleb's memory – black and white, yellowed with time. A morning train is a trial for those seeing you off. Evening departures are followed by night, and night is a great consoler. You can get used to a lot overnight. A morning train divides the day in two: with and without the person who's left. If this means seeing that person off for a long time, the day turns into a lifetime, its concise presentation. The departer's absence is gaping, his silence deafening. The unfinished tea on the table, the damp towel on the hook. He's still here, sort of, and that makes his disappearance so patent. The whole way, Gleb thought about his mama and grandmother. But when he arrived in Piter in the morning, he saw Liza through the wet window. She immediately boarded the car and helped him carry out his two suitcases and guitar; all this baggage was why he'd taken the train, actually, and not a plane. Liza led him to the taxi stand. The taxi driver talked to her lazily, almost disdainfully. And suddenly Gleb noticed that Liza was poorly dressed. It wasn't that her appearance had changed so strikingly in the past year – Gleb had. He'd grown up. He'd started to figure out who was dressed how and what it meant to dress well. The taxi driver had sized up Liza instantly. Like anyone drumming up clients, he had unerringly calculated his and Liza's financial capabilities. His entire look showed he didn't expect much from them. But he would go. He nodded for them to load the suitcases in the trunk. When Liza picked up one by the handle, Gleb said the driver would do that. A pause ensued. The driver, sitting in the taxi, faced a knotty choice. He could say he wasn't a porter and they could go to hell, or he could get out and load the suitcases. He looked at Gleb, who was determined and unwavering. Standing on widely planted feet. The taxi driver was no longer young, and he didn't have the energy for a scene. Whistling under his breath, he put both suitcases in the trunk. When he saw the instrument in Gleb's hands, he smiled. "Guitarist?" "A virtuoso," Liza confirmed readily. On Builders' Bridge, right by the dorm, she handed Gleb her wallet for him to settle the bill. The wallet was flaking and hard to open. Gleb returned it to Liza. He got out his own; supposedly his mama had given him money especially for the taxi. When the car pulled away, Liza said, "You're a grown man now." A year ago those words would have made him happy, but now he felt a certain awkwardness even. After filling out the paperwork with the dormitory's resident director, Gleb and Liza got his room key and took his things there. There were three beds in the room, a desk, and a dining table. "They assume only one of you three has any interest in his studies," Liza joked. She didn't invite him to move in with her. Gleb wasn't offended because he didn't want to live with Liza. From her letters he knew that in addition to the many cats she now had a maimed fox cub living with her. The cub wasn't the problem, of course. The presence of cats in those numbers was already a diagnosis to a certain extent, and the cub just added a bullet point. Liza turned out to have a thermos and sausage sandwiches in her bag. They had a bite to eat. As she was walking away, Liza told Gleb that if anything came up he should call, but he could already tell that it was highly unlikely to. So could Liza, it seemed. She lived in the north of the city and was now planning to go to the nearest metro station, Vasileostrovskaya. Gleb offered to walk her there. It was the gesture of a gentleman, and moreover, he felt like the walk. There's a special charm in taking a walk on the day you arrive. They walked in silence. Liza was thinking her own thoughts (about her cats, Gleb suspected), and he was surveying his new domain. He had no doubt that this city would belong to him from now on in all its glory and wistful beauty. Privately, he compared the city to a tubercular woman in need of his warmth. And here he'd arrived, a hot-blooded southerner, and now he was going to put his arms around her and give her his sun. He and Liza descended from the bridge and started down the embankment. Liza pointed out a monumental building with columns: "Pushkin House. Pushkin didn't live in it, but they do study Russian literature here." Gleb nodded silently. Too bad Pushkin hadn't lived there. Sometimes it seemed to him that Pushkin hadn't lived at all, that he was the fruit of the Russian imagination, a nation's beautiful dream about itself.

JUNE 16, 2013, NEW YORK

I wake up late. Beside me, Katya has her laptop on her stomach. I open one eye and watch her finger slide across the touchpad. Any moment and Katya will turn toward me; she always senses my gaze. She turns. Kisses me on the forehead. Turns the screen toward me.

"A triumph!"

Katya is beaming. I open the other eye and scan the text.

"Let's eat something."

We order room service breakfast. The waiter materializes almost immediately. What, was he waiting outside the door? He asks whether he should open the drapes. Yes, if he would, open them. Broadway appears in the huge window, a beautiful and amazingly narrow street. Do they prefer breakfast in bed (he has trays in this case) or at the table? At the table, they prefer. The waiter lays the table. Before leaving, he fans out the morning newspapers on the coffee table.

Katya, chewing, reads out the headlines.

"A new peak for the virtuoso. . . . He is as stupendous as ever. . . . A magic show at Carnegie Hall. . . . Yanovsky's concert: a twenty-minute ovation. . . . How are you feeling?"

I make a limp gesture.

"Dizzy with success."

"By the end of the banquet you didn't look so hot." Katya hands me a caviar tart, but I push her hand away. "Just too drunk to make sense."

"Really?" I feel that smiling at full strength still isn't working. "I didn't even take my evening pills?"

Katya laughs.

"No. Everyone liked you tremendously. The mayor gave you a big kiss."

"The mayor was there?"

"Yes, he came later, very preoccupied, kind of on the gloomy side. But when he saw you he melted. Won't you eat something?"

I drink a glass of apple juice. Lingering, I take a tartlet from Katya but immediately give it back. The juice has made me even dizzier. I'm going to have to lie back down. Here's what abusing apple juice leads to (I throw my arms behind my head). Katya heads for the bathroom.

Next to me on the bed is Katya's abandoned computer. When I hear the sound of water, I enter the search program. I'm not looking for anything in particular – just pure curiosity. What they're writing in America about a topic that interests me, for instance. A tremor in both hands (it's affecting my legs, too, maybe my jaw and tongue as well). It's striking. . . . The facial muscles' failure, the face becomes like a mask. Another well-known phenomenon. Aha. Exercise the facial muscles, make faces. Why not? Without ceremony.

I'm at the focal point of three mirrors. One Mr. Yanovsky in each, and all three are making faces. Virtuosi.

The expression "maximum jollity": slit eyes, two rows of teeth. The sight of three jolly Yanovskys makes me laugh.

The expression "blessed sorrow" is even funnier: drooping eyes, bowed lips.

"Poorly concealed irritation": turned-down corners of the mouth, even the nose noticeably hanging. An unsightly picture, strictly speaking. Apparently it's better to conceal your irritation.

Fine, then, "unconcealed hatred": furrowed eyebrows, clenched teeth, pulsating temples.

"Love for children": a thick-lipped half-smile, wide-open eyes.

"Thoughts of the homeland": pursed lips, sharpened cheekbones, eyes focused toward the bridge.

"Bewilderment": mouth half open, eyelashes batting.

"Sensuality": mouth also open (very slightly), eyes half-closed, nostrils trembling.

"Playing Beethoven": the face consumed by grimaces, the ears wiggling a little. People playing Beethoven are a disaster; better not to look at them, honestly. Virtuosi are better to listen to, especially violinists and pianists. The eyes rolling, the hair tossed back, the tongue running over the lips – and that's the best they have to offer.

"Despair": a face like a rumpled jacket, tears rolling down the cheeks.

I don't notice when Katya comes in. She has a towel around her neck, and her hair smells of unfamiliar hotel shampoo. She sits on the bed and watches me silently. She wipes my tears with the edge of her towel. Turns off the computer.

1981–1982

Gleb adjusted to the dorm amazingly quickly. His years in a communal apartment might have been considered good training, but this was a somewhat different experience. Yes, strangers in the kitchen, yes, a shared washroom and (a very unpleasant) toilet for everyone, but the main living space – the room – he'd always had a separate one. Gleb's easy entry into his new life was explained more by youth than experience. He didn't mind that he was going to have to sleep, eat, and study in the presence of outsiders. The fact that all this ceased to be a regular thing simplified his adaptation to his new circumstances. His roommates were two other philology students, Yuri Kotov from Irkutsk and Sofia native Krasimir Duichev. Both were in their second year and remarkable people in their own way. Deep down, Gleb regretted that he was the third in this crowd. Once he'd met his roommates, he discovered for himself that difference does more to bring you close than similarity does. Given the degree of their dissimilarity, Kotov and Duichev undoubtedly were a pair. They might well have been in the movies, sung comic couplets, or performed acrobatic exercises. Kotov was short with light brown hair and glasses. Duichev's height (which he would mention offhandedly) was six-two, his hair and beard were pitch-black, and the only glasses he'd known in his life were sunglasses. As his name's etymology – which he shared with the word "beauty" – implied, Krasimir was handsome and well-liked by the girls. He even liked himself. That was why they called Duichev "Dunya." But no one liked Kotov, so he was just called Kotov. After lectures he stayed in the library until closing – not so much out of a love of knowledge as of a fear of possible surprises at home. More than once, returning to the dorm, he'd found the room's door bolted from the inside. The response to his lengthy knocking was silence or muffled laughter. Sometimes a recommendation would come from behind the door to come back in an hour or two. The recommendation was issued in Dunya's voice, but the voice was unusual – feeble and languid – which sent Kotov into a fit of loathing. The voice named movies he could go see and listed the exhibits that were open and their hours of operation. The Bulgarian visitor – and here Kotov gave him his due – was up to date on the city's cultural life. Kotov himself had no interest in cultural life and so did not follow this advice. He would sit on his briefcase in the hallway and patiently wait for the room to be free. No one in the room was in any hurry. Meanwhile, sounds came from within that sent Kotov into an even greater fit of loathing. Frequently he heard a muffled rumble as if heavy objects were being moved across the floor. Perspiration would bead Kotov's forehead. If he could explain the creaking of the bed's netting and the accompanying sounds on the basis of stories he'd heard about *it*, then the rumble resisted all interpretation. Kotov understood only that something outrageously cynical was going on in the room. Against his will, his imagination drew a heavy woman being dragged across the floor. Two women even. . . . Eventually the door would open, releasing a young creature in a crushed skirt, a creature almost every time new and always frail. He could only assume the worst, that they'd dragged Dunya himself across the floor. Dunya would appear after that and, feigning unnatural surprise at Kotov sitting there, would invite him in. Kotov's woes didn't end there, though. After these visits he would discover, for example, that his bath towel was damp. Yes, Kotov had used it the night before, but the towel should have dried out in a day even in rainy Leningrad. While estimating the speed at which towels dry, Kotov sometimes would notice wine left on the bottom of the glass where he kept his toothbrush. Sometimes there were red lipstick traces. Dunya's pathological distaste for washing dishes compelled him to use all the reserves there were, including personal hygiene ones. Kotov would wash his glass for a long time, with disgust, and he wouldn't use his towel until the next change of linens, patiently air-drying after his shower. The disgust he felt didn't allow him to criticize Dunya. Kotov found any discussion of *it* just as unacceptable as *it* itself. Gleb had a different attitude toward what went on. The first time he encountered the closed door, he took the advice to go to the movies. The second time, he kicked the door open. This happened in the presence of Kotov, who was sitting on the floor (but immediately stood up). The scene revealed to them as they entered was especially nasty for Kotov. In the middle of the room was the double bed pushed together from Dunya's and Kotov's beds. The source of the mysterious sound was immediately determined – Kotov's bed, which they'd dragged up to the other – although this discovery was hardly reassuring. Spread out on the bed was a naked Dunya, and sitting next to him his half-naked girlfriend. Despite the situation's drama, the young woman introduced herself: "Lidia, but you can call me Lida." She'd thrown Gleb's shirt over her shoulders for modesty's sake. Grabbing his shirt off the visitor, Gleb threw it in Dunya's face. "Not very gallant of you," Lida noted. Dunya jumped to his feet on the bed and to the creak of the netting took a step toward Gleb. The netting didn't withstand his next step. It gave way, bringing Dunya to the floor with it. With a deafening clang, one of the bedframe's sides fell in. A second later the metal headboard collapsed on him. "TKO," Lida certified. In this moment of conflict, she alone kept her cool.

Following her gaze, Dunya and Kotov saw a knife in Gleb's hands. It was a kitchen knife, thin from years of honing, which Kotov had brought from Irkutsk. Just a second before it had been lying on the dining table. "We're going to get dressed now and leave," Lida said. "Please wait for us outside." When the lovers appeared in the hallway, Dunya looked at Gleb darkly: "What, did you really want to knife me?" "No" – Gleb smiled – "just castrate you." Lida ran her finger across Gleb's cheek: "Boys, anything but that." That evening Kotov figured out how to repair the lock; he turned out to be a handy guy. The bed, though, was beyond repair. The hooks that held the netting in place had broken off from the headboard and had to be soldered, and even Kotov couldn't do that without a soldering iron. Dunya tried to exchange his bed or at least the headboard and went to see the resident director with that goal in mind. The resident director had neither; everything had been handed out long since. "What on earth are you doing with those beds?" the director barked, but Dunya declined to explain. Returning to their room, he took the bed apart and slept on the floor for another two months. Just before New Year's, Kotov noticed a lonely headboard on a trash heap and brought it to Dunya. The headboard looked completely different from the broken one. Everything about it, from the nickel-plated tubes to the knobs, was different. But incredibly, the hooks for the netting were in the right place. Dunya greeted the new year on a serviceable, albeit somewhat garbled bed style-wise. His previous escapades with ladies were never repeated. What had happened had taught Dunya a good lesson. He may simply have been embarrassed to bring anyone to a bed like that for fear of accusations of eclecticism. All he could use it for now was sleeping. After Dunya and Lida were driven out, life calmed down for Gleb and Kotov. Not that Dunya devoted himself to asceticism; he just found somewhere else for his trysts. He knew beforehand from the resident director which rooms had to be freed up temporarily – as a rule, before repairs. The director, whom the Bulgarian student generously treated to rakija, would put off the repairs for a day or two and give Dunya the keys. One could conclude from the fact that plaster sometimes speckled Dunya's hair that in some instances the repairs had already begun. But even in these difficult situations, Dunya was in no hurry to return the keys. Generally speaking, keys became as inevitable an attribute of Dunya as a stethoscope is for a doctor. Now he was always carrying them in his pockets, and a melodic jingle signaled his approach. Apart from dorm room keys, he kept the keys of Leningrad friends who entrusted him with their garages as well as their apartments while they were away. Dunya carried one garage key in his hand for a week because it didn't fit in his pocket. An object of Dunya's special interest was the key to the Lenin Room, which was usually empty. This was the one key the director refused to give him. He rejected Dunya's insistent requests as "ideologically unfocused." The puzzling formulation flummoxed even native Russian speakers, but Dunya figured it out. What helped bring focus was a liter bottle of rakija; once he'd received it, the director gave Dunya the key. The Lenin Room had the main prerequisites: a large sofa and the possibility of locking himself in all night. Like all rooms in the world, it had its pluses and minuses. Thus, Dunya found the dominant red bunting in it erotic, but the decor as a whole was somewhat bombastic. Particular doubt in this sense was raised in him by the bust of Lenin in the corner and the enormous wall map with the coats of arms of the cities from which students had come. After his first night, Dunya stated that he felt uncomfortable making love in Lenin's presence. After that he complained many times that the inhuman dimensions of the leader's head made him feel he was being watched – so Dunya had to turn it around each time. Gleb was surprised that Dunya managed to turn such a big sculpture around by himself, but inside, it turned out, Lenin was hollow. One person really could turn him around. Actually, this fact was fateful for Dunya. One night he woke up Gleb and Kotov, banging on the door. Gleb was prepared to tell Dunya off, but when he saw his comrade he stopped short. Dunya was extremely upset. Closing the door behind him, he told them in a whisper that Lenin had fallen and he needed help. "Who? Lenin?" Kotov asked, also in a whisper. Dunya gave him a nasty look but realized Kotov wasn't fully awake yet: "No, me." Lenin was beyond help. He'd broken into many pieces, and it was impossible to glue them together (Kotov, now awake, confirmed that). At the same time, the pieces hadn't fallen apart, they were still held together by the sturdy fabric base to which the plaster had been applied. Lida sat over the pieces, this time wearing Dunya's shirt. She greeted the arrivals with a delight that didn't correspond to the occasion. Gleb made a mental note that Dunya was becoming a one-woman man. The lovers, it turned out, had already tried to take the broken sculpture out in parts, but their (the parts') inseparability prevented even that. Without a word, Kotov left the Lenin room and returned a minute later with a sack. In the other hand, he held a hammer. Kotov suggested smaller pieces, so you couldn't tell what the destroyed sculpture was, and this seemed politically far-sighted as well as sensible to everyone. They tried to work quietly, setting the plaster on fluffy bunches of newspaper. An hour later, Dunya and Gleb carried the sack to the nearest construction site. There they put it with the other sacks, which looked amazingly like Kotov's. Struck by the resemblance, Dunya even suggested they look to see what was in them, but Gleb talked him out of it. He realized that any resemblance has its limits. In the morning, Dunya went to the director to report that the bust of Lenin had been stolen. The director swore and then was just gloomily silent. For ideological reasons, he couldn't express his doubt that anyone might have need of the bust. He was reconciled to the loss only by the fact that, unlike beds and headboards, he did have busts in reserve. He told Dunya to take a new Lenin to the Lenin Room and return the key. The assignment was carried out with the help of Gleb and Kotov. Carrying Lenin out of housekeeping, Dunya now familiarly jingled his rings of keys. Lida awaited them in the Lenin Room. While they were installing the bust, she examined the wall map. Her shoulders were shaking noticeably. Gleb almost thought she was crying: like it or not, she and Dunya had lost their only private housing. When Lida turned around, it was clear that the young woman was laughing. Pointing to one of the images, she said, "It's good, at least, that Dunya's family coat of arms will stay here." Dunya moved closer to the map with a mistrustful smile. Gleb and Kotov were right behind him. On a heraldic shield, to the left of a lion standing on its hind legs, there were two crossed keys. It was the coat of arms of his hometown in Grodno Province.

AUGUST 20, 2013, MUNICH

The Aumeister restaurant. The flickering hour of transition from hot to cool. A chestnut leaf is lying on our little table like a spread palm. I put it in a bottle of mineral water. I cut some Bavarian sausage and wash it down with beer.

"I'm telling you, the writer Thomas Mann liked to come to this establishment."

"What is he remembered for here?"

I call the waiter over:

"What is Thomas Mann remembered for here?"

He casts a brief glance at the bottle. This is a tacit reproach. You don't have to drink the water brought, but leaves in it, you see . . .

"I haven't been here long, Herr Yanovsky, and I don't know all our customers by name."

"Not a bad customer," Nestor says in English. "On the other hand you do know Mr. Yanovsky, and that's something."

The waiter bows his head.

"Who doesn't know him?"

Nestor winks at me: there you have it, fame. Seeing a pack of cigarettes on the table, the waiter brings an ashtray. We're sitting outside because here you can still smoke. You can't inside anymore. Nestor lights up, and the first puff of smoke is slowly lost in the chestnut's crown.

"You've said very little about the time of your fame."

"Really?" I flick Nestor's lighter and look at the flame. "You know, I'd prefer you did without that in your book."

"Is this modesty?"

"No, it's just no longer about me. It's about my admirers, the press. My double, if you like. Everything I've achieved, not just in music but in general – everything happened before this. What you're talking about is an image."

"Not bad. But it's *your* image."

"It separated from me." I point up. "More or less the same way the smoke has from your cigarette. Tell me, Nestor, what does this cloud look like?"

Nestor stares carefully at the puff of smoke hanging over our table.

"Maybe a famous musician" – he takes another drag – "a diplomaed philologist."

"There, you see. And I think it looks like a certain famous writer. I suspect the cloud brings to mind all famous people simultaneously. But that has nothing to do with you or me."

Nestor sips from his mug and runs his tongue over his lips.

"Gleb, my dear man, the last thing I would want is for my book to be a story of success. Success in the crudest sense. That would be too simple."

"Especially since life is never the story of success." I raise my mug. "*Prosit!*"

"Even yours?"

"Especially mine."

1983

Fallen idols have an affinity for revenge. In this category, even Lenin was no exception. Smashed to smithereens and even dust, he rose from the ashes on September 1, 1983, when the Philology Department decided to open the first day of classes with a "Lenin lesson." Lessons like that were an ordinary event in high school, but up until now the university program had not envisaged anything of the kind. The reason for the plan may have been an uncertainty that had arisen in Party minds with the change of Party General Secretary. Newly in power, Andropov revealed no more signs of life than his predecessor Brezhnev had. Given the situation, it was decided to look to someone who had the status of the eternally living. The Lenin lesson at the Philology Department was led by a certain Burtsev, who taught Scientific – known to students as Antiscientific – Communism. Deep down, Burtsev guessed that the students' designation did not lack foundation, and over the years this guess had led the teacher to an ambivalence and then to a frantic zeal. People said that his one love was fat failing grades on his test, which he assigned right and left, regardless of the respondent's knowledge or ideological firmness. The waverers got them for their wavering; the convinced, on the contrary, for their conviction, inasmuch as you can't be an idiot and believe in fairytales, Burtsev thought maliciously. For some reason, he began his talk to the students with a criticism of religion. Burtsev might have criticized something else (he liked to criticize), but he forced himself to stick to what was allowed. After an extended introduction he began to cite

167

the statistics on Lenin's executions of clergy. While his audience was pondering whether this was what the Lenin lesson consisted of, Burtsev moved on to the third part of the event: each person had to stand up and say whether he believed in God. Execution certainly did not threaten those who confessed, but expulsion from the university seemed a definite possibility. As for Gleb, expulsion would automatically have led to him being sent off to the army as well. With a chill in his stomach, he realized that the exchange of opinions had lost its academic character. There was something to consider here, only there was barely any time left to do so. His classmates stood up one after the other and said they didn't believe in God. Renunciation began with the first row, but this time Gleb had sat in the last. A stopwatch started in his head, click after click coinciding with the pounding in his temples. Father Pyotr used to tell him that only one thing had been demanded of the first Christians. To the question, Do you believe? answer no. Then go believe quietly; your entire life is your reward. They answered yes because a life after no lost all meaning for them. For some reason, Gleb looked at his neighbor, Dasha Perevoshchikova, who had come from the obscure town of Totma. Totma comes from *to t'ma* – obscurity – Dasha would say about her hometown. She calmly observed what was going on in the classroom. The calmness of clarity, Gleb thought irritably, as if she were going to say something. Sing something, maybe. I don't understand how anyone can believe in God, she might say. But he did understand, only he didn't know whether he'd admit it. Because the same Father Pyotr had said that judgment can be made only about someone in his natural state. He'd said, you can't hand someone a bill if he's being tortured. And isn't this torture? Dasha stands up as if in slo-mo; he's next. "I do believe in God. How could I not?" This isn't him speaking, it's Dasha. Burtsev doesn't react. With a bored face he looks through his papers for something. The dean's secretary appears in the door: "Gennady Nikolaevich, you're wanted immediately in the dean's office." Burtsev nods. Goes out. And doesn't come back before the two hours are up. What was that? Gleb asks himself later. A miracle? And the dyed blonde from the dean's office is God's instrument, the Angel with Golden Hair? Ultimately, what do we know about angels? Yes, it was a miracle. Gleb found out the name of the one who'd saved him when he was delivering the newspaper to the dean's office: Krylova – from *krylo*, wing. Thus his third year began. That year Gleb became obsessed with Bakhtin. Now he knew everything about carnival and Rabelais, and about how the narrator differs from the author, but what made a special impression on him (as should have been expected) was Bakhtin's work on polyphony in the novels of Dostoyevsky. Polyphony had interested Gleb back in music school, but only with respect to music. Now he had discovered for himself that the whole world is polyphonic. The many-voiced sound of trees in a grove, automobiles moving down a street, conversations in a line. Gleb thought about how this could be expressed in his thesis. In third year, Philology Department students chose their specialization and had to choose between language and literature. Gleb chose literature. Moreover, he found an advisor who, in his opinion, suited the goals of the research he was contemplating. Unlike many of his classmates, who tried to write under professors' direction, Gleb asked to have appointed as his advisor a graduate student, Ivan Alekseyevich Sergienko. Ivan Alekseyevich had just been an undergraduate and was noted for his rare erudition, and, not unimportantly, for his literary name and patronymic. Strangely enough, Gleb chose as his mentor a person with those professional virtues for a quality that had nothing to do with literature: Ivan Alekseyevich played the guitar. Not that he was a virtuoso, but he played with feeling and was the life of the party. He played and sang – Okudzhava, Vysotsky, Kim. In trusted company – Galich. He wore an elegant three-piecer, not baggy professorial suits.

Once he showed up in an ascot, but after the dean's stern criticism he went back to his usual tie. Only a person like that could have a correct understanding of polyphony. And could defend it as well. Once, in Gleb's presence, Dean Chukin walked up to Ivan Alekseyevich and called polyphony a false doctrine. Chukin had built his scholarly career on his dispute with Bakhtin. A polemic with a deceased opponent was convenient and reminiscent of a chess game against yourself. Coming up with moves for his opponent, Chukin would race around the board like an enraged queen and take out piece after piece. Observing Chukin's perpetual battle, many began to fear him. But not Ivan Alekseyevich. He responded wittily to all of Chukin's anti-Bakhtin speeches. When they got to the French poststructuralists, who had promoted Bakhtin, Chukin began to huff and puff, and Gleb got the definite sense that he hadn't read their works. True, Gleb hadn't either, but he wasn't the one disputing Bakhtin. It ended with Chukin accusing Ivan Alekseyevich of a preference for bourgeois theories and kowtowing to the West. Gleb's advisor paused and then noted that he had one more weighty argument he might present to Chukin in private. An intrigued Chukin withdrew. Since then, Gleb had run across him in the department corridors several times, but the topic of Bakhtin never came up again. In the end, Ivan Alekseyevich had succeeded in convincing Chukin. Sometime later, Gleb asked his advisor what his decisive argument had been. He replied that his argument had been of an extraliterary nature. Not strong in terminology, Gleb only understood that the proof had been weighty, and he started taking pride in his teacher. Gleb also liked the fact that, unlike the advisors who were professors, Ivan Alekseyevich didn't harass him with strict oversight. They met rather rarely – and not at the department but at the Brigantina, a beerhouse. His mentor was satisfied with oral reports from his ward. Listening closely, he sometimes interrupted, asked for clarification. And always gave good advice. Sometimes Ivan

Alekseyevich's attention would become all-consuming, and his stark eyes would focus on a single point – most often the chandelier, executed in the shape of a ship's wheel. Sometimes he would notice the wheel turning and report this to the waiter, Lyosha, a towheaded boy missing his right index finger. Lyosha would shake his head contritely and suggest Ivan Alekseyevich not drink anymore. Alluding to the lost finger, Ivan Alekseyevich would say that Lyosha was in no position to be making any suggestions to anyone. A while later, he stopped Gleb's report and called over Lyosha to ask whether the Brigantina was on course. "Aye, aye, captain," clever Lyosha responded, since he knew this would be reflected in his tip. On days like that, Ivan Alekseyevich had few words and no advice at all, he just sipped his beer silently. Very quickly it became clear that the beer was the final link in a chain that had its start in the morning hours. But Gleb was happy for this silent attention because it was invariably good-natured. It was then that he allowed himself to lay out his boldest ideas, confident that they would be accepted without objection. Gleb saw polyphony not only in the parallel voices of the heroes but in counterposed plots, in the different narrative timeframes whose point of contact might be found in the text of the work or outside it – in the reader's mind. The young scholar could not always cite examples of such works, but on his better evenings his advisor would suggest those examples to him and even cite scholarly works devoted to them. On one such evening, Gleb repeated his question regarding the decisive argument for Chukin. Carefully considering the question, Ivan Alekseyevich said, "I just punched him in the face." He brought the lighter to his extinguished cigarette. "Read the poststructuralists, my friend, and you'll avoid a lot of trouble." Generally speaking, Ivan Alekseyevich's best evenings with Gleb were those when he did not come alone. As a rule, he was accompanied by young women – lecturers and university students. In their presence Ivan Alekseyevich shone with erudition and wit, quoted from memory page after page, and regardless of how much he drank his gaze didn't fix on one point. It's quite likely that he brought the ladies on purpose, inasmuch as there can be no better backdrop for a teacher than the presence of a pupil. Gleb understood that his academic advisor was spreading his tail for the ladies, but that didn't bother him in the least. Ivan Alekseyevich's tail was wonderful. Moreover, a companion's presence meant the evening's continuation. From one bar they'd move on to another, and Ivan Alekseyevich's wit was never depleted – and most of all, neither was Gleb's wallet – because his advisor paid for everything. A few times Gleb tried to chip in, but Ivan Alekseyevich reminded him that in this case it was a teaching process taking place for which he, as the advisor, bore full (including financial) responsibility. This was simultaneously the most joyous and most fruitful learning process in Gleb's life. Much of what Ivan Alekseyevich said Gleb wrote down, so that the notepad next to his beer was no surprise to anyone. At the same time, his advisor's generosity reached such heights that he was often in no shape to get home without help. More than once or twice Gleb helped the ladies put Ivan Alekseyevich in a taxi and sped off with them through nighttime Piter to Fourteenth Line on Vasilievsky Island. He would help his advisor up to the fifth floor and say goodbye. To the suggestion he stay until morning he would respond with a polite no. He explained that it wasn't at all far from Fourteenth Line to the Mytninskaya Embankment. And it really wasn't far, except for the bridges. Often Gleb had to wait – for a short time or all night – for them to come down but that didn't really bother him. Gazing at the black mass of the bridge, he realized these nights would remain with him always, and his heart felt a tug for his future memories. He knew he would remember the checkered tablecloth with the ring left by the sweating mug, the rickety Viennese chairs, the loud toasts and the laughter in the room. Thirty years from now, for instance, would they all be laughing? And if so – where?

OCTOBER 20, 2013, MUNICH

I half-recline on the sofa, hands clasped behind my head. Katya is in the swivel chair at the computer, finger on mouse.

Biting her lip, she scrolls through text on the screen.

"Tomorrow is the last warm day. Then it's winter, by the way." She sighs and turns the screen around. "Winter, Gleb."

The window of the neighboring cottage reflects a red evening ray, which glances off, like a soccer ball, into the Yanovskys' living room. And trembles on the ceiling.

I say, "Write Mayer that I'm canceling the Berlin concert." Pause. "That I'm canceling my concerts in general."

Katya does a half-turn in her chair. Looks at me silently.

"What are you staring at!" I glance at Katya and change my tone. "Write . . ."

Katya opens the mail program.

"Are you going to give him a reason?"

"Let's skip the reason." I walk up to the window. "The reason is that I can't play anymore! I can't. Do you understand?"

"You know even with diseases things can go different ways. There are known cases where everything passes by itself."

I laugh loudly and artificially.

"I practiced for four hours yesterday. A total crock. Did you hear that gurgling? You did: when you walk up to the door the floor creaks loudly. And you know why it creaks?" I head for the book-shelf, move aside a volume of Goethe, and take out a flask with two fingers. "Because alcohol makes you fat. I know all your stashes."

"I'm a fat old sot. If that makes you feel better."

She says this almost in a whisper. Stares hard at the screen. I put my hands on Katya's shoulders and press my forehead to the top of her head.

"Forgive me. You're not old and you're not fat. But you are a sot."

Katya covers my hands with hers. She looks up at me.

"Gleb, darling, bear in mind, I haven't touched spirits for two weeks. Didn't you notice?"

"No, because yesterday you smelled of it."

The computer signals incoming mail. Katya touches the mouse, and the dark screen comes to life.

"I had a drink yesterday when I heard you playing."

Email from Anna Avdeyeva.

I go back to the sofa.

"To hell with Anna Avdeyeva. Write to Mayer."

"She writes her maiden name."

"To hell with her maiden name."

"It's a funny name: Lebed."

Swan.

I run my hands across my face. The skin stretches like a rubber mask.

"And what, I wonder, does Anna Lebed write?"

"'Dear Gleb, despite all the years that have passed, I hope you remember me. I'm sure you do, although your memories are probably not the nicest.'"

"Not the nicest. And her style is straight out of Turgenev. What a fool."

"Just a sec. . . . 'I was married twice but never did manage to have a child.'" Katya looks over briefly at Gleb. "'So. Marrying for the third time, I moved to Leningrad. And had a daughter, her name is Vera. Soon after Vera's birth my husband died.'"

"What do I need all this slobber for? Trash it!"

"Wait. 'Vera started having liver problems, and recently they gave her a diagnosis of cancer.'" Katya continues to read the letter silently for a while. "The girl is thirteen. Anna writes that she studies at music school. Piano. Amazingly talented. . . .'"

I look closely at Katya.

"Anna was my first woman."

Katya continues to run her eyes over the lines.

"'After the way we parted, it's probably wrong to turn to you, but I'm beyond proprieties. I'm snatching at any straw.' She's asking for help, Gleb."

Amazingly talented. And what parents don't think their child is talented? Maybe only my father.

"What can we do for her?"

"For now, nothing, but she might need a liver transplant."

I watch the gardener push the wheelbarrow into the shed. When he steps outside, he slowly pulls off his gloves.

"Are we going to help her, Gleb?"

"Do you want us to?"

"Yes."

"Then write her that we'll help. Only in your name."

1983–1984

Gleb greeted the new year of 1984 in Leningrad and, for the first time in his life, not at home. On the morning of December 31, Gleb took his last exam and went straight from the university to the airport, hoping to fly to Kyiv. Unfortunately, there weren't any tickets. En route to the dorm he tried to buy champagne, but he failed in that department as well. Gleb was filled with confidence that both (this is how life works) had wound up in the same hands. He could even picture quite well those lucky people flying into Kyiv and toasting with champagne. The dorm was half empty. Gleb's roommates (now they were students from Novgorod) had left, actually, for Novgorod. It took them three hours to get to their hometown by train; they had no need of air service. Gleb wasn't even sure there was such a thing between Leningrad and Novgorod. Stretching out on top of the bedspread, he remembered how, just a week before, Novgorodian Valya had told Novgorodian Kostya he'd bought two bottles of champagne for the occasion. To Kostya's suggestion that they drink them immediately, Valya said sternly that he was taking the champagne home. Kostya fell silent and with cool dignity advised him to keep the bottles in the refrigerator. Already half-asleep, Gleb managed to marvel at the Novgorodians' foresight. When he woke up, it took him a while to realize what time it was: the clock not wound yesterday had stopped. Ten thirty, came a suggestion from the hallway. Late already. Damn. The door slammed and he heard steps accompanied by clinking bottles. Gleb thought sadly that, unfortunately, he wasn't late. Sitting on the bed, he rocked, and the springs lamented in response. The light in the room was turned off (it had been daytime when Gleb fell asleep), but the ceiling reflected the streetlamps. Their lunar flickering was even sadder than the springs' creak. The flickering fell on the calendar with views of Kyiv that hung over Gleb's bed. The Kyiv views did not cheer him up. They reminded him of the inaccessibility of the city where, had things turned out differently, he might have been right now. A pitiful ersatz reality, a drawing of a hearth in Papa Carlo's little room. Gleb stood up decisively and turned on the light. He heard quiet steps outside the door. These weren't the steps of someone rushing somewhere; their general rhythm did not speak to the existence of a goal. They piqued Gleb's interest and even amused him. Leaning back against the door, he tried to imagine the person moving – maybe even creeping – tentatively down the hall. The unknown person would stop by a door, and evidently peer at it. Gleb felt uneasy. What was there to look at in doors? Locks! Taking advantage of the dorm's desertedness, a thief was walking up and down here. . . . Gleb abruptly opened his door and saw a young woman in the hall. Gleb's unexpected appearance frightened her. He recognized her. It was Katarina, a German from East Berlin. She was studying Russian philology, two years behind him. They didn't know each other, and he doubted Katarina had any idea who he was, but Gleb knew her because everyone knew this tall, skinny German. Foreigners were a rarity at the university. Actually, this wasn't just about her being a foreigner. Katarina was remarkable in and of herself: straight blond hair, a cartoonish teenage walk, and a turned-up nose on a Gothic face. Behind her back she was called the Rail, as in "skinny as a." Ill will has a keen eye. The nickname reflected, besides Katarina's features, the hurt felt by those she'd rejected. Despite her entertaining appearance (in fact, because of it), Katerina had won the hearts of a few philological youths. They all knew, though, that she had a fiancé in Berlin, to whom she remained faithful. This elicited legitimate respect, yet couldn't help but annoy. This was the Katarina who now stood in front of Gleb. She smiled in embarrassment, her initial fright dissipated. She was looking for her girlfriend. "I vas supposte to tselebrate New Year's vif friends of my parents, but they got sick. *Grippe.*" "*Grippe.* That's bad," Gleb agreed. Her parents had asked her not to celebrate in the dorm. They said there'd be terrible drinking and carousing. "But it's empty here." Gleb cast an eye over the hallway. "No drinking, no carousing for you." "Ferry dull." Katarina laughed. "That's not the word for it," Gleb confirmed. She gestured: "I always get it wrong. I still don't know Russian well." "Not at all. Your Russian's fine, quite okay even." Gleb pretended to think hard. "I never did manage to come up with any alcohol, but I'm prepared to invite you for tea. We could celebrate the New Year with tea." "Do you have tsugar?" Gleb looked down, afraid Katarina would see something that had nothing to do with sugar in his eyes. "Yes." "Then we can tselebrate." He heard a smile in her voice. Gleb looked up – and there it was. She'd been smiling the whole time. Letting her into his room, he said, "You have a wonderful smile." Pause. "Really?" This time she didn't smile, and Gleb thought he'd spoiled everything. He got busy, looked in his nightstand for his box of refined sugar and put it on the table; the unevenly torn carton jutted up like a piano lid. The sugar as proof of the purity of his intentions. His thoughts pure as the driven snow, so to speak. Now she was going to ask who'd opened the box so barbarically. *Russische Arbeit.* No, instead she asked, "Do you have anything besides sugar?" He nodded. "Of course I do. Bread, sausage." He feverishly tried to remember. "Marinated mushrooms, for instance." Katarina said she had something, too, she'd just go get it. . . . It was clear as day. He'd scared her off. Why did he say that about her smile? He'd scared her and she'd found an excuse to leave. He got it. She had a fiancé in Berlin, and here he'd started in on the compliments at this time of night. Watching Katarina go made Gleb sad. He picked up his guitar and started strumming. He thought he heard steps outside the door – no, the window. . . . Enough time passed for her to get to any room and return. She could have done it ten times. No point in waiting. Gleb lay the guitar on the bed and turned on the radio so he wouldn't miss the New Year. He heard light scratching at the door. Katarina. Katarina! She was standing there with a plastic bag – a genuine Snow Maiden, a real Schnee Mädchen. Now she was dressed differently, and she smelled of something not from here. Not Red Moscow, for instance, the perfume Gleb's grandmother used. That was why she'd taken so long. Entering the room, she started putting her German provisions on the table. "There's so much!" Gleb said admiringly. She replied that this was her little apology for taking so long. Gleb opened the refrigerator and took the liter jar of mushrooms off the shelf, put it on the table, and realized he'd noticed something unexpected in the refrigerator. A return visit to the refrigerator made everything clear. Lying on the Novgorodian Valya's shelf were two bottles of champagne. When he was packing, Valya forgot the champagne. "I spent my time well, too," Gleb said calmly, as a true magician should. With a snap of his right hand a bottle appeared in his left. "Champagne? Really?" Katarina was amazed. "No." Gleb shook his head. "Two champagnes." Katarina opened the refrigerator. "Confess, you had them!" Gleb still maintained his serious face. "No, I didn't, or rather, *I* didn't." Katarina said that one bottle was enough, and Gleb immediately agreed. "Of course it is." The main thing was that she shouldn't think *carousing* was about to ensue. When the General Secretary's congratulations came over the radio, Gleb started opening the bottle. He did it without a bang, so no one would have any doubts about the evening's peaceful nature, but Katarina expressed disappointment. To her mind, champagne should be opened noisily. Gleb apologized and promised to open the second bottle that way. That was the last thing Katarina wanted, though, since then they knew what would happen. When the congratulations ended, Gleb poured champagne into two dark blue enameled mugs. They also had a faceted glass and a half-liter cup with a view of the Novgorod kremlin, but Katarina rejected those volumes as unpaired. The mugs were true twins (the mole that differentiated them was a chip in the enamel on one), which, when clinked, made the metallic sound of a cowbell. They clinked a second before the bells' peal, as Gleb and Katarina saw out the old year. To the hymn of the Soviet Union the metallic sound was repeated: now they were ringing in the new year. Soviet music hall tunes started playing. After listening to a few songs with all seriousness, Katarina pointed to the guitar: "Will you play?" And added: "I've heard you play well." Gleb was surprised but tried not to let on. Katarina turned out to know more about him than might have been expected. He switched off the radio and picked up the guitar. He glanced at Katarina with a certain pride; her words were still ringing in his ears. Might she have known that he was here? Might she have been roaming the hall not at random? He started playing. He purposely chose a couple of difficult pieces to demonstrate his technique. He wondered whether her fiancé could do that. Whether he played the guitar at all. Gleb seriously doubted he did. With these thoughts, he moved on to simple, melodic pieces. When he played "The Story of Love," Katarina sang the lyrics in English. Quietly at first, shy, but when Gleb joined in with his humming, she started singing in full voice. He'd never heard a voice like Katarina's before, powerful and low. Suddenly she broke off singing and said she wanted to drink to Gleb, a stupendous musician. Feeling himself blush, he poured what was left of the champagne into the mugs. Katarina glanced briefly at the empty bottle, and Gleb thought she was about to take back her toast. She didn't. Then she set about slicing the salami she'd brought. Gleb asked whether that beauty was from Berlin. When Katarina answered in the affirmative, he asked whether it was a present from her fiancé. She smiled with restraint: "You mean in the USSR fiancés give presents of salami?" A second later she couldn't hold back anymore. She laid out the neatly sliced pieces on the plate and let the laughter shake her. Subsequently, Katarina admitted that it was neither Gleb's guitar playing nor his humming but the salami that had finally won her over as a bridge to the main question. She said her fiancé was moot. Because she didn't have one. Gleb felt a surge of happiness and didn't even ask why not. The main thing was she didn't. And maybe never had. He'd been made up so she could reject admirers. Katarina asked permission and took the calendar down from the wall. She sat on Gleb's bed and started leafing through it. "Tell me about Kyiv." Gleb sat down beside her. He watched Katarina's hands, watched her eyelashes tremble. "This is the university." "Why is it that red?" "I don't know, I've been used to it that way since childhood. At the word 'university' I always pictured something red. The word itself was red, even." Katarina's pale fingers slid over the red building. Gleb no longer dared look up and looked only at them and loved them infinitely. He covered them with his hand – and Katarina didn't pull them away. Her fingers were trembling. He squeezed them lightly – very lightly, to reassure her. He sensed the moment when he and Katarina turned into a single whole and he pressed his forehead to her shoulder. Katarina leaned toward him, and he felt her breath. He didn't feel his own. "Can I kiss you?" The pause that arose was filled by a car outside. "I'fe nefer made luff." Gleb slowly raised his head and touched his lips to her half-open lips. Forget any fiancé. . . . The calendar slid to the floor.

DECEMBER 1, 2013, MUNICH

Katya is behind the wheel; I'm sitting next to her. Nestor and Nika are in the back seat. We're heading to our alpine home, where we plan to spend a few days. The car is going up the switchbacks, and Nestor isn't feeling so good. His whitened fingers are squeezing the strap above the window. Nika is stroking Nestor's knee. In the rearview mirror – Katya's worried look.

"We have another twenty minutes or so to the dacha, but we can stop."

"Better stop . . ." Nestor says this, barely unclenching his lips. Trying to smile.

At the next switchback, the car swooshes onto the gravel. Nestor and Nika get out. Nika is holding a packet of tissues; she's expecting the worst. Nestor makes a reassuring sign. He slams the door and leans his back against it. Breathes deeply, with an open mouth. I roll down the window.

"Winter's technically here, but the weather is like early autumn," Nika reports.

I reach out to Nestor.

"Better?"

"Much." Nestor takes another gulp of air and gets back in the car with regret.

After the last switchback we drive into the alpine village. At our massive iron gates, Katya clicks the remote and they open soundlessly. Nestor perks up before our eyes. He asks what century the house is from. Katya says the sixteenth (we just happened to buy it). The Nestorovs are full of admiration; they've never happened to do any such thing. The house is indeed fine: spacious, two-story, with a garret under a gabled roof.

We put our guests in the garret. Taking a shower in the marble-fitted bathroom, Nestor finds that when it comes to comfort the sixteenth century is in no way inferior to the twenty-first. At dinner he asks what in the house is original.

"The walls," Katya answers. "Also the doors and locks."

She leads our guests to the front door and shows them the whimsical mechanism on the inside of the door. The lock looks like an ornament, pure and simple, useless, like anything beautiful. Katya takes keys of cyclopean proportions off a nail and disappears behind the door, and the ornament goes into motion, its creaking musical.

During dinner, blocks of wood crackle in the fireplace – outsized blocks, like everything in this house. The chairs are thrones, the glasses goblets. Wine in a three-liter carafe. That's how it came to us.

"You feel like you're in a movie," Nestor says. "A butler should come in now carrying candles."

Katya goes out and a minute later appears with two candelabra.

"Our butler is Geraldina, but she stayed in town."

"If you like, we'll pretend you're Geraldina," Nestor proposes.

Nika smiles.

"She doesn't look resentful enough for Geraldina."

It's hot in the room, and Katya opens a window. Brings a finger to her lips. In the ensuing silence we hear a cowbell.

"They don't bring the cows in at night here." Katya looks out the window. "The grass in December. . . . I'd graze myself."

Nika comes to stand next to her by the window.

"So would I."

"We will together." Katya turns toward the men. "Only don't call us cows."

"And we'll ring for you," Nika adds. "A magical sound."

"The sound of a metal cup. Our very first night, Gleb gave me champagne to drink from a metal cup."

I look around Katya's back and out the window.

"You make it seem I was trying to get you drunk."

Katya pours herself some wine from the carafe.

"No, I wanted it myself. I'd wanted to meet you for a long time. Didn't you know? I saw you coming back to the dorm from the airport, and someone said you'd wanted to fly to Kyiv. I realized you hadn't. I didn't know where you were going to celebrate." Katya takes a big sip. "All of a sudden I went and called the people I was supposed to celebrate New Year's with. A really stuffy couple. I said I'd taken ill."

"*Grippe,*" I clarify. "You were more cunning than I'd thought, Katya. And I was so afraid you wouldn't come back."

"That's true." She turns to Nestor and Nika. "My boy was very worried. So was I, and my Russian wouldn't obey me, and then I felt he didn't like me."

"Yes, your Russian was a lot better in the morning."

"It wasn't all that bad, my Russian."

"Don't flatter yourself."

"Well, maybe small problems with pronunciation. Gleb used to tease me about my s's being all over the map. But mine were, like in German." Without looking at me, Katya pours herself another from the carafe. "He used to tease me. . . . How did you tease me, Gleb dear?"

"Shtillnesh in ze grove, not a rushtling zound. That's exactly how you sang it, by the way."

"Doesn't sound so bad." Nestor lights up by the window. "I like it even better that way, don't you, Nika?"

"No comparison."

Katya polishes off her glass.

"Katya, you've had enough."

I reach for Katya's glass, but she doesn't let go.

"Too bad you didn't tell me that our first night." Katya's voice is getting peevish. "We polished off a bottle of champagne in one breath. Without any lectures."

"You had two bottles there," Nestor prompts.

Katya pours herself some juice.

"The second bottle is a whole other song. When Gleb started opening it, it exploded. I'd never seen so much foam before."

"Maybe it was the fire extinguisher?" Nika conjectures.

"No, it was Sovetskoye champagne. I tried to plug it up" – I pick up a bottle of cola and cover the neck with my finger – "like this . . ."

". . . and aimed the stream at me! *Meine Mutter!*"

"I didn't realize what had happened. The bottle came from the refrigerator and no one had shaken it, but it spewed like in Formula One."

"I ended up drenched from head to toe – wet and sticky!"

"So the champagne was sweet," Nestor concludes. "Semi-sweet at worst."

"I wanted to take a shower and change clothes, but Gleb said I couldn't show myself in the hallway looking like that."

"Katya, darling..."

"He was awfully convincing, so I started washing myself in the room sink. The boy chastely turned away. I was trembling from the cold, and he offered to wrap me up in his blanket, and we had tea. And I still couldn't get warm."

"I think" – I put my hand on Katya's shoulder – "we might have some tea now too."

"Did you remember all that when you shagged your Hanna?"

Katya pushes my hand away and blows out all the candles in turn. Her sobs are muffled and dry-eyed. Nika puts her arm around Katya and takes her to the bedroom. Nestor and I silently watch as smoke streams up from the candlewicks.

1984

On January 1, Gleb and Katarina woke up in the same bed. From that day on, their life changed completely; they were never apart, not only in the year just begun but in all the succeeding years. Waking at two o'clock in the afternoon, Katarina asked in a whisper that he call her Katya. Her fusion with Russia was so profound that she could no longer use her old name. After breakfast, the couple decided to get some fresh air. They walked with their hands pulled up into their sleeves. Their steps crunched on the streamers and confetti scattered over the snow in honor of their sudden meeting. The snow was trampled and neither fresh nor clean, but it was festive snow. From time to time snowflakes would fly by, tiny and stinging. On a bridge, Gleb breathed on Katya's hands and admired her long fingers. He asked whether she'd studied music. No, she hadn't. Mittens dangled childishly on an elastic under Katya's hands. Gleb put a mitten on her right hand, and she slipped her left into his jacket pocket. He squeezed Katya's hands and gasped from happiness. Gasped because his happiness was enormous and vaporous, it no longer fit inside him, and its excess came out in flying puffs at every exhale. Privately, he thanked God for this gift. There was no other word for it because only gifts can be so unexpected and beautiful. Gleb never tired of wondering at how someone who was a stranger just yesterday had become so close today. Become a part of his *I*, and now he loved Katya with a double love – as his neighbor and as himself. Words failed Gleb, they were inadequate to the love that had gripped him. He wished he could express his feeling in action, and his bed was too small for that, he wanted to *do* something. Maybe even suffer. Unsurprisingly, an occasion soon presented itself. It arose in the person of Dunya, who by then had parted with Lida and had even managed, as became clear, to notice Katya. It was he who had been told that Katya had a fiancé, inasmuch as Katya's goodheartedness wouldn't let her reveal the essentially simple reason for her refusal: she didn't like Dunya. News of the new couple flashed through the department. Dunya felt deceived and became enraged. He said hello to Gleb in as friendly a way as before, but the hour of his revenge was at hand. Choosing a moment when Gleb and Katya were standing in a crowd of students, he walked up to them, smiled, and said it turned out someone was already hanging on the Rail. The people standing around fell quiet. Gleb looked silently at Dunya's smile, which had nothing natural about it. Dunya's lips were twitching. Gleb turned away, hunched over, and became even smaller compared to the mighty Dunya. Everyone thought he was leaving, so they cleared the way for him. Straightening up as he turned, Gleb punched Dunya in the jaw from below. Dunya's legs buckled, and he dropped to the floor. Gleb pulled his arm back for another punch, but Dunya gestured limply: no contest. He sat in a heap, near to fainting, senselessly looking straight ahead. When the ambulance took Dunya to the hospital, it turned out he had a broken jaw. At check-in, when asked the reason for the trauma, Dunya nobly said he'd fallen down the stairs. The doctor shook his head dubiously but said nothing. The next day, Gleb and Katya visited Dunya. They brought him vegetable purée and asked his forgiveness. Dunya indicated with gestures that he was the one who should be asking forgiveness. The silence lingered because Dunya, usually so talkative, could only participate in the conversation as a listener. In his mute gesticulating one felt a certain excessiveness; there was evidently something he couldn't say, but for the most part there wasn't anything to talk about. To fill the pause, Gleb told the joke about bringing the man with the knife between his ribs to the hospital: "What, does it hurt?" the doctor asked him. "No," he answered, "only when I laugh." The joke turned out to be very appropriate. Dunya started to laugh – and immediately clutched his jaw. Moreover, at the mention of a knife, the thought flashed that by Russian measures he'd gotten off lightly. To the general relief, five or so minutes later the patient was sent off for procedures. When Dunya was discharged, Katya kept making purées and soups for him. Actually, just a week later, moved by pity for the sufferer, a student from the Polytechnic Institute took her place. One might say that Gleb and Katya were once again left to their own devices, if it hadn't been for Gleb's two roommates, who returned to their beds on January 3. They managed to avoid explanations, and the drunk (and undrunk) champagne was quickly replaced, but with the Novgorod students in the room, Gleb and Katya couldn't do anything. Never before, it seemed to Gleb, had their presence been so indefatigable; when it wasn't both of them, it was one and then the other. Katya's roommate was a homebody, such a homebody that the couple had very few trysting opportunities. They didn't have the money for a hotel, and even if they had, that wouldn't have changed anything: guests of opposite sexes were admitted only with a marriage stamp in their passport, which Gleb and Katya, understandably, did not have. They spent nearly all their time together, meeting in the evenings on the Neva embankments, in cheap cafés, and in dormitory halls where, leaning against the wall, they had long, half-whispered conversations. Gleb later recalled those weeks of forced abstinence as the happiest time of his life. Never again were their feelings so delicate and ringing, never did their touches reverberate in such trembling. The immateriality of their relationship probably didn't suit Gleb in every way because one day, overcoming his reluctance, he knocked at Dunya's door and asked whether he would give him one of his famous keys. Dunya replied that the key he had was in use, inasmuch as he, Dunya, at present was having a stormy romance with the girl who'd been looking after him. Saying this, he mechanically felt his jaw. As Gleb was getting ready to leave, Dunya wavered and said that he actually did have one other, special key. The word "special" was uttered with such emphasis that Gleb got upset. His imagination immediately drew a stokehole, a building awaiting capital repairs – even a tugboat cabin (he'd heard of the like). "This place is very nearby," Dunya added, drawing out the mystery. But the answer was definitely worth it because it trumped Gleb's most daring fantasies. "It may sound surprising," Dunya said with modest dignity, "but it's the Rostral Column." Gleb decided to act nonplussed: "There are two of them." "What do you need two for?" Dunya asked. "We're talking about the right-hand column if you're facing the Naval Museum. The columns' watchman gave me the key to the utility room. I'm warning you. It's cold there, you have to take a heater with you. And an air mattress too. There's no canopied bed there exactly." Dunya took a key out from under *The Resistance of Materials* (by all accounts, resistance was minimal at the Polytechnic). "Will that do?" Gleb didn't think twice: "Yes." Rummaging in his clothes cupboard, Dunya (who decided to be noble to the end) pulled out a neatly folded air mattress from a stack of sweaters. He didn't have a heater. On the other hand, Katya did, and this exotic enterprise thrilled her. They went to the Rostral Columns that very evening. Crossing the Malaya Neva, they stopped in front of the column they'd been offered. At its base, covered in snow, sat two mighty figures, allegories for the great Russian rivers – which ones, exactly, Gleb was at pains to determine. Over the allegories' heads, growing straight from the column, were pointed ship prows, the technical term for which is "rostrum." Their selfless outward direction implied that no one would stick their nose into what was going on inside the column. Opening the lower door in the pedestal, Gleb felt for the light switch to the right of the door. Two Fledermaus lamps ("Are there any bats here?" Katya whispered) lit the square space (more likely rats, Gleb thought) and the spiral staircase in the middle. There was a table and two chairs by the staircase and a bed placed right in the corner – the door had been taken off its hinges and set on trestles. First thing, Gleb plugged in the heater – a heating coil. Aimed at a person, the heater gave off a minimum of heat but had no effect whatsoever on the space's overall temperature (which was the same as outside). The second means for getting warm was the bottle of brandy Katya set on the table along with some snacks. Trembling more from impatience than the cold, Gleb got out the air mattress. His attempt to inflate it with air was utterly exhausting. All those deep breaths made Gleb's head spin, while the mattress remained pathetically dystrophic. Not only that; the rubber and the fabric covering for this summer item had stiffened and categorically refused to straighten out: the materials' resistance had reached its apogee. The dizziness and cold somewhat dampened Gleb's initial enthusiasm. Their previous plans notwithstanding, he wearily agreed to Katya's suggestion that they eat. Katya sat in his lap, and they set up the heater right next to his chair. Together with a few shots of brandy (the same mugs performed this role), these measures warmed them up a little, but when they took off their jackets and sweaters, their hard-won warmth instantly melted away. Katya put her clothes right back on. Gleb tried to persuade her not to be in any hurry, promising swift warming, but his voice no longer held its former confidence. In the end, he hastily put his clothes back on as well. Half an hour later, the couple had packed up everything they'd brought and started walking toward the dorm. In the morning, the key was returned to Dunya.

DECEMBER 20, 2013, MUNICH

I'm reading the newspaper. Katya is checking the mail.

"Gleb, a letter from Anna Avdeyeva. I was just thinking about her. She apologizes for going missing."

"This isn't the first time with her."

"She writes that things aren't going in the best way. Vera has already been hospitalized twice. Then she goes on about what she's taking. . . . Her daughter continues to study piano quite seriously. . . . She writes about her repertoire. . . . Winner of international competitions, for your information."

"I was never a winner. Is there a specific request?"

"She doesn't write about any. Shall we help her with money?"

"Well, if she's a winner, let's help."

"Gleb . . ."

Katya falls silent.

"Yes?" I look at her over the newspaper. "I'm still listening, Katya darling."

"The thirty-first will be the thirtieth anniversary of us meeting."

I set aside the newspaper and observe Katya. She's spinning on the swivel chair.

"Gleb, dearest, we have to celebrate the day in Piter."

"*Abgemacht!* Let's do it. I'm a free man now."

Katya comes over. I bury my face in her sweater.

"Yes, you truly are a free man. You see? We can go wherever we want. Whenever we want."

"The only question is for how long. This morning my right leg was trembling. That's a bad sign, you know."

"Mohammed Ali got Parkinson's when he was around forty, and now he's over seventy."

"Yes, Mohammed Ali, people have told me. The banner for everyone with Parkinson's." I cautiously move Katya back and stand up. "The race is over, Katya. Now it's not quite clear why I ran it in the first place."

"The race is, yes. But movement continues."

"Movement where?"

I watch big wet snowflakes fly past the window. The house across the way has its Christmas lights on.

"Gleb . . . why don't you try to sing?"

"Better to dance, eh? My left leg still isn't so bad."

"You didn't hear me, Gleb. I said 'sing.'"

Geraldina brings in the tea. I sing:

"Geraldina, Geraldina, oy oy oy, a package from Peking-a, oy oy oy!"

"What a pretty song!" Geraldina tries to hum the melody. "It's just too bad I don't understand the words."

I lean toward her ear:

"Geraldina, a simple Russian girl, gets package after package. At the end of the song, she's accused of dealing drugs."

Geraldina smiles guardedly. She gives my shoulder a few quick pats. I kiss her hand. Geraldina leaves the room on wings.

"You see? Geraldina likes you." Katya presses up to me.

"Well then, I'm going to sing for Geraldina. Until my voice goes: the disease includes that too. After that, the gardener will sing to her."

The gardener is walking past the window. He's holding fringe tree branches he's trimmed.

1984

On April 17, Gleb celebrated his twentieth birthday. The party was held in the Lenin Room, where the guests were met by the backup Lenin, who differed in no way from the smashed one. From time to time, Dunya, the duly appointed toastmaster, would look around at Lenin (directly behind him), and they would exchange hostile looks. No matter what Dunya said, his words were greeted with an identical critical squint, which drove the toastmaster wild. Later he wrote off both his quick intoxication and his sudden falling asleep to that nagging stare behind him. At first, Dunya made toasts you had to drink to standing. On the subject of ladies, love, loyalty, and science. Then he mentioned the birthday boy and proposed a toast to him. After some hesitation he called for this to be done standing as well. Once he'd run out of steam a little, he started ceding the floor to the guests. No matter what the toast, he would say, "We have to drink to this standing." Each time the call was quieter and quieter and at a certain point they stopped altogether. Dunya rested his head on his arms and slept. For a long time the toasts proceeded without his accompaniment. Close to the end of the celebration, there was an almost intimate toast. Gleb's classmate hoped that in seventy years the girls would love him the same way they did now. At these words, Dunya lifted his head; an interrupted dream splashed in his eyes. "We have to drink to this lying down," he said, and fell back to sleep. When in the morning Gleb and Katya came back to clear the dishes, Dunya was still sleeping. Like a true toastmaster, he had remained at his post just in case someone might return and decide to give a toast. That morning, Katya and Gleb learned that new housing awaited them.

The friends of her parents whom Katya had not joined for New Year's were leaving for Berlin's Humboldt University for two semesters. The ornithology professor couple was going to tell German students about Russian birds. They proposed that Katya stay in their apartment on Bolshaya Pushkarskaya Street. Not believing her sudden good fortune, Katya agreed. As with everything sudden, her good fortune turned out to have a back story. The invitation from Berlin had been organized by Katya's parents, also ornithology professors. It was they who had felt it appropriate that their daughter look after the professorial nest in Petersburg. Knowing her parents to be unsentimental people, Katya suspected that this proposal had been the goal of the Russian ornithologists' summons to Humboldt University. One way or another, immediately after the ornithologists' departure for Berlin, the young couple moved into the apartment on Pushkarskaya. An hour after, to be precise. The only thing Gleb and Katya took with them on their first visit was sheets. The next day, with the help of the two Novgorodians, they brought over the rest of their things. Actually, the professorial apartment had nearly everything necessary, but the new residents preferred to bring a thing or two with them. In the end, it wasn't that difficult. The building on Pushkarskaya was not very far from the dorm. The Petersburg scientists' apartment reminded Katya of her parents' apartment in Berlin, so for her the move was a kind of homecoming: crammed bookshelves, book stalactites on the floor, and pensive stuffed birds on the dressers. Katya didn't like birds. Since her childhood they'd stood as the embodiment of immobility. At first she believed in the flight of their domestic fledglings, and at five, sometimes, she'd toss them in the air from the stepladder. As if contemplating a victim, they dropped like a stone to the floor, where their prey was her Legos, a gift from her West German relatives. In time, though, it became clear that these birds were not fated to soar. She found their absolute inability not just to fly but even to walk, and also their dirty yellow stuffing (the little girl had dug out one of the stuffed birds) depressing. Little Katarina, of course, did see birds capable of flight, but primarily sparrows and pigeons, which could not be compared with what was preserved at home. Unlike Katya, Gleb had never lived in an ornithologists' apartment, and the birds on the shelves amazed him. Gleb didn't toss them up or dig them out, but he couldn't deny himself the pleasure of stroking the delicate fluff under their wings either. Actually, the biggest surprise in this apartment for him was another bird: Katya. The opportunity to touch a hawk or a golden eagle didn't engender in Gleb the tiniest portion of the happiness he felt touching Katya's soft neck. She was a crane in the sky who had suddenly descended into Gleb's arms, and he had found not the slightest desire to fly away. Waking in the morning, Gleb would experience a momentary fright that his happiness was just a dream and his firebird had flown away. But Katya was by his side. Usually she was no longer sleeping and lying quietly so as not to disturb his sleep. Watching Gleb. Sometimes reading. Seeing his eyelids flutter, she would touch them with her lips. Gleb would embrace her, wouldn't let her go, and Katya's body would unbend on his body, tense like a guitar string – stomach to stomach, legs to legs. . . . The morning would begin with a very long kiss. After getting up, Katya would go take a bath, and Gleb would flop over onto her half of the bed and burrow his nose into her pillow and the scent of Katya's hair. The big cast iron tub filled slowly. In order not to waste time, Katya would get in when the tub was a third full. She liked to feel the roiling of the water with every cell of her body, and she liked it when Gleb would leave their bed, sit on the edge of the tub, and hold her hand. Once, pretending to lose his balance, he slid smoothly into the water and announced he had no plans to get out. You see, he was convinced that the professorial tub was too big for one person. That the architects had conceived of it as a pool that should be seen as a manifestation of traditional Russian collectivism. Katya (an expression of strong doubt) hesitated slightly but then slid to the other end of the tub and made room for Gleb. After that, he shared Katya's morning bath without further explanation. Katya (what wouldn't you do for the sake of tradition) did not actively protest, but she did set one condition: that they use their time in the bath to study German. She was dissolving completely in Gleb and wanted to see reciprocal movement as well. Katya's condition was accepted enthusiastically. Gleb very much wanted to learn German, which for him consisted at the time of about thirty words and expressions he'd heard from Katya. And the teaching method proved effective; never before had he memorized vocabulary so quickly. Katya built her teaching method on the principle of agglutination. First she used the verbal material presented by the bathroom, including the names for the parts of the human body. After the bathroom came the hallway and kitchen, then the dining room, bedroom, library (including the names of the birds), and the professor's study. The professor's wife's study was the library, which allowed them to repeat yet again the book and ornithological lexicon. The question of why the professor's working conditions were better gave them the chance to touch upon the problem of gender equality. Further topics were their building, Bolshaya Pushkarskaya Street and the stores on it, the city, and the Land of the Soviets. Thus, while regulating the hot and cold water (the pressure in the pipes was constantly changing), Gleb and Katya reached the international level, where the topic was primarily Russo-German ties, which the couple were strengthening by all available means. Here ended the course in the oral study of Germany, which clinched Gleb's fine German pronunciation once and for all. Meanwhile, it had become obvious that the beautiful-sounding words were wholly absent for him in their written guise. In this German course, the eye had clearly lost out to the ear. Inasmuch as reading and writing in the tub was inconvenient,

Katya and Gleb moved their grammar exercises to the evening and the table in the library. That left only conversational topics for their morning bath – for Gleb, especially precious.

DECEMBER 31, 2013, PETERSBURG

Katya and I land at Pulkovo Airport. A Petersburg blizzard greets us. The car speeds toward town, leaving snowy vortexes in its wake. I feel Katya's look.

"Maybe now you'll tell me where we're going? Okay?"

I turn. The expression on her face: *Where we were happy.* I answer: "We're going where we were . . . where we were, in short."

Katya laces her fingers through mine.

"You know, Gleb, I tried to call our old dormitory. It was razed. And built all over again afterward, but it's something different now."

"You've managed to do a lot, Katya."

"It's just that we began thinking alike long ago. I immediately realized where you wanted to take me, you see. I'm thinking, you know: there is no dormitory in that building anymore. It was moved to Peterhof."

"I know."

"There are elite apartments for sale, and they're impossible to rent – even for a star like you. Imagine! When I called the sellers on your behalf they were very cool."

"We'll get even."

Katya holds the pause.

"Are you saying you actually rented an apartment there?"

"No, Katya. I bought it."

The concierge meets the car as it pulls up. He takes our suitcases and carries them to the elevator. In the lobby are representatives of the municipal authorities in an excited mood. Flowers, a bucket of champagne. French, I note, two bottles: the Novgorod students are back on their feet. Welcome home (a firm civic handshake). Happy New Year (embraces). Happy New Home, I joke, and everyone laughs.

The apartment has four rooms, magnificently decorated, and windows on the Neva. It bears little or no resemblance to the dorm rooms we once came to live in. Katya compares our apartment to the halls of the Hermitage spread out on the opposite bank of the Neva. I make a face (an expression of slight disbelief) and openly express my disagreement.

I think the main difference from the Hermitage is that the choice of furniture is more ascetic. Three rooms are empty, and the fourth (the living room) has two iron beds, two nightstands, two desks, a bookshelf, and a refrigerator into which I immediately put the gifted bottles. Hanging on the wall is an ebonite radio – almost identical to the one thirty years ago. Katya turns it on, and a song plays, "Oh Field, Dear Field." I press one of the buttons. A disc slides out: the radio is a CD player.

"I haven't heard Soviet songs in such a long time. And the choruses . . ."

"The Red Army Chorus," I respond. "Crème de la crème."

I pull Katya to me and touch my lips to her forehead.

"Thirty years ago, you kissed me on the lips."

"I couldn't bring myself to right away. Don't you remember?"

Katya does remember. She goes over to the bookshelf and picks a book at random. Bakhtin. *Problems of Dostoevsky's Poetics.*

"Your polyphony is here too. You didn't do so badly with that."

"Now I can pick up where I left off."

Katya puts the book on the shelf.

"Why not?"

Through the window, the Hermitage lighting blazes up. The blizzard blurs its outlines, and the window turns into a painting. Now the Impressionists are exhibited on both sides of the Neva: on the third floor of the Hermitage, and on the fourth here.

At about ten o'clock, there's a ring at the door. Two waiters accompanied by the concierge bring in baskets with New Year's refreshments. Without the slightest hint of surprise, they spread a tablecloth on the desks moved together and light the candles. From the baskets they extract pickles and tomatoes, mushrooms and ramson. Black caviar. A small, toy-size suckling pig on an oval platter. The rest is left unwrapped for now. Biting her index finger, Katya follows what is happening.

"And where is the Olivier salad? Where are the mandarins?"

As if on command, something peeks out in foil, under the foil: a salad bowl with the Olivier. Mandarins are heaped into a bowl brought in.

"Now everything reminds me of New Year's in the dorm." Katya's eyes shine. "Especially the black caviar and suckling pig."

At eleven, they bring a package wrapped with a ribbon and give it to Katya. Untying the ribbon, she unseals it: it's a dress. Exactly the same as then, light and translucent. Katya silently buries her face in the dress.

"I have to spill something," I explain.

Katya puts on the dress.

"I don't understand how you guessed the size. You don't even know your own."

"Geraldina helped me."

At five minutes before midnight, the standard Brezhnev smacking comes from the speaker, accompanied by a New Year's greeting. I don't think Brezhnev was still smacking in 1983, so most likely they've presented a recording of the 1981 version. An anachronism.

I pour champagne into aluminum mugs, and we celebrate the thirty years gone by. With the last peal of the bells, we drink to another thirty years. Katya expresses the hope that the matter won't be limited to thirty years. I nod silently. At a quarter past one, Katya's dress has champagne spilled on it with the greatest care. Like it or not, she has to take it off. We push the beds together. The night is no less incandescent than what happened here thirty years ago. Almost.

1985–1986

For Gleb and Katya, life in the ornithological apartment was like hovering freely over the everyday. Ever since, thoughts of good fortune have been connected in Gleb's mind with birds, especially stuffed ones. Their stay on Bolshaya Pushkarskaya lasted two years instead of one: the professor's contract with the Berlin university was extended a year. After the first year, the couple came home for a month, and for that time the young couple decamped to the dorm. Katya's things stayed at the ornithologists', but they decided to remove Gleb's. It wasn't quite clear how the apartment's owners would feel about Gleb's presence, and Katya's parents even more so. Or rather, Katya was well aware of their attitude. They hadn't wanted to let her go to the USSR, having a presentiment that their daughter would find herself a Russian husband there. Katya was forced to agree that her parents' presentiment had not misled them. She had gone to the USSR, she reasoned in her morning bath, and found a Russian husband. No need to tell them the good news before she had to. Her Russian husband maintained a diplomatic silence. He didn't try to clarify why being a Russian husband was so bad. Most of his country's women had precisely that kind of husband, and you can't say that distressed them particularly. The answer to Katya's parents' prejudice was Gleb's study of German, which he pursued with doubled effort. On the other side of the border, though, they had their own prejudice with regard to the German Katarina Gärtner and her relationship with Soviet citizen Gleb Yanovsky. Acting in loco parentis here was the university's Young Communist organization, whose obligation it was, according to its charter, to know who was sleeping with whom. The organization summoned Gleb to a meeting. When Gleb received the invitation, he decided to consult with Dunya, whose liaisons had been primarily international. Without hesitation, Dunya suggested that Gleb accuse the bureau of "political myopia." He had come across this phrase once in a history of the Communist Party textbook and had immediately decided it would come in handy. Finding the expression effective, Dunya repeated it on every suitable occasion, and sometimes without any occasion. He showed Gleb how to say it: sternly and a little bit pensively. Maybe even with a squint – myopia and all that. Dunya also took a shine to the expression "vestige of Zinovievism," but in this case (Dunya looked at Gleb dubiously) that seemed less appropriate. At the meeting, it was brought to Young Communist Yanovsky's knowledge that his behavior was amoral and that he must immediately separate from the GDR citizen. In response, Gleb stated that he would not part from Katarina inasmuch as they intended to marry. Looking into the eyes of the bespectacled presiding officer (behind those thick lenses they were comically small), he accused those present of political myopia just in case. After these words, silence fell. Strictly speaking, the Young Communist organization was opposed to international marriages, even with representatives from socialist countries. Such marriages invariably ended with the Young Communists going abroad. Those who left were fainthearted enough to prefer their ties with foreign citizens to their ties with their native organization. But the case of Gleb and Katya seemed ambiguous. The determination Gleb had shown made the bureau members hesitate. That determination threatened a scandal, and a scandal was undesirable – and ultimately, Katya was inside the socialist camp. Overzealous insistence on their part might be viewed as deafness to the ideal of internationalism, a deafness that led, as should be expected, to political myopia. An unreassuring diagnosis. Gleb (as if Dunya had foreseen it) had made an ineradicable impression on them. There was in it something unbecoming, intellectual, uncharacteristic for a genuine Young Communist. In his confusion, the presiding officer removed his glasses, but even this decision was not distinguished for its farsightedness. His short-sighted, helpless look became in the eyes of those gathered the most vivid illustration of myopia. Its apotheosis, you might say. The energy of angry condemnation dried up instantly; he had no strength left for even a formal reprimand. In view of current circumstances, the Young Communist could only be given a fatherly scolding. On the way home, Gleb bought a bottle of wine and proposed to Katya that very evening. Katya burst into tears and said yes. These were tears of hurt as well as joy. It turned out she'd been waiting for his proposal for a long time and didn't understand why it had taken so long to be made. Gleb himself didn't understand either. Maybe he was afraid of jinxing the infinite happiness that had come into his life with Katya. A few months later (not without some trouble), they were married at one of Leningrad's registry offices. Arriving in sweaters and jeans, they asked the officiant not to say anything. "From our point of view, it's fairly unceremonious," Gleb said into Katya's ear. "Exactly so" the officiant, who had excellent hearing, confirmed. After that she maintained silence. She indicated where to sign with a pointer. "Why didn't you propose a wedding?" Katya asked once, having realized she had to clarify everything for herself. "Because we belong to different churches," Gleb answered. A few days later, Katya told him she'd decided to convert to Orthodoxy. "I don't want us to end up in different places after we die," she said firmly. This time Gleb teared up. This was what he hadn't been able to bring himself to ask. A month later, the prayer blessing her conversion was read over Katya, who had learned the Orthodox symbol of faith. One letter was changed in her name: Katarina became Katerina. This took place in Prince Vladimir Cathedral, which Katya and Gleb attended on Sundays. Their wedding later took place in the same church. They sensibly did not invite guests. The Young Communist organization, which had done so much to bring about their marriage, would never have forgiven a wedding. At another meeting of the organization, even "vestige of Zinovievism," the most biting definition from his collection, wouldn't have helped, in Dunya's opinion. It should be said that the wedding would not have happened without his support. As an Orthodox Bulgarian, he and a young woman by the name of Alexandra had participated in the mystery as witnesses. Dunya and Alexandra were taller than Gleb and Katya, which came in very handy when they had to hold the crowns over the couple's heads. At the end of the service, Alexandra complained that the crown was heavy and that if she'd had to hold her arm high (which she didn't), she might not have lasted to the end. She also supposed that if Gleb and Katya ever had to hold the crowns, say, over her and Dunya, they'd never be up to the task. At these words, everyone looked at Dunya, but his eyes locked on the dial of his watch. Dunya was the soul of concentration, as if time had stopped on his watch or, for all anyone knew, started going backward. In a certain sense, that was true: all Dunya's romances repeated each other and ended in a conversation about marriage. As for the young woman, nothing was known about her besides her name, and neither Gleb nor Katya had ever seen her before. Nor did they in the future. Katya tried to picture the height of those who would hold crowns over Dunya and his girlfriend. Alexandra's disappearance attested to the fact that no such people were ever found. Actually, before her disappearance, she managed to stop in at the Brigantina with the newlyweds and celebrate the event among a select few. Naturally, Dunya was there too. And so in his life was everything desperately repeated: once again he was toastmaster and once again he fell asleep in an awkward pose, although this time he did not have to talk about Leninist intrigues. Gleb and Katya recalled this pose a few years later when they learned of Dunya's tragic death in Sofia. After returning to his homeland, he finally married and had a son. In a difficult period, when the threat of famine arose in Bulgaria (as in Russia), Dunya showed himself to be a loving father. The child needed milk, and people got in line for it in the middle of the night. Every night, Dunya started up his rickety old Zhiguli and drove to the milk store. And returned in the morning. One of those nights, he drove into a trailer hauling pipes. The taillights were out on the trailer, there wasn't even a flag on the pipes, and Dunya didn't notice the pipes. People said he lay with his head on the steering wheel, sprinkled with shards from the windshield – more or less the same pose as on the celebration table once upon a time. Katya and Gleb mourned him terribly and could not imagine Dunya dead.

JANUARY 2, 2014, PETERSBURG

Katya and I are on our way to see the Avdeyevas. Katya has already called Anna; they're expecting us. Turning off Nevsky onto Pushkinskaya Street, the car stops at a building. The lobby is dim. The apartment doors are amazingly varied. A true gallery of doors – from armored to flimsy plywood, some with holes from old locks. Like the Avdeyevas'.

Anna opens up. Shapeless, ungroomed, mother-of-pearl lips taking up half her face. Fear – mixed with coquetry – in her eyes. She asks whether she's changed a lot. Oh no, not a lot – and I squeeze out a smile. Consider yourself unchanged. I try not to look at her. To think I'd once been in love with this dumpy old woman. Anna leads us into the living room. A girl comes out of the next room. Pale. Very thin. She smiles nicely.

"Vera" – and she holds out her translucent hand.

She looks like Anna as a child, but without her vulgarity. Light brown hair with subdued features. Strange though it seems, in this she reminds me of my mother.

"We're recuperating after the latest hospital stay," Anna says. "We're terribly tired."

The living room is spacious but neglected. A high ceiling, cracked molding. In the corner, where the piano is, the wallpaper has separated noticeably from the wall. In the corner, naturally. Where else? He'd known that before he ever met Anna. An aquarium next to the piano. Two bookshelves from the 1950s with glass doors covering the books. The windows are unwashed. Anna catches my gaze.

"With all I've had to do, I haven't gotten around to cleaning."

I nod. It's obvious that Anna hadn't gotten around to it for much longer than that.

She invites us all to the table. Olivier, vodka, and Sovetskoye champagne. Mandarins at the edge of the table. Katya must be asking herself whether they've been initiated here into my retroplan – that's the expression on her face. Sometimes Katya jokes with herself.

Picking up a fork, I feel a slight stickiness. So that Anna doesn't notice, I wipe the fork on the slightly used napkin. I catch Vera's distraught look. I feel an awkwardness but to an even greater degree a sympathy for the girl, who (this is immediately evident) is not made at all like her mother. I'm just about to say I'm not hungry, but Vera's look stops me. I serve myself some Olivier salad, which bodes nothing good for my stomach. I have no doubt the Olivier is made the same way the forks are washed. The glasses too. I notice dried soap spots on mine. While I'm talking with Anna, Vera quickly exchanges her glass for mine. Red drops appear on the tablecloth. I'm still contemplating their source while Katya is already taking Vera to the bathroom. The girl has a nosebleed. Anna takes cotton balls out of the cupboard and joins them.

A few minutes later, everyone returns. There's cotton in Vera's nostrils. Her forehead is wet from the towel on it. I think that Vera is worse, much worse off than I am, only she's being stoic and I'm not. Suddenly I want to hold this child close and breathe life into her. That's how you pull a person out of any pit. You can scramble out yourself too. It all depends on strength of will.

"Excuse the meagerness." Anna points to the table, and this gesture seems habitual. "Were my parents alive, it would all look quite different. Everything now goes to treatment."

"Mama."

"This is life, daughter dear, nothing to be embarrassed about."

I make a sign to Katya, and she puts a miniature leather case on the table. I hand it to Anna.

"I hope you won't object if we help out a little?"

Glancing at Vera, Anna sighs.

"No, I won't. I don't have the option to object." She comes over to Katya and me and hugs us in turn. "Gleb means everything to little Vera. She listens to him all the time. And the fact that he and I studied together. . . . After all, she herself plays the piano. Right, Vera dear? She's performed in London, Helsinki, and Prague. She's won prizes in Moscow."

"Please, don't, listen to me . . ."

Vera's face is sad and drawn somehow. Katya squats next to Vera's chair. She takes her hand and presses it to her cheek.

"Will you play? Please."

Vera looks at me.

"In front of Gleb Fyodorovich?"

"Gleb Fyodorovich" – Katya turns around – "you'll support us in some way, won't you?"

I walk over and squat next to Katya. Right now my wife and I probably look like a pair of large birds. Or something similar. Stuffed birds, for example.

"You have no idea how badly I played as a child. And that was okay; I wasn't afraid. Whereas you play brilliantly, I think."

"I don't know what you mean by badly." Vera looks into my eyes seriously. "The whole world listens to you."

"It's just they've grown used to it." Anna makes a sound of protest, but I return to Katya's request. "What are we going to listen to?"

Vera turns away and takes the cotton out of her nose and wants to stick it into her dress pocket. Katya cuts her off with a quick movement. Puts it in her purse. Vera's brief glance at Katya. The girl sits down at the piano. Fingers on keys, seconds of concentration.

We hear the first chords of Albinoni's Adagio. I stand up, lean my elbows on the piano, and watch Vera. I notice my right hand trembling and change pose. I'd expected a schoolgirl's music-making, but Vera's technique is magnificent, no doubt about it. I contemplate words of praise. The tone I'd adopted now seems idiotic to me. Vera is essentially an adult. Her music speaks to that. Her face. Played a thousand times, the well-traveled piece is performed as if for the first time. There is no affectation in Vera's playing: you can tell she understands what she's playing about. And whom.

I worry she may decide to strengthen the impression and be ashamed of her performance's simplicity. That she'll start embellishing music that should be only simple. No, she hovers at the maximum height. At a point where the musical pattern changes, my voice rings out. Vera doesn't look up, as if she'd been expecting it.

And I experience the uplift I'd lost the habit of. A perfect confluence in music.

I wish I could dial up Brisbane and let my mother listen. To console her a little, maybe. I'd say, look, there's music in my life again, and this is happiness. On the other hand, it's a sadness, too, inasmuch as this perfect music will also come to an end. And then my mother (don't I know her?) will object that something perfect never ends, it simply transforms into something else. Not necessarily music – a word, a landscape, a gesture. Aren't there many perfect things in the world? Finally, into silence, inasmuch as silence alone possesses complete perfection. Actually, I would call for the sake of that explanation. But it's awkward. Awkward in front of everyone.

1986

This was Gleb's final university year. He wrote his thesis on polyphony, the topic he'd started studying once upon a time under Ivan Alexeyevich. By now, Ivan Alexeyevich was no longer at the university: fired for drunkenness. Actually, people said that wasn't the sole reason. According to people in the know, his firing was to a much greater extent provoked by the teacher's anti-Soviet statements. Indeed, Ivan Alexeyevich had no love for Soviet power and spoke out hostilely against it. Alcohol's role in this story consisted in the fact that the teacher's statements became increasingly frank and, what was even worse, public. At times, his criticism had no logic to it. He reproached Brezhnev's nearly twenty-year rule for endlessness and condemned the leadership of the quickly dead Andropov and Chernenko for brevity. To a wall-newspaper report about how General Secretary Chernenko had taken over the governing of the country, Ivan Alexeyevich, who had also had time to take something on, added in red marker: "without regaining consciousness." The newspaper was taken down, and the annotation's author wasn't found, although he had borrowed the marker from the dean's office. His passion for alcohol and women notwithstanding (or, rather, because of it), Ivan Alexeyevich was a great favorite. For a while, a blind eye was turned to his comments on the "half-lit Politburo" and the "zombies on the mausoleum tribune." When it reached the point of the mausoleum, the higher-ups' patience ran out. To avoid a scandal, they suggested to Ivan Alexeyevich that he resign at his own wish, to which he replied that he felt no such wish. Then they fired him for violating teacher ethics. And aesthetics, too, the dean told Ivan Alexeyevich, pointing to his wine-stained tie. Neither Lenin nor Chernenko, who had died by then, figured in the directive. It was decided not to mention the deceased, considering the character of Ivan Alexeyevich's statements. Gleb was assigned another supervisor, eighty-year-old Professor Besedin. The professor didn't invite his charge into a world of nocturnal escapades, although for all his memory problems, he may well have had memories of his own. With every year lived, the past presented itself to him more and more like something preposterous and unrelated to him directly. His one companion was his carved cane; they seemed created for each other. His knobby fingers entwined its knob like roots, making obvious the striking similarity between the professor and his cane – in design, color, and material. Polyphony aroused no protest in him, but no particular delight either. He would have preferred Gleb write a thesis based on textological methods and even proposed a few topics. Gleb was able to stand his ground, though. Actually, he didn't need to insist. In the interest of his blood pressure, Besedin had long since stopped getting into debates. "Polyphony is just fine," he said curtly. "The main thing, young man, is one's health." Watching a female student walk by, the professor added nostalgically, "Oh, where are my seventy-five . . ." Gleb was left to his own devices and quite calmly finished the research that had engendered such heated discussions with his former advisor. At his thesis defense, he first thanked the rebellious Ivan Alexeyevich. Gleb was vaguely concerned about a possible speech by Dean Chukin, polyphony's most virulent enemy. The sole person capable of countering with arguments was no longer working at the university. Taking advantage of Ivan Alexeyevich's absence, Chukin did in fact speak. When at the discussion he stood up and said that he disputed everything the work's author had said, the hall exhaled. Katya, sitting in the first row, turned white. In the ensuing silence, Professor Besedin's voice rang out, unexpectedly loud and imperious: "I do not think we are going to argue." "And why is that?" Chukin inquired ironically, "if you bear in mind that truth is born in argument." "Truth is not born in argument," the professor interrupted him. "Aggression is. And not only that, you, Chukin are not arguing with the stated theses but with your own phantoms." "I see, if you will allow –" (Chukin leaned hard on the second syllable). But Besedin did not allow. He didn't like arguments and he didn't like Chukin. He informed Chukin that the most shameful thing was to build a scholarly career on smearing great men. And even nongreat men – Besedin nodded toward Gleb standing at the rostrum. "Are you ill?" Chukin asked. The professor thought a moment, agreed, and said that at eighty that comes with the territory. In his opinion, Chukin was much more dangerously ill. This was followed immediately by his diagnosis: delusions of grandeur. Chukin turned bright red. You could tell he was preparing an extended and stern rebuke. His eyes filled with bitterness. "You're my former teacher. . . ." The audience started to get restless, but the professor calmed them with a gesture. "As your former teacher I'm telling you, Chukin, sit down. Sit down!" Chukin sat down. A minute later Chukin walked out to disapproving shouts. Gleb defended his thesis with the highest mark and a recommendation for graduate studies. To general astonishment, Gleb turned down graduate studies. Philological theories – even such a marvelous one as the theory of polyphony – interested him more in the practical dimension. In explaining his rejection, Gleb cited *Faust*, which for some reason came to him in Ukrainian: *Theory is always gray, my friend, and the tree of life golden.* Goethe in Ukrainian made a great impression on those present – much greater than had it been said, say, in German. It was obvious to everyone that it was pointless trying to change his mind in this situation. Gleb himself did not doubt his decision. The result of five years of study had for him been the realization that scholarship was not his path. What was his path was rather vague. The biographical literature about Gleb Yanovsky usually asserts that this was the second path Gleb rejected. It is believed that the first such path was music. It's noteworthy that the research subject disagrees with that interpretation. He thinks that his years of separation from music played the deciding role in him becoming a musician. Those years kept him from getting habituated to his own playing. All those years he kept hearing heavenly music without experiencing any attachment to its earthly embodiment, which is always imperfect. Not only that, he once said, the main thing music lacks is silence. Music can only exist in harmony with silence. Without a pause a sound is incomplete, as is speech without silence. Gleb's musical pause lasted for many years, but it was only a pause. For his understanding of music, they proved more important than years and years of playing.

January 7, 2014, Petersburg

By Orthodox Christmas, they bring some furniture to our Petersburg apartment, and, moreover, a keyboard synthesizer. Our home should have a musical instrument, but that instrument cannot be a guitar. Why it was a synthesizer that was ordered neither I nor Katya know exactly, just as we don't know why the apartment was bought, apart from celebrating New Year's. Truly for celebrating, apparently, since we don't intend to live in it. Or maybe we do, Katya speculates, we just aren't admitting it to ourselves. We have no particular business in Munich now. Nor do we in Petersburg, actually.

Anna and Vera are coming over for Christmas. Anna never ceases to thank us for the gift of money. Now she can buy the high-quality food Vera so needs. When it comes to food, she finds perfect understanding in the persons of Katya and me. The dishes for our Christmas dinner have been ordered from a health food restaurant.

Raising her toast, Katya suggests we all switch to the familiar "you." Anna nods, pointing out that she and Gleb did that long ago. To Katya, her lips look more vivid than before. Katya says that Vera should set aside her formal "you," too. The girl is embarrassed, but Katya explains to her that otherwise we won't have equality. Otherwise I, too, would have to use the formal "you" with her. Vera promises not to use the formal "you" and drinks (fruit drink in her glass) with everyone. Something tells her the toast has been made for her sake.

Everyone gets up from the table and goes into the next room, where the synthesizer has been set up. Vera is unfamiliar with this thing, and she listens closely to my explanations. She tries to play it and likes it. Anna asks Katya about our Munich life. She listens with pleasure, not denying herself the thought (of this I'm nearly certain) that it might have been her in Katya's place. Anyway, Katya has a documentary film about our life by Munich television. Anna shows the liveliest interest in the film, and they go to watch it on the computer.

Vera's fingers feel as confident on the synthesizer as on the piano. After playing another melody, she breaks away from the keyboard.

"Do you play the piano?" she asks me.

"No. All I know is you should hold your hand like a little house."

I demonstrate my knowledge on the keyboard. Vera gives my hand the correct shape:

"Like this."

"Now I'm going to tell everyone you set my hand." I sit in the creaking rocking chair, brought this morning. "But why did you play Albinoni then?"

With one hand, Vera plays the Adagio's first measures.

"Because I'm afraid of dying."

"Anna said your therapy went very well." I look into the girl's calm face.

"Well. But not very. She just doesn't know it. The doctors told me I can expect anything."

I catch myself rocking harder in the chair. I fall still.

"Wait a minute. Why doesn't she know?"

"I asked them not to tell her anything. She has . . . Basically, once a year she gets admitted to a psych hospital. If they tell her the truth, that will be the end of her. She's failed so badly over my illness." After a silence, Vera looks up. "But where's your guitar? Show me?"

I spread my arms.

"No guitar."

"A rest?"

"You might say that. I have Parkinson's and can't play anymore."

Vera comes over to me and takes my hands in hers.

"Is this the disease that makes your hands shake?"

"Shake and move poorly, especially the fingers."

She examines my fingers. Bends them cautiously.

"When will you be able to play again?"

"Never." I wink. "You and I are trading secrets, right?"

She grazes my fingers with her lips.

"Does your secret scare you?"

"Yes."

"Don't you have anything besides music?"

"This isn't just about music. In a while I'll become helpless. And that frightens me."

Vera returns to the synthesizer and picks out a few notes. She looks at the frozen Neva.

"When are you and Katya leaving?"

"In a week."

We hear Anna and Katya's steps in the hall.

"So soon . . ."

1986–1987

The end of university gave rise to three urgent questions simultaneously in Gleb's life. The first – and most important for Gleb – had to do with the fact that the ornithologists had returned to their apartment, and the young couple had to find themselves new housing. The second involved the feudal institution of the residency permit. Gleb's temporary residency permit in Leningrad ended with his studies, and he did not have the right to a permanent one. Finally, the third question he had to resolve was work: in the USSR, the right to work was the strictest obligation. What made these questions so difficult was the fact that they were indissolubly linked. That tight knot could not be undone. It could only be cut, but the line of dissection, unfortunately, lay between him and Katya. In order to stay in Leningrad with her, Gleb needed to have a residency permit, if only a temporary one. Without that he couldn't get a job, and that meant he had no money to rent housing with, which, by the way, he couldn't have done even if he had money. They refused to give him a permit on the basis of his marriage to Katya because Katya was a foreigner. As in the case of his thesis defense, help came unexpectedly from Professor Besedin, who called someone on the municipal executive committee – a former student, it turned out – and asked him for a residency permit for Gleb. The permit was issued immediately. Another student of Besedin's, the dean of the Philology School, directed a separate room be given to Gleb and Katya in the dormitory and saw to his graduate getting a job in a Leningrad high school. Gleb was left with the impression that the city was made up of the professor's students. When Gleb shared this observation with him, Besedin clapped him on the shoulder, modestly noting that he was not equally pleased with all his students. In August, what Gleb had long feared happened: his grandmother died. In June, after his studies ended, he and Katya had flown briefly to Kyiv. Katya wanted to meet all of Gleb's family. She didn't manage all of them (Fyodor and his family were in the country), but Katya did meet Gleb's mama and grandmother. Once, when Katya and Irina had gone out on errands, Antonina Pavlovna suddenly said, "I'm going to die soon." Gleb knew she was not one to cast words on the wind, but he was at a loss for a reply. His grandmother – so it seemed to him – was waiting for a response, but what could he say? Gleb was also silent because a lump had come to his throat. He realized it had been said in all seriousness. His grandmother had changed greatly, withered, become all white and even immaterial. She wasn't Antonina Pavlovna anymore, she was his grandmother. On their day of departure, she told Gleb and Katya again, "I'm going to die soon." This time Gleb replied with forced equanimity: "Everyone's going to die. I'm going to die too." His grandmother looked at him sadly and said, "But, you see, I will before you." At the time he thought this intentional rudeness would shake her up and not let her become listless. Later he realized he'd made a cruel mistake. He never forgave himself that sentence. For the first time in her life, his grandmother had asked him for support – in what is probably the hardest thing. And he had left her alone with death. He flew to Kyiv for the funeral alone; Katya was in Berlin at the time. His grandmother's funeral was held in St.

Vladimir's Cathedral. The priest prompted the young deacon on the texts of the prayers, so it was like a funeral training. Gleb felt something vague and dark, which he later recognized as a presentiment of disaster. The problem wasn't the deacon, of course. To Gleb it felt as if the floor was rocking, and the Vasnetsov fresco he'd known since childhood was leaving the walls, as if fleeing impending changes. A dragon freed itself first from some dark spot, declared it was taking the church under its wing, and circled through the cathedral space, gallant and fire-breathing. The candle flames swayed in horror at the airstreams driving them, the garments of those standing by the coffin fluttered, and sparks flew over the vestments of those conducting the funeral. Only his grandmother maintained her self-possession. Her look calmed and inspired optimism in everyone present. Two days later, Gleb flew to Petersburg. Irina saw him off at the airport. Sitting in the Boryspil Café, she told him that Cook had proposed to her long ago, but she hadn't been able to accept, naturally, while she was looking after his grandmother. Last night she'd called Cook and said yes. This didn't mean she was going to Australia immediately. There were lots of routine issues to be settled. But she had set her course. Irina spoke without expression, as if embarrassed. Not knowing, possibly, what her son would think of this, although it was clear what he would. Gleb congratulated her and proposed a toast to Irina and Cook. "That sounds good," Irina approved. It was worth marrying him just for that. And then Gleb saw how happy she was. She told him about Brisbane's subtropical parks and constant rain, about the Aborigines and convicts. What was most interesting (Irina ordered another glass of wine) was that Cook was a descendant of an English convict – and he was also her fiancé. Gleb nearly missed his flight. On the plane, he thought about his grandmother. Pressing his nose to the window, he stared at the clouds. Eventually he saw her. She was winding her way, hunched over, up a sloping cloud. Life beyond the clouds reminded him of ordinary life in a way: buildings, trees, animals. Everything, including his grandmother, was made of something white, flying, moist. His grandmother was walking toward a big cloud-house where she was evidently awaited. She was holding her shopping bag, although she hadn't really done any housekeeping for a long time. One day she didn't make it all the way to the grocery store (she was helped getting back) – and she never went out again. Only to the courtyard. Since then, the store had been the job of Irina, who did whatever was required to take care of her mother. His grandmother understood everything, of course. The two people closest to her were starting lives of their own, and there was no room for her in either of those lives. So she died.

January 13, 2014, Petersburg

Katya and I are having breakfast in our Petersburg apartment. The microwave with our rolls pings. Katya's mobile echoes a response.

"A text from Vera. She asks whether we can stay a few days more." Katya puts the rolls on plates. "Why don't you say something?"

"It's not easy for the girl."

A call from Nestor interrupts me. Tomorrow he's planning to go with us to the airport. When should he come? I promise to tell him this evening. I put the phone on the table.

Katya pushes the phone toward me with her teaspoon.

"Call Geraldina and say we're detained?"

"Geraldina will lose her mind."

"If anyone's lost her mind, it's Anna. When we were sitting together – you know, at the computer . . . at first I wasn't going to tell you." Katya stirs the sugar in her coffee. "She described your adventure to me."

"Adventure's a good word for it."

"In every detail, by the way. I got the impression she wouldn't mind repeating it."

"Anna is truly ill. She's on the books at a psych hospital."

"I'm not surprised. . . . And a child is fighting for her life under these conditions." Standing, Katya abruptly pushes her chair back. "I'm going to call Vera."

I shrug.

"What are you going to tell her, Katya darling? That we're going to take her mother's place? Let's think this through."

But Katya's already calling. She puts the phone on speaker. Vera answers a little sleepily. Yes, she sent a text. Anna had a breakdown last night. Vera's voice is drowned out by the kettle's whistle. What kind of breakdown? Nervous. They took Anna to the hospital. Katya looks around at me. She tells the girl we're on our way.

Half an hour later, we're with Vera. Katya doesn't know how an apartment looks after a nervous breakdown and looks cautiously from side to side. All's well, apparently. No, it isn't. Katya's glance falls on a crack in the aquarium wall. It wasn't there the last time. She would have noticed. Katya makes a decision she's not about to discuss with me now. She puts her arms around the girl and asks her to stay with us – until Anna's return. Katya speaks calmly but inwardly she's upset.

Vera needs time to collect her things. An old duffle gets packed with clothing, books, cassettes. . . . The aquarium. How can she leave the fish? Or leave them and come every day to feed them? It's my belief that the cracked glass could break at any moment, so the water should be drained. While Vera is collecting everything she needs, I fill two three-liter jars with aquarium water and start transferring the fish into them.

From time to time Vera and Katya look to see how I'm handling the net.

"A virtuoso" – Katya can't help herself.

It's an unusual spectacle, but the audience thinks it's impolite to laugh. After moving the fish into the jars, I take the hose out of the base, plunge its wide end into the water, put my lips around the other end of the hose, and breathe in as hard as I can, which should bring the water with it – there's a bucket on the floor for it. Upending my notions of the movement of a liquid (I'd pictured it unhurried, like the Volga), the aquarium water ascends the pipe instantly. Before I can direct the stream into the bucket, it gushes into my mouth and soaks my face and clothing. Katya and Vera laugh loudly. After I spit the water into the bucket, so do I.

The first thing we do upon arrival at the Mytninskaya Embankment is search the Internet for a new aquarium. Vera chooses it with the fishes' tacit approval. Katya calls the store and asks them to deliver the aquarium immediately. When she hears they can't deliver before the day after tomorrow, she hands me the phone.

They'll bring the aquarium in an hour – the display model, with a handsome stand to fit and a set of everything the store clerk believes to be dear to fishes' hearts. Katya and I fill it with water, bucket after bucket (fortunately, this does not require a hose). Vera pours sand into the aquarium and sets out the grottos. Last, the lamps, air compressor, filter, and heater are installed. Now the water has to settle.

Nestor and Nika arrive that evening. A man of his word, Nestor tries to confirm the time of our departure tomorrow as soon as he walks in, but his question goes unanswered. He doesn't give up and repeats the question a different way. When everyone sits down at the table, he raises his glass and wishes Katya and me a pleasant journey to Munich (by the way, what time are we leaving?). Katya stops him with a gesture, suggesting for starters that we drink to the Old New Year; she values this odd Russian holiday highly.

"You're leaving tomorrow?" Vera asks.

Her equanimity makes Katya feel bad. She strokes Vera's back.

"No, not tomorrow."

"Nestor is making his toasts for future use." I clap Nestor on the shoulder. "It's just he's writing a book in which we eventually have to go to Munich."

Nestor maintains his gravity.

"I was just trying to clarify exactly when. But of course not tomorrow." He casts an extended gaze over those sitting. "That would ruin the entire book."

1988–1989

Gleb and Katya lived in the dorm for another year. Katya continued her studies, and Gleb went to work as a teacher in a school on the Petrograd side. He awaited his first teaching day with a certain excitement. Ultimately, he'd been only a pupil his entire albeit brief life. Gleb's first months in the school did not disappoint him. He would go into the teacher's lounge like an adult, pick up his class journal, and head for class. He taught language and literature. Eyes that had not yet lost their childlike clarity and perhaps even trust were aimed at him. Shining through the readiness (tongue on upper lip) with which the children wrote down the words he pronounced was an unshakable confidence in the rightness of the world order, a part of which was he, Gleb, and his lessons. Out of an excess of zeal, his pupils constantly asked more questions and clarified points – and he liked that. Looking at them, Gleb thought that there was hardly a person in the world now whose words he would write down so wholeheartedly. Everything changed in the winter, when due to a colleague's illness his workload was increased and they had him teach an older class in addition. The questions – and most importantly, the eyes – were completely different there. When they asked questions, his new pupils would look away or, just the opposite, look without blinking, and this gaze (so it seemed to Gleb) held nothing but insolence. The questions were asked by the boys, but the girls laughed the loudest; they realized all the boys' efforts were made for their sake. In the class on *Crime and Punishment,* they asked Gleb why he was defending the criminal. Falling for the question, Gleb explained in detail why studying a murderer's psychology is never his vindication. From the other end of the classroom, someone immediately remarked that Gleb Fyodorovich knew this psychology suspiciously well. When the laughter died down, a sorrowful voice asked, "Have you ever killed anyone, Gleb Fyodorovich?" The question belonged to Kryuchkov, a tall, pimply lad from the back row. Realizing the time had come for action, Gleb asked him what Raskolnikov's patronymic was. The answer was given in the same mournful tone: Fyodorovich. The glee was universal, and his despondent "Sit down or fail" only raised the temperature. The answer was not only funny, it was heroic. At the next class, when the topic was Sonya Marmeladova, an inspired Kryuchkov again asked a question. Now that they'd clarified everything about murderers, he wondered whether Gleb Fyodorovich had studied the psychology of prostitutes. The other students responded with quiet laughter. As their English teacher would have said, this was a little *too much.* Gleb Fyodorovich looked at Kryuchkov, feeling pure hatred. "Are you trying to grandstand for the girls?" Gleb walked slowly toward the pupil. "You know, you'd better not do so at my expense." "Or else what?" Kryuchkov clarified with restraint. "Grandstand" had made an impression on him. Gleb slammed the volume of Dostoyevsky shut and brought it right up to Kryuchkov's eyes. "I want you to know that punishment follows a crime." With these words, Gleb moved on to the image of Marmeladov. At the end of class, as usual, he asked if there were questions. Kryuchkov raised his hand again. Gleb nodded dispassionately. "I have a question, Gleb Fyodorovich. Why do I need Russian literature?" The teacher came out from behind his desk and slowly headed toward the pupil. The class fell silent in anticipation of assault and battery, which seemed perfectly natural to everyone at this stage in their relations. Approaching Kryuchkov, Gleb said quietly: "*You* don't. It's obvious you're not going to be engaging in brain work, my friend. You're going to be a trained shitcleaner – you'll be good at replacing toilets. Your head will be filled with something completely different." The bell rang, and Gleb returned to his desk. Watching his pupils silently leave the classroom, he knew he was going to regret what he'd said. Kryuchkov was mortally offended and stopped talking to him. True, he didn't open his mouth in class anymore. Convinced that the novel's title was not empty words, all the rest quieted down too. But victory did not gladden Gleb, and school began to weigh on him. He realized that the tree of life was not at all like it's described in Goethe. Properly speaking, these were Mephistopheles' words. If you thought about it, that was who Professor Besedin had been opposing in trying to talk Gleb into going to grad school. Perhaps he'd been wrong not to go; now he could be dealing with dry theory and enjoying life. But it was too late to change anything. He'd signed on for this assignment and had to work in the school for three years, and soon after Gleb's defense, the professor died, unfortunately. After but not because of, Katya had joked morbidly at the time. Meanwhile, she too graduated. After some efforts by her husband (for the first time in his life he was pulling strings), she managed to get a job at Gleb's school as a German teacher. Now they had to find housing immediately because after graduation there could be no legitimate (and with Besedin's death, illegitimate) reason for staying in the dorm. They circled acceptable options in the classifieds, and in the evening, armed with two-kopek coins, they went to the telephone booth on the embankment and called around to apartment after apartment. The payphone swallowed their coins unconscionably without making a connection, but even worse was the fact that five minutes later people started pounding on the door. Then Gleb and Katya came up with a ruse. They would take turns going into the booth, like strangers, but this increased their talking time only a little. Soon after, they managed to rent an inexpensive one-room apartment in Rzhevka – a bedroom suburb that was very much Leningrad and had nothing to do with Petersburg. After a life lived in the center of the city, it took Gleb a long time to get used to the monotonous precast structures. Unseen giants kept setting them out with the indefatigability of domino players. Sometimes he thought he saw their gigantic calloused fingers, smelled their cheap cigarettes, and heard their pathetic domino jokes. The names of the Rzhevka avenues and streets seemed to Gleb like one of those jokes. Shockworkers Avenue. Preceptors Avenue. Pacesetters Street. Industrial Avenue. Their building was on Industrial. After a few months, the name no longer irritated them; they didn't notice it. The same thing would probably have happened with the shockworkers, pacesetters, and something even more hopeless. They easily came to feel at home in the world, that is, they made the world their own, filling its cracks with their love. Industrial Avenue became *their* avenue, and in it they found signs of architecture, their cramped apartment became *their* apartment; it got bigger and cozier. In old age, that quality fades. At a certain age you can't warm up your environment anymore. Old people freeze. They can't even warm up their own bodies.

January 20, 2014, Petersburg

Katya, Vera, and I are eating supper. Vera neatly places her knife and fork on the edge of the plate.

"I wanted to ask . . . Does your driver really have to take me back and forth to school?"

"Since we've hired a driver, he has to drive someone." I pour juice into glasses. "We barely go anywhere now. The boy's going to lose proficiency."

"I'm being serious. Everyone in class already knows it. It's kind of . . . well, it's sort of embarrassing."

Katya fixes the bang that's fallen on Vera's face.

"If they know that in class, that means they also know it's all a matter of medicine, not that, what do you call it . . . ?"

"Braggadocio?" Vera guesses.

"That's it. Braggadocio. Almost sounds Italian." Katya kisses her forehead.

"I tried to visit Anna today," I say. "They wouldn't let me in. They said it's still too soon. Especially for you, that is, me. I didn't quite understand what that meant."

Katya looks at Vera. Vera looks down.

"Well, you see, mama lit a fire there."

"Lit a fire . . ." Katya repeats thoughtfully. "Was it *she* who broke the aquarium?"

"Yes, with a flower pot. She threw it at me, but missed."

"Why?"

"She said I was trying to take Gleb away from her." Vera covers her face with her hands, and her voice sounds like an announcement on a trolleybus. "She said Gleb was crazy about her and I was standing in their way. She told me about how she and Gleb . . ."

"Vera dear" – I hold out a handkerchief to her. "Let's play something."

Katya's phone rings.

"Ja, hallo. . . ."

Vera and I go into the next room with the synthesizer. Vera sits down at the instrument and runs her hands over the keyboard. I cautiously play a chord in the same key. My fingers tremble noticeably.

"My little house is teetering." I play another chord. "It's threatening to collapse."

Vera puts her hand on top of mine.

"I'll hold your hand until it gets better, okay?"

"I'm afraid you'll be holding it for a long time."

She turns my hand palm up, like a fortuneteller, and looks intently.

"Your hand just has to get better. Otherwise where's the justice? Your fingers played such a tremolo, and now they have trouble with a knife. I was watching you at dinner." She squeezed my hand. "I wish I could reanimate your fingers because right now they're like some kind of mechanism."

"A mechanism for scooping up prizes." I carefully free my hand. "What prize do you want?"

Vera thinks about that.

"I played Albinoni for you, and you joined in at the end. Maybe we can try it now from the very beginning?"

I puff out my cheeks and close my eyes tight. She plays a few notes from the Adagio.

"Don't you like this music?"

"Of course I do! It's just I've been prescribed to make faces. Doctor's orders, by the way."

"That's great. How about the music?"

"I'm not going to lie. It's dismal."

"When you performed, it was like . . ." Vera makes a half-turn on the swivel chair. "Well, it's like you're riding along in a car and suddenly it takes off. Can you imagine a good car taking off? A Mercedes, say?"

"Easily. Even a Zhiguli. If someone gave it wings."

Vera presses her hand to my lips.

"You were those wings! Let's try one more time."

"Aye aye!" I switch the synthesizer setting. "Organ?"

"Organ." She tries the unusual-sounding keys. "And your voice."

After the intro measures, I come in with the theme. Against the organ background, my voice sounds better than I'd expected. The harshness on the upper notes is balanced out by the velvet on the lower ones. From the vocal standpoint, it's totally wrong, starting with the sound production. Katya listens to us on the threshold holding her mobile. Her face, a mirror, breathes tragedy. Her eyes are wide open, her nostrils are trembling, and with her this means more than tears. When the last note of the Adagio dies down, she silently embraces us – first Vera, then me.

"Mayer just called. He's come around to your duet. I pitched the idea to him a few days ago, but he had his doubts. Now he's prepared to produce it, though, and he's asking what we're going to sing. The Adagio!"

I look at Katya through an imaginary lorgnette.

"And that's all?"

"No, it's not. You and Vera prepare the repertoire, and Mayer organizes the tour. This will pull both of you out of your mire. Vera is still young, of course, but that's where her strength lies."

"Where does mine then?" I wonder. "I'm not young, after all."

"In the fact that you're such a smokin' old dude. Who, no matter what he does on stage, people will still come to see. My girl, do you agree?"

Does she agree? My girl. She nods a few times and blushes so that her entire childish essence comes through.

"Tomorrow I'll tell Mayer you agree." Katya tweaks my ear. "You agree, right? I'll tell him about the Albinoni at the same time."

"People say Albinoni didn't write the Adagio," Vera informs us. "That it was someone else."

Katya shapes her hands like a megaphone and for some reason says in a whisper:

"Remo Giazotto. Gleb met him shortly before his death."

"He did?"

Vera shifts her eyes to me.

"I used to play that piece. At first I couldn't figure out how to approach it, so I went to Florence to see Remo." I turn off the synthesizer. "But at the time I still didn't know he was the author."

1990

Life in Rzhevka was hard, but years later they remembered it with gratitude and love. They had to forget their habit of walking everywhere. In the morning, Gleb and Katya faced an overcrowded bus that took them to an equally overcrowded metro. In fact, they didn't always get to do that. Frightened by the hordes of people at the stop, drivers often went by without stopping. On the way back, Gleb and Katya had the opposite problem: sometimes they couldn't get out and the bus would take them an extra stop. They would get out on an avenue they called Post-Industrial because it was even farther than Industrial. For the first time in their lives they were genuinely afraid of being late, as it wasn't a university teacher waiting for them but two whole classrooms. More than once they had to take a taxi, which made the teaching staff very uneasy. At best, these trips spoke of Gleb and Katya as people who got up late; at worst as darlings of fate and burners of candles at both ends. The latter suspicion looked especially bad. It wasn't easy for teachers fighting for every hour of teaching load to reconcile themselves to the fact that Gleb had been given an additional class, for example. And although Gleb's raise was expressed in just a few rubles, those rubles did count. There was, in his colleagues' mind, another source of his sweet life: Katya. The professor's daughter

226

from Berlin was surely getting support from her parents. His colleagues also speculated about the approximate sum of that assistance. Otherwise people were sympathetic toward the young couple and even gave them teaching advice. The sympathy might have gone even deeper if they'd known the details of Katya's parental assistance, which had been modest even during her student years. When Katya wrote them that she'd found a job, that assistance stopped. Instead of the next transfer, however small, congratulations arrived on the start of her working career. Although Katya did like the work itself. She liked children (she imagined that she and Gleb would have some of their own), her colleagues to some degree, and even the janitors who greeted her with a puzzling array of sounds – loud but good-natured. These people liked to think they were greeting the teacher in German. Katya was especially moved by the portraits of German classic writers on her office walls. Since the war, they'd hung slightly skewed – not that anyone had any thought of blaming them for anything. Katya was aware of the awkwardness of their position and so invested all possible warmth in her own greeting. The classics responded in kind: they'd long grown bored of the firm German *Guten Morgen*. The whole school knew about the morning exchange of courtesies, and the attitude toward Katya only improved because of it. She was out of the ordinary, and usually people don't have bad feelings for people like that. Moreover, Katya was simply a good person. This evidently was the main reason why her colleagues didn't say malicious things, the janitors said hello, and the pupils didn't disrupt her lessons. As it turned out, Katya's German class ended up taking in Kryuchkov, now disenchanted with Russian literature. Apparently his disenchantment did not extend to the German language. He conscientiously completed the hardest homework assignments and with a certain brilliance. For their geography lessons he readily helped set up the screen and slide projector. Thus Gleb was amazed to learn from Katya that Kryuchkov was capable of being a competent fellow and not grandstanding at all. But Katya didn't limit herself to this information. One day she asked Kryuchkov to help her carry two packages of books home. Without another word, Kryuchkov, deep down a gentleman, picked up the heavy bag and headed off to accompany Katya. Evidently he sensed a trick because he set the bag down at the apartment door and tried to beg off. Katya ("What do you mean, leave?") said that now she simply had to treat him to tea. Kryuchkov saw you-know-who in the apartment but didn't leave. That would have been too much like running away. Without looking Gleb in the eyes, Kryuchkov mumbled something. Gleb held out his hand: "Are you angry with me?" Kryuchkov didn't say anything, but he did shake his hand. When they sat down at the table, Gleb said he wanted to ask his guest's forgiveness. Kryuchkov turned red. He drew a triangle on the tablecloth and looked at Gleb for the first time. "Oh, that's all right, it was my fault. I was grandstanding. It's forgotten." "Grandstanding," Katya whispered. She turned to Gleb: "Did you ever grandstand in school?" "Did I ever," Gleb replied. "To beat the band." From the movement of Katya's lips, it was clear the expression wasn't lost on her. Then they had tea and cake. Considering the suddenness of the request, it must be admitted that Katya had prepared well. After cake it somehow came out that Kryuchkov could eat a cheese sandwich. Maybe some pelmeni, too, which Katya immediately started to cook. Privately she berated herself for not offering the boy dinner from the very start. When the sandwich and pelmeni had been eaten, Kryuchkov told them how he and his stepfather had been ice fishing on the Gulf of Finland when their ice floe split off and they were carried out to open sea and a helicopter rescued the fishermen. He also told them that fish in the gulf is tasty but freshwater. The Neva dumps so much fresh water into the gulf, there's no chance of it remaining salt. The Neva (at this, Kryuchkov asked for another sandwich), strangely enough, isn't a river but a natural canal between Lake Ladoga and the Baltic, and that's why it doesn't have springtime riverine floods. The Neva floods when very strong winds from the Baltic drive it back upstream. Kryuchkov would have liked to tell them the story of the floods, too, but he was gently stopped. Gleb expressed admiration for the pupil's erudition. He admitted he'd had no idea what a profound and multifaceted person Kryuchkov was. Excusing himself for a minute to go to the toilet, Kryuchkov upon his return informed them that the word for toilet, *unitaz,* came from the company Unitas, which had produced this unpretentious but important object. Their conversation lasted until after midnight, so that they sent Kryuchkov home in a taxi. After that, it was as if the boy had been replaced. When during Russian literature lessons he was first to raise his hand, no one was laughing anymore. Everyone knew that Kryuchkov's answer would be the fullest, although perhaps a little overlong. After that memorable evening on Industrial Avenue, Gleb's teaching life returned to its peaceful course. The rebellions were not repeated, his relations with his colleagues grew stronger by the day, and he was even able to touch up his Russian literature syllabus, which Gleb didn't like. Without saying so specifically, he shortened his teaching of the stuffy Soviet classics and in the time saved read Leskov to his pupils, more rarely Platonov and Bulgakov. His pupils liked it. One weekend, he took Kryuchkov's class to Akhmatova's grave in Komarovo, and the pupils took turns reading her poems out loud, passing the tattered little volume from one to the next. That trip could have been called the shining hour of Gleb the teacher, had it not been for one strange circumstance. That very same hour, Gleb suddenly felt a weariness. Even more: indifference and disappointment. He was beginning to feel that the path he'd started down had exhausted itself. Thus, for the first time in his life, Gleb became aware that a success can simultaneously be an end. One of those autumn evenings – at supper, as usual – Gleb and Katya were watching television. When he saw people storming the Berlin Wall, Gleb said, "That's where we should go now. That's where life is. Shall we make the leap?" "Let's make the leap," Katya echoed. Dinner continued as if nothing had happened, and they talked about other things. But Gleb's words – regardless of whether they'd been spoken seriously or not – had stunned Katya. The very possibility of going somewhere had not occurred to her. It turned out, that possibility did exist. And also: Katya hadn't thought revolution was capable of making an impression on Gleb. He'd always seemed to her a private person, indifferent to the public sphere. In the end, she explained Gleb's statement by his weariness with school. Katya had started to weary of it a little herself.

FEBRUARY 1, 2014, PETERSBURG

In the middle of the night I'm awakened by the sound of footsteps. I throw on my robe and go out in the hall. Light is coming from the room where the synthesizer is. Wearing headphones and with speakers off, Vera is running her fingers over the keys. She doesn't hear me come in. To keep from frightening her by a touch, I turn the light off and on. Vera turns around and takes off the headphones. I kiss her on the forehead.

"What are you playing?"

"I'm practicing the Adagio."

"At night?"

I sit down in the rocking chair.

"You said you'd seen Giazotto. What did you think of him?"

"An ordinary gentleman who looks like a school principal. He worked in radio somewhere. Taught. In the late 1950s he announced he'd found a fragment of an unknown Albinoni composition – six measures or so – and had restored it."

"On the basis of six measures?"

"That's what he said. Do you want some fruit juice?"

Vera nods and I bring two glasses of juice from the kitchen.

"It's so odd" – Vera's lips shine from the wetness – "to credit your own music to someone else."

"Maybe. Usually it works the opposite way."

"But since we know the truth now, it's wrong to call his music Albinoni's."

"I agree. Our performance could be announced like this: Remo Giazotto, Albinoni's Adagio. Although how we announce it doesn't matter to either one anymore. Nor does it for the music."

Vera walks across the room and perches on the windowsill.

"I was playing and thinking that music like this can only be written right before death."

"Giazotto lived another thirty years after his Adagio. But you're right in a certain sense. I think he really was preparing for death. Getting used to the idea."

"Can anyone get used to death?"

"You've got a lot of time to do it. An entire life."

"And if you can't?" The girl gets up from the windowsill and goes over to the coffee table. "An Italian real estate catalog. . . ."

"Yes, Katya and I wanted you to look at it."

Vera sits in an armchair and I settle on the arm.

"Pozzuoli. Where's that?"

"Outside Naples. This here" – I point to a photo of the port – "is where the Apostle Paul disembarked on his way to Rome."

"Great photograph."

"You can even feel the heat, right?"

"That's because of the lizard on the rock. And the air above it, look, it's hazy."

"And this is the villa. Do you like it?"

"I thought it was a museum. Right on the shore. Very cool. You wake up and see the sea." Vera turns the page. "This woman looks like Katya. Katya told me she'd had an addiction."

"Yes. Thanks to you, everything's changed. . . . And this is in Calabria, also in the south. Scalea. A little music-box town."

"It even sounds like a fairytale: Scalea. Do you want to go there?"

"Why 'you'? *We.* If you have no objections, of course."

"What about Mama? Katya and I visited her the day before yesterday."

"I know. They'll move her to a private clinic in a few days, and then we'll see."

Somewhere down below the first trolleybus is going by. The rods clank where the wires cross.

It's good Vera doesn't have to go to school tomorrow. On the doctors' recommendation she's been given leave until September. Music, on the contrary, they've advised her not to give up – just to practice without overdoing it.

"Is that true?" Vera looks out the window. "About you and her, when you were young?"

"Yes."

"Mama's told me that story a few times. She's certain you still love her."

1991

August 19, morning. Gleb was awakened by his father's call. Dispensing with any greetings, Fyodor asked, "*Do you have Swan Lake, too?*" This was a kind of password, but Gleb didn't know the right answer. Of course, he could have countered him with a question – "Are you maybe back to hitting the bottle, Fyodor?" – only he didn't have the right to ask his father those questions. Anyway, it was clear from his voice that Fyodor was sober. He told Gleb there'd been a coup in the country, and they were airing *Swan Lake* continuously on television. "*I never liked that ballet. It's sickly sweet, and I'm no fan of sweets.*" Knowing his father, Gleb prepared himself for a detailed analysis of the ballet, but Fyodor was to the point. "*God alone knows how this story will end. I'll just say one thing: Be careful, son, and remember you have a brother Oles. Help each other.*" After a pause, he added: "*Here's the declension of* put' *for you. From now on, they'll do it in the plural, because there isn't going to be a single path for Russia and Ukraine anymore.*" Gleb hung up, turned on the television, and listened to "The Dance of the Little Swans." He liked the coup's choice of musical accompaniment. He looked out the window: everything was as usual. Even the line for glass recycling was no shorter. At the time, Gleb was on his own; Katya had flown to Berlin to visit her parents. The fact that she was making the trip alone perplexed him. Her first trip he could explain by the fact that they weren't married, but now there was no explanation. Katya shook him off with a brief "it's better this way," and Gleb felt questioning her beneath his dignity. When he'd finished watching *Swan Lake* to the end he went to school rather than wait for the repetition. He himself didn't know why he was going there specifically. Maybe because everyone he might call was out of town and he didn't feel like staying home. Complete calm reigned at the school, which smelled peacefully of paint: the painting crew was laying down its final brushstrokes. The teachers were preparing their classes for the start of the school year or silently collating handouts. Sometimes exchanging whispers. Only the teacher Kruglov, who taught State and Law, was pontificating about what was going on in the country. Moving from classroom to classroom, he informed his colleagues that the state and law were finally returning. To the least reliable of the collective's members, among whom he included Gleb, he limited himself to saying that the innocent would be spared. This promise made the two English teachers burst into tears; they realized that the main accusation against them would be their subject matter. Kruglov let Gleb know that he was in possession of information about how exactly Gleb had been teaching Soviet literature; however (you could hear the steel in Kruglov's voice), this did not mean Gleb would automatically be considered a saboteur. As he was leaving, he turned around: in short, this had to be sorted out. When Gleb inquired who exactly was going to be doing the sorting, Kruglov glumly remarked, "the organs" – and moved on to the next office. In the second half of the day, the principal assembled the teaching collective and read out the clarification of current events he'd received from the regional Party committee. The only sentence that belonged to the principal himself was the assertion that *this* had been bound to happen. He said this in a steely Kruglovian tone and as he spoke looked loyally at Kruglov. His intonation made his statement wholly loyal to the putschists, so that even Kruglov nodded his head approvingly. But the principal proved more far-sighted than anyone might have thought. In the future, this same sentence, spoken with bitterness and distress even, served as proof of his opposition to the conspirators. Kruglov was fired a week later for his support of the putsch. Actually, on August 19, no one, including Kruglov, had the least inkling of this, and the matter seemed hopeless. Gleb left the school and wandered through the city for a long time, arriving home only at dusk to hear the telephone ringing from the front door. It was Katya, and she was crying. The fact that Gleb hadn't answered the phone all day had led her to assume the worst. Katya begged him to be careful and told him she was flying in tomorrow evening. Gleb protested. Rejecting the very idea of her return, he called Katya a Decembrist's wife. Judging from the snuffling in the receiver, the irony was lost on her. Evidently people in East Germany didn't know enough about the Decembrists.

It's great luck that you're in Berlin, Gleb explained, since it's unclear what's going to happen here tomorrow. That's exactly why I'm coming, Katya replied. The background of this sentence was indignant German. In all likelihood, Katya's parents were on Gleb's side when it came to her return. After he hung up, he started boiling a jacket potato. He was going to turn on the radio, but the usual wavelength greeted him with the silence of the grave. Gleb felt lonely. Peeling his potato, he remembered with sadness Katya's excellent meals, which were nothing like his present intake of food. When nearly the entire potato had been eaten, a rustle came from the forgotten radio, accompanied by quiet mumbling, an effect comparable to the first radio signal sent by Popov. Gleb stopped chewing. Someone cleared his throat and announced that Open City, an underground radio station, was on the air. The voice was replaced by a rustling (who are you, you dwellers of the underground?), but a minute later, by an effort of will, it came back on air. Through crackling and signal attenuation, it reported that Pskov Division tanks were on their way to the city. It called on all the city's men to go to St. Isaac's Square and come to the defense of the city council. It advised bringing warm things and an umbrella, inasmuch as they would be there all night. Crackle. Silence. But Gleb had heard the main thing: St. Isaac's Square. He didn't even notice how he came to be holding an umbrella: that meant he was going after all. For a second he felt awkward because of Katya; he'd promised her he'd be careful. He thought about that. He would keep his promise by being careful there, on St. Isaac's Square. As he was leaving the building, he discovered he'd left the umbrella by the front door, but he didn't go back. A tank division was on its way to the city, and there he'd be with an umbrella. Pretty ridiculous. He looked around. Industrial Avenue was deserted. Gleb looked at his watch: just after midnight. How long does it take to eat a potato? He decided to hail a taxi, and fifteen minutes later he caught one. He got in the backseat, which is what people do who don't want to get into a conversation. Gleb didn't. That morning he'd been looking for people to talk to at school (he'd found Kruglov), and now he was grateful to the taxi driver for his silence. On Bolshaya Morskaya the driver told him briefly: "Barricades, on foot from here." This summoned up a fairytale vision in Gleb: I can't go any farther, now it's you, Ivan the Tsarevich, you yourself, somehow. . . . The car's headlights wrested details out of an amorphous structure that stretched from sidewalk to sidewalk: a heater, a legless chair, and on top the northern leafless vine – barbed wire. Great, they'd found barbed wire somewhere, Gleb muttered, getting out his wallet. "Everyone's had enough," the driver responded. He categorically refused to take money. The taxi pool had decided not to charge for driving people to St. Isaac's Square. Gleb went around the barricade next to the building wall and headed for the square. It was crowded there and even rather festive. The last gleam ran over the barricades that closed off the adjoining streets. Where there wasn't enough material for a defensive structure they'd parked a No. 22 city bus. Militiamen with good-natured faces were pouring Molotov cocktails. A man in camo came up to Gleb and said it wasn't going to be possible to shut the square off entirely; there were too many open spaces here. Not only that (he lit up), bear in mind that *tanks* are coming here. Tanks. He said it with a short, angry "e": *tenks*. Getting through barricades was child's play for *tenks*. Anyone trying to run away when the *tenks* burst onto the square would get tangled up in them. "Your suggestions?" Gleb responded like a soldier. The man shrugged and walked away. Gleb lost all interest in conversation. On the square, where everyone was talking to everyone else, no one spoke to him again. This fraternal stand, arm in arm, in view of impending danger, did nothing to warm him. He felt acutely that death is filled with loneliness and sunders any arms, scatters those who have embraced the same way a tank does a barricade. *Tenk*. Looking at the monument to Nicholas I, Gleb thought that when the tanks did enter the square, it would indeed be pointless to run away. Better to press up to the pedestal, exhale, and wait. A tank couldn't drive right up to the monument; the cannon was in the way. Or wasn't – Gleb found that funny. Meanwhile, the Pskov Division was getting closer, as the loud-speaker on the wall of the Mariinsky Palace announced. It was a grim loudspeaker, with a weakness for black humor. It started talking about Moscow and mentioned that the first victim had already been crushed under a tank's caterpillar tread. As he walked by an ambulance, Gleb tried to picture the injuries. He couldn't. He was tired. His imagination didn't function in the middle of the night. Had the entire division shown up right now, Gleb didn't think he'd be frightened; torpor had set in. But the division did not show up. At dawn it was announced that everyone could go home. Next to Gleb, someone said that en route the tankists had sabotaged their vehicles so that ultimately they had to order them to stop. Tankists. Taxi-ists. . . . Gleb imagined taxi-ists. On Nevsky he had no trouble catching a taxi. Leaning back, he felt himself falling asleep. Taxi-ists (he thought) wouldn't sabotage their vehicles. They had a different objective. And he felt a quiet joy.

FEBRUARY 6, 2014, PETERSBURG

Nestor and I are having dinner in a restaurant on the Petrograd side.

"Let's go back to what you were telling me about St. Isaac's Square, if you don't object?" Nestor slowly sinks his spoon into his mushroom soup. "I want to pin down some details. How did you end up there in the first place? You don't seem like a fan of gatherings like that."

"It's only now I don't. At the time I could still take part. Nestor, at the time I was completely different. Plus, once again, the underground radio, the fatherland in danger, all the city's men – that gets you going."

"You mean you wouldn't go to St. Isaac's now?"

"On no account. Eat your soup. It won't taste good cold."

"I'm eating. . . . Or maybe you've just become more cautious?"

"The way my life has developed lately, I'm less afraid." I catch Nestor's attentive gaze. "Dear man, it's very hard to frighten me now. As it is to get me to go anywhere."

"But what about for an idea, say? Any great idea needs defending."

"It doesn't need a single thing! Defend it in yourself."

"I'm afraid you're not going to solve the problems of the whole nation in yourself alone."

"Nor is there any need. You see how this usually ends. Solve your own. Let each person solve his own, and everything will be fine for the nation."

"That's awfully neat. . . . Ultimately, the book isn't about me, though. My job is to tell your stories without error."

"What I've read so far is irreproachable." I finish chewing a piece of meat. "Like this steak."

"That means you weren't wrong to fight the putschists. They would never have allowed a steak like that."

"You think?"

"Food wasn't supposed to taste good. That was the whole point of the putsch."

I wipe my mouth with my napkin.

"You know what your mistake is? You believe the system should be changed for the sake of a good steak. Whereas I think we just have to learn how to cook well. And the system will catch up."

"That's why it's a system, because it covers many objectives!"

"Well, yes, it does. Only they aren't mine. Thousands risk their lives, it turns out, so that in the end a few gentlemen can privatize oil wells dirt cheap."

"Don't you think you're exaggerating?"

My face takes on an expression of *unshakable certainty*. And is replaced by a *readiness to concede*. I don't mind.

"Of course I am."

The waiter brings ice cream and coffee. He serves everything with exaggerated deference. He hesitates and asks for my autograph. The possibility of getting an autograph lifts several people at nearby tables from their seats. I ask his name, sign pages from a notepad, napkins, and a menu. Last to approach me is an elderly lady. She has tattoos on her bare shoulders. Chain earrings, a good fifteen bracelets – all silver. Black jeans, a vest, rivets.

"To Tsaritsa Ira, please." Meeting my gaze (*poorly disguised surprise*), she reaches into her purse. "That's how it is in my passport. Here."

I nod and write. Jangling her bracelets, Tsaritsa Ira holds out her hand to me. Elegantly, regally, you might say. I graze it with my lips.

"What did you write for her?" Nestor wonders. "Did you wish her a peaceful reign?"

"Huh? An enchanting coup!"

1992

One clear April day, Kleshchuk popped up in Gleb's life again. He called and asked if he could fly in for a conversation. Without waiting for an answer, he told him he had a plane ticket for the next day. Gleb finally realized what this was about. Music school, solfeggio, triad construction. All this seemed so far away now that it didn't come to mind immediately. Killed tens of times by Gleb in duels, Kleshchuk turned out to be not only alive but firmly intent on showing up in Petersburg. "Come," Gleb responded unenthusiastically. He didn't understand why they couldn't discuss everything over the phone. Kleshchuk did come. He was still fat, but now he exuded the specific scent of money. This was expressed not only in the literal sense (cologne not made here) but in the creak of his expensive leather jacket, in the watch casually dangling on a chain, and, ultimately, in the way he behaved. There was the sense that the man was a success. Maybe he learned how to construct triads, Gleb thought, but he was wrong. The reason for Kleshchuk's prosperity was of a very different nature. He told Gleb how up until recently he'd been playing the accordion in a Kyiv restaurant. One day he had a rare bit of luck. Ivasik was dining in the restaurant and got the urge to sing so he asked him, Kleshchuk, to accompany him. Kleshchuk was astonished to hear that Gleb had no idea whom he was talking about and plunged into a detailed story about Ivasik, one of the day's most prominent businessmen. He spent such a long time listing what Ivasik had sold and resold that Gleb was starting to lose the narrative thread. Kleshchuk could probably tell that, because the thread suddenly broke with the information that right now the businessman was working in *retail* produce. Here Kleshchuk fell silent in order to assess the impression he'd made. Seeing that Gleb was silent as well, Katya politely praised produce as healthy. In no hurry, Kleshchuk took out his pipe and lit it. "You see . . ." Aromatic smoke issued with each new portion of Kleshchuk's words. You see, the profit from produce was more significant than is usually thought: it had made Ivasik a millionaire. And millionaire Ivasik (smoke rings) loved to sing. Always had. He was no Pavarotti, but you couldn't call his voice unpleasant, and for the most part he sang in tune. And now, a month after this historic meeting, millionaire Ivasik invites him, hack restaurant musician

Kleshchuk, to his restaurant. French cognac, caviar, a separate room – in short, everything produce has to offer a man. At the height of the feasting, his host casually asks, "You remember how great we sang?" "How can I not?" Kleshchuk replies (his lips covered in caviar). "How you accompanied me?" "Not bad at all," Kleshchuk recalls. Right then a flunky brings in an accordion, and Ivasik says, "How about we sing, brother?" And he sang all evening, drenched in tears, and was amazed that Kleshchuk could accompany any melody. When he finished singing, he asked, "Do you like my singing, Kleshchuk?" At that, Kleshchuk forced out, a catch in his throat: "Very much!" The performer glowered: "You know, some people in the conservatory, dammit, they don't." "That's just envy," Kleshchuk said indignantly, "envy for your genuine talent." "Bastards," Ivasik agreed. "Supercilious pricks. You play just as well." Kleshchuk wasn't about to object, failing to mention, of course, that he hadn't been accepted by the conservatory back in the day. "Triads?" Gleb asked. "You got it." Kleshchuk sighed. He went on to tell Gleb that Ivasik, it turns out, had decided to afford his friends some pleasure and prepare a little concert for them. Kleshchuk immediately expressed surprise that such a talented man didn't want to afford that pleasure to the broad public. Ivasik, who still nurtured a spark of healthy doubt, asked whether his singing really would be of interest to the public. In response, Kleshchuk was at a loss and seemed to choke up from an excess of feeling. Of course it would! Because if Ivasik's singing didn't interest them, then what could interest a public like that? "I can't even read music, though," Ivasik admitted. At that moment Kleshchuk saw something vulnerable in him. But, Kleshchuk admitted, the black caviar had rushed to his head and he no longer had control of himself. He told Ivasik that as best he knew, Pavarotti didn't read music either, but even so he was far from the least in the vocal arts. Ivasik timidly suggested that his voice didn't compare with Pavarotti's, to which

Kleshchuk replied that Ivasik was a born lyric tenor, something he himself might not even have guessed. Indeed, Ivasik didn't – especially since he had no inkling that such a voice even existed. Kleshchuk began persuading the businessman to start a solo career and offered to put all his, Kleshchuk's, effort and ability into that – in the name of art, naturally. A plan formed instantly and consisted of the following. Create a quartet to accompany the rising star: accordion, violin, guitar, and double bass. Actually, the quartet could have been a quintet or even a sextet, but as he sorted through possible candidates in his mind, Kleshchuk only came up with four. The collective practically named itself: the Ivasik Quartet. The lyric tenor smiled perplexedly but didn't object. He only asked that they not bring in conservatory musicians. Kleshchuk – this was his hour of vengeance against the conservatory – assured him that that was ruled out. None of the candidates for the Ivasik Quartet had studied a day in that institution. So, your triads helped you, he thought as he listed the musicians' names for Ivasik. Among them, Gleb's. It was for Gleb that Kleshchuk had flown to Petersburg. The quartet leader's pipe had been filled a few times, and the smoke rings he was putting out now seemed like the zeros in businessman Ivasik's millions. At first Gleb refused. He called it a crazy scheme and said he wouldn't be part of it. But Kleshchuk had been right to favor an in-person conversation to the telephone. Here Gleb couldn't hang up, couldn't even just say no. Hundreds of kilometers traveled lay behind his visitor, and he had the right to a discussion. Which he took advantage of. Lightly accepting "crazy scheme," Kleshchuk asked how much teacher Yanovsky made a month. "Say what? Say what?" Kleshchuk asked twice, his hand cupped to his ear. The amount was so small, he simply couldn't hear it. The quartet leader offered Gleb a salary fifteen times more. Plus fees. Plus an interesting life. "What do you call an interesting life?" Gleb wondered. "Traveling, performing . . ." Kleshchuk turned to Katya for the first time. "I think any life is more interesting than school life, right?" Katya shrugged. "You say that because you've never worked with children." "No, I haven't," Kleshchuk agreed. "Drink to our meeting?" He reached into his bag and – as his final means of persuasion – took out cognac and caviar. Macaroni and sprats appeared on the table from the Yanovskys. Gleb had to hand it to Kleshchuk; he didn't make any other attempts to pressure him. He reminisced about music school. At his request, he and Gleb acted out for Katya the scene of their duel, and Kleshchuk fell just as clumsily. On the other hand, he produced a second bottle of cognac from his bag. Toward the evening's end, Gleb asked what kind of repertoire Ivasik envisioned for himself. Before answering, Kleshchuk poured himself a full glass. "I'm afraid there's nothing here for you to like. It's not Stravinsky or even Shostakovich." He drank it down. "But we can play good things even without Ivasik." Kleshchuk's plane didn't leave until morning, and Katya suggested he stay for the night. "A hotel," Kleshchuk told her in short. "The Evropeiskaya." He was visibly drunk. As he was leaving, he left Gleb his business card. "I'll think it over," Gleb promised. "You're just saying that to get rid of me now," Kleshchuk sighed. "But I know you really will think it over. And you'll agree."

FEBRUARY 24, 2014, PETERSBURG – KYIV

Early in the morning, Oles calls from Kyiv. Katya picks up the phone, but Oles asks for me. I pick up the receiver, although I know what he's going to say. Oles has never called so early. To be precise, he's never called.

"*Father died,*" Oles says. "*We're burying him the day after tomorrow.*"

"I'll be on the next flight."

"*Listen, brother . . . Things are a little dicey in Kyiv, so be careful.*"

I promise. I can't wrap my mind around the idea that my father's gone. It hurts.

I get a ticket for an evening flight. Katya wants to go with me, but I forbid it. Ultimately, someone has to stay with Vera. Katya has her doubts. She remembers the events of 1991 and is afraid I'll get mixed up in something.

"You know, I'm going to bury my father. Their turmoil has nothing to do with me. Even Russia's wouldn't."

"*It* might have something to do with *you.*"

"Katya darling..."

I nearly miss my plane what with packing and arguing with Katya. I arrive at Pulkovo just minutes before boarding ends. No, after: they've waited for me. Shortly before midnight I land at Boryspil. The border guards smile politely. They've recognized me.

"*Purpose of your visit?*"

From their pronunciation I can tell they aren't quite steady with their "native tongue." I speak the language much better.

"*I'm burying my father.*"

"*Our condolences.*"

The border guards shake my hand in turn. Why did I switch to Ukrainian with them? I never did with my father. Maybe because our relationship went deeper than politeness?

My father. Witness to my past life. He's gone, but the past remains; it, the past, needs no testimony evidently. When an antique sculpture is stolen from a museum, that doesn't cancel the history of antiquity. Antiquity just becomes one sculpture poorer.

If I'm guided by the usual order of things, then what stood between me and death was my father. He was that first rank that perishes in battle. Now that first rank is me. And the battle is obviously lost, understandably; no one has ever yet won it.

A taxi takes me to my hotel. Riding over the Dnieper, I cross myself when we go by the monastery – as I always do, every visit. The Dnieper's water is black, and dirty white ice floes glide down it. I didn't tell Oles when I was getting in so he wouldn't meet me. Otherwise I'd have to spend the night with him and Galina, and I didn't want that.

The hotel is on Vladimirskaya Street. I'm met at the entrance, and they ask permission to take a photograph with me. I leave my bag in my room and head out for a short walk. Just a few hours ago I was at home, and now I'm in a completely different place. Or rather, in both places simultaneously. Delight in space disappearing, a keen emotion. I hurry to enjoy it because tomorrow it might disappear.

"I'm going for a short walk," I say as I walk past the desk clerk.

"Allow me to give you some advice. Don't go to Kreshchatik, it's dangerous there now."

"Certainly."

I walk down Vladimirskaya to Proreznaya and turn toward Kreshchatik. I'm calm at heart. I'm part of the nighttime city. I spent my childhood here, and that childhood is my defense. I walk, invisible to everyone, in a cloud of memories. I touch the buildings with my palm because I know – went into or just walked by – each and every one. I stopped and chatted with someone – When? Who? I put my foot on a stone pedestal. The words in my memory latch onto the place, not the person. It's decades later but the words are here, hovering just like before – on the buildings and the trees – like new.

But the pedestal is gone. To say nothing of that someone.

It starts to drizzle and I step into the nearest doorway. The drops are mixed with snowflakes, like winter. This is another unforgettable moment: hiding from the rain in a doorway. Under an archway, there was a lightbulb on a wire. Swinging, moving the shadows. (The rain is gradually stopping.) Now there's an energy-saving light here, totally still. No one preserved the lightbulb of my childhood, it just swung, and it's gone.

Maidan is lit up by fires burning in front of tents, in what was once a thoroughfare. One of the tents is surrounded by a wattle fence, and behind it are an old man and an old woman. Felt boots and sheepskin coats, a pot on the fire. A rooster tethered by the foot. I've seen all this before, and more than once. What was that? A summer in a village? An open-air museum? Maybe, if it weren't for the pile of tires behind the tent.

I slow down. Say hello.

"*Have some tea?*" the old woman asks.

"*Yes, thank you.*"

The old man (a cigarette in his gnarled fingers) pulls up a crate for me. The old woman puts a teabag in a mug, scoops water out of the pot, and hands it to me.

"*And what's that?*" I point to a strange contraption in the distance.

"*The catapult,*" the old woman says.

She's probably amazed that I don't know the simplest things. I feel a rush of gaiety because I realize this is a dream. Or no, a set for some play. The end of the story: Kreshchatik, the wattle, the catapult. But these two are the real deal; they exude warmth.

The mug of tea warms my hand. I ask:

"*How's living here? Not easy?*"

The old man crushes his cigarette on the crate.

"*No, not easy.*"

"*There's nothing to do, and we're not used to that.*" The old woman takes out a handle-less broom from behind her back. "*I'm weaving brooms, but where's for me to sweep? What am I supposed to do with them?*"

"*Fly!*" The old man's mouth spreads into a smile; his face is an accordion.

"*So how come you're sitting here?*"

The old man and woman exchange looks. A figure in a greatcoat steps out of the darkness.

"*So who do we have here?*" The new arrival is grim. "*Papers!*"

I get out my passport. I have two, a German and a Russian, but I left the German one at home. I'm beginning to realize this is bad. I examine the commissar's excellent greatcoat. Usually greatcoats are shapeless, but this fits like a glove. So do his boots. A dandy.

The old woman comes to my defense.

"*Mikola, leave him alone, he speaks Ukrainian.*"

"*Ukrainian, you say? Even worse.*" He shows them my passport cover. "*Mother Russia. You're flapping your gums, and this is a provocateur and a spy.*"

To me: "Stand up. Follow me."

I stand up and bow to the old people.

"*See you,*" they say.

Mikola looks at them sarcastically:

"*See you in the next world.*" He takes his gun out of his pocket and pokes it into my side. "*One false step and I shoot.*"

"*Mikola. . . .*"

He turns toward the old folks:

"*We'll deal with you too. Contras. . . .*"

I walk past the tents, feeling the gun poking into me. I hear the hem of his greatcoat flapping against his boots. No, this isn't a summer in the village. It's not even August 1991; everything here seems much graver. Mikola takes me to a big tent with a yellow and blue flag. The questioning begins. My consciousness refuses to believe what's happening and offers options of its own. It's a dream.

A movie in a dream. A dream in a movie.

But what's happening is happening, that's its nature, and I'm standing in the middle of the tent, and in front of me, sprawled in a chair, is Mikola. He reminds me of a picture – of someone's interrogation, as in my case. Mean and dark-haired. *Why, oh why, did you ever love, ever love Ivan the Black?* Why indeed? No good reason, apparently. I wonder whether there'll even be a concert with Vera. If so, we absolutely must include that song.

"*Who are you working for? I know Moscow, but who specifically?*" His speech is clipped, his intonation irreproachable.

I wish this were a dream. I wish that the morning that began today in Petersburg was continuing and I was still in bed. There are extended dreams like that, when you think you've woken up and are out of bed, gone to the airport, say, flown somewhere. I'm gripped by apathy. If Mikola shoots me, that will spare me many unpleasant things in general. A Tokarev pistol as a cure for Parkinson's.

"*You won't talk?*" He raises his gun.

I shrug.

"*I'm asking you, you Moscow bastard, why did you learn our language and why were you questioning those fools? Were you trying to make traitors of them?*"

"Of course not."

"*Are you trying to get on my nerves? I know for a fact you're a spy, but I won't take you to court, because the court won't shoot you. I will, though.*"

Mikola is turning red. And black at the same time, although you'd think that wouldn't be possible. A menacing angel of revolution.

"Listen, we're one people after all. . . ."

"*Is that so?*" Mikola suddenly switches to a calm tone. "*One people?*" He pensively blows on the barrel. "*No, not one people. In this you're badly mistaken. You're my people's enemy. And now listen to me carefully.*" He cocks the pistol. "*I'll give you a minute to answer my question. In a minute, I'll shoot.*"

He theatrically pushes his sleeve off his watch. He's going to shoot me just as dramatically, I think. I regret Kleshchuk's absence; at last he'd see how people actually fall. In the literal sense, the teacher's final attempt.

Confess? To what? Anything at all? And give him grounds to shoot me? If he has the slightest doubt now . . . But Mikola doesn't look like someone who has doubts. He's sure he's right.

Steps and the rustle of canvas. Mikola looks at the person who's entered.

"*I see there's a rather tense atmosphere here.*" He points to the gun in Mikola's hand.

He turns to me. He looks like Egor, whom I haven't seen since high school graduation. Egor? He looks at me. Winks. Egor. So this is where he is.

"*I caught a spy.*"

Mikola sounds displeased. He's been interrupted.

"*What spy?*" Egor laughs. "*This is the virtuoso guitarist Gleb Yanovsky, my step-brother.*"

"*I saw what kind of virtuoso he is. . . . Calls for betrayal.*"

"*There was no such thing,*" I object.

"*Silence!*" Mikola suddenly yells. He stands up. "*Pan Egor, you know how much I respect you. . . .*"

"*I'm glad you respect me. Now drop that thing.*"

"*So I'm asking you, don't interfere.*"

Pan Egor is as cheerful as before. He gets out a cigarette and brings a lighter up to it. It all happens suddenly: the movement of a foot, the gun strikes the tent's stretched top and falls next to me.

"*Is that any tone of voice to use with me, you nit?*"

Egor's not laughing anymore. His gaze is calm and angry. It's clear he wasn't laughing before. Mikola stands up, but a little uncertainly.

"*Now pick up the gun*" – Mikola's lips are trembling – "*and give it to me.*"

"*Give it to you?*"

"*And why not?*"

Egor knocks Mikola down with a blow to the face. Mikola feels around the floor, and I remember those movements. The bald driver. The ashtray. Egor lifts Mikola by the nape to hit him again but at the last moment stops. Mikola's face is bloody. Egor flings him to the floor.

"*Want more?*"

"*No,*" Mikola rasps.

Egor leads me out of the tent. We walk past the fires, which now seem fewer. Kreshchatik dozes off at some point too. It smells like spring.

"How did you end up here?" Egor switches to Russian.

"I came for my father's funeral."

"So he died. Too bad. I'm not going to the funeral. Sorry." He winks, but a little unnaturally. "Not that anyone informed me."

He winks again, and it occurs to me that he has a nervous tic.

"It's been years since I've heard anything about you."

"And thank God. Honestly, it's better you didn't." Egor slaps me on the back. "And all these years I followed you, Mr. Virtuoso, from afar."

Near the turn onto Shevchenko Boulevard, Egor stops.

"All right, we'll say goodbye."

"Thanks, brother." I embrace Egor, or rather, I try to, since Egor isn't budging. "I think he would have shot me."

"Well, that's unlikely. Mikola's a former artist, a harmless creature. All he wanted was a showy scene."

"Too bad he didn't use the catapult. Didn't he think of it?"

"I guess not. Gleb, bro." Egor looks at the dark, hulking chestnut trees. "Step back, otherwise I'll shoot you myself. 'If you didn't hide, it's not my fault,' remember?" He lights up. "Say hi to your mother. She always dreamed of going somewhere. Did she?"

"Australia."

"The land of convicts. Tell her I'll visit her."

"You're planning to go to Brisbane?"

He takes a deep drag and shoots the cigarette into the air. Sparks flare in the chestnut's bare branches.

"Most definitely." Egor takes a few steps into the darkness. He turns around. "When I'm deported. Now we have Australia instead of Siberia."

1992

Kleshchuk turned out to be right. Gleb thought it over – and agreed to play for Ivasik. Gleb felt that his life was at an impasse, so he decided to take a detour. Even if this meant a major retreat – which was exactly how he thought of the job with Ivasik. The decision was taken jointly with Katya. She had gladly taught school but just as gladly gave it up. This new stretch on her life's path promised discoveries, inasmuch as, unlike other Germans, Katya knew that in Ukrainian the word for journey – *put'* – is feminine. At the school principal's request, Gleb and Katya finished out the school year and on July 1 left for Kyiv. A two-room apartment on Solomenskaya Street was put at their disposal. Kleshchuk explained that this was one of the apartments Ivasik used for informal business meetings. Judging from the erotic posters on the walls and the supply of contraceptives in the cupboard (all given to Kleshchuk), the deals made here had nothing to do with vegetables. At first, the Empire furniture and gilded doorknobs that decorated the paneled apartment irritated them. But the furniture was soft and the knobs sturdy, and a reconciliation came about with those objects. What was harder to reconcile with was Ivasik's repertoire – Ukrainian pop tunes, mostly. Gleb could never have imagined playing anything like that. Actually, this wasn't about playing, nor was it about the music and lyrics. It involved retrieving three chords and about as many words. Ivasik was responsible for the words. He was a solid man nearly two meters tall who sang in a high, weak voice. The voice Kleshchuk had called a lyric tenor quivered, and on the upper notes strayed into falsetto. Ivasik made up for his lack of a tenor with his lyricism: he would purse his lips into a Cupid's bow and wiggle his thick eyebrows. His gestures looked artificial, labored, and made Gleb think of a puppet theater. When he met Ivasik, Gleb tried to imagine the puppet master of this huge, beetle-browed puppet – and failed. Meanwhile, Ivasik possessed unpuppetlike feelings and never let slip a chance to shed tears. This happened when he sang "The Last Forced March," which took him back to his army youth. The cruel ballad "Letter from Murmansk" told of a young woman cheating on a soldier doing his mandatory service. "Born in the Village of Avangardny" and "Once Again I Visited" were lyrical sketches, and their emotional tension derived from the fact that the soloist had grown up in that obscure Avangardny. But the song that really got to Ivasik was "Bergamot Perfume," so much so that after he sang it the man's large face glistened with tears. In criminal business circles he even got the nickname Bergamot, which defined his musical tastes and, simultaneously – because the Russian word for "hippo" is nearly identical – the performer's build. What remained unclear was what exactly provoked the tears – the songs' content or his own performance. Maybe both. The rehearsal period was brief, two weeks. Rehearsals were required primarily for Ivasik-Bergamot. His problem as a vocalist was that he didn't sing the melodies quite accurately. Not that he was entirely and crudely out of tune, just that some notes diverged slightly from the composer's. The divergence wasn't huge, but it was this approximateness that drove Gleb craziest. It would be better if this were total rubbish, Gleb thought. That would be more honest. At the word "rubbish" he remembered his music teacher and rejoiced that she didn't know about his musical career. Gleb wanted to visit her very much, but he knew that then he'd have to tell her about Bergamot. So he didn't. There was someone, though, whom Gleb couldn't not visit: his father. Gleb and Katya went to his place for dinner, and Fyodor greeted them perfectly good-naturedly. While Galina and Katya were talking in the kitchen, he asked softly: *"How's your mother?"* "In Australia," Gleb said reluctantly. *"She got married?"* Gleb nodded. *"To someone from there?"* "Yes. . . . I haven't seen him." Oles came into the room, and Fyodor told him: *"Go help the women." "I already helped."* (A creak from the chair he sat in). *"Go help some more."* When Oles headed for the kitchen, after rolling his eyes, Fyodor asked: *"Son, why did you get mixed up with that Ivasik? He's an idiot."* Gleb shrugged: "I know." *"Money isn't everything. Develop what you were given – and you were given a lot."* This was the first time his father had admitted he had talent. He was wrong only with respect to the money. That wasn't the main reason Gleb had taken his decision. Gleb would have liked to have told his father that everything that was happening was his attempt to give fate a nudge, but that was hard to explain. So he didn't. His attempt – Gleb had seen this for himself – had failed, but not wishing to thrash about, he hadn't changed anything yet. Generally speaking, the new environment into which Gleb plunged was in a certain sense of interest. Remarkable people were playing in the Ivasik Quartet. The violinist Tereshchenko – a tiny, freckled fellow – he remembered from music school. He'd often been spoken of as a wunderkind and rising star. Everyone knew that Tereshchenko could hear a short piece and then repeat it without a single mistake. He took pride in the fact that, unlike the others, he didn't have to sit over his music for four hours a day. People said that this gift had played a nasty joke on him, though, because a deep understanding of a piece comes only after its hundredth repetition – it simply enters the pores. A hundredth repetition wasn't something that happened to Tereshchenko. His musical career never did gel, and he did not become a star. In a certain sense, Tereshchenko remained just that, a wunderkind. For some reason he failed to develop in the physical as well as the musical respect, never growing taller than a meter and a half. But his ability to remember a piece after the first time remained. The violinist had demonstrated it on various television programs, from musical to gastronomical, Ukrainian and Russian. Everything has its limits, though. Even a very short person has a hard time playing the child indefinitely, and his memory trick gradually got boring. Invitations started coming in with decreasing frequency. In this respect, the Ivasik Quartet could not have come at a better time. The fourth in the quartet, its rhythm and power, was a double bassist with the sonorous last name Targony. The name sounded Roman to Gleb, and Targony himself – swarthy, with an olive cast – reminded him of an ancient Roman. True, soon after it became clear that the noble color had an alcoholic origin. The bassist was always drunk. His smoldering alcoholism led to neither scandals nor fistfights. It came through in his lackluster gaze, guiltily lowered head, and taciturnity bordering on muteness. At the same time, Targony poom-poom-poomed with the precision of a metronome. He didn't miss a single rehearsal and was never once late. After their two-week preparation, the performances followed in quick succession. Bergamot was seriously enthusiastic about the vocal arts and nearly every evening appeared on stage in a tuxedo and bow tie. At first this was the stage of a restaurant he owned. To start, Kleshchuk the emcee would come out and inform the audience about their incredible luck. Which consisted of the chance to hear an outstanding performer who, despite his busy schedule, had found the time to entertain his restaurant's customers. As a small bonus to the main gift, and in honor of the rising star's performance, a twenty-percent discount on their orders was announced. Uncertain of the interest in Bergamot's art, Kleshchuk had come up with the discount. The lyric tenor, in whom the produce dealer would awaken from time to time, tried to lower the discount to ten percent, but when Kleshchuk reminded him that art demanded sacrifices, he ceased his resistance. This measure did in fact increase the restaurant's business on performance days. Many were prepared to listen to Bergamot for the discount. Soon, he himself came to believe that everyone really was looking forward to his performances, and in his absence the restaurant would look like an orphan shelter. "I cannot be hostage to my art and perform there every day," he would say in a peevish tone, Meanwhile, he liked being a hostage to his art. He liked it very much.

FEBRUARY 25-26, 2014, KYIV – LOZOVOYE

I wake up late and call Oles.

"*Where are you?*" Oles asks.

"At my hotel."

"*Everything okay?*"

I rub my forehead. Good question. Oles says we have to go to the morgue tomorrow at eight o'clock to pick up our father's body. Galina has decided to bury him not in Kyiv but in Lozovoye, the village his mother was from. Fyodor had spent the past few summers there.

"*Father liked it in Lozovoye,*" Oles explains. "*My mother says he'll be at peace in the village cemetery.*"

Katya calls. She says Vera has shown her a remarkable song she's written about ducks. They've already sent it to Mayer, who is thrilled.

This is exactly what's needed for the concert. Vera and I will sing it together. Katya asks me not to leave the hotel; I promise. And don't.

Life, which seems to have taken a downhill turn, is precious to me, it turns out, even like this. I think about how suddenly and stupidly it could all end. That artist could easily have sent a bullet into my forehead. Getting into his part *à la* Stanislavsky.

The next morning I arrive at the morgue at a quarter to eight. Oles and Galina are already there. We embrace silently. At eight o'clock, they roll out a trolley with the casket. Like a sculptor tugging the canvas off his sculpture, the morgue attendant flips the tulle back from my father's face. My father is calm and doesn't look in the least like a dead man. There even seems to be a ruddiness playing on his cheeks. Oles catches my look and whispers:

"Toner cream."

"*I wanted him to be handsome in his coffin, too,*" Galina strokes Fyodor's face.

"Take over," the author proposes.

I give him a few bills and a thumbs-up. They close the casket lid and load it into the Gazelle. Galina gets in too. Oles invites me to ride with him. It's 150 kilometers to Lozovoye. Oles's car is the first to leave; he's showing the Gazelle the way. As we leave Kyiv, clouds stretch along the horizon.

"*At least it didn't rain. Snow's better.*"

I look questioningly at my brother.

"*I'm afraid his makeup's going to wash off,*" he explains.

It seems to me Oles looks less like our father than I do. His features lack the precision I inherited from Fyodor. His personalty is milder, too, I think. Essentially, I know nothing about my brother. Almost nothing. My father once said he was an engineer. Unbeknownst to Oles, I start observing him. His eye is on the road. He's not talkative. He's biting his lower lip.

"How are things with you in Russia?"

"There?"

"Well, not here. All the sickness comes from there."

"You're hasty with your conclusions."

"Just don't say this was all America's idea."

"Sometimes you don't have to invent anything. It's enough to light the match and it all goes up itself."

Oles turns toward me.

"Tell me, brother, do you miss Ukraine just a little? You were born here, after all, grew up here. Doesn't your heart ache?"

"It does. For me, Russia and Ukraine are one land."

"For us, they aren't."

"Don't say 'we' so often. 'I' means much more."

Without taking his eyes off the road, he shakes his head.

"Sorry, brother, that's your fantasy. When thousands are at war, 'I' means nothing."

"Win peace, and thousands around you will be saved."

"Did you make that up yourself?"

"It's Saint Seraphim of Sarov. In our case: peace between men begins with peace in one man."

"Seraphim's a Russian." Oles laughs. *"I don't know whether I can believe him."*

I twist my finger at my temple. My brother puts one arm around me.

"Father said I should listen to you."

The rest of the trip passes in silence. Right before Lozovoye rain starts falling, mixed with snow, and Oles turns on the wipers. With their first sweep the rain stops. Oles can do a thing or two too.

We drive through the village and stop at the church. A minute later, the Gazelle pulls up. People walk toward the vehicles. Then they walk away. Exemplary Brownian movement. They greet each other, slap each other on the shoulder. They come to a stillness, arms crossed at the chest (or stuck in their pockets), sometimes scratching their cheeks, making an emery board sound. They smoke. Oles opens the Gazelle doors and we pull out the casket. A few men come over and grab the handles, and we carry the casket into the church. They remove the lid and at the head place a wooden frame with slots for candles. I've never seen the like.

Oles says we have to go to the next street for Yavdokha. I don't know who Yavdokha is or whether I need to go for her too. Nonetheless, I get in the car with Oles. We slowly drive up to Yavdokha's hut. A few minutes later, Yavdokha herself appears in the doorway. She's bent ninety degrees at the waist and walks leaning on two crutches. Her arm and leg movements remind me of a skier. A very old and estimable skier for whom there are no more worthy competitions in this world. Yavdokha asks me to let her have the front seat because she can't get in the back with crutches. I realize that Yavdokha's presence has some particular, though as yet unmanifested, purpose.

Before the service, a woman approaches the casket with two ropes and ties my father's legs at the ankles. She wants to tie the arms, too, but the right arm has stiffened alongside the body. More or less like mine.

"It won't bend."

Yavdokha's voice rings out:

"I'll bend it."

As she approaches the deceased, Yavdokha hands the woman her crutches. I look away, but with my peripheral vision I still see Yavdokha bend my father's arm with unexpected force. The bent arms get tied together. Once upon a time he carried me in those arms and his tears flowed from under those eyelids. Now his arms aren't bending and his eyelids aren't lifting. Was this the man who carried me? This the man who wept?

The service begins. The church is full of people, and I feel dozens of gazes on me. I get the unpleasant feeling that I'm the deceased at this funeral. Oh well, ultimately my father is a part of me, no matter how life turned out.

After finishing the service, the priest asks:

"You bound his hands and feet?"

"We did, father."

"Then carry out God's servant Fyodor."

The casket is lifted by six men (this time Oles and I do not take part), who carry it out of the church without closing the lid. There's a Zhiguli at the door with a trailer. The casket is set on the trailer. Like on a gun-carriage. Lozovoye pays my father its last respects by forming a funeral cortège.

The procession gets under way. At the head is a man with a cross, a little behind him two men with gonfalons, behind them the priest and chorus, then the Zhiguli with my father on the trailer, behind the trailer Galina, Oles, and I, behind us Yavdokha on crutches, one mongrel to either side, and after that the whole village. The Zhiguli goes slowly, but the dirt road is bumpy. My father's arms (especially the right one bent by Yavdokha) start lifting. His elbows are already resting on his stomach, and now his wrists are hovering in the air. Lying in his casket, you have to think my father is talking to heaven. His arms are swaying, which lends a peaceful and even casual look to the conversation.

It's about half a kilometer to the cemetery. Every hundred meters, the procession stops and the priest, accompanied by the singers, recites prayers for the repose of the dead.

"Your mother called him," Oles says. *"About six months ago. They talked for a long time."*

259

I walk, head down.

"What about?"

"I don't know. He was sad. All he said was he'd had a call from Brisbane."

When the first clods of earth strike my father's casket, I'm shocked at how loud they are. They're like a drum, not at all appropriate for the funeral's silence. After the grave is filled in, everyone goes to the funeral repast at the station buffet straight across the ceremony. I'm about to head off after everyone, but someone stops me:

"The relatives have their own path."

They show me the way only relatives of the deceased are supposed to go. A little behind me is Oles. About thirty meters behind us comes Galina. She's talking on the phone.

Oles catches up to me.

"Brother, I keep wanting to ask, what's wrong with your hand?"

"Oh, it's nothing."

At the meal, Oles and I are sitting on either side of Galina. She doesn't move or speak. As the meal is coming to a close, Galina pulls our heads toward her and quietly says:

"Boys, weep. . . . Tonight Egor was killed on Maidan."

"What did you say?" Oles squeezes her hand.

"Shot in the back. While we were burying your father, there was a call for me."

For some reason she gets out her phone and sets it in front of her. Oles looks thoughtfully at the flickering display. *"Whatever he did, he was your brother. You're alive, and he's dead. Forgive him."* Galina stands and crosses herself. *"And forgive us, Lord, for being afraid of him all our lives. Your father took him with him so he wouldn't cause any harm here."*

It turns out, all those years they were frightened of Egor's vengeance over having Oles. Over sending Egor to a home after he tried to kill his brother. They waited for him to come and finish what he'd started.

I tell Galina:

"I know an instance when he saved a man."

She hugs me.

"I believe he'll be forgiven a lot for that."

For the first time, I can see tears in her eyes.

"Who killed him?" Oles asks.

"He was shot in the back. No one knows."

No. I know.

1992

In late September, Kleshchuk was able to reach an agreement for a concert by the Ivasik Quartet and soloist at the House of Officers. This wasn't particularly difficult, since vegetables were supplied to the army as well. Representatives of the armed forces expressed the liveliest interest in Bergamot's art. When the matter of compensation for their support of art was clarified, they promised to ensure him a full hall. They guaranteed the audience would be hanging from the chandeliers. So as not to create the impression that the quartet's admirers were exclusively men, the junior officers were told to show up with their wives. It goes without saying, all the support staff, which consisted primarily of women, was enlisted too. The total number of women was promised to be as much as thirty percent. With his natural gallantry and humor, Kleshchuk asked that the women not hang from the chandeliers. They laughed. When they started to talk about applause, it was made clear, to Kleshchuk's surprise, that they followed separate pricelists, with rates from "warm reception" to "stormy ovations." Kleshchuk paid for stormy ovations, and also for "bravos!" and "encores!" – which were paid for according to the number of shouts. Moreover, a significant sum was allotted to the concert's organizers for purchasing bouquets at a flower shop. The concert's success was tremendous. Standing in front of the stage, the conductor directed the applause with military precision. Due to the undying ovations, the lyric tenor was unable to start a new song each time. Sweating and happy, he calmed the audience with a gesture, but the audience still wouldn't calm down because they had orders to obey only the conductor. The conductor couldn't see what was going on on stage and focused on the timer. "Bravo!" and "Encore!" shouted the officers' wives, which lent the audience's reaction a slightly hysterical tone. The hall was exhausted. The audience really did get wound up, and in the first section there were even unpaid-for shouts. Seeing his boss's happiness, Kleshchuk the accordionist beamed too. His fingers slid over the keys like a Geiger counter, and the heavy instrument practically flew – until they started bestowing the flowers. There were lots of bouquets, even more than anticipated, but they were all daisies exclusively. There was no mystery for Kleshchuk in what had happened: there wasn't a hint of any flower shop here. From the height of the stage, he clearly saw the nearby field where the mobilized companies had picked these daisies. Kleshchuk started playing with determination and anger, his eyes glued to the major general, the likely author of this idea. The major general looked at the stage without blinking. From time to time he would put his palm to his lips, as if lost for words, crushed by Bergamot's magical lyre. But even the daisies made the soloist happy. How romantic, he commented in passing to Kleshchuk, who was very much relieved. The one major slip-up was the absence of applause after the encore. This sudden silence was explained by the fact that only the scheduled part of the concert had been paid for, and the conductor, having no separate instructions concerning anything additional, called off the stormy applause. He called off all applause: after the first encore song, a ringing silence hung in the hall. But only after the first. After the second, Kleshchuk came stage front and started clapping rhythmically, managing at the same time to shake his fist at the major general, who was starting to doze off (whites in the slits of his half-closed lids) but roused instantly, gave the conductor the middle finger, and applause started up again the equal of which there had not been before. The next morning, all the Kyiv newspapers wrote about Bergamot's triumph. The reports evinced a uniform style – Kleshchuk's. In a confessional manner, the authors admitted that they had gone to the concert thinking of the warm reception that might be given the rising star but had never counted on that turning into absolutely stormy applause. That was the headline for half the articles: "Stormy Applause." Some noted the emotional tension, which ran so high that after the first encore the audience lost their ability to applaud (which then returned). The newspapers were silent on the subject of the massive gift of daisies, an unaccountable fact. Bergamot sobbed reading the articles, which actually worried Kleshchuk a little. Bergamot knew the organization of the concert down to the last detail (he being the one who'd paid for it), and he knew who'd written the boilerplate for the reporters, but he was still uneasy until he'd read all the identical articles. And shed copious tears over each. Kleshchuk tried to interest all kinds of social groups and placed reviews in Ukrainian- and Russian-language publications, pro- and anti-West, music, sports, and gardening publications. Only *Palindrome* escaped him, a newspaper that published items under palindrome headlines. The editors (there were only two of them) didn't come up with the palindromes but cleverly used existing ones. Small and not proud, the newspaper itself approached Kleshchuk with an offer: under certain terms to run a positive review in their pages (which, matching the number of employees, were also two). Not properly appreciating the palindrome's role in public life, Kleshchuk told the newspaper where to get off. As a result, the only negative publication about the concert came out in *Palindrome*. It was headlined, "Nod Off, Obese Boffo Don." The next height Kleshchuk aimed for was the October Palace of Culture. Hearing this, violinist Tereshchenko and bassist Targony asked why the October specifically. Because the concert's going to be held in October, Kleshchuk replied. Gleb shook his head and said the palace was too big, that gigantomania would be the organizer's downfall. Doubts came over even Bergamot, who, despite his triumph, retained remnants of good sense. Natural modesty made him protest a proposed taping of the concert for television; he obviously did not expect his popularity to be that great. But there was no stopping Kleshchuk, who was filled with spirit, as he put it. He called them to leave behind their defeatist moods and told them he knew the secret of success, which this time meant changing the target audience. This time, it should be pensioners. Kleshchuk had supposedly found the key to their hearts. To Gleb's surprise, Kleshchuk's calculation was right on the mark. Pensioners' hearts turned out not to be indifferent to two things: free tickets (distributed through social services) and free food packets. Noting that these two components – tickets and packets – almost rhymed, Kleshchuk put them in a ladder-poem à la Mayakovsky in a poster pasted up all over town. He even tried to rhyme the contents of the package, but in the end had to give up. If he got away with "oats"/"groats" (a nod to the pensioners' tastes), then, in Gleb's opinion, "lettuce" and "radish" did not rhyme, and although Kleshchuk disagreed, the assortment appeared in an asterisked list. It also said there that the packages would be distributed on the way out. Gleb advised Kleshchuk to take that part out, but Kleshchuk objected vociferously. He was afraid the pensioners (he knew them) would take the packets and evaporate. Even worse. Foreseeing it would be harder to get stormy ovations from an audience like that, Kleshchuk announced a contest for the most spirited audience member. An authoritative jury was supposed to determine the winner and give him a big bag with samples of what the soloist sold. The muses did pitch in at first (bean/aubergine), but when it came to "marinated cabbage," which was hopeless, they fled like cowards. Kleshchuk, who had found the impressive rhyme "can't manage" (without marinated cabbage), could do nothing about the meter. If it were just "cabbage," then fine; but with "marinated" – no way. He was prepared to substitute a head of cabbage for the marinated cabbage in the assortment, but Bergamot forbade him; he only wanted to offer highly processed foods. Actually, the concert at the October Palace was a kind of product too. The processing concerned the lyric tenor above all. They made a recording for each song; moreover, Bergamot's voice was reinforced by the voice of USSR People's Artist Solovyov. The opera soloist had won this right by winning a private competition for the best imitation of Bergamot. The competitors got to know his performance style and mastered his characteristic features. Bergamot lisped, so they lisped; he sang "enuv" (in "Enough Tears"), so they sang "enuv." At a certain point, the singers had questions about the word "azvalt." The voice coach, after weighing the pros and cons, concluded that in this context (the song "Rolled into the Asphalt"), that pronunciation was the only one possible. Why pretensions arose against that word specifically was a mystery; among the peculiarities of Bergamot's pronunciation, this was not the most striking. When all the songs were recorded, ten days were spent on rehearsal, and Bergamot learned to sing to the recording. Preparations for the performance were multifaceted and took a lot of time and money, but the concert, as already noted, was scheduled for October. Bergamot was fine. He would open his mouth inspiredly and let out, note after note, the free-flowing sounds from the speaker. Between songs he would say a few sentences, quoting, as if just happening to recall, Dostoyevsky, Joyce (Kleshchuk chose the texts to learn), and also Gianni Rodari, who'd been read to him as a child. Quotes from *The Adventures of Cipollino* roused the hall and allowed the audience to view the vegetables with new eyes. Apart from the main hero, Bergamot acted out Signors Tomato, Radish, and Bean. Not Godmother Pumpkin, since pumpkins weren't part of the assortment. Later the press noted that the performer successfully combined profound erudition with a refined sense of humor. Generally speaking, Bergamot's refined taste won special praise in the reviews. The performance of a nonclassical (to put it mildly) repertoire in an operatic manner was declared a new musical style: operatic *chanson*. The pensioners didn't let him down either. According to the newspapers, in hopes of winning the audience prize, they *lit up*, leaving rock fanatics in the dust. *Palindrome*, though, responded to the event with a devastating article accusing the organizers of pandering to the pensioners and even bribing them. The headline in the first column, "Bombard a Drab Mob," reflected the content rather precisely. At the same time, the newspaper did not limit itself to general criticism, not disdaining ad hominem attacks. In the same issue they ran an artistic portrait of the violinist Tereshchenko ("Avid Diva") that was highly negative and contained, among other things, allusions to his stature. These publications (it's easy to hurt an artist) genuinely grieved Bergamot. He got in touch with *Palindrome*'s editor and asked whether he liked baseball. As it happened, as the editor was responding, several individuals entered his office carrying baseball bats and smashed all the newspaper's equipment. The editor's feelings about baseball never were clarified. Three weeks later, the high-profile concert was broadcast on television. Half of the long shots were devoted to the elderly. Pensioners dancing in their seats, rushing the stage, throwing flowers to the performer (this time Kleshchuk prudently purchased bouquets himself), and swinging him in their arms. These frames went all over the world as an example of sprightliness at an advanced age. They were shown in Vladivostok, where they drew the attention of ophthalmologist Sudarushkin, who had once been the victim of a financial pyramid. In the Ivasik being swung by the pensioners he recognized the pyramid's builder, Vitaly Bezborodov, known in Vladivostok as Tutankhamen. Yes, the artist's name and appearance had been altered somewhat, but this did not prevent the ophthalmologist from spotting his offender. Sudarushkin immediately realized whose money was swinging Bezborodov and telephoned the prosecutor's office. When the prosecutor asked whether Ivasik was definitely the once-vanished Bezborodov, he replied that you could tell with an unaided eye. The closed fraud case was reopened, a request for extradition followed, and in mid-December Ivasik-Bezborodov was being extradited to Vladivostok. Right before New Year's, the Ivasik Quartet gathered for the last time. Without their instruments, at Cricket's, a restaurant. The soloist's arrest had been a shock for everyone, especially Kleshchuk, who had begun negotiations with Montserrat Caballé for a duo performance with Bergamot. He recalled bitterly how the lyric tenor hadn't wanted to be photographed. As if he'd sensed something, bassist Targony, who was already very drunk, suggested. Gleb smiled: "Our Bergamot is a victim of his art." "He craved fame," violinist Tereshchenko said contemplatively. A tear rolled down Targony's cheek: "He was sacrificed to that craving . . . or no, he craved that sacrifice. . . . It's dreadful. . . ." Failing to find the right word, Targony drew a strange figure in the air. "Dreadful for a bug living on a branch," Gleb prompted. Targony raised his suffering eyes to him: "The bug, you know, it, it used to smile so calmly and dreadfully. . . . I don't remember who said it. . . ." "Bugayev," Kleshchuk piped up. Sweeping his plate from the table with his elbow, Targony shouted loud enough for the whole restaurant to hear: "Life is cruel, and every bug is a victim! Every bug is a victim!"

I'm fifty. We've decided to celebrate at home in the most intimate company possible. Besides the birthday boy and Katya, sitting at the party table are Vera, Nestor, and Nika. And Anna. Katya gets the credit for inviting her. Inviting Anna seemed like insanity, literally, but Katya said it was important for Vera. I relented.

After long negotiations, the attending physician let us take Anna from the clinic for one evening – on my responsibility. He warned it was a risk and categorically forbade her alcohol, even the smallest quantities. He said "alcohol," which made the danger even more obvious. Yes, for the past few weeks Anna had been calmer, but this calm was less the result of any improvement in her condition (which there wasn't, essentially) than it was the effect of the tranquilizers. Before the social event they give her a double dose.

Sitting at the table, Anna looks somnambulistic. She's scant of words and movements, her back is straight, her gaze aimed straight ahead. The waiter invited to serve the feast looks at Anna respectfully. Tonight he sees her as an honored guest, a model of restraint and aristocraticism. He puts freshly squeezed orange juice in front of Anna.

"Juice." Anna's comment is dry and to the point.

Katya brings in an armful of congratulatory telegrams and starts reading them out.

"Katya, darling" – I halt her reading with a conductor's sweep. "Let's do without that. And turn off the phone, all right?"

Katya dumps the telegrams on the windowsill.

"Gleb, darling, we can't. What if someone truly important calls?"

"Who, for example?"

I adopt an ironic look.

"What if it's the president of Germany?" Nika straightens Anna's napkin on her lap. "Or your mama, eh?"

"Knock, knock," I say pensively.

"Who's there?"

"Atch."

Having given her version of the answer, Anna is once again listless.

Nestor proposes a toast to the birthday boy. Everyone but Anna drinks. Nika hands her her juice, but Anna firmly deflects her hand.

"Mom, have some juice," Vera asks. "Please."

Her request is not granted. Katya makes an imperceptible sign to Vera not to insist. The waiter brings the entree.

And then I speak.

"I want to drink to our debut. Which is equally important to both Vera and me. We've been rehearsing for two months, and for me this has been sixty days of happiness."

Katya announces that Mayer phoned her and said we should focus primarily on the pieces Vera knows – those she's played in competitions. And he advised including a children's song in the repertoire, to underscore young Vera's age. Mayer asked something else, too, but Anna suddenly interrupts Katya.

"Sixty days of happiness. Daughter, aren't you ashamed?"

Vera sits up straight and looks at her mother. Anna isn't looking at anyone. Katya realizes that the plan to make Vera happy was a mistake, but there's nothing she can do. Nestor and I throw lap robes over our shoulders and go out on the balcony to smoke. We shut the door behind us and sit in the woven chairs.

"Are you really going to sing at the concert?" Nestor asks.

On the other side of the glass we observe the inaudible conversation in the room.

"Nestor, I wanted to tell you something. This isn't much of a celebration, perhaps. . . . I have Parkinson's."

There's no surprise in Nestor's eyes.

"I know that, Gleb."

"Katya told you? Actually, what does it matter."

"I figured it out myself. A couple of months ago, from your right hand. You put your knife into it with your left. I noticed how you write: with difficulty. And then there's the trembling, of course. It's not very noticeable yet, but my father had Parkinson's, and I see it."

"Katya's suffering from my disease more than I am. I tell her everything's all right for now. Though she sees everything, I think."

"Don't doubt it."

"She rushes to get me my coat, helps me put on my shoes. I start hissing at her, saying I'm still capable of doing everything independently. But it takes me three tries to find my sleeve. Nestor, what am I supposed to do?"

"You see, this disease isn't just physical. It's accompanied by deep depression. You need to deal with that at least."

The women in the room are silently watching the smoking men. Suddenly, Anna grabs my glass of whiskey and polishes it off in three swallows. The ice cubes jump out of the glass and bounce down her chin. Anna laughs. I see the waiter take away the bottles at Katya's request – everything but the mineral water. He's managed to realize that Anna's stillness is by no means a sign of her restraint. Rather just the opposite.

Nestor (he's sitting with his back to the window) lights another cigarette off the previous one. He notices nothing.

I notice but don't want to interrupt him.

"From time to time my father would refuse to take his medicine; he'd say he preferred croaking as soon as possible. So my mama and I would have to come up with reasons for him to live."

"For example?"

"Well, we'd say we needed him. Yes. . . . We'd say that and he'd shout, 'As a ball and chain?' My mama had the patience of an angel. She would stroke his head and say we needed him in any capacity, just so he was with us. My father knew this was the truth and he'd calm down. Sometimes. Sometimes not. From shouting he'd switch to quiet tragic speech. He'd say yes, he realized we were right, but a person of his temperament and profession wasn't created for life inside four walls any more than a bird is for a cage."

"What was his profession?"

"Actor. Understand? Actor. Herein lay half his woes, I think – and half ours too. We were his sole audience, and he put his all into it. A ball and chain, a caged bird. Theatrical intonations." Nestor tucks in the lap robe tighter. "I should say that he locked himself in the cage himself. He didn't want people to see his mask-face and shaking hands. By type he'd been a hero-lover, people were used to seeing him that way."

"You keep saying 'was.' Did he die?"

"Yes. But not from Parkinson's. During one of those performances his heart gave out. In a certain sense, he died on stage. Acting is a dangerous profession."

"Oh, yes it is." I think of Mikola.

"It's not easy for me to tell you all this, but that's my experience." Nestor stands up and brushes the ashes from his lap. "Maybe it will help you in some way."

"Probably I first have to deal with my mind; then things will be simpler with my body."

"Yes. That's exactly what my father couldn't do."

We return to the dining room. Katya indicates Anna with her eyes. I make a sign that I saw everything.

"You were talking about Mayer's request," Vera turns to Katya. "About the children's song. I have one song, only I don't think it will suit."

"Why, Vera, dear?"

"Well, it's my song – words and music. It's meant for home. I feel awkward performing it with Gleb."

"She feels awkward!" Anna grabs the glass of juice and throws it at Vera. "She wants to take you away from me!"

The glass hits Vera in the shoulder and smashes on the floor. There are yellow drops of juice on the faces of everyone there. Nika picks orange pulp off her nose. Retaining her self-possession, she smiles: it's freshly squeezed, not concentrate. Anna's hand reaches for the bottle of water, but Katya manages to intercept the bottle. A moment later Nestor and I are holding Anna by the arms.

She tries to break away and howls. Nestor shouts that we need to tie up Anna, but no one knows how that's done. A coil of rope is brought from the kitchen and they start unwinding it. Katya protests that the rope might squeeze her veins. She disappears for a moment and comes back with a couple of my belts. I try to wrap them around Anna's arms, but the patient resists with surprising strength.

The waiter comes to our aid. Telling the men to hold Anna firmly, he quickly ties up her hands and feet and lays her on the rug. Left in peace, Anna quiets down. She looks up at those standing around her without blinking. Everyone exhales. Nika respectfully calls the waiter's use of the belts an art. He readily explains that he learned that art in the police, where he worked before the restaurant. He's the only one who retains any presence of mind. He asks when to serve dessert. Everyone but Anna refuses dessert. She's not opposed. They say goodbye to the waiter, adding a bonus for his additional services.

I call Anna's attending physician, but he doesn't answer. We confer and call an ambulance. The arriving crew gives Anna an injection and carries her to the bedroom. When Anna dozes off, they untie her. She should sleep through until morning, but someone has to watch her constantly.

The attending physician phones; he found the missed call. She made a scene? Oh well, that's very regrettable. He had warned us how this might end, and if it hadn't been for Gleb Fyodorovich's personal request he would never have . . . No need to disturb the patient now, but in the morning he'll come with an orderly to pick her up.

Nika goes home, but Nestor – in the event of something unforeseen – stays to keep watch with me in the bedroom.

"You know why I feel so bad, Nestor?" I pour us each a glass of whiskey. "There's no damn hope."

Anna groans without opening her eyes.

"Children, get ready for school. Vera, get up!"

I switch to a whisper.

"I remember when I was ten my dream came true: they bought me a radio. Cheap and crummy, but I was so happy! And then that same radio fell off the shelf and broke to pieces. That's what can happen to dreams. My grandmother and I took it to the repair shop. For some reason I firmly believed they'd fix the radio. It didn't look that hopeless. But the repairman turned it over in his hands and said, 'This isn't something you repair.' At first I didn't understand the words. I asked, 'What's to be done?' He shrugged: 'Throw it out.' This guy explained exactly which parts had broken and I burst into hysterics."

"Children, get ready for school!" Anna orders in her sleep.

Nestor and I clink glasses without saying a word.

"Even now, when I think of that story, that idiotic sentence is still the most awful part: 'This isn't something you repair.' Had he said something simpler, like, I can't fix it, or something like that, it would have been easier. But what he did say meant absolute irrevocability: I couldn't listen to the radio now and there wasn't money for a new one. I can hear those words in my head right now. Your body, they told me, isn't something you repair. They didn't say, Throw it out, but that's understood. And there's just nothing to pin any hope on!"

"Gleb, my dear man, fortunately you're not quite right. This time your radio hasn't broken. It does work worse, but it works."

"And it's going to keep working worse and worse until it gives up the ghost."

Anna opens her eyes.

"Atch sang long ago . . . choo choo, choo choo." Anna's eyes close. "Bass trumpet."

"Things could be very bad." Nestor nods toward Anna. "Compare."

"Scant consolation."

I straighten the blanket that's slipped off Anna. She sits up on the bed. Her hair is disheveled, her gaze wanders.

"Children, school. Vera, where are you, daughter? Atch . . ." – she waves her baton – "choo choo, choo choo. Four quarter time."

She lies back down and falls asleep.

Nestor's asleep now too.

And I'm writing.

1993

After Bergamot's arrest, Gleb and Katya spent another few weeks in Kyiv. They had no idea what they should do next. They didn't feel like going back to Piter; clearly that phase of their life was over. The matter solved itself when one sunny January morning bailiffs rang the doorbell and demanded they vacate the apartment in an hour's time; it was going under the gavel to pay Bergamot's debts. The bailiffs watched captiously as Gleb and Katya packed up their things, but they let them take everything. They may not have been counting on taking control of the territory so easily. After a couple of hours, a laden taxi set sail from Bergamot's building. Gleb and Katya spent the night in a hotel, and the next day (Gleb already had a German visa) they boarded a train for Berlin. They chose a train rather than a plane due to the large quantity of luggage. As for the decision to go to Germany, it wasn't sudden – witness the visa, actually. This turn of events had not been ruled out, although you couldn't say the Yanovskys had done anything to hasten it. It occurred to Gleb, and especially Katya, that Berlin might present its own complications. But neither Gleb nor even Katya foresaw the degree of those complications, which began right at the Berlin train station: Katya's parents did not show up. Katya tried half-heartedly to explain this non-welcome, although they both understood perfectly what was going on. They'd never spoken about Katya's parents, but Gleb understood that it was no accident Katya had never invited him to come to Berlin with her. Gleb met his new relatives in the doorway of the apartment on Vinetastrasse. They greeted their son-in-law without any particular delight and then watched silently as Katya and Gleb carried their things in from the taxi van. Katya seemed not to notice the cool reception. She smiled her disarming smile and told them how hard it had been to convince the border guards that she and Gleb weren't smugglers. She didn't disarm anyone. Her parents kept standing there with stony faces, and the story about the border guards did not amuse them. And anyway, that hadn't happened. Gleb felt excruciating pity for his wife. And love. Katya's mother quickly asked Gleb something. Even too quickly, he thought. Was she checking up on his German or something? Seeing Gleb's confusion, Katya interpreted immediately: "Mama wants to know what you would like to do in Germany." "You, for instance, could be your husband's interpreter" – and Gärtner père smiled for the first time. "If someone will give you a paycheck for that, of course." And what was he going to do? Germany doesn't have a profession like that: counting crows. Gleb was about to give some thought to an answer, but he realized no one was expecting one. From then on they ignored him and the conversation between the two Gärtners continued. With the first sounds of the television news, they shut themselves in the living room and didn't show their faces again that evening. Only before bedtime did Gleb run into Frau Gärtner near the toilet, and she said something to him quickly. Again Gleb didn't understand – and she gestured hopelessly. When Gleb called to Katya, Frau Gärtner said distinctly that Katya now really did have an excellent job, rendering Gleb her services as interpreter. Along with all her other services, of course. Katya blazed up, but Gleb concluded that his mother-in-law could speak distinctly, it turned out. When she wanted to be heard. Katya asked what exactly her mother wanted to tell Gleb, but she herself couldn't remember now. Frau Gärtner went to her room (her parents slept separately), and Gleb and Katya went to their, formerly Katya's, room, a small room with a cupboard, a desk, and Katya's childhood bed, on which Gleb didn't fit. Katya found a cot for him in the storage room. Before going to bed, they each ate a bar of chocolate. To Gleb's silent amazement, Katya had bought the bars at the station. Now it was clear to him that his wife knew they might come in handy. Then they set up the cot. Gleb bedded down on it, in a manner of speaking, but sleep wouldn't come. From Katya's restrained sighs, he realized she wasn't sleeping either. His pity for his wife turned to tenderness. To the creaking of springs (though the idea had been to be silent), Gleb rose from the cot and rested his knee on Katya's bed. It really was hard to lie down beside her; he had to throw his arm and leg over Katya. "Put up with my parents," Katya whispered, "even though they're nothing but repulsive." Gleb brought his lips to Katya's: "I don't find them repulsive because they had you." Katya wound her arms around his neck. "I'll have someone even better for you. Kiss me. . . ." When they emerged from the room in the morning, Katya's parents were having breakfast in the kitchen. They said they'd be finished in about fifteen minutes and then Katya and Gleb could have breakfast. They also told them that for *this* breakfast they could take food from the refrigerator; in future they had to buy everything for themselves separately. A separate shelf had been cleared for them in the refrigerator. Katya wanted to go to the store right away, but Gleb quietly squeezed her arm: Don't make matters worse. Katya didn't. Everything was bad enough as it was. Gleb saw her lips trembling from time to time. She felt hurt and ashamed simultaneously. She hadn't expected anything good from their arrival, so her hurt was more like anger, but shame was shame because it was all unfolding right in front of Gleb. They had plunged into an airless space. A breath of fresh air arrived that evening in the person of Uncle Kurt, who was uncle only to one person, essentially, Katya's father, being the brother of his deceased father. Uncle Kurt, who had the same last name as his nephew, was, according to Katya, his complete opposite. The fact that she defined her father as Uncle Kurt's nephew did not escape Gleb. Observing relations in the family, he realized that of all the Gärtners, Katya loved only this old man. He showed up without an invitation. Or rather, the invitation followed after he said he was going to come see Katya and her husband. Kurt Gärtner was a famous artist, his paintings were expensive, and he was lonely. These were the three reasons that, in Katya's opinion, compelled her parents to reckon with him. They often speculated on what kind of estate he would have, and in interacting with him displayed their best qualities just in case. Actually, Uncle Kurt didn't look like someone planning to die in the near future. He was a tall, stately old man, who looked a little like Hemingway. He hugged Katya (she hung on his neck) and firmly shook Gleb's hand. He asked, in Russian, "How's it going, comrade?" "It's going great," Gleb replied and praised his Russian. "A good school," Frau Gärtner said (a sigh of sympathy). "Yes, a good one," Uncle Kurt confirmed, and he added that he had the best memories of Russia. Katya, smiling, explained that her Uncle Kurt had spent several years as a Russian prisoner of war. Her uncle nodded with a serious expression on his face and remarked that captivity wasn't the worst way to study a country. Maybe it wasn't a resort (he winked at Gleb), but the experience he'd gained had hardened him for life. And helped him understand life. Uncle Kurt loved Bulgakov and Tarkovsky and – what was most important for Gleb – once upon a time had supported Katya's decision to study in Russia. When they started getting ready for dinner, Katya asked her mother whether she and Gleb needed to cook something separate, but Frau Gärtner replied that of course they didn't. She laughed. Blushed. "We have our little family jokes." Uncle Kurt smiled at Gleb. "Every family has its jokes" – Gleb smiled back – "and that's fine." Katya shrugged: "Ours are a little strange." She was clearly going on the attack, but Uncle Kurt introduced conciliation: "Let Gleb get used to it. After all, he's a member of our family now too." He made a toast to the family and the dinner. He complained that Katya's sister Barbara was so far away now. "She escaped, poor thing," Katya whispered to Gleb, "to study medicine in Manchester." Before leaving, Uncle Kurt found it necessary to speak in private with the young couple, so they went into Katya's room. The old man's face was sad. "You have to get the hell out of here," he said suddenly. "These fowlers are going to pluck you clean." Katya turned away. Uncle Kurt patted her head: "I'll try to come up with something. But for now" – he took out a fat envelope and handed it to Gleb – "take my wedding present. How does that go in Chekhov? The belated flowers . . ."

Vera and I are preparing for our concert. Vera is sitting at the synthesizer, and I'm looking at the music over her shoulder.

"I'll sing the first verse and then we'll try it together, all right?"

"All right. Listen, why don't you sing this song alone?"

"Don't you like it?"

"On the contrary, very much. It just seems to me that this needs to be sung in your angelic voice, and my humming will spoil everything."

"That's clear, then. The song is out." Vera slaps the music. "You know I don't like it that much myself."

I put my hand on her shoulder.

"Vera, dear, whatever you decide is how it will be. Sing me the first verse."

Vera shakes her head. She musses the hair on her forehead. Her face has a yellowish cast.

"Please." I fix her bangs.

Vera slips out from under my hand and looks at me carefully. She opens the music and runs her fingers over the keys. Then she touches them. And starts to sing.

I start in on the second verse: "The ducks have left the lake."
Vera takes her hands off the keyboard:

"The verse starts on C, not A."

"Right, the even verses start on C: The ducks have left the lake, /
Morning has broken / The sky is pink –" I break off singing. "After
this let's try taking turns: 'Soaring up, without a sound / a voice....'"

"Soaring up, without a sound / a voice, / Aiming, / As if the lake
were in the sky / Just the same."

"As if the lake were in the sky / Just the same," I join in on the
repeat. "And now me: 'They drift up there, becalmed, / For symmetry – heads down....' Not bad! 'For symmetry / heads down.' We try
it together. 'Then they languish / Over their good luck. / And what
they've left behind, / Ever shall they mourn.' On the repeat, just you."

"And what they've left behind, / Ever shall they mourn."

A beaming Katya is standing in the doorway. Both thumbs
up – her trademark gesture. Vera is flustered; she still doesn't know
how to accept praise. I kiss Katya and go to my room. I'm about to
go to my study, but Katya stops me. She closes the door.

"They just called from the hospital. When you were out we went
there for testing." Her throat catches. "It's all pretty bad. Pretty bad.
Do you understand?"

"Wait up. What did they say specifically?"

"Vera's bile circulation is impaired. Bile is starting to spread
through her body. Have you noticed how yellow she is? The blood
isn't getting filtered properly. When unfiltered blood reaches the
brain, the person becomes aggressive and unpredictable. They
warned me that this would all start showing up in the near future."

It already has. A medical prognosis is one thing, but the changes
you observe yourself are another. What Katya faces with respect
to me.

"What are they suggesting?"

"Immediate hospitalization. I couldn't tell her that now."

I get my phone out of my pocket, dial Mayer, and tell him what Katya said. He promises to call back in an hour.

Me to Katya:

"They'll call us back. Sit down, no need to stand like that."

"How 'like that'?"

"Hopelessly."

Katya sits down in the armchair; I on the swivel chair by the instrument. I play the song's melody with one finger. Vera appears in her pajamas; she's come to say goodnight.

"So the song's okay?"

Katya smiles:

"As you see, he can't stop."

Katya and I give Vera a kiss and she goes to bed.

Mayer calls, exactly an hour after our conversation. He's punctual. Effective. Sparing of words. There's a place for Vera in a Berlin clinic. Two days to pack.

1993

Meeting Uncle Kurt inspired hope. It wasn't even that his royal gift (the 20,000 marks in the envelope) gave us the chance to escape. The very idea that somewhere nearby, in the same city, there lived someone who would find a solution if worse came to worst, gave us much-needed support. And the worst was swiftly approaching. The three weeks we spent in Berlin did not differ especially from the first day. In dealing with Gleb, Katya's parents kept up their rapid speech and eye-rolling when he didn't understand. Sometimes they switched demonstratively to slowed speech where the verbs were in the infinitive and the nouns in the nominative: snow shoes to dry; light to shut off. Everything nasty about him was spoken in a clear, measured recitative – to Katya, in his presence. One day, Frau Gärtner made a sign inviting him to the toilet. She opened the door and pointed to the toilet seat: "Drip, someone to drip." Hearing her mother's foreign constructions, Katya appeared immediately. At that moment Gleb was trying to explain that when he used the toilet he always raised the seat. Katya told her mother that the person who poured out the old tea leaves from the teapot into the toilet could have dripped (it was forbidden to pour the tea out in the sink). According to Frau Gärtner's version, however, only someone "peeing standing" (she used the word *Stehpisser*) could drip "like that." When Katya reminded her of the presence in the apartment of one other *Stehpisser*, Frau Gärtner shouted that her daughter had better not talk about her father that way. Gärtner père emerged at these shouts. Hearing about the suspicion that had fallen on him, he nearly choked with indignation and even raised a hand at Katya. Gleb, who had been on guard, was instantly by his wife's side. Katya pushed Gleb into their room and closed the door behind him. Through the door he heard the shouts of Frau Gärtner and, among other things, a mention of the Battle of Stalingrad, which he, Gleb, was just about to start here. The shouts were suddenly replaced by Katya's quiet words, which were barely audible. Gleb cautiously pushed on the doorknob and an imperceptible crack formed. Katya was saying unevenly that if she and her husband left now, her parents would never see her again. By all accounts, such a development of events did not frighten them. The conversation's end was obviously near, and Gleb stepped away from the door. Katya came in and said, unexpectedly calmly, that they had to pack. Gleb didn't even ask where they were going. The main thing was: pack. He immediately took a suitcase out of the closet. Katya picked up the Yellow Pages and started calling around to hotels. She found one of the cheapest and reserved a room. Then she dialed Uncle Kurt: "We're clearing out. We're going to a hotel right now." Uncle Kurt welcomed their decision to clear out but was categorically opposed to a hotel. He told her to cancel the reservation and come to his studio. It might not be five stars, he said, but it has its own exotic quality. When Katya and Gleb were standing in the doorway, Katya's parents appeared. "Have you thought this through?" her father asked. "That's all I've been doing these three weeks," Katya said. "*Schluß.*" Enough already. And it really was *Schluß.* She never went to see her parents again. She saw them a few times at family occasions – at Uncle Kurt's – but she never went to see them. Like her sister Barbara, who also never went home. When she finished her studies in Manchester, Barbara found a job in a Munich clinic; she chose Munich in order to be closer to Katya. And Katya and Gleb ended up there thanks to Uncle Kurt. After visiting relatives on the day of their arrival, he immediately turned for help to a friend and admirer, the Munich gallery owner Anna Kessel. After listening carefully to Uncle Kurt, she agreed that the young couple's situation could be described as critical and promised to ask friends if they might be able to help. Everything favored the search. People from the most widely flung spheres gathered at Anna's gallery, including some capable of providing a practical solution to the question, and she certainly knew how to pose the question. Anna completed her assignment fairly quickly. She told Uncle Kurt that the position of *Bundeskanzler* was taken, but two vacancies had been found that could bail out the young people for now. Katya was offered a job as a Russian-German interpreter, primarily for exhibits. Gleb they were ready to take on as a tutor at St. Thomas Theological College. Uncle Kurt announced all this news in the presence of the many famous people hanging in his studio. The famous people (some of them still lacking eyes and mouths) reacted with restraint, but Katya and Gleb's gratitude knew no bounds. The tutoring job Anna had found for Gleb was not very remunerative, but it had an important advantage: it solved their housing problem. For his token wage, Gleb and Katya were presented with a small two-room apartment at the college itself. After spending a few more days in Uncle Kurt's studio, they left for the capital of Bavaria. Gleb was traveling on a high-speed train for the first time. He admired the blurred lines of the buildings, trees, and stations and their varied colors. Just one thing was missing: sounds. The train moved in absolute, almost studio-quality silence such as Gleb remembered from making the recordings for Bergamot. At the Munich train station they took a taxi. Making quiet, doleful sounds (added to the Yanovskys' own things were presents from Uncle Kurt), the car merged with traffic. Half an hour later they drove through the college gates – with seemingly similar songs, but now in a major key. Their new life greeted them with the automobile's joyous crunch. Over the course of their trip, its dulled paint's shine had been restored, and the driver was now a little younger.

MAY 5, 2014, BERLIN

A deluxe hospital room. Vera has been here for more than two days, undergoing a thorough examination. The doctor appears and with his apologies asks me to step outside for a while.

"Go for a walk somewhere," Vera says. "Why should all three of us be cooped up here?"

On the whole, the doctor understands what's been said from her expression. He speaks to Vera in English:

"In your papa's place, I would go to the Tiergarten, it's nice there now. And your mama can help us with German."

A smile appears on Vera's face.

"Hear that . . . Papa? To the Tiergarten this instant, Papa."

She likes the word. I stand at attention and salute. Katya straightens my collar:

"Our papa is very accommodating. Such a good papa."

"What about Mama?" the doctor asks. "She won't let us down?"

Katya pauses and says:

"Things are very complicated for us when it comes to mamas."

The doctor puts on his stethoscope. Implacable.

"Let's open our mouth, yes. . . . Parents are nothing but trouble. Say ah. . . . What creatures parents are. Again: ah . . . Excellent, Netrebko can relax. Now, let's undress to the waist."

I leave the room. A taxi quickly takes me to the Tiergarten. It's green and sunny there. Why is it green and sunny everywhere in the world except Petersburg? The leaves there are only starting to come out, but here they're in all their glory. I won't even mention the sun. I step off the path and sit on a bench by the pond. Rare passersby on the path and ducks on the water. Park life and pond life. Not hospital life.

An old man asks my permission and sits at the other end of the bench. Hat and cane: receding Berlin. "The ducks dive comically for food – only tail and feet on the surface. They drift up there, becalmed," – I feel the old man's eyes on me – "For symmetry – heads down. . . ." What's going to happen to Vera? I'm a stranger to this beauty, but Vera is even more so.

"Parkinson's?"

I turn to the old man and don't hide my surprise. He lifts his hat.

"Do you have Parkinson's?" The old man points to my trembling hand. "Forgive me, I'm asking out of love, not curiosity."

Is that so. I feel a surge of energy – exactly as much as I need to say something rude and leave. But the old man radiates good will. His hand, resting on his cane, is trembling – much harder than mine.

So be it, then. Is this sufficient cause for interrogation, especially in Germany? And yet my irritation passes.

"Are you a colleague?"

"A colleague!" Smiling, he lifts his hat again. "Colleague Martin. And you are colleague Gleb. A famous man. You look very sad; you're thinking about your illness."

"There you're wrong."

"That means you're thinking about how to live now."

I look into Martin's blue eyes.

"And are you going to explain that to me?"

"Naturally! Because I've already been through all that. Otherwise there'd be no point in me striking up this conversation."

Martin falls silent, his eyes are closed. Ripples cover the water, and the wind drives last year's leaves toward the little island in the middle of the pond. The ducks head there too.

"What's your main problem with the disease?" Martin asks without opening his eyes.

"That it's incurable."

"You mean old age is curable? And death?" He looks at me with his former sprightliness. "They're no less real than our disease, but you have no acute fear of them. There's the calm understanding that one fine day –"

"That's quite true. Only people don't talk about old age or illness being incurable. An utterly hopeless word! More hopeless than death."

"That means you're afraid of the words, not the phenomena."

"Old age and death – those are sad but natural. Whereas illness . . ."

"Illness is natural too."

I'm quiet for a while.

"For whom?"

"For you and me. Who else? Don't look on the illness as something external. Love it, it's yours, all yours!"

"An optimistic view. You mean I'm going to shake like an autumn leaf and be happy about it?"

"You're going to think, I'm all aflutter."

I find that funny.

"Martin, you forgot about the accompanying phenomena! I don't even want to bring them up."

"You can be proud to have so much accompanying you."

"The day will come when it's going to be hard even to walk around the room."

"Sometimes a room is bigger than the whole world. The main thing is not to grieve over what hasn't happened yet. Because then you've got double woes: first, Parkinson's; and second, your grief. Start helping someone, and that will help you yourself. There are people in the world much worse off than you."

"I have. It just happened."

"Easier?"

His clear gaze makes me uneasy.

"Harder, Martin. Much harder."

1993

St. Thomas Theological College was an educational and philanthropic institution. Its educational component provided a theological education and was viewed as supplemental to university instruction. The college's philanthropic activity was expressed in its care for people with psychological disorders and physical disabilities, who lived there in special wings. On the day of his arrival, Gleb met with the college's rector, Pater Peter (known as PP for short), and signed a seven-page employment contract, which listed the new tutor's duties and rights with German painstakingness, including all exceptions from said duties and rights. In short, Gleb was given two main assignments: teaching Russian to future theologians; and (surprisingly) guitar lessons. Both were considered essential for a theological education.

The Russian language gave students access to Orthodox theology; the guitar to the beautiful, since (here PP allowed himself to smile) a true theologian cannot manage without the beautiful. PP suggested he and Gleb use the informal "you"; the brothers and sisters did not address one another otherwise here. Gleb replied, "Gladly." PP asked him to tell Katya this too. Gleb promised he would. He and Katya immediately felt at home here, and he liked that. They were given the option of ordering breakfast and dinner in the common kitchen – inexpensive but tasty. All in all, Gleb and Katya quickly became convinced that theological daily life was arranged wonderfully sensibly. Those who think about the heavenly organize the earthly well too. The main plus of their current situation was the absence of Katya's parents. Their three-week life under the same roof with them had felt so endless and hopeless, they simply couldn't believe in the possibility of change. The main victim of those three weeks had been Katya, on whom it had been hardest of all. As the years passed, Gleb was amazed that Katya, good and all-forgiving Katya, didn't change her attitude toward her parents. Once Gleb asked whether she didn't want to forgive them, but Katya replied that forgiveness was beside the point. She just couldn't see them. Even later on, when Gleb (as it happened) paid for their expensive treatment and the Gärtner couple behaved quite differently, Katya tried to keep her personal contact to a minimum. Gleb realized this wasn't about the three weeks but about her childhood spent with her parents. Katya's sister Barbara never brought a husband (which she never did acquire) to meet them, but her attitude toward her parents was no different from Katya's. In Munich, Gleb and Katya simply forgot about her parents. Both of them liked their new jobs, which might not have been that good but did give life a new impetus. Katya translated exhibition catalogs and documentation into and out of Russian for several Munich firms collaborating with Russia (Gleb corrected her Russian). She also did consecutive interpretation, which at first was quite difficult. The people being interpreted ("speakers" here) frequently forgot about the interpreter and she had to interpret what was said in large chunks. In this event, Katya's colleagues advised her to bring a notepad to jot down key words as an aide-mémoire. But there were also speakers who waited for interpretation after every sentence, which you'd think would simplify things. In reality, it didn't. Interpreting sentence by sentence made the interpreter's tiniest mistakes more noticeable. What saved her was that, as time passed, Katya made fewer and fewer mistakes. Gleb gained experience too. If at first he worked from his school memories in his guitar classes and mainly urged them to play with nuance, later on the list of his requirements expanded considerably. Three people volunteered to study with him, one of them a beginner. A female beginner. Beata Bauer, a tall (taller than Gleb) blonde native of Hamburg. The call to play with nuance didn't affect her since she couldn't play at all yet. Beata faced a simpler task, learning the methods of sound production, so she couldn't join the regular group. For now, Gleb was placing her hand the way Vera Mikhailovna once had placed his. The right hand has to form a little house over the strings ("a little house," Beata repeated seriously), and its roof can't collapse in the process. Using Vera Mikhailovna's method he stuck his finger into Beata's little house to show how badly her roof had caved in. His finger got trapped there. Gleb (a carefree bug who had penetrated a predatory flower) raised his eyebrows, but Beata didn't let go of his finger. "It won't work to play like that," he said calmly. "But I want to play," the young woman objected. "Very much." Gleb realized a nonmusical situation was taking shape and decided that in this case the best thing was to stay calm. Which was not all that easy, actually. He was embarrassed, and Beata (his finger was still in her possession) sensed that. But Gleb was older, and in these situations that counts for a lot. He saw in his pupil something that wouldn't let him take her seriously. When Beata let go of his finger, Gleb smiled: "Well then, shall we study?" "Yes," Beata snorted, "the only question is, what?" "Your left hand." He pointed to her left hand. "You have just as many problems with it as with your right." Beata shook her left hand and her wooden bracelets slid toward her elbow. "Yes, my left, of course, my left, I completely forgot about it." Amazingly, Beata was twice a beginner: she also decided to study Russian with Gleb. In this sphere, a situation took shape symmetrical to the musical one. Three people were studying Russian. Two turned out to have some familiarity with the language, and it was decided to put them together. Beata required private lessons here too. Her ability to grasp anything new was phenomenal. Beata was pursuing two majors – theology and psychology. Gleb didn't know how she'd done at university, but judging from her success in his lessons, she was doing just fine with theology and psychology too. The parallel lessons in music and language struck Gleb with their similarity; they were even held in the same classroom. The main thing was that music was language and language music. Beata learned basic note reading quickly and the Russian alphabet just as quickly. After a couple of lessons she was already playing simple musical phrases, accompanying them with phrases in Russian. She trained her digital dexterity with études and her linguistic dexterity with tongue-twisters: *Shla Sasha po shosse i sosala sushku* – Sasha walked down the road sucking a cracker. "Why was she sucking it and not gnawing on it?" Beata wondered. "Was it a very hard cracker?" "Yes, double-baked. A cracker made from a breakdown in technology. Also, Sasha may just not have had teeth. So. *Na dvorye trava, na travye drova* – Grass in the yard, logs on the grass." Beata immediately pointed out that logs are kept in a shed; on grass, they quickly get damp. If you're going to put anything on the grass, then it's that unfortunate cracker, to soften it up a little. When she heard *zhutko zhuku zhit na suku* (dreadful for a bug to live on a branch), the young woman just laughed. "Why does he live on a branch if it's so dreadful?" Gleb looked at her thoughtfully: "Because that's his homeland, Beata."

MAY 25, 2014, BERLIN

Vera and I are leaving the clinic. The gates spring closed behind us. The car heads for the airport: we're flying to Petersburg. Two days ago, Katya flew there to arrange everything for Vera's arrival. Vera's condition has been stabilized, but her illness is continuing to develop. More than likely, she'll need a liver transplant, and oh, how complicated that is. They proposed keeping Vera under observation in Berlin for the next few weeks, but she wanted to spend that time in Petersburg. She can be followed by the doctors there. At the first sign of deterioration, we'll fly back to Berlin.

The car comes up to a light. Vera rolls down the window. Red light. A group of cyclists is crossing the street. I discreetly watch Vera: she's smiling. Yellow light. Vera's face has a yellowish cast too. I feel a lump rise in my throat. The car begins to move and starts without waiting for the green light. It's first in the stream of cars.

"Did they say we can't rehearse for the concert?" Vera asks.

"Who?"

"The doctors."

Basically they did, of course. They wanted to, but I managed to dissuade them. Canceling the concert, I argued, would be the harshest blow for the girl, while rehearsals, quite the opposite, are a stimulus for recovery. If she doesn't overdo it. The doctors agreed reluctantly, demanding specifically that she not overdo it.

"The doctors welcome any activeness. So that as of tomorrow we start rehearsing again. Unless you've changed your mind, of course."

"Don't get your hopes up." She leans up against my shoulder. She laughs. "Papa. . . . You are my papa, aren't you?"

I kiss her temple.

"And you're my daughter."

At the psychiatric clinic's recommendation, Anna has been stripped of parental rights. She has an indeterminate time ahead of her there. The question arises about guardianship or adoption – I'm not clear on the distinctions. Whatever it's called, we consider her our daughter.

The plane gains altitude. Surfacing from a puff of vapor, it emerges on the other side of the clouds, reminding me of the duck in Vera's song. Its true dimensions are lost in the infinite space, and from below it's smaller than a duck. Vera looks out the window. She turns around.

"Listen, that Giazotto . . . I keep thinking, why did he ascribe his music to Albinoni?"

"That, I fear, we will never know."

The attendant brings cranberry juice and asks for my autograph.

"Maybe he thought he wasn't worthy of the music?" Vera holds the juice up to the window and the clouds turn crimson. "That it was too great for him?"

"Well, yes, probably. For instance, he might have thought, 'Look what an undeserved gift for me.' Or something of that sort."

"Do you think it was undeserved?"

"Any gift is undeserved. It's just important to use it correctly. Giazotto found his solution."

The flight attendant pushes the newspaper cart. Vera takes one. She starts leafing through from the back. She nudges me in the side:

"Look, they write here that there is no Australia."

"Splendid."

"No, it's true, some Swedish girl proved that Australia is a fiction, a mirage. Who has ever seen it with their own eyes? Have you?"

"No, I haven't."

"It was made up in England when they carried out mass executions of convicts. To keep their relatives from rioting, they were told, You see, it's like this, he's been sent to Australia. Go check whether he is or isn't in Australia." She laughs. "Do you still believe Australia exists?"

"Now I don't even know. Maybe there is no Australia."

1993

Daily life at the college was arranged as follows. From 7:30 to 10:00 you could have breakfast in the common room. To do so, you had to add your name to the breakfast list the night before. Dinner opened at 1:00 p.m. For those taking part in the common meal, there was a dinner list with a checkmark for "hot entrée." Those who planned to eat later or in their room went on the "cold entrée" list. In that case, dinner awaited its owner in one of the refrigerators (each person had his own shelf) and could be heated up in the microwave. The college kitchen didn't make supper, evidently assuming that an evening feeding was bad for you. Gleb and Katya preferred having breakfast and dinner in company. They liked the shared conversations. They didn't have any friends in Munich, and the collective meals made up for the shortage of contact. The dinner table conversations were even more interesting because there were not only Germans but foreigners living at the college, and the meals sometimes went on for a few hours, during which Gleb learned a lot about Germany and Western Europe as a whole. About the United States, Brazil, and two emphatically southern nations, South Korea and South Africa. At the same time he thought that with each such conversation he knew less and less about Russia, which wasn't like any other country in the world. It didn't have the German painstakingness or the American wealth, didn't know how to play soccer, and had no black-skinned population. When the others asked Gleb what defined contemporary Russia, he had no clear answer. He might have spoken about its natural resources, but they hadn't made the population richer, so their very presence in the bowels of the earth had begun to raise doubts. He might have mentioned Russia's vastness, but it was quickly shrinking – and not only due to exotic Asia but also due to his native Ukraine. Ukraine was a part of his homeland in the deepest sense of the word. Abroad, Gleb got the physical sensation that his once united country had fallen to pieces that were now separating beneath him, like in an earthquake, while he stood right over the abyss feeling he might fall in any minute. This sensation was so strong that once at dinner he even told PP about it. He painted a vivid picture of the earth moving under his feet and him (a snatching movement) having nothing to hold on to. "Hold on to heaven, my friend," PP advised, swirling spaghetti on his fork. "When something like that's happening beneath your feet, it's better to hold on to heaven." He put this so simply, as if this went without saying. He sipped his coffee, wiped his mouth with his napkin, and hurried to his office. The phrase could well have become a maxim, had it been spoken in Russia. But the ground doesn't separate under Germans' feet, and there was no one to repeat it to here. There was another phrase in the college essentially no worse than the first; it was a kind of daily greeting. It had been spoken by the gardener, Pilz, as he poured unfiltered beer down the side of his glass: "You Russians, are you still Romans or already Italians?" Formally speaking, this was a question, but Pilz said it like a set phrase because, put this way, it meant that the empire had collapsed and they'd become Italians. The first time he asked Gleb this question while running his finger over a newspaper; subsequently he pretended he'd thought it all up himself. In the purely human sense, Gleb would have preferred to be an Italian, but the comparison with the Romans had its merits too. It put a toga on him, his grandmother, Lesya Kirillovna, Kleshchuk, and anyone who had ever lived in the Soviet Union. Lent them a tragic note, you might say. Pilz repeated this statement about Romans and Italians dozens of times. Actually, not every time. On another occasion there was a statement about how there is no physical law that says gas goes from east to west, so the Russians would do well not to provoke us. The gardener only repeated this phrase for a few days. Meanwhile, there was an individual in the college who did nothing but provoke the Russians. Beata. Her success at learning the language dramatically expanded her opportunities to affect Gleb. For instance, while studying verbal aspect (the hardest part of Russian grammar), Beata paid very close attention to the information that the imperfective aspect can mean not only incomplete action but also repeated action, as well as a round trip. "Am I correct in understanding," she asked thoughtfully, "that the description of actions of an erotic nature use the imperfective?" She swung her long finger like a metronome. "Yes," Gleb said politely, "especially if those actions are incomplete." The more he dealt with her the better he understood that these little outrages were not inviting something bigger since Beata didn't need anything bigger. Speaking to this was the fact that Beata played her games right under Katya's nose, thereby imposing a limit on them from the outset. His pupil was what the Russian language refers to with the industrial word "dynamo." She revved to the maximum revolutions but fired blanks. When Beata moved from constructing separate sentences to creating coherent texts, Gleb suggested she choose conversational topics. Beata asked whether she could make her first sexual experience a conversational topic. Gleb said she could, of course, if she had one. So Beata started sharing her experience. Her broken Russian together with a certain fantastic quality to her descriptions created the impression of pure fiction. And when Beata (a blue-eyed "What do you think?") fell silent, Gleb said briefly: lies. He said, "I'm certain that there is no experience in this instance – even a first. That

295

the action in the story was successfully replaced by words and that all this, obviously, is serving to release psychological (sexual?) tension." Beata would never allow a release like that with her fellow countrymen (Gleb took off his sweater and was left in his jersey) because the relations she'd constructed with her fellow countrymen were not subject to review. He, Gleb, was another matter. Gleb undid his watch strap and stated that he and Beata were people from different planets and their relationship was not regulated by conventions of any kind. This was why Beata had the right to behave the way she did. But inasmuch as she was so interested in the erotic theme (Gleb took off his jersey), he was prepared to provide her with some experience. Gleb undid his jeans belt. Just to supply you with material for your conversational topic. He undid the button and zipper. Holding his jeans up, he walked to the classroom door and bolted it. He let go – and his jeans dropped to the floor. When he grabbed his underpants, Beata said, "Please, stop." Her face was beet-red, such as only happens to thin-skinned blondes. Beata was nervously twirling her pencil, as if prepared to make a list of what Gleb had taken off. "If I'd known you'd take it all so seriously . . ." "Beata, my dear, I take it absolutely unseriously. That's the point. Nothing's going to happen between us, not a first experience, not a second." Gleb slowly put his clothing on in reverse order. When he was already at the door, Beata suddenly told him she'd made up the erotica as part of a scientific experiment. Her thesis combined Beata's two specializations and was called "The Psychology of Sin." The scholar admitted she'd gotten totally lost in the material. The pencil broke in her hands. Gleb sat Beata on a chair, gave her a kiss on the forehead, and walked out of the room. In a standing position, he didn't reach her forehead.

A week before the concert, Vera, Katya, and I fly to Munich. Mayer meets us at the airport. He'd come to Petersburg before this. He'd listened to Vera and me and refined the concert's concept and pre-sentation in the press a few times. Now that Mayer's plans are firmly in place, he's starting to implement them.

From his standpoint, if we're going to turn to something new, we have to say a loud farewell to the old. The first thing he asks me in the airport is to tell the reporters about my illness. I express doubt, but more out of politeness. On the airplane I myself had told Katya that it was time to come clean. Katya knows coming clean means admitting it. She agrees. It's time. Otherwise it becomes a guarded secret.

Which is silly.

The producer also asks Vera to talk about her illness. Here I'm prepared to argue with him, but to my surprise, Vera takes his request as natural. Mayer tells her that the performance by an ill girl on stage could support thousands of ill people, encourage them to fight for recovery – and that's why she needs to talk publicly about her infirmity. Vera agrees to do so when she has the chance. The chance, as becomes clear, has been planned by Mayer for today, and there will be a press conference in just four hours.

My view of the producer's plan is less romantic. I understand that Mayer isn't sure of Vera or even me. He's putting out the medical theme as justification for a possible failure. Different criteria apply to the ill, you see. Here people look not only at quality but at the very fact of the singing. They're sick, yet they sing. No matter how we perform, no one is going to ask for a refund, and Mayer knows that.

His main discovery is Vera and her talent. She has marvelous playing technique and natural charm. Mayer's particular impression is connected to Vera's song, which he himself has had translated. Vera is going to sing it in English. Moderately childish and emotional, this song is exactly what he was hoping to see.

After dinner, Mayer and I go to Olympiahalle, where we will be rehearsing all week with a symphony orchestra and a children's chorus. For now, there are only reporters here. They've sat in a half-circle, more or less, in the parterre. A table with name cards has been set up near the first row. In the middle is Vera; Mayer and I are on either side.

I'm anxious. Nothing like this has ever happened to me before. At the most important concerts I've dealt easily with any anxiety, but today for some reason I can't. I'm going to have to tell them about the end of my career as a musician – after so many years of success.

Mayer says a word of introduction. Under the lighting here he looks like Luther. Fat, thoughtful, he sets out his points, which are very few. When he finishes, he suggests that the reporters ask questions. Someone comes up to the stage with a bouquet and shouts that this is for me. I accept the bouquet and rather than go back to my seat, perch on the edge of the table. I look at Katya, who nods: Yes, my husband, that's exactly how you should sit. Formality at times like this is ruinous. Mayer brings me the microphone, on tiptoe for some reason. In an outstretched hand.

A question is asked by a young reporter – out of the half-dark, the backlight haloing her head.

"Mr. Mayer has alluded to certain medical circumstances. . . ." Her notepad rubs the microphone, producing a loud screech. "Can you speak in more detail about these mysterious circumstances, inasmuch as –"

The microphone falls with a crash and rolls under a chair.

"I understand your question. Actually, this is why I came today." I push up on my hands and sit fully on the table. "I want to announce that I'm ending my guitar career." A gasp passes through the hall. A few indecipherable exclamations. "For reasons of illness."

"What kind?" – a shout from under the chair and (the microphone is found) a rustling. "What illness?"

Mayer waves to the invisible reporter.

"Hey . . . come back, ma'am!"

Laughter in the hall. The reporter, breathing hard, gets up off her knees.

"I have Parkinson's disease, and my right arm is out of action." I raise my right hand and shake it, like in a gypsy dance. "The left is catching up. My tremor . . . is almost a tremolo. An unending tremolo."

A stir in the hall. This they hadn't expected. The microphone is handed to the opposite flank.

"I see you haven't lost heart."

"No, I haven't."

Trying to block out the footlights, I try to make out who has asked this. He's twenty-five or so. Jeans and a pullover. Sleeves rolled up to the elbow.

"Respect. However. If I'm not mistaken, the voice is affected as well by Parkinson's."

"This isn't a medical conference." Mayer stands up. "Is there a question?"

The young man calmly indicates there is, of course.

"Given this state of affairs, is there any point starting a career as a singer? Forgive me, but this is the natural question."

"The main thing is to be humane," Mayer comments. "Sometimes you don't notice when a journalist turns into a butcher."

"It's all fine," I reply. "I'll sing until I lose my voice. I'll raise my daughter" – I point to Vera – "with hand signs."

No one laughs. At Mayer's signal, the microphone is handed to an elderly lady.

"Might one say that your daughter is the new meaning of your life?"

I extend my upturned palm to Vera, who gives it a loud slap.

"One might."

Now it's Vera's turn. Mayer talks about her illness. They ask her to tell them how she's fighting it. Vera shrugs. She consults doctors, that's clear. And she and Gleb rehearse. Rehearsals are the best medicine, without them she might already . . . Sometimes she's not up to it, and sometimes she's afraid of dying. Then neither music nor rehearsals help. Nothing does. She doesn't know why she's telling them all this. It's not at all what she'd intended to say. Yes, Gleb and Katya took her to get baptized recently.

Mayer asks Vera and me to sing something. Vera sits down to the piano, and we perform "The Ducks." At the final note there's a burst of applause. The reporters and stage workers applaud us. Lifting their hands from their instruments, the symphony orchestra musicians, who are starting to gather for rehearsal, salute her. Coming out on stage in an organized fashion, the members of the children's chorus wave colorful ribbons. Olympiahalle's still empty rows of chairs are overtaken by ovations, but only Mayer knows this. Right now only he is enjoying the exultation of the hall's many thousands. He has a way of hearing what others can't yet.

1994–1995

Approximately a year after they arrived at the college, the Yanovskys got to know its mentally ill residents. These people lived in three separate wings, but their life did not look one bit separate. They took walks in the common yard, peeked into the theologians' wings, and sometimes took part in the common meals. The term "mentally ill" did not fully describe their condition. Many were ill in body as well as mind. Some barely had a body: twigs and husks with twisted fingers raised to the sky lay in wheelchairs. At first Gleb was afraid of them. This was explained by the fact that at first he had no contact with the residents of the three separate wings. Unlike Katya, by the way. Gleb was near to fainting when she would go up to them with her handkerchief and wipe their drool. Or straighten the knit caps on their heads, as small as decorative gourds. When PP arranged dinners together with them, food would stick in Gleb's throat. Actually, it didn't even get as far as his throat. Looking at their disease-mutilated faces and hands, Gleb couldn't force himself even to swallow. This changed with time. Observing the mentally ill, he clarified that they were all ill in different ways and each had his own special personality. There were also people living at the college who didn't look ill. Their appearance barely reflected their psychological deviations. The Yanovskys made friends with one of them, Franz-Peter, whom they had seen for the first time during their introductory tour of the college led by PP. An open car was racing along the road alongside the soccer field. Fortunately, it was racing at a moderate speed because it didn't have a gas pedal. It had two pedals, which were connected by a chain to the wheels – and pushing the pedals made the vehicle move. Simply put, the car moved thanks to the work of the driver's feet. This driver was Franz-Peter. Neither the speed nor the expression on Franz-Peter's face allowed one to say that the car was "racing." It was his zeal in pushing the pedals. He simply flew past the tour and stopped about ten meters away. With a weary driver's gait, Franz-Peter approached the halted group and said, "You have to tend to friendship." Admiring the impression he'd made, he added: "Now I'm on my way to see a certain *Fräulein* in order to rehabilitate myself, so to speak." He slapped his gloves on his hand and held a match in his teeth. That movement, that intonation, and even the match in his teeth – Gleb had seen that once, only he couldn't remember where. Katya had the same feeling. Later they realized that Franz-Peter's gestures and words came from the television. Franz-Peter was not just a viewer but the most exact and merciless imitator of television hosts and soap opera actors. The more convincingly these people appeared in his performance, the more banal and primitive they looked on the television screen. Franz-Peter conveyed with special success the speech of the officials who flashed by on the television no less often than the entertainers. Many "it does not appear possible," "in the current circumstances," and "it should be emphasized" phrases flew out of him with the steadiness of a musical robot – not indulging us, perhaps, with any purity of sound but always turned on. From time to time he would drop by the Yanovskys' and they would offer him tea and cake. Franz-Peter would tell them about the hard fate of someone in constant demand. The administration of the bus plant where he worked were constantly consulting with him. "You mean you work?" came out of Katya unexpectedly. "Day and night," Franz-Peter confirmed with a steely expression. What was most surprising was that he really did work there. Twice a week, as a form of work therapy, he was taken to the bus plant, where he swept up the metal shavings. One time, arriving at the Yanovskys', Franz-Peter found Gleb alone. In Katya's absence, the host could offer his guest only a roll and milk. "This I categorically reject," Franz-Peter said with dignity. Moving toward the exit, he said he hoped to get cake from little Daniela. Gleb wished him success with little Daniela, remarking at the same time that he didn't actually know who he was talking about. Franz-Peter admitted with a sigh that he didn't either; he was extremely honest in his relations with friends. As he was leaving, he said: "Life is the long habituation to death." Said it in passing. Without any particular connection to the preceding conversation. Gleb saw his guest out, put on his light jacket, for some reason went over to the calendar (April 15), and slipped his wallet into his jeans pocket. He went downstairs and crossed the yard. "You Russians, are you still Romans or already Italians?" Pilz the gardener asked him. Gleb waved to Pilz, not even attempting to answer. No, Franz-Peter was clearly cooler: the long habituation to death. . . . Gleb stepped under the awning where the bicycles were parked. He threw his leg over, got comfortable in the saddle, and rode out. Where he was going, he didn't know. Something had driven him out of the house. He knew only that he would remember everything he'd just now seen. Even the most unremarkable things. This had happened to him before, and each time in spring. His memory, like a video camera suddenly turned on, focused sharply and began filming all by itself. Just like a BBC series, he caught each blade of grass with its raindrop, a clinging leaf on a tree, a trembling spiderweb, for instance – everything they so love to film. On top of that, a cat licking itself on a car's still-warm hood. Lying under the car, a man with a radio (tuned to classical music) and a set of tools. Symphony for violin and crescent wrenches: each clinked its own way, depending on its number. The cat stopped its washing, wondering at the impression it made. Stretched. Admired the legs poking out from under the car. To Gleb: I told him this morning, basically, to check out the gearbox, you can take the radio along, I told him, and listen to classical, class-i-cal, none of that Bavarian tilly-tilly-bom-bom, I've had it with folk art, especially those damn bagpipes, worse than a nail across glass, and he says to me, don't worry, puss, half an hour's work, like, and that's it, we'll lie in the sun half the day, half the day, because if arms don't grow out of there, then how can you repair anything? The cat winked at Gleb and fell silent. He moved on; the camera was rolling so you could see its red light. April 15, diffused sun. He rode past the tennis court; a wall of twisting grapevines hid the players. You could hear rackets striking the ball. Life is the long . . . Please tell me, how, philosophically – it couldn't have been Franz-Peter who made that up. Maybe little Daniela? Gleb was sure she wasn't made up. The girl had probably stepped into Franz-Peter's twilight consciousness out of some Latin American soap. Little Daniela. That's what all the young women were called in those serials. Like his own two names, Franz-Peter had combined fiction and reality in his mind. And come up with a reality. The ideal viewer. Gleb coasted down Ludwigstrasse, cutting through puddles on the bike path. Beata's surprised face flashed by. A little puffy and hurt: after they'd had it out, she'd behaved like a jilted wife. Why had Beata turned up here? he wondered. Why was she tramping down Ludwigstrasse with her backpack? What was she hoping for: to stick in his memory? Above all he would remember the spring in all its details: the whooshing of the tires, the road workers in their helmets of different colors, the sunbeams in the fountain, maybe even Beata. Past the library he turned into the Englischer Garten. I'll remember it all one day, Gleb promised himself, inhaling the scent of the first greenery and last year's rot and listening to the artificial waterfalls and the natural birds. Thinking about how at that same moment little Daniela might be treating Franz-Peter to cake.

JUNE 24, 2014, MUNICH

Concert eve in our Munich home. The three of us and Nestor, who flew in the day before. He's writing his biography of me slowly but painstakingly. Now the biography is developing right before his eyes.

Before the concert no one can sleep, including Geraldina, who has her own reasons. When she was given a complimentary ticket to the concert, she asked for one more – for the gardener.

"We'll go together," Geraldina says. "It's the first time we're going somewhere together."

As I give her the second ticket, I try to guess whether the gardener knows about this. Previously he was interested in nothing but flowers – not concerts and not Geraldina. But then, in their employers' absence life did not come to a standstill here.

Imperceptibly, everyone gathers in Vera's room. Geraldina brings her a sleeping pill on a tray.

"It's dangerous for performers to take sleeping pills," Nestor warns. "There's no way to know its effect the next day."

Ultimately, no one takes the medicine. To relax Vera, we take turns telling funny stories. Vera doesn't relax, rather quite the opposite.

When she hears how once by accident I put a flannel house jacket on for a concert (the hall decided it was planned that way), Vera rushes to check her own performance dress. The story about how I once forgot the notes and made up the melody as I went turns into worry over the current repertoire.

Vera's nose starts to bleed, she gets put to bed, and she lies there with her head back. It takes a long time to stop the blood. Geraldina brings ice wrapped in a towel, which they put on Vera's forehead and the bridge of her nose. Just as Katya is about to call an ambulance, the bleeding suddenly stops. There are crimson drops on the bed and the sheepskin next to the bed: Vera tried to get up a few times.

Katya is becoming quietly hysterical. While Nestor talks to Vera, Katya whispers to me:

"This concert will be the end of Vera, it has to be canceled."

"If anything's going to be the end of her, it's canceling the concert," I reply, also in a whisper.

Katya's hysterics end as suddenly as they began. Nestor says goodbye to everyone and leaves. Katya pulls the covers over Vera and lies down next to her, on top of the blanket. I sit on the sheepskin, leaning back against Vera's bed. I start telling bedtime stories. They're in no way remarkable, and therein lies their power. Calming and soporific. I heard many like that in my childhood.

I tell them how I didn't sleep the night before my final exam in history. I studied the questions and fought sleep with the help of coffee. At dawn, I decided to get a little rest, but I couldn't fall asleep by then. Then my mother sat down next to me and told me about Brisbane, where there is a very long rainy season. The climate there is subtropical, and the rains are apparently warm. They fall around the clock so that the Brisbane River overflows and floods the valley. It's nice to think when it's raining. To read. And, of course, to sleep. As I drifted off, I felt my mother cover me with a throw. Through half-closed eyes, I see that Vera and Katya are sleeping. I don't feel like going to our bedroom so I settle down on the sheepskin. Draw my knees up. My anxiety is gone. Calm and coziness.

Vera dreams of the concert. After a week of rehearsals, she knows everything about it down to the tiniest details. She's dreamed of nothing else in the past few days. Katya dreams about an ambulance arriving: Vera's bleeding just won't stop. Everything turns crimson: the bed, the floor, the windowsills, she and Gleb, and even Geraldina and her gardener. Katya forces herself to open her eyes but doesn't fully wake up. She sees that everything is all right. She notices me curled up on the sheepskin. She tries to smile but before the corners of her lips can turn up she's sleeping again and she dreams she's smiling.

I dream of how, many moons ago, as I rode into the Englischer Garten that spring day, I promised myself I'd remember everything. Here I am crossing a stream over a log bridge. The logs knock melodiously under the bicycle wheels, one after the other. It's like a big xylophone from which the touch of rubber elicits deep, muffled sounds. Then the asphalt. After that, the tamped dirt of the bike path. When the wheels run over roots, the tools jingle freely in the bike kit. The chain flies off the gears. Putting it back on, it's impossible not to get grease on your fingers. Carefully, so as not to touch my jeans, I ease a tissue out of my pocket with my pinky. I wipe my dusty face and soiled hands. My face gets narrower, my chin sharper, my veins no longer entwine my hands with the same determination they demonstrated when I was entering the park. I get younger incredibly quickly. My gray hair immediately starts getting darker, and the wrinkles under my eyes and nose disappear, but the main thing – the main thing – is that my hand doesn't tremble anymore. My movements are sure and smooth, my shoulders are back, I'm in top form. Handsome as can be, as the song goes, I ride into the college – and don't recognize a thing. PP is long gone, promoted, his further destiny unknown. How can it be unknown, I say, astonished, if you say this person was promoted? After all, anyone higher up can be seen from everywhere, right? This was a modest promotion, I'm told, not one that many would notice, frankly. Fine, I go on, now younger, and how are Beata and Franz-Peter doing? You aren't saying they've been promoted, too, are you? Very much so, they say, a theologically accurate definition, for they have passed away. Beata ran a philanthropic organization in central Africa, caught something, and died. Pause, sigh. Don't go to Africa to play, children. . . . The only joy is that she died here, they managed to get her back home, although at that point she didn't recognize anyone. And Franz-Peter? He died for no reason at all. Up and died. I shake my head. He just got thoroughly habituated to death, I think. What did you say? they ask. "Franz-Peter thought" – I clear my throat – "that life is the long habituation to death." They drill an astonished gaze into me. "Really? He said that?" "Yes, word for word."

The novelty of college life slowly wore off. And became so familiar as to cease to feel like life. It started to resemble memories that have both good and bad to them but all of it is past. It can't surprise you. Of all the people around them, only Franz-Peter retained the ability to surprise Gleb and Katya. He regularly appeared at evening lectures and watched the speakers with the unblinking gaze of someone whose convictions are firm, if not indisputable. Franz-Peter listened closely to talks on the most complex theological topics, but his questions were simple and maximally specific. He asked one of the speakers why they crucified Christ and, most important, why he was resurrected. She replied that these were undoubtedly key questions, but limited herself to that. The auditor told another speaker that his mother had died two years ago and asked where she was now. The answer was vague enough that not only did Franz-Peter not understand it, but neither did most of the classroom. Actually, individual disappointments could not affect his devotion to knowledge, and he continued to attend the theological sessions. He listened raptly, which was why there was always a shiny spot under his nose. This had no effect on the process of cognition, but it did interfere with Franz-Peter's other important enthusiasm – his weakness for kisses – and very much so. The young women at the college didn't want to kiss him. When Franz-Peter's embraces caught them unawares, they would shout indignantly: *"Oh, diese feuchten Küsse!"* What wet kisses! He didn't kiss married women, which allowed him to visit the Yanovskys and eat their cake with a clear conscience. It must be said that Franz-Peter was nearly the only person Gleb and Katya shared a meal with because they had long since refused the shared breakfasts and dinners. There were still exceptions when it came to dinners, but they had breakfast only at home. In the morning it's incredibly hard to talk to anyone.

It's impossible to say an elementary *Guten Morgen*. Fatigue began to overtake Gleb and Katya. Their living conditions were fine – the best in their entire married life, perhaps. They themselves couldn't have said properly what weighed on them exactly, but they definitely felt a weight. It was becoming increasingly clear that weariness comes not only from an excess of effort. It comes from not moving, too. The Yanovskys began to overcome their immobility at the exact same spot where it initially arose. That point (if it's appropriate to speak this way of a tall and plump lady) was the gallery owner, Anna Kessel. All these years she had frequently invited Gleb and Katya to parties at her gallery. At Anna's request, Gleb would play the guitar at these parties and even get a small honorarium for it. Gleb liked these performances. They didn't obligate him in any way, and as was his habit, he played calmly and hummed, not particularly concerned about the impression he made. At first, Anna asked him not to hum too much (this seemed like something unusual to her), but her guests liked his humming, so she left Gleb in peace. Let him hum, she decided. Present at one of these *jours fixes* was Stefan Mayer, who, unlike the other guests, who were engaged in conversation, spent the entire evening listening closely to Gleb's playing. When everyone was dispersing, he asked Anna to introduce him to Gleb. "In my opinion he plays quite well," Anna said, and Mayer nodded. "Although he does hum a little," the gallery owner added, so as not to overpraise the musician. "He hums phenomenally," Mayer murmured. "I've never heard a voice resonate so amazingly with an instrument." "I always thought there was something to his humming," Anna said as she introduced Gleb to Mayer. The producer gave Gleb his business card and invited him to come to his office the next day. "With my guitar?" Gleb asked. The German glanced briefly at Gleb's guitar: "No, no need." The guitar from the Leningrad Musical Instrument Factory (Gleb suppressed a smile), you see, was not to his liking. When Gleb arrived at Mayer's office, Mayer went to a mahogany cabinet and opened it without further ado. Lights turned on inside. Gleaming in the beams, secured on special clamps, was a guitar. Mayer clicked them open and took the guitar out of the cabinet. "José Ramirez, the Stradivarius of the guitar." He held it out to Gleb: "Play." And Gleb did. One after another he played pieces from the classical guitar repertoire – Tárrega, Giuliani, Sor. "Now play nonguitar classics," Mayer requested. Gleb played a fragment from *The Magic Flute* that he'd learned back in school (in Sor's transcription for the guitar) and the Fugue from the Sonata in G minor (transcribed by Tárrega). He played and luxuriated in the instrument. So resonant! So fragrant. It opened up like the bouquet of a noble wine. "Voice," Mayer said quietly. "What?" Gleb asked. Mayer looked vaguely out the window. "What you call humming." Mayer was immediately presented with the voice. "*A bocca chiusa,*" the producer commanded, which in Italian means singing with mouth closed. Gleb sang as requested. It was utterly impossible to tell from Mayer's face whether he liked Gleb's closed-mouth singing. Not very much, evidently, because after a little while he said, "And now part your lips." Gleb did, but, as became clear, too much. "You're not at the dentist." Mayer bared his ideal teeth. "Not so widely." When Gleb was ready for the disappointed Mayer to tell him goodbye, Mayer spoke. What the producer said so failed to correspond to his face's weary expression that at first Gleb thought he'd misheard. Mayer called Gleb an outstanding performer and saw it as his mission to allow Gleb's talent to unfold. Gleb's power was not in his supernatural technique or ear (which he didn't have) but in the prodigious symphony of his voice and instrument. This was the result of Gleb's special energy, which, if you liked, could be called a gift. Where and how the performer had come across this exceedingly rich energy stratum, Mayer didn't know, nor did he care. The main thing was that he could see the tremendous potential of that stratum and the nature of its energy streams. As an intelligent person, Gleb remained guarded. The half-smile on his face attested to his readiness to consider all this a send-up at the first sign of such a revelation on Mayer's part. But those signs didn't come. Moreover, Mayer described in detail the characteristics of the energy streams supposedly pouring out of Gleb. One did not feel subtlety in them, and they weren't connected to musical intellectualism (the conventional Debussy, Stravinsky, Schnittke) – that enchanting fountain that shatters energy with its virtuosity. No, these were mighty waves, all-consuming waves. According to Mayer, waves of this kind could be ridden only by well-tested surfers like Bach, Mozart, Beethoven, and Tchaikovsky. If you like – the author of Albinoni's Adagio. This company would send the future star's energy along its true course. "You want me to play popular classics," Gleb said in amazement, "but this is ... banal." Mayer looked at him sternly. "Is that so? Well, all the principal truths are banal, only that doesn't make them any less true. Banal material played nonbanally – what could be better? You have to play these guys as if for the first time. Making it clear, of course, that you know this has been played already. Rootedness on their part, flight on yours. This is like an enormous, deep-rooted tree soaring upward – that's what art is. Have you seen a storm twist trees out by the root?" Mayer didn't wait for an answer: "I have. You probably think they shoot up like a rocket." (Gleb thought no such thing.) "No, they rise slowly into the air as if dragged out by a crane. They turn on their axis." Mayer extended his arms and turned as well. He looked like a bear at a fair. "And they rise higher and higher. It's a fantastic sight." Mayer flew up a little and then returned to his modest height. "It's that might you have to achieve! I'll pay for consultations with conservatory professors (guitar, voice), but in the scheme of things they can only spoil you. So listen to them with half an ear and strive only upward. They won't understand your humming, but they'll give you useful advice on performance technique. That's all." He lowered himself into a chair. "No, not all.... I'm giving you this guitar for temporary use. Don't refuse." (Gleb wasn't refusing.) "We both have an interest in the result. Just take good care of it, that's all. It's insured, of course, but I'd be sorry to lose it. I saw the shovel you were playing. We aren't going to conquer the world like that. Now that's all. I'm starting work on your first concert."

JUNE 25, 2014, MUNICH

"When I started work on his first concert . . ." Mayer is helping Katya and Vera out of the limousine.

On the other side of the vehicle, Olympiahalle staff meet me. As does the roar of fans. I wave to them energetically with my left hand. It doesn't work with my right anymore. Everyone starts down the red carpet to the stage door. Mayer and Vera lead the procession.

". . . at first it was hard because Gleb was nervous." Mayer takes a bouquet from one admirer and hands it to Vera. "He thought he was unprofessional, uninteresting, unworthy. And who, one wonders, is worthy? Who is professional? Somehow I've never heard of a conservatory department of humming."

Mayer speaks English with Vera. She doesn't understand everything in his English, but she nods anyway. Indeed, there is no such department because she hasn't heard of one either. No one has.

"Meanwhile, your song is first-class – about the birds."

"Ducks," Vera prompts him.

"Aren't ducks birds?" Mayer, who does not like being contradicted, laughs.

"Ducks are ducks," Vera says firmly.

Katya to Mayer:

"You don't call Gleb a human. You say 'Gleb.'"

Meine Mutter, Mayer thinks in Bavarian. How subtly all this is arranged. *Meine Mutter*. Vera's behavior seems capricious to him, but one glance at her and he starts realizing that this might not be so. Her face has a yellow cast and in the light of the sconces it suddenly looks wan.

A few reporters try to get into the rehearsal room. Mayer puts them out unceremoniously.

"We're warming up our voices and fingers." He hugs Vera and me. "Warm up lightly, at half-strength."

Vera and I sing a couple of verses from a few songs. Vera is very nervous. Mayer reminds her once again that in the event of a mistake she should get pianissimo, and one of the orchestra instruments will immediately pick up the theme. If nothing at all works (these things happen), Vera should pretend to perform: the director will start the recording. She says she'll remember everything. Mayer is brought a shot of brandy. He's nervous, too, especially about Vera. He tilts his head to the side and looks into her eyes.

"This is Gleb's premiere as much as yours, by the way. He's a vocalist now." Mayer rolls the brandy under his tongue and swallows. "And it's fine, he's not panicking."

He regrets having said that. Vera's eyes fill with tears.

"You were starting to say something about the ducks," Katya reminds him angrily.

"I was. It has an attractive melody and a fine rhythm."

Mayer's smile makes his wide face even wider, but Vera is serious.

"You feel close to compositions in two four?"

"Very. It's my favorite meter." Winking at Vera, Mayer polishes off the brandy in one swallow. "There aren't that many meters that correspond to human rhythms. Two three, four four, six eight . . ."

A man in a tailcoat approaches Mayer and tells him they need to begin. He says there are fifteen thousand in the audience, that they're hanging from the chandeliers. Mayer asks him to draw up separate statistics on the hanging ones. He suggests they increase the number of chandeliers. The man in the tailcoat laughs politely. Simply because he can't not – such is Mayer's humor. They've been having this back-and-forth about chandeliers for many years. Everyone involved in concert organization is in on it. That's their way. With a military sweep, Mayer commands them to take their positions. The man in the tailcoat leads the procession.

The well-lit corridor suddenly goes dark. A light appears in the leader's hand. Vera and I realize we're already in the wings; we have come out this way many times in rehearsal. A few meters from us there is animated movement in the darkness. With the agility of crack commandos, black figures scatter across the stage. This is the large symphony orchestra that has been called here in order to provide cover for us.

Why do this? I think. Why do what I've never done before – sing?

Why have we involved Vera in this? Katya thinks. She may not be able to take it.

The symphony orchestra will keep us afloat, Vera thinks. It simply won't let us sink to the bottom.

At the edge of the stage, Katya gives Vera a good hug: It will all be fine. Vera keeps walking, holding my hand – in the total darkness. Afraid to let go. So am I. If we let go, we won't be able to find each other again. An icy fear grips me; it's put a lock on Katya long since. The fear that this girl's hand will slip out of our hands and Vera will head off into the darkness all alone.

A figure appears in front of me: "You stay here." I hug Vera and give her a kiss: "It will all be fine." The person who stopped me takes Vera's arm: "And we will continue." Behind my back, the last musicians are crossing the stage. The faintest wave of eau de toilette reaches me. I hear the floor creak under their feet. Plunged in darkness, the enormous hall is absolutely quiet. It knows it won't see me as I used to be and is awaiting the new me. Waiting for someone because it doesn't want to say goodbye yet. It knows an ill girl is performing with me, and they love her compassionately already. Only the lights – the exit signs – speak to the gigantic dark space up ahead.

A powerful shaft of light strikes from above. It rips the piano and Vera standing next to it out of the dark. The light brings sound with it:

"Fera Afdeyeva!"

Instantly, everything Russian leaves those two simple words. The hall bursts into applause. Vera bows woodenly. Her angularity underscores her young age. The change from darkness to bright light makes Vera blink. It's all put on a large screen, close-up and genuine.

A second grouping of stage lights is turned on thirty seconds later, like a light cannon. Aimed straight at me.

"Fera Afdeyeva *und . . .* Gliyeb Yanofsky!!!"

An ovation: fifteen thousand performers, and all standing. As the newspapers would later write, a four-minute ovation. And that's even before the performance.

The light goes on over the symphony orchestra and conductor. They're announced twice, but it all drowns in the general din. I take my right hand out of my pocket; it's not trembling anymore. I raise it, subduing Olympiahalle – as I'd always done in the past. I feel myself fill with strength, feel my blood being restored.

The agreement was to choose the first piece once we were on stage. Index finger – Chopin's Nocturne; index and middle – Bach's Toccata and Fugue in D minor. The choice is mine. Index and middle: Bach. The sign for *victory*. I show it to Vera and Huber, the conductor. Vera nods and Huber repeats the sign for the orchestra. He raises his baton. The hall dies down, and a half-dark sets in once again. There are three lit points on stage: Vera, me, and Huber. The conductor's baton is aimed at Vera. A sweep of the baton. A sweep of Vera's hands.

The first and most famous ten notes of the Toccata whirl over the orchestra like a tropical flower that grows in a single night. In response, seven notes, sung by me and rising to the same height. A few pensive phrases on the piano, and the music comes crashing down like a waterfall. The arrangement virtuosically unites the different streams – orchestral, piano, and vocal – first intertwining them, then letting them sound separately, but each time with a force that gives birth to a profound, earthly rumble the composer never envisioned.

With the last note of the Toccata a few seconds of silence ensue. The music was so saturated that with its conclusion the space still can't accommodate other sounds. In those seconds, the antemusical, antesonic nature of the earth surfaces. The performer knows the value of this silence; it precedes hurricane ovations. Thus, before a tsunami strikes, the sea retreats hundreds of meters and the dry land is bared. But somewhere far away, all the way at the horizon, a gigantic, albeit as yet invisible, first wave is already rushing in.

1997–1998

The preparations for Gleb's first concert took about six months. Professor Richter refined his guitar playing, and Professor Lemke trained him in humming. If the former was doing something ordinary, the latter's assignment was more complicated. Before consulting for someone on humming, he had to learn to hum himself. Being a professor, Lemke started humming fairly quickly. He was no blind defender of tradition, this voice specialist. After evaluating the unique timbre of Gleb's voice, Lemke began working enthusiastically on improving the quality of his humming and raised it to perfection so that it entered into perfect resonance with the guitar. Professor Richter did not let them down either. He went through with Gleb not just every note of his chosen repertoire but every grace note and harmonic. In lessons they played each piece many times, and each time Richter seemed to find one flaw or another in a seemingly irreproachable performance. After the lesson at the conservatory he demanded another four hours' practice at home. Gleb took the repertoire of his future concert to the point of automatism – the state when it's as impossible to stumble as it is to stumble when walking (as he thought before his illness). This music sounded in his head when he was riding his bicycle to the conservatory for his next lesson. It felt as if he were explaining the rules of Russian grammar to his German pupils to the music's rhythm. The music sounded in him in his sleep and was the first thing he heard upon rising in the morning. But one day Richter told him to stop studying and not touch his instrument. A week later, to Gleb's surprise, he began to miss the melodies – which by this point had been giving him nothing but a toothache – desperately. When he told the professor this, he said that was good. And asked Gleb to continue not playing. Toward the end of the third week, Richter himself called Gleb and asked him to come see him with his instrument. Gleb did. And when the professor suggested he play the first three pieces from his repertoire, Gleb nearly wept from happiness. He played them very well, better than he ever had in his life. Before, you'd learned the notes to perfection, Richter said, but you lacked an emotional relation to it. Love, if you like. In order to feel love, you need separation, because the strongest passion is the result of restraint. Now the separation is behind you and you're ready to perform. In any program, Richter advised him to have options that would take into account the emotional and energy backdrop, the state of his health, and so on. So, if you're feeling on the ascent, you can begin your concert with Vivaldi's *Seasons* ("Summer"). This gives the performance an emotional tension – if, of course, you have the strength to maintain it to the end. If you don't have strength for the entire concert, you need to raise the temperature gradually, starting, say, with Schubert's "Ave Maria." At his first concert, Gleb chose Schubert. As he came out on stage, he knew he was going to have to accustom the audience to his strange performance style gradually. It was later, when he and his audience had studied each other, that he gave no special thought to what he would begin with. Gleb merged with his audience, the way old lovers merge into a single organism, simultaneously entering a state of ecstasy. In those anxious moments, Gleb saw discharges of electricity in the dark hall – high up, at the level of the top tiers. They hung over the loges' velvet like tiny, cascading sparks. Sometimes several times in a concert. The wave of success didn't reach Gleb immediately. As he later told Nestor, at the first concert it barely got his feet wet. At the time, Gleb didn't know anything at all about waves or electric sparks over upper tiers. There weren't even any tiers because his first performance took place in a small hall on the outskirts of Munich. The audience had no idea what exactly Gleb was offering, so at the end of the day, no such electric effects were anticipated. And Gleb was mastering himself, not his audience. Neither his repertoire nor the modernized performance style Mayer had chosen seemed convincing to him. And if Gleb had made his peace with the beginning musician's textbook, as he called his repertoire, without any special effort, then the elements of rock music (for example, the accentuated use of percussion) raised serious doubts in him. Accessibility to everyone does not mean bad taste, Mayer tried to persuade him. At various times he went over in detail performances by Francis Goya, Vanessa-Mae, and David Garrett, closely analyzing their strong sides and, even more closely, their defects. Mayer shook Gleb up then, but he was unable to change his mind entirely. It took years of performances before Gleb stopped blushing in the presence of *classical* guitarists. He realized that what was truly important was only what elevated a person, and what you called that was of no consequence. There are no bad genres, Mayer often said. There are bad musicians. He also said that good musicians make their own rules, on which they should be judged. Germans are not indifferent to bons mots like these, and Mayer was a true German. For the first years of his performing career, Gleb invariably listened to his producer. Mayer may not have been much of a theoretician, but he possessed an unerring feel for success. With time, Gleb's work with textbook pieces changed. He used modernization less and less and to a significant extent rejected modern rhythm. He filled classical compositions with his own spiritual experience, and this was his second inspiration. Not a single critic could explain this inspiration, but they could feel it the way you smell the undoubted scent of spring on a February day. This had nothing directly to do with his performance technique or even the (outstanding) material being performed. However, Gleb's repertoire was not limited to classical music. It included folk and even pop songs. The stamp of inspiration lay on them too. Mayer saw all this as well. His characteristic feel for success suggested that here there was no call to intervene.

JULY 1, 2014, MUNICH

For Vera, the concert was an incredibly powerful upheaval. Actually, it's not that the concert *was* because inside her, it continues. Every day she sits down at her instrument and plays the entire program from beginning to end. Katya says the girl needs to assimilate what happened emotionally. Not happened, happens, because Vera does not simply play the entire repertoire time after time – each time she lives it anew.

The hall's darkness and the stage's floodlight. A pause follows the Toccata's last chord, and then – a tsunami. Only it's not a tsunami because the wave of ovations that hits us doesn't throw us back, it fills us. Vera waits for the wave to subside, casts a glance at me in the circle of light, and starts the Nocturne. I sing in a harsh, unmusical voice.

I walk into the room and Vera turns around. She says she would start the concert with the Nocturne. I agree. I promise next time we'll start with the Nocturne. Or, say, the Adagio. I explain that besides its classic-folklore-pop composition, the concert has an internal rhythm. Yes, after the Toccata we just needed to rest. Vera nods distractedly; she's already heard all this.

I know what she thinks about "next time." When will that be – and will it? In the past few days her condition has deteriorated. The tests say so.

I watch her surreptitiously: wan, yellow. You don't need tests to see it. I keep talking, to fill the silence. I feel an awkwardness, shame even. Vera moves on to the Adagio. Everyone who gave her flowers after the Adagio had wet eyes. They pitied me, and they pitied her – the two sick people. What's surprising in that? Well, and the music, of course, is luminous and tragic.

Now, no one cries for *Four Seasons*, "Summer." When she performs that piece, Vera pictures two waterfalls. Emerging in the morning from behind the cliff, the sun shines amber through them, and fine sprays create a rainbow. The waterfalls rush downward in direct proximity to each other, and there's something human in that. Unwaterfallish. They're never in unison, it's always one after the other, and they sing very different things. While Vera is picturing these waterfalls, she doesn't feel or think about her illness, even though her liver hurts more and more every day. She doesn't step away from the piano because the piano acts as a kind of painkiller for her.

I tell her Mayer called. On November 15, there will be a benefit concert in the Royal Albert Hall for children with cancer. Taking part will be Paul McCartney, Elton John, Mick Jagger, and Sinéad

O'Connor – not bad company as a whole. Yes, she's been invited and someone else too. Who? Vera asks with just her lips. You and I. And do you know what they're asking us to perform? Vera does, of course, but she quickly shrugs: "How am I supposed to . . ." I play her song's melody with one finger: This. (The doorbell rings and I hear Geraldina's hurried steps.) This song sounds incredibly fine in concert. The lyrics sail across the big screen in German. And now in the Royal Albert Hall those words will sail by in English. I watch Vera's fingers, fine and white, glide over the keys. It's easy to imagine them dead, no longer bending. Crossed on her chest.

In the vestibule is Katya's sister Barbara. Katya's muffled sobs. Vera hears them but pretends not to. Katya is at the end of her rope, and she always smells of nutmeg. She always eats a little after alcohol, believing for some reason that you can't smell the alcohol then. She also believes that we're to blame for the deterioration in Vera's condition, that Vera overdid it on the concert.

Vera tells Katya that's not true at all. There's been no overexertion. In the first place, she rests sometimes, when the orchestra is playing. Secondly, there are pieces with easy piano parts, and she rests on those too. "The Sun Is Already Low," slow and very sad. My favorite song. Now that it's clear she can't go to Katya, Vera tells me about her pains. I promise that everything will be fine, and my calm is conveyed to her. A calm I don't possess.

Vera also looks to Barbara. In addition to all the invited doctors, Barbara comes to see us nearly every day and examines Vera. Intelligent, very slightly inebriated, with a smoke-damaged voice. You can talk to her about anything at all, including music. It's Barbara who once suggested we include in our repertoire Khachaturian's Waltz from his *Masquerade* – now one of our main hits.

Vera picks out the first notes of the Waltz. She plays it with the same passion as in concert. But neither she nor I dominates in the

Waltz; here the orchestra's full might unfolds. The melody takes a turn around the hall, like an airliner over an airport. It makes one circle, and another, and a third, and still won't land – not because it can't but because it doesn't want to leave the sky.

Vera is facing a churning ocean. Wave after wave crashes over the hall, and these blows (drums) make the rows of chairs shake, and the foam on the waves' crests (cymbals) inspires the audience with awe. In the center of the storm is Huber, the conductor. His desperate attempt to master the elements is echoed by the listeners, who leap in their seats, their movements synchronized with the conductor's. Their combined efforts manage to tame the elements a little. A sigh of relief runs through the hall. And in that moment, against the background of receding horror, Vera's piano (fortissimo) and my voice shoot up, like two arrows of one blinding lightning bolt. Someone in the parterre cries out.

In halls I've conquered, I've been known to cast shafts of sparks; I was skilled when it came to electricity. But never before had I brought down lightning from the skies. And now two men in white jackets are leading someone by the arms down the center aisle. They've lit their way, and you can see the sufferer's legs – in the beginning lifeless and seemingly having forgotten the joys of ambulation – gradually start feeling for the ground. For now they are noticeably splayed, and the group still reminds me of skaters, but a favorable outcome is not in doubt. Glide, skater, glide, Vera whispers, and remember Aram Ilich Khachaturian.

Katya and Barbara are standing in front of Vera with joyous faces. The girl realizes that she is in much worse shape. The doctors say (Katya's voice is unthinkably cheerful) that you need a liver transplant. I'm going to the clinic right now to discuss the details. Barbara plays a C. She turns to Vera: "A transplant is a good thing because it means there are no metastases. Otherwise they wouldn't have agreed to the transplant. They didn't know before." Silence. Another C from Barbara. Only a C. What will they know after?

Vera plays the first notes of the Adagio. I get in the taxi to this music. I hear it during my conversation with the clinic's chief physician. The problem is the transplant. Not being a German citizen, Vera has no right to any medical programs financed by Germany.

Tearing her eyes from the keys, Vera sees the thousands in the hall rise to their feet. They put their arms around each other's shoulders and start swaying. The chief physician puts his hand on my shoulder: "You know, I was at that concert, I heard that music, and I swayed along with everyone else. It's phenomenal. Vera is still just a child. We can put her on a waiting list at home, of course, but as practice shows, not everyone lives to see their turn come up. Broadly speaking, there are various ways to acquire a transplant, but the question again comes down to money." When I say money is not a question (the doctor's respectful look), we move on to discussing the medical problems: the transplant's compatibility with the patient's organism (determined by a shared blood type), its preparation for the operation, and so forth. A transplant could show up in a month or two, or tomorrow, and you have to be ready at any moment.

The chief physician thinks very highly of his patient's talent. He hopes that the art of the local doctors will be as high. At his request, he and I sing the last part of Giazotto's immortal music. In the doctor's version, it isn't as immortal, but I delicately do not say so. From far away, from Am Blütenring Street, I hear the piano part.

1999

As Mayer predicted, Gleb skyrocketed. In one interview, the producer even called Gleb a vertical-lift fighter jet. This comparison appealed to Mayer for some reason and started appearing in most of his interviews, which actually worried Gleb a little. Yes, he'd seen those planes in war reports, but the comparison to a fighter plane was not obvious to him because, he once asked Mayer, who was he supposed to destroy? You're going to destroy your competitors, the producer explained. What's not to understand? If you think the music market is undersaturated . . . No, Gleb didn't think that. He didn't have much of an idea about the music business. Mayer, on the other hand, did – and gave detailed explanations. You can't amaze people with supernatural technique. You don't even have absolute pitch (the German was a master of the compliment). However. Mayer paused and held his protégé's chin. You have an incredible energy, a radiance, what in German is called *Ausstrahlung*. And naturally, this is your vocal effect. Effect or defect, call it what you like, but it resonates with the guitar and most orchestral instruments – to say nothing of human souls. That's what Mayer said. Time proved him right. Unlike the bellicose Teuton, Gleb had no plans to destroy anyone, but he had to admit his flight was vertical. The aviator's field of vision expanded extraordinarily, and as he gained height, St. Thomas College began gradually to shrink until it vanished from view altogether. Before it did, though, it blazed up in his and Katya's life with a touching farewell dinner. For the dinner, to which everyone living at the college was invited, the cook was asked to prepare a Russian dish of his choice. After long thought, he settled on beef Stroganoff. Getting a taste for the food, this master of his trade also made "Russian salad," known in its country of origin as Olivier salad. The cook's knowledge of Russian cuisine was extensive, although it had its quirks: for dessert he suggested serving ice cream coupes with roasted sunflower seeds. Gleb and Katya dissuaded him. To heighten the Russian flavor, along with the usual wine and beer here, they bought a few bottles of vodka. The guests drank it with pregnant looks – taking small sips and savoring it. Gleb wanted to tell them that vodka isn't savored in Russia; on the contrary, people take a deep breath before drinking it down, but at the last moment he stopped himself. Gleb couldn't have explained to them what kind of drink this was if it was better not to taste it. Only two people didn't drink, Beata and Franz-Peter. Beata had a complicated theory about sobriety that hardly anyone listened through to the end, and alcohol was strictly forbidden Franz-Peter. The young woman was sad because she still wasn't used to goodbyes, to say nothing of the vertical liftoffs of people who were part of her daily life. Usually people filter any event, even the most tangential, through themselves, and Gleb's success automatically meant Beata's lack thereof. As for Franz-Peter, he arrived in an elevated mood since he didn't know the reason for the occasion. Even before, he hadn't been interested in reasons; delicious food and well-dressed people made him happy in and of themselves. When Gleb and Katya told him they were leaving, Franz-Peter said, "I'm very, very sorry, but not to worry." Then he smiled, but tears rolled from his eyes. Katya got out a tissue and wiped his nose. "Good timing on your part," Franz-Peter said, and he started complaining about the neighbors of his father, whom he visited periodically. The married couple, both over sixty (a bird's low flight), wouldn't look Franz-Peter straight in the face. "What am I supposed to do, you think? Throw a bomb?" Franz-Peter narrowed his eyes and enjoyed the effect he'd produced. While Gleb and Katya tried to talk him out of bomb-throwing, the essence of the charges changed. These neighbors, it turned out, had harassed him with their questions and requests, pestering him day and night. You see, their lawnmower wasn't working. And this was a reason to drag a person out of bed at night? Understandably, Franz-Peter had no wish to get up. But he also didn't want to leave his neighbors unaided. He shouted sternly to them to check the lawnmower's electrics. They did and – what do you think? – the mower started right up, and they immediately mowed their entire lawn. "Immediately. You mean, at night," Katya clarified. "Immediately. I mean, at night," Franz-Peter confirmed, and he lapsed into thought. When Gleb brought him some apple juice, Franz-Peter sadly said, "Finally something positive." At his request, Gleb went to get a straw. Sucking up the last drops (the straw snorting at the bottom of the glass), Franz-Peter praised the juice. Only little Daniela gave him such delicious juice. With a sigh he added that life is the long habituation to death. Saying goodbye, he hugged Gleb and Katya. According to him, they were the only people he could talk intelligently with. "Evidently you can with little Daniela too," Gleb corrected him. "Evidently," Franz-Peter nodded. "I never tire of emphasizing that. Despite how insanely busy I am, she still loves me." A week later, Gleb and Katya moved to the apartment Mayer had rented for them.

JULY 8, 2014, MUNICH

At 9:30 p.m. we get a call from the clinic asking us to collect Vera immediately for a liver transplant. The organ's arrival in a state of cold ischemia is expected shortly; an emergency vehicle with the container left Augsburg half an hour ago. Clinic personnel have been called in urgently. The operation has to begin tonight or else the donor organ will perish.

Half an hour later a mobile ICU pulls up to the building to start preparing Vera for the operation immediately. Its flashing light is reflected on Geraldina's face as she carries out a bag with Vera's things. Her eyes are lowered, her steps wooden. Nestor and I come out next, Katya and Vera behind us.

The July night is cool. The rustle of trees. Nothing unusual, but everything is carried out so very precisely, not a single extra stroke. Strictly speaking, everything in nature should be ordinary; only then is it recognizable, only then does it touch the soul. It's reflected subsequently in various unfading things, like the *Four Seasons*.

My right hand is trembling harder than usual. I catch Vera's look and stick my hand in my pocket. Lately I haven't been thinking about my illness and only now realize this. Vera squeezes my hands and Katya's. The mobile ICU doctors interpret this gesture incorrectly and warn that only Vera is riding with them. Vera knows the others will come in another car, but this warning makes my heart sink for some reason. She lies down on the stretcher, as she is told, and the doctor draws the curtain. Katya and I are left with just her voice:

"If I pull through, let's go to Scalea, okay?"

The slamming door drowns out our response. Katya is worried that our "Let's!" wasn't loud enough for Vera to hear. I reassure her that it was and that she did hear.

Our car starts out after the mobile ICU. We make a strange pair: a medical van larded with equipment and a luxurious Cadillac with the top down because it's summer. They sail through the nighttime city, and the silent flashing light lends their movement an otherworldly look. Somewhere between Augsburg and Munich a van is speeding with the donor liver. On Ludwigstrasse, where the traffic is intense even at night, the mobile ICU turns on its siren. A minor second – there's no greater dissonance in music. The clinic gates pull aside as if in slow motion. The mobile ICU pulls up the ramp, and they show our car where to park in the lot.

The clinic gates keep opening again and again; personnel summoned urgently keep driving in. Transplant surgeons, vascular surgeons, anesthesiologists, nurses, technicians, and many others without whom the operation can't happen arrive. They get out of their cars and head for the entrance in a shared deliberate rhythm. Everything opens automatically: the gates, the clinic doors, the mobile ICU's doors, from which Vera rolls out on the stretcher. The four orderlies take the stretcher (which turns into a gurney) with the same lack of haste and move it toward the clinic doors. Her fingers pressed to her lips, a pale Katya observes what is happening from the parking lot. This general movement merges into a single, soulless mechanism that bewitches her and swallows up our little girl. Katya seems about to collapse. I take a step toward her and grab her arm.

"We didn't have time to tell her anything," Katya whispers. "Gleb, we didn't have time to kiss her."

I feel my chin twitching. Nestor puts his arms around us both.

"She knows you're here."

Katya abruptly frees herself.

"She went through those doors completely alone."

The operation is beginning in three hours. Katya, Nestor, and I wait in the corridor leading to the OR. We stand – because we can't bring ourselves to sit. At a certain point Katya says she needs to get away. I'm surprised she takes her purse, but Katya explains that a woman needs her purse everywhere. When she comes back, I detect a whiff of brandy. Judging from Nestor's quick glance at Katya, he does too. We don't let on.

After six hours of surgery, one of the surgeons comes out to see us. He's changed into street clothes. He'd been asked in to consult on the first stage of the operation, and that stage has been a success. There's no need to guess about the mood in the OR: he's smiling.

"Everything's going according to plan. I'm dying for a smoke."

I shudder at "dying." There are words not made for surgeons.

"May I join you?" Katya asks.

The doctor understands completely. He invites her to walk him to his car. Out in the fresh air, he lights up and tells her how, first, Vera's diseased liver was removed. Shunts were put in to support her circulation (he takes his cigarette in two fingers and demonstrates how), and a pump implanted to pump blood to the heart. The next stage was putting the transplant in the removed organ's place. Now they're finishing sewing up the arteries and veins, and it's already clear the new liver is going to work. The question remaining, essentially, is bile circulation, since the donor liver is transplanted without the gall bladder.

To Nestor's question about the donor, the surgeon says that's a medical secret. He can only say that it involves a car wreck in Augsburg. Such is life. Philosophical notes appear in his story: only yesterday, a person didn't know his liver would be sent off to Munich without him. His relatives gave permission to remove the organ, but they had to be convinced. That's all. *Auf Wiedersehen.* He gets into his car and drives up to the gates and waves a brief goodbye to the guard.

The wall clock. The operation has been going on for more than eight hours. No one else comes out of the OR, but the earlier tension has lifted. At the chief physician's instruction, they bring us a cart with coffee and croissants. We sit down at a little glass table under a palm. The chief physician had invited us to join him, but Katya says she prefers a tropical breakfast. In fact, she doesn't want to leave her post. This is the only thing we can do now for Vera. We even take turns going outside to smoke.

It's my turn now. I'm sitting on a bench under a maple. A light wind rustles the maple leaves. My clothing is dappled with sun, like camo. An arena for the struggle between light and shadow. If it weren't for the air moving, it would be hot. Doctors and patients walking by look at me with curiosity. Some smile and say hello. So I won't have to respond, I drop my head and look down.

My very life is there. A group of ants is dragging some winged creature toward the lawn. Everywhere the same thing. The minute they discover your wings, they try their best to hide you away somewhere. My personal experience doesn't confirm this, but it's a good image: one winged someone and a mass of socially oriented ants. I realize fatigue is starting to tell in me.

I go back to Katya and Nestor.

"A nurse was just asking me something," Katya says, "But first she asked me, Are you Vera's mama? For the first time in my life I was called mama. It's an incredible feeling!"

I kiss Katya.

"I can imagine. . . ."

Katya touches my nose with her finger.

"Can you? Have you ever been called mama?"

2000

Bicycling through the Englischer Garten, Gleb fell and broke two fingers on his left hand. When the bones mended, it was clear that one finger moved as before but the other didn't. That is, it moved, but not fully. That's not enough for a musician. Good fortune had turned its back on him this time. The foolish accident took everything away: his celebrity status, his celebrity fees, but mostly – the meaning of life, which he now found in his performances. Mayer arranged medical consultations, but nothing intelligible was said there. And although he urged Gleb not to lose heart, asserting that it was all fixable, as time passed this was said with decreasing confidence. One day, when Gleb said his vertical lift had ended in a nosedive, Mayer said something in protest but didn't object. And this was a blow for Gleb. He realized that despite his awareness of the disaster that had befallen him, he firmly believed in his producer's ability to solve any problem. This ability turned out to have its limits. For the first time, Gleb began to suffer from depression. He tore down the posters for his performances that Katya had hung up, threw away her collection of newspaper reviews, and returned Mayer's guitar. Gleb was getting rid of everything that reminded him of that vivid slice of his life. To Katya's timid question about what he wanted to do now, a brief answer came: nothing. Stormy emotions quickly wear you out, especially if you lack strength. The hysterical period of Gleb's depression was replaced by total apathy. He started sleeping a lot. Just like all those years ago, in his difficult adolescence, when he didn't feel like getting up in the morning and kept his eyes closed as long as possible. Katya creaked the doors and banged the drawers, but Gleb knew that as long as his eyes were closed she wouldn't disturb him. After breakfast he would settle on the couch with a book, read a few pages, and fall back to sleep. He would liven up a little only late in the day, when he and Katya watched detective shows at dinner. Gleb didn't care for new films – he liked German serials from the sixties and seventies. They had wise but weary commissars who looked like Mosfilm's Communist Party secretaries, and good always vanquished evil. Thus Gleb discovered for himself a different Germany, one he hadn't known anything about before. In this country, the same veneer cupboards creaked open as had in the communal apartment of his childhood. Carbon copies of his Uncle Kolya smoked at open windows, and shoes worn to holes were regularly taken in for repair. One of those movie nights, the phone rang. Gleb, who hadn't answered the phone for a long time, did not betray himself this time either. Nor did Katya answer, since she had strict instructions on this subject from her husband. But the phone kept ringing and ringing, and Katya eventually did pick up. It was Fyodor calling. After saying hello he asked to talk to his son. He asked how Gleb was doing. When he got a curt answer (fine), Fyodor said: "*Your grandfather is dying.*" Mefody was lying in a Kyiv hospital. There was something wrong with his blood. "*There's something wrong,*" Fyodor clarified. "*If you want to say goodbye, come now.*" "I'm on my way," Gleb said. He was terrified Mefody would be gone. His grandfather had been weak for a long time, and Gleb couldn't remember the last time he'd talked to him, but Mefody's very existence brought peace to his soul. Gleb knew there was at least one person who prayed for him daily. And now he would be gone. The next day, Gleb flew to Kyiv. Katya reserved a hotel room for him next to the hospital; this was a good excuse for not staying with his father. Gleb dropped off his things in his room and walked over to the hospital. He inhaled the fragrant Kyiv summer. Made fragrant by the bushes near the hospital building. They reminded Gleb of his childhood. Marigolds, pansies, tobacco plant (this accounted for most of the fragrance), cosmos. Gleb found his grandfather weak of body but strong of spirit and in the mood to talk. His grandfather preferred not to discuss his health – and immediately moved on to Gleb's life. Gleb brushed him off with generalities, but Mefody unerringly sensed something wrong. He asked his grandson to be open, the way their relationship had always been, and Gleb realized that he had, in fact, been waiting for this invitation. If he needed a word right now, it was his grandfather's. Talking about the disaster that had befallen him, Gleb felt ashamed for his weakness but, simultaneously, relief. After hearing out his grandson, Mefody took his hand and examined it for a long time. "*I worry not for your fingers but for your immortal soul. Don't despair, Gleb.*" Gleb (hesitating): "I don't know how to explain it. You see, my life has always had development. It's been exactly like a magic carpet being rolled out for me. And all of a sudden it's stopped. Do you understand? I'm standing here and have no idea what to do. Absolutely no idea. What's the point of standing like this?" Mefody (switching to Russian): "You're starting from the assumption that you can only move forward on the carpet. But that's not true. Developing means untwisting what's twisted. It's the carpet itself. So it's stopped, and you're standing looking ahead. But behind you are woven designs – walk over them as much as you like." Gleb: "In that case, you can only go backward, then, from today to yesterday. What's the point of that movement?" Mefody: "From the standpoint of eternity, there is no time, no direction. So that life isn't the present moment but all the moments you've lived through." Gleb: "You're talking about the present and the past but not about the future, as if there weren't one." Mefody: "In fact, there isn't. Not at any one moment. Because it comes only in the form of the present and is very different from our notions of it, believe me. The future is the scrap heap of our fantasies. Or, even worse, our utopias: people sacrifice the present to make utopias come true. Everything nonviable gets sent into the future." Gleb: "But it's characteristic of man to look to the future." Mefody: "That man would do better looking to the present." A nurse came in and asked Gleb to wait in the corridor. He went out and moved to the other end of the corridor, trying to step inside the linoleum squares. He stopped. How tactless, really, to talk about the future with a dying man. Even if there is no future. Returning to the ward, he tried to change the subject. He told a joke about Russians and Ukrainians, but it wasn't funny. To break the protracted silence, he said that sometimes he himself didn't know whether he was Russian or Ukrainian. Although he had known from childhood, of course. "*You are you,*" Mefody went back to Ukrainian. "*As the song goes: a man is like a tree, he is from here and nowhere else.*" As he said goodbye, Gleb asked his grandfather (he had a hard time getting it out) to get better soon. Mefody promised to try. He realized his grandson didn't want to talk about death, and Gleb knew his grandfather realized that. Gleb felt a burning shame for what he'd said, for his tone, for his inability to take with his grandfather the few steps that separated his grandfather's life from death. It had been like this when his grandmother was dying, and nothing had changed. On the plane, his face up against the window, Gleb recalled what his grandfather had said about the future. He thought about everyone who had placed their dreams there. His mother in Brisbane, Bergamot in fame, Franz-Peter in little Daniela. Had that brought them happiness? The attendant served Gleb orange juice. At last something positive. . . . Returning the glass, he asked:

333

"What do you dream of?" "A safe landing, Mr. Yanovsky." Gleb told her her dream would come true, and she cheered up. What was important was that he had Katya and their love. That was in real time. And real. A month later, Mayer arranged for an operation in Israel. Two months later, Gleb started rehearsals.

JULY 9, 2014, MUNICH AND ELSEWHERE

The operation is in its tenth hour.

I try to speak calmly.

"The chief physician called me. Vera is having some problems with her heart. They've sent in a team of cardiologists."

"We saw them," Katya speaks in an ordinary tone.

Nestor puts his hand on her shoulder.

"There are highly qualified doctors here, Katya."

Katya nods.

"I'm going out for a minute."

"Katya, darling, if you need a drink" – I point to her purse – "drink here."

Katya goes behind the palm and takes her flask out of her purse. She puts her lips to the neck and then offers it to me and Nestor. We each take a sip. Before screwing the cap back on, Katya puts her lips to the neck one more time.

"How can you not understand" – Katya suddenly shifts to a raised tone – "that if he felt he needed to tell you that, that means things are very bad! And why didn't he say so in person? We're right here! I'm asking you, why did he report this over the phone?"

She hits the flask again, not offering it to anyone else. Two doctors are walking down the corridor, one a half-step from the other. Katya leaves the flask in the pot with the palm and rushes toward them. She catches her foot on the palm's wide tray. She falls.

334

Nestor and I pick her up and the doctors are lost behind the doors. Attendants push an enormous cube nearly at a run, and Katya blocks their way. They're just boys, and they look at her scared.

"What's going on there?" She shifts to a shout. "What are you moving, damn it?"

"Additional equipment for the resuscitation experts. Let us by, please."

The corridor is full of medical personnel and patients who have come out of nowhere. Katya covers her face with her hands. She takes a step back. Nestor and I hold her up by the arms. Someone's phone plays Bach's Toccata. The clock's hands stop and start moving backward.

An elderly surgeon comes out of the OR. They chose him. He walks slowly. "Her heart stopped. . . ." Katya covers his mouth so she herself can scream. A nurse runs up to her with a pill and a glass of water. Katya knocks the glass out of her hand. One of the patients shrieks. The glass hits the floor and explodes in a mix of glass and water. "They tried to start Vera's heart for two hours. . . . They did everything they could."

Katya turns and walks, swaying, toward the exit. The crowd parts for her like the sea. Downstairs are dozens of reporters. She slips on the stairs and is caught under the arm by a cameraman. Nestor and I catch up with her. Katya is heading toward the car. She has trouble opening the door. By the car she kisses Nestor and indicates he should go away.

She looks at me:

"Get in, Gleb."

The chief physician:

"She can barely stand! Mr. Yanovsky, I beg of you, get behind the wheel."

"You see" – Katya ruffles the chief physician's hair – "he doesn't know how to drive. Not at all."

And we have to go together.

She starts the engine. I get in the front seat.

"Stop this farce." The chief physician leans over me. "I won't open the gates."

I don't look up:

"Then we'll ram them."

Katya guns the engine in warning. The chief physician says something to an attendant, who runs toward the garage. A moment later, the mobile ICU pulls out of the garage and stops in front of our car. The gates start to open, and the mobile ICU turns on its siren and flashing light. The attendant sticks his head out and indicates that Katya should follow him. Katya nods to say she understands. She gestures to him to turn off the siren.

When it's quiet, she turns to me:

"Put on the song about the ducks. Louder. Like that."

With the first beats of the song, the mobile ICU starts moving. Katya follows it. We leave the clinic grounds. Making way for the cortège, cars squeeze up to the sidewalks.

I look at Katya. Straight spine. Gothic face. Firmly pressed lips. Her frozen features are enlivened by the flasher's dancing lights. Katya-Immobility-Itself suddenly starts swaying to the rhythm of the song. She puts her hand on my shoulder, and we sway together. Television vans join up with our car; they're reporting live. Then they fall back. The mobile ICU turns off somewhere too. After that, Katya and I continue alone.

In complete solitude, we drive into Scalea, where we'd promised to take little Vera. During the day, we gather impressions; in the evening, sitting on the balcony, we share them with our little girl.

Nestor can't rule out her being able to hear us. Talk to her sometimes, he advised, it'll make things easier for you, and maybe even for her.

The first day, I tell Vera that the water is very warm.

"Too warm, to my taste," Katya adds. "There are motorboats and yachts on the water" – Katya's hand moves like a wave – "such peace. Even though Gleb's arm is a little worse, today he swam the crawl and breaststroke."

I whisper: "Tell her about the cliff."

"Oh yes," Katya recalls. "In one place there's an underwater cliff. It's important, when you're swimming, not to run into it. Simply pay attention. The water's so clear you can see it from far away. One part of the cliff comes up over the surface, covered in brown seaweed – like a mop of hair being combed by the waves, right, Gleb?"

"I can imagine how tiresome that might be" – I run my hand through my hair – "thousands of years of uninterrupted combing."

The next day we go to the medieval part of town, which is on a hill. We turn off via Roma and come across a Byzantine chapel – that's what Katya's tablet tells her. Eighth century. Frescos intact. San Nicola di Platea. The chapel in private hands. Katya runs through a few references. Here, I've found it. Lucia, who lives next door, has the key. We knock at Lucia's. The neighbors say she's gone visiting. We follow her trail and in one of the houses we find Lucia, an elderly Italian lady. We talk with her in relative English. "Yes, I can show you. Why not?" She has the key on her.

We enter the chapel. The lighting is natural; the structure has no roof. There really are frescos in the apse. They're damaged, but the paint in the preserved fragments hasn't faded. In the middle is a mill-stone (there was a mill here at one time), a kind of exhibit. When our eyes get used to the dim light, we notice a human figure in the corner. Perfectly still. Yet another exhibit.

"That's Father Nektary," Lucia says in a whisper. "A Russian." The figure revives and crosses himself. Katya shudders. Also in a whisper:

"Is he here ... all the time?"

"He comes to pray. He has his own key."

Nektary lights a candle and kneels. Lucia exits silently.

We lose track of time. We watch Nektary and his candle. He recites his prayers very quietly, and we hear only snatches. Just so he doesn't stop. We don't want to leave here because here there's no time. And outside is the future, which I basically don't have. Stand by this murmuring for eternity and plunge into its peace. Cheat the future that awaits us outside the doors.

Nektary stands in front of me, small and gray-haired. Round eyeglasses in a metal frame. Catching my gaze, he smiles:

"The glasses are vintage. I got them from a certain monk." His smile melts. "You were thinking about the future just now, weren't you?"

"Are you clairvoyant, father?"

"No, just voyant – thanks to the eyeglasses. Your hand is shaking. I suspect you're seriously ill."

"Not that long ago I was afraid the illness had robbed me of my future. But now, you know, it hasn't."

"It's easy to steal the future because it doesn't exist. It's nothing but a dream. It's hard to steal the present, and even harder the past. And it's impossible, I'm telling you, to steal eternity." He puts his hand on my head. "If your days are shortened by this disease, then know that then your days will be given depth instead of length. But we will pray so that their length is not shortened."

Katya and I climb to the top of the hill. From high up, the sea isn't uniform. The currents and shoals are neatly marked by different colors. The white dots of yachts by the shore are the same size as the liner on the horizon.

The path down starts right at our feet. Who uses it? Beasts, humans, angels? It's steep – how can anyone go down that?

"Katya, I keep thinking we need to tell Anna about Vera's death."

Katya shrugs:

"The point being? Anna's living in her own world. Why disturb her?"

I dial Anna's hospital to consult with the doctor, who, like Katya, has his doubts. He asks why. "It's my duty," I answer. Without enthusiasm ("That's your right") he asks me to call back in about fifteen minutes. He says that more than likely she simply won't recognize me.

Katya and I are silent. Looking at the path running downhill, I suddenly remember a downhill slope in my early childhood. Which scared me for life. Leaving no details whatsoever in my memory. What place was it on earth? Mount Sinai? Ararat? Or maybe Kamianets-Podilskyi, where we once visited my father's family? I have no earlier memories. It's like the fresco in the chapel – a large part of it has been wiped away. All I remember is being in someone's arms. And that someone going downhill, balancing, sideways. Foot to foot, foot to foot. And the tragic music corresponding to that descent: two-part phrases. What music was that? *Lacrimosa?* Herbert von Karajan conducting? Unlikely. . . . Unlikely Karajan was ever in Kamianets-Podilskyi. Memory's tricks, the habit of thinking in musical figures.

Once again I reach the hospital. I put it on speaker so Katya can hear. The doctor (emphatically dry) says he's handing Anna the receiver. Despite expectations, Anna recognizes me. She tells me about the importunate attention she's getting from men. She complains that yesterday for the first time Vera didn't visit her.

Katya raises her head and looks at me. Covering the receiver with her hand, she whispers:

"Say she went away."

In a raspy voice I repeat that Vera went away.

For a long time. After a pause, a voice from the phone:

"Where did she go?"

I look at Katya.

"Bris-bane," Katya whispers in syllables. "It's in Au-stral-i-a."

Anna receives my answer and thinks about it for a couple of minutes. When it already seems as though we've been cut off, she asks:

"Did she get married?"

"Yes."

"There, in Australia?"

I clear my throat.

"In Australia."

"Who to? Well, why don't you say something?"

"An Australian."

PS

Vera's funeral is attended by a narrow circle and without press. The girl who became famous overnight takes her final rest in a Munich cemetery. The Yanovskys have been unreachable ever since. They don't pick up the phone or answer letters. When the mentions of them are solidly tied to the word "disappearance," they suddenly appear in public.

This happens on November 15, 2014, at a benefit concert in London's Royal Albert Hall, where Gleb and Vera were supposed to perform. The great Santorini is conducting. Gleb comes out on stage and the hall rises in silence. One after another, they start turning on their phone lights. A minute later, the hall has become a flickering sea. Santorini (there is an electric arc over his baton) looks at Gleb inquiringly. So does the hall. Gleb indicates with just his eyes that he's ready. Santorini comes up to Gleb, embraces him, and says something in his ear.

A sweep of his baton. The orchestra. Gleb's throat seizes up and he can't sing. Even from a distance you can see his hand trembling. The orchestra starts playing again, and at the right place the conductor gives Gleb the signal. To no avail. Gleb doesn't sing this time either. Not a sound comes from his half-open mouth, and tears run down his cheeks. The orchestra plays Vera's song, and the lyrics slide across the big screen. Gleb is silent.

The next morning, the newspapers write only about him. Under the headline "Silence in Two Four," there is an interview with Santorini.

Question: "Before the performance you embraced Yanovsky and told him something. What exactly?"

Answer: "Nothing special. We hadn't had any rehearsals, and I only indicated the manner, *andante cantabile* – slowly and melodiously."

Question: "And it was emotionally and silently?"

Answer: "Can there be a better ending to a musical career?"

Question: "Are you joking?"

Answer: "I haven't joked for many years. The ideal music is silence."

Gleb Yanovsky's name surfaces once again in 2018. This time it appears in Kyiv in court hearings in the famous Case of the Taxi Drivers. Taxi drivers had been handing over single passengers shuttling between airports to a criminal gang. The robbed passengers were killed – which was why the search for the criminals took so long. In his testimony, one of the taxi drivers mentions the name Irina Yanovskaya. When he'd asked where she was going, Irina had answered, "Brisbane." When he'd asked why no one was seeing her off, she laughed and said that seeing people off just encouraged dampness.

When he finished with his prepared questions, the taxi driver asked out of pure curiosity what awaited her in Brisbane. "Happiness," Irina replied briefly. "But why Brisbane exactly?" the man wondered. "Because," Irina said, "it's on the other side of the globe."

She described the city the whole way. To this day the taxi driver remembers her story word for word, her shining eyes in the rearview mirror. Never before had this man ever heard anything comparable to her information and incandescence about Brisbane. Continuing at the prosecutor's request to give testimony, he says that just before getting to the airport he turned into the forest at the appointed place and left the car there for half an hour. When he returned, Irina wasn't in it anymore.

In the course of the investigation, it also becomes clear that immediately after his mother's disappearance, Gleb went to Kyiv and since then has flown here regularly. Now wealthy, he hired private detectives and promised rewards to the police, but with zero result. Irina never was found. At the last session, Gleb gets up and says that he does not believe his mother is dead. That's his only statement in the trial.

Knowing that a book about him is in the works, Gleb gives the publishers the diary he's kept for the past three years. These notes will be published in the book. They ask Gleb whether he wants to add anything relevant to the story of his life and career. He thinks it over and says that he might just add something.

He remembers the cliff. Tall grass stirs at the very edge. Uneasily. Somewhere past the grass is the path down. Beyond the grass – an abyss. Clouds of smoke rise from there, as if there, below, they were burning last year's leaves. Gleb, two years old, is being held by a stranger, a woman. He feels her cold hands. His mother is afraid. She's afraid to go down herself, let alone carrying her child. The boy wants to say that maybe they don't have to go down, but his verbal resources are vanishingly small, and it becomes clear that they do have to go that way; no other paths are foreseen. "I'll carry the baby," the woman says, "and you get yourself down, Irina." Apparently this woman is her own person here and seems used to the descent, but this frightens Gleb even more. In his eyes, horror. His mother reaches out for him, and now he's in her arms. In tears, they begin their movement down. Irina goes down sideways, taking slow, chassé steps. She looks like a tired crab. He hears music born from the rhythm of this clumsy and terrible descent. Does anyone but Gleb hear it? His mother is breathing hard. She shields her baby from the abyss with her hand. Time after time they're enveloped in smoke, while the stranger stands lookout on the bluff.

 **Eugene Vodolazkin's** second novel, *Laurus,* won both of Russia's major literary awards, the National Big Book Award and the Yasnaya Polyana Book Award, and was shortlisted for the National Bestseller Prize and the Russian Booker Prize. His debut novel, *Solovyov and Larionov,* was shortlisted for the Andrei Bely Prize and the Big Book Award. A third critically acclaimed novel, *The Aviator,* has also been translated into English. Vodolazkin is the 2019 winner of the Solzhenitsyn Prize. He was born in Kyiv in 1964 and has worked in the department of Old Russian Literature at Pushkin House since 1990. He is an expert in Russian medieval history and folklore and has numerous academic books and articles to his name. The author lives with his family in Saint Petersburg, Russia.

 **Marian Schwartz** translates Russian classic and contemporary fiction, history, biography, and criticism. She is the principal English translator of the works of Nina Berberova and translated the *New York Times* bestseller *The Last Tsar,* by Edvard Radzinsky, as well as classics by Mikhail Bulgakov, Ivan Goncharov, Yuri Olesha, Mikhail Lermontov, and Leo Tolstoy. She is a past president of the American Literary Translators Association and the recipient of two National Endowment for the Arts translation fellowships and numerous prizes, including the 2014 Read Russia Prize for Contemporary Russian Literature, the 2016 Soeurette Diehl Fraser Award from the Texas Institute of Letters, and the 2018 Linda Gaboriau Award for Translation from the Banff Centre for Arts and Creativity.